S0-AKP-433

David Lurie is the hero of Potok's new novel. Through David's eyes, through the recall of his beginnings, we relive our own: the sheltering strength of family ... schooltime best friends and bullies ... the dawning of intellectual adventure ... the first frightening battles with the gods of our childhood (the all-powerful parents, now suddenly fragile) as the moment arrives to make our own moral choices, our own decisions about what our lives will be.

With this book, Potok has given us back all our beginnings.

_____

Fawcett Crest Books
by Chaim Potok:

CHAIM POTOK

IN THE
BEGINNING

FAWCETT CREST • NEW YORK

To
ADENA
my wife

and to
ROBERT GOTTLIEB
my editor and friend

IN THE
BEGINNING

———————————

One

All beginnings are hard.

I can remember hearing my mother murmur those words while I lay in bed with fever. "Children are often sick, darling. That's the way it is with children. All beginnings are hard. You'll be all right soon."

I remember bursting into tears one evening because a passage of Bible commentary had proved too difficult for me to understand. I was about nine years old at the time. "You want to understand everything immediately?" my father said. "Just like that? You only began to study this commentary last week. All beginnings are hard. You have to work at the job of studying. Go over it again and again."

The man who later guided me in my studies would welcome me warmly into his apartment and, when we sat at his desk, say to me in his gentle voice, "Be patient, David. The midrash says, 'All beginnings are hard.' You cannot swallow all the world at one time."

I say it to myself today when I stand before a new class at the beginning of a school year or am about to start a new book or research paper: All beginnings are hard. Teaching the way I do is particularly hard, for I touch the raw nerves of faith, the beginnings of things. Often students are shaken. I say to them what was said to me: "Be patient. You are learning a new way of understanding the Bible. All beginnings are hard." And sometimes I add what I have learned on my

9

own: "Especially a beginning that you make by yourself. That's the hardest beginning of all."

I marvel that we survive our beginnings. Mine was filled with strange accidents. In the very beginning there was the accident that occurred about a week after I was born: my mother, bringing me home from the hospital, tripped going up the front stoop of our apartment house and fell forward heavily onto her knees and then sideways onto her left elbow before my father caught her and helped her to her feet. My nose and the left side of my face had struck the stone edge of the top step.

Of course I have no memory of that accident; but that accident has much to do with what I am able to remember of subsequent years.

My mother's knees and elbow were badly scraped. I appeared to be uninjured. The blanket I had been wrapped in had protected my face, and only very little blood, as if from a small scratch, had come from my nose. Our family doctor—a short, pink-faced, red-haired man who spoke Yiddish and English fluently and wore a pince-nez—came quickly, conducted his examination, and announced that no injury had been done to me, I was lucky, we were all lucky, at least twice a week he had cases of mothers tripping on stoops while carrying their babies in and out of buildings and sometimes the babies were badly hurt. But I was all right. However, if my nose swelled, or my mother's knees or elbow swelled, they were to call him. My nose did not swell and my mother's scrapes healed rapidly.

Dr. Weidman had spoken with authority, and neither my mother nor my father had thought to question his judgment. They had the European immigrant's awe of doctors and reverence for medicine. It was a few years before they discovered that our doctor had erred.

Then there were the bird and the dog I killed accidentally when I was about four. The bird was a canary, a gift of my father's to my mother. She loved that bird; she would sit in the living room and listen to it sing. After a few minutes she would begin to smile, her tight, nervous features would grow calm, and her darting eyes would slowly relax and become limpid with joy. Once a week my father would close all the windows in the apartment and let the canary fly around the house. I lay ill in my bed one hot day, unable to breathe through my clogged nose, my throat painfully tight and dry. I forgot about the bird and opened my window. The bird flew out and was gone. My father hit me for that accident. A cat would now eat that bird, he said. Only feathers would be left of it, he said.

The dog belonged to a downstairs neighbor, Mrs. Horowitz, who let him roam our New York block. Everyone liked him. I would sit alone near my brother's carriage and watch the children playing with him. One day he got up on his hind legs and poked his shaggy head into the carriage while my brother slept. I hit him and he ran into the street and was hit by a car. Mrs. Horowitz shrieked at me when she saw her dog crushed and dead along the curb. "But it was an accident," I kept saying. "It was an accident."

There was Eddie Kulanski, the boy on my block who hated Jews with the kind of mindless demonic rage that remains incomprehensible—and terrifying—to me to this day. He was only six years old but his hatred bore the breeding of a thousand years. A few months before my sixth birthday he accidentally came near to killing me.

The street we lived on—before our world fell to pieces and we plunged into the decade of the Depression—was wide and tree-lined and lovely. It was a quiet, sunny, cobblestone street filled with well-to-do families who owned cars, went to their synagogues and churches, spoke English civilly to one another —the senior members in the heavy accents of their European lands of origin—and who felt that, at least for them, the immigrant's dream had been realized, they had been right to abandon the blight of Europe and gamble on golden America. Somewhere in the city things were different for immigrants, they lived in a black nightmare of tenements and a miasma of squalor and degradation; but the immigrants on our Bronx street had succeeded: they were all naturalized citizens, proud of their new country, their new wealth, and their children who romped on the sidewalk, played happily, and chattered in an English that seemed to immigrant ears accent-free.

Those should have been sweet years for me, those first years of my life. But they were not. I did things and things happened to me that brought dread into our lives. All through those early years and on into my teens, accidents trailed in my wake like foul-breathing specters. Often my accidents were very narrow escapes; but sometimes they resulted in serious physical injury to myself or to others—and this despite the fact that I lived and played with caution because I was slight of build, always short for my age, and often ill from the injury our family doctor said had not been done to me when my mother tripped and fell with me in her arms.

The injury that had not been done to me by that fall is called a deviated septum, the breaking of the cartilaginous tissue that partitions the nose and aids the delicate and vital filtering processes of the nostrils. Once it was broken, I became fair game for the viral and bacterial pirates of our world. The break widened as I grew older, and the septum began to block my right nostril; but the damage was not discovered until I was almost six. By that time the break was reparable only by potentially serious surgery, which could not be performed until after I had stopped growing.

I spent my early life growing a little and being ill a lot. I thought and dreamed a great deal. I lay in my bed and watched and listened. I turned my long lonely days and nights into nets with which I caught the whispers and sighs and glances and the often barely discernible gestures that are the real message carriers in our noisy world. But it was years before I could shape what I saw and heard into a pattern that made some sense of the lives of my aunt and uncle and cousin, the alternately withdrawn and volatile natures of my parents, and the mysterious comings and goings of the now ubiquitous, now vanishing Mr. Shmuel Bader.

There was the cracked and yellowing photograph I found one afternoon on the desk in Mr. Bader's study when I was almost six years old.

About forty men had posed for the photograph somewhere in a forest. The men were in three rows. Those in the first row were seated with their legs crossed; those in the second row were kneeling; those in the last row were on their feet. The earth in the foreground was covered with snow; in the background there were thick-trunked trees and a dense brocade of snow-covered branches from which hung stilettos of ice. The men wore dark coats or parkas, and boots. Some had on hats, others wore Russian-style fur caps. All were clean-shaven; two in the last row held flags. Partially concealing the chin of one man and the head of another was a sign with the Hebrew words Am Kedoshim printed on it, together with some additional Hebrew letters and the numbers 1919.

No one in the photograph was smiling. Most of the men held in their bare hands either a revolver or a knife; some held both. The hands and the knives seemed starkly white against the blackness of their coats. On one of the flags I thought I could make out Hebrew letters, but I was not certain. The flag must have stirred in the winter wind of the forest at the very moment the photograph was taken, and the letters had blurred.

I first saw that photograph on a Shabbat afternoon in the spring of 1929. My parents and I had walked through a heavy rain to the Baders' apartment a few blocks from where we lived. Mr. Bader was leaving for Canada that night and from there to Europe on Tuesday morning and my father needed to speak to him. A neighbor's teenage daughter had come in to sit with my baby brother. I remember that my mother had not wanted me to walk in the rain but I had refused to stay home without them. I was very frightened of remaining in the apartment without my parents. I lay on the living room floor and cried. In angry desperation, my father had finally permitted my mother to take an umbrella, an infraction of the Jewish law that forbids the carrying of objects on public property during Shabbat. But someone's life was involved in that visit to Mr. Bader, and Jewish law not only may but must be broken if it stands in the way of saving a life; and so we walked in the rain to Mr. Bader's apartment, my mother keeping me close to her beneath the umbrella.

Mr. Bader himself opened the door to his apartment. He seemed surprised to see us but said nothing. He helped my parents off with their coats, raised his eyebrows at the sight of the dripping umbrella, glanced at me, and nodded faintly. He was a tall, thin gentleman in his early forties, courteous, soft-spoken, and with the graceful air of an individual who is at home in many worlds. He had thick brown hair, which he combed fastidiously and parted in the middle; his features were craggy and deeply tanned; his eyebrows were lighter than the brown hair on his head, and very thick; they formed a dense, straight, and almost uninterrupted line above his sharp, direct, penetrating dark eyes. He wore a maroon silk smoking jacket over a dark red cravat and dark trousers. On his head was a small dark skullcap. He nodded graciously to my mother, greeted my father as an old friend, and led them into his living room, where Mrs. Bader, a tall, well-dressed, kind-mannered woman, greeted us warmly and began putting out little cakes and cookies and cups and saucers on the ornately carved coffee table near the sofa. My parents sat on the sofa, looking small and uncomfortable. My mother's normally drawn features and shifting eyes, which never focused directly on the face of the person to whom she spoke, seemed particularly tense and darting that afternoon. The rain drummed with a dull, wearying sound on the large windows of the room. I saw it falling on the tall trees outside, the dark bare early April trees of the neighborhood which my mother had promised me would soon be green with leaves. I could not remember them ever having had leaves before.

"It will be a dreary trip to Canada if this rain doesn't stop," I heard Mr. Bader say.

"You are traveling by train?" asked my father.

"Yes. And part of the way by car. I must stop off in Boston for half a day."

"And you leave on Tuesday?"

"Tuesday," said Mr. Bader, nodding.

"That will be a very big job," said my father, nodding his head briefly.

For some reason my father's expression of approval, reticent as it was, seemed to fill Mr. Bader with enormous pleasure. He lowered his eyes in a gesture of modesty.

There was a silence.

"Please have some tea," said Mrs. Bader. "Ruth, let me pour it for you. And I have cookies for David."

My father raised his cup of tea to his nostrils and sniffed at it briefly. Then he put it to his lips and said, "Then you will be in Lemberg."

"Of course," said Mr. Bader.

My father put his cup down on the coffee table and leaned forward slightly on the sofa. A wedge appeared above the bridge of his nose between his small eyes. He was a little shorter than medium height with very broad shoulders and short, muscular arms and legs and a trim, narrow waist. He had brown wavy hair and gray eyes and a square face with a protruding lower jaw. He cleared his throat.

"There is illness in Ruth's family," he said very quietly, looking down at the coffee table. "There is difficulty obtaining proper medication." He paused. "It is complicated, very complicated. Matters have to be explained carefully to Ruth's mother and father." He paused again. "And to her brothers," he added.

Mr. Bader nodded. "Of course," he said. "I understand perfectly. You brought the medication?"

"Yes."

No one seemed disturbed by this further infraction of Jewish religious law.

"You will tell me what to do and I will do it," Mr. Bader said. "But, first, please have another cup of tea. David, take another cookie. I am glad to see you are over your bad cold. Take some more tea please, Ruth. Please."

They chatted amiably. My father had spoken with clear discomfort and hesitation to Mr. Bader, as if he were distressed to be asking help from so important a person; yet Mr. Bader had responded promptly and with deference, as if the important person in the room was really my father. It seemed mildly confusing to me.

"Yes, I will be in Lemberg and Warsaw and Lodz," I heard Mr. Bader say. "It will be no problem to go from Lemberg to Bobrek. Believe me, I am happy to do it for you."

I remembered those names: Lemberg, Bobraw, Warsaw, Lodz. My parents used them often when they spoke together in the nights. Often when I lay ill, my mother would tell me stories of her years on a farm near Bobrek, a town of about five thousand people, almost half of whom were Jews. The town was situated four miles southeast of Lemberg, which was the major city of the Polish province of Eastern Galicia. Her parents owned the farm. It was located on the outskirts of Bobrek. She would tell me stories of the games she had played in the forest that adjoined the farm, of winter ice skating on the river that was the western boundary of the farm, of sleigh rides in the snow, of the way the forest and the rolling hills beyond turned slowly green in the spring, of the birds in the trees and the fish in the river. In her stories birds would have sweet human voices, dogs would be loyal to their masters, lead children out of deep forests, and never paw holes in the earth or dirty the paths used by people, and the wind would be the bodies of angels moving invisibly within our world. She would tell me only happy stories. She never told me stories about accidents or illness or death.

"Tell me the details," Mr. Bader was saying. "Is there any more hot water left, Miriam? Thank you. Tell me carefully all the details."

I finished my cookie and grew bored and slipped from the room, casting a swift, sidelong glance at my mother, whose eyes were fixed on her short thin hands clasped tightly together on her lap. She looked tense and forlorn, her gaunt features very pale against the darkness of her severely-combed-back, lusterless hair. My father was talking quietly in rapid Yiddish, and I could no longer understand what he was saying. I went into the hallway of the apartment, wandered through the kitchen and a large bedroom, and came into Mr. Bader's study.

It was a large room with glass-enclosed bookcases, a thick Persian rug, an easy chair, a huge dark-wood desk with a tall dark-wood chair behind it, and two tall windows behind the desk. On both sides of the windows stood wooden filing cabinets. Dark velvet drapes lay across the windows; one of them had not been fully drawn and through it I saw the rain falling steadily on the trees and the cobblestone street and the traffic below. It seemed a bleak and dirty rain. The afternoon was slowly growing dark. Dim light came through the window from the wet world outside and fell weakly upon the one partly visible windowsill, upon the dark-wood chair, and upon the neat piles of papers and books and pamphlets on Mr. Bader's desk.

It was then that I saw the photograph. It lay on top of one of the carefully arranged piles of paper. I glanced at it; then I stood on my toes and looked at it. Then I reached up, took it from the desk, and peered at it closely in the dim light of the study. I brought it over to the window and looked at it intently, at the faces of the men, at the guns and knives in their hands, at the forest, at the snow on the ground and the ice on the branches of the trees. When I looked up, the afternoon had darkened perceptibly, there was a vague pain behind my eyes, and Mr. Bader was standing in the doorway of the study.

The room lay wreathed in shadows. His features were indistinct in the darkness that had drifted across the section of the study that was farthest from the windows. I watched him move in a sudden swift glide across the room, as if his feet were not touching the floor; suddenly he was beside me, towering over me and looking down at the photograph I held in my hand.

"Well," he said gently in his soft voice. "We wondered where you had taken yourself off to, David. Isn't it awful the way big people will sometimes talk and talk and forget that there is a little boy around who can't understand them?" He had placed a thumb and forefinger on the photograph and was removing it from my hand. "That isn't nice of big people, and I apologize. But they were important, the things we talked about." I watched the photograph disappear into a pile of papers. "There is a little pamphlet here I wanted to show your

father. Here it is. Come, let's go out. It's so dark in here I can
barely see you. Would you like a glass of milk and another
cookie?" He had his arm on my shoulder as he spoke and I
felt myself moving and when he was done talking we were
outside in the hallway. Behind me the door to the study closed
with a soft click. I looked up at him. He was so tall I had to
bend my head far back to see his eyes. His thin craggy features smiled down at me benignly. "We may even have a
game for you somewhere. I'll ask my wife. I'm very sorry we
ignored you, David. Come."

He brought me back to the living room where I found my
parents talking earnestly together on the sofa. They stopped
talking when I came in.

I spent the rest of the visit in the kitchen with a game of
dominoes Mrs. Bader found in a drawer somewhere, and
thinking of the photograph in Mr. Bader's study.

We stood at the doorway. Mr. Bader helped my mother on
with her coat. He seemed strangely reverential now in the
presence of my father, as if he was parting from him with
great reluctance.

"I will take care of everything, Max," he said reassuringly.

"You have left your umbrella," Mrs. Bader said.

"It has stopped raining," my father told her. "I will come
back for it tomorrow. Have a safe trip, Shmuel. Be careful of
the crazy Bolsheviks and the bastard Chekists."

"I am always careful, Max. It's a reflex by now." He turned
to my mother and bowed slightly. "Goodbye, Ruth. Don't
worry about anything. But of course you will worry anyway,
won't you, until you hear from them?" He smiled down at me.
"Goodbye, David. Stay well. Do you hear me, David? Stay
well."

We went slowly down the stone stairway and through the
ornately decorated and furnished entrance hall into the pale
early evening street. The rain lay in dark, dirty puddles on the
sidewalk and along the curb. A cool wind blew remnants of
rain from the trees.

My mother helped me button my coat. Her fingers were
cold; I felt them cold and trembling on my neck as she raised
and buttoned my coat collar.

A car drove by on the cobblestone street, sending rain onto
the sidewalk. My father stepped agilely between us and the
oncoming car and took most of the cascading rain onto his
coat and trousers.

"Are you wet?" he asked me quickly.

"No, Papa."

"Bastard," my father said. His short, thickset form and squarish features had hardened in a sudden flash of rage at the rain-splashing automobile that continued along the street, heedlessly sending waves of water onto the sidewalk.

"Max, please," my mother murmured.

He took her arm. They were both short, but my father's thick shoulders and muscular frame reduced my mother's height even further. He patted her hand. "Everything will be all right, Ruth. Let's go home."

But we did not go directly home. We had walked one block when, on an impulse, my father decided that he wanted to see his brother. "I feel a need to see him," he responded to my mother's feeble protest. We detoured two very long blocks to a wide cobblestone boulevard lined with wet trees and dense with traffic. The sky, leaden with clouds, had brought early darkness to the day. We walked quickly, keeping close to the elegant apartment houses on the boulevard and away from the traffic near the curb. A trolley car jammed with passengers went by in a clattering rush. Abruptly all up and down the street the lamppost lights came on. Gauzy yellowish halos formed themselves out of the evening and hung like ghostly balloons over the wet pavements and bare trees. We turned into an apartment house and climbed two flights of stairs. As my father knocked on the door to his brother's apartment, my mother bent and unbuttoned my coat. The vague pain behind my eyes, which had left me when we had come out onto the street from Mr. Bader's apartment, now returned. I felt it throbbing softly. It was a familiar pain and I dreaded it.

My cousin, a tall, shy boy four years older than I, opened the door and smiled in surprise when he saw us.

"Who is it, Saul?" I heard my aunt's voice from somewhere within the apartment.

"Uncle Max and Aunt Ruth," my cousin called back over his shoulder. He gave me a warm smile and a pat on my arm. "Hello, Davey." He was always solicitous of my needs. He helped me off with my coat. "Is it very cold outside?" he asked me quietly.

"Yes."

He looked at me. "Are you okay, Davey?"

I nodded.

He gazed at me intently and I saw he did not believe me.

My aunt and uncle came into the hallway and there were greetings.

"I need a glass of tea," my father said.

We went into the living room and sat on sofas and easy chairs by the soft light of a tasseled floor lamp, for the Shabbat was not yet over, and the other lights in the apartment would not be turned on until after the Havdalah Service. There was more tea and cake for my parents, and more milk and cookies for me, and, served in little dishes, a jamlike concoction of strawberries and sugar for all of us, and more subdued conversation, which I did not bother to listen to this time. Then I heard my uncle say, "You couldn't have gone yesterday?" His faintly nasal voice registered mild reproach. "The letter came this morning," my father said. My uncle nodded. I felt bewildered: my father had torn open a letter on Shabbat and no one seemed shocked. I recalled that my father had quickly left the house when we had returned from the synagogue and had been away a long time. We had eaten Shabbat dinner late.

Now they were talking about my mother's mother. Their voices became very low. I looked away and noticed Saul. He had paid no attention to the conversation between our parents but had sat quietly all the time, watching me from across the room with a look of concern. I avoided his eyes and gazed at the intricate design on the rug and at the rococo whorls and gyrations in the wooden arms of my easy chair. Then I saw Saul get to his feet. He came over to me and whispered in my ear, "I've got a new midrash for you. I just read it today." We went quickly through the dark hallway into his room.

The room too was dark save for the pale yellow street lights that came through the window. It was a fairly large room, with a dark-wood bed, a chest of drawers, a small desk, a bookcase, and two wooden chairs.

"Lie down, Davey," he said to me. "You look a little tired."

"We had a big walk, Saul. We went to Mr. Bader's house."

"In the rain? It was like a flood outside today."

"Papa let us take an umbrella."

"On Shabbos? It must have been important."

"It was about Mama's mother. Mr. Bader is bringing her medicine for her sickness."

My cousin was silent. I could dimly see him regarding me through his shell-rimmed glasses. For a moment I thought to tell him about the photograph. But I sensed that the photograph should not have been seen by me, that its presence on the desk had been an inadvertence on Mr. Bader's part. I remained quiet.

"There's a new elephant in the zoo," my cousin said, breaking the silence.

"Really?"

"And a new billy goat. A friend of mine told me. I thought I would go today. But I stayed home and read because of the rain."

"Saul?"

"Yes, Davey?"

"What does Mr. Bader do?"

"Do? What do you mean?"

"Like Papa sells houses. And your father is a lawyer. What does Mr. Bader do?"

"He's in a business called export and import. He buys things in countries outside America and sells them here to Americans. Like rugs and jewels and things like that."

"But he reads the Torah and teaches Mishnah in the synagogue."

"A businessman doesn't have to be an ignoramus, Davey. Your father also reads the Torah. Mr. Bader went to yeshivas in Europe when he was young."

"Does he travel so much because of his business, Saul?"

My cousin fell abruptly silent. The street lights glinted dully off his glasses. Around us the darkness seemed to deepen in the wake of the sudden silence. I had begun to notice that people who knew Mr. Bader did not like to talk too much about him; they spoke with glances and gestures rather than with words.

"Can I tell you that midrash now, Davey?"

I settled comfortably on the bed and closed my eyes.

"I heard it first when I was a little boy in the yeshiva. But today was the first time I actually read it."

He told me the story of Abraham smashing the bodies and heads of his father's idols. I listened and was suddenly frightened. Heads lying smashed on the ground; noses and ears and eyes. Idols.

"What is that?" I had once asked my mother, pointing to the statue of a woman in front of one of the Catholic churches in our neighborhood.

"That is one of the idols of the goyim," she said.

"An idol? What the Torah talks about?"

"Yes, darling."

I had thought of idols as belonging to a misty time when patriarchs and prophets walked through a pagan and Israelite world. I shivered with the thought that there were idols in my neighborhood, as I shivered now with the vision of broken stone bodies littering the sidewalks. I opened my eyes. It was a strange, cruel story.

"That was an awful thing he did, Saul."

"Why was it awful? Abraham did it because he believed in God."

"But he broke their heads and bodies, Saul. He broke them into pieces."

I could feel him looking at me. I stared at the dark shadows on the ceiling.

"Why did he have to break them all to pieces, Saul? Couldn't Abraham have done something else?"

"But they were idols, Davey."

"It was awful, Saul. Abraham should have found another way. Breaking them with an ax all over the sidewalks and the streets. Wouldn't the goyim get angry if we did that, Saul?"

"Take it easy, Davey," I heard him say in a quiet voice.

I lay on the bed and closed my eyes. The pain had settled into a weighted dullness. I shivered again. The room moved faintly.

"It's time for Havdalah," my uncle called from the living room.

I sat up and the room moved again.

"Are you all right, Davey?" my cousin asked.

I let him lead me into the dining room where our parents stood near the head of the table, watching my uncle light the long braided candle. A wick sputtered, taking the flame given it by the match; then the remaining five wicks caught and a single tall flame burned and smoked in the dark room and sent a reddish glow across the faces near the table. In that glow I saw my cousin whisper into my mother's ear and my mother glance at me with a helpless, resigned, forlorn look. I stared at the night outside the window.

"David," my uncle said, and handed me the candle. Molten wax slid down the candle onto my fingers. I watched and felt the faint trembling of my hand, and shivered once again. I stared at the flame, at its red and yellow and blue brightness, at the way its tip danced and spiraled and reached out into the enshrouding darkness; then I stared through the flame at the faces reddened by its glow, at the hard, strong-boned, squarish face of my father, at the pale, weary, nervous face of my mother, at the smooth-skinned oval face of my aunt, at my uncle's face, so much like my father's but softer, gentler, without the flaring moments of rage that seemed to have cut deep lines across my father's brow and into the corners of his eyes, and at the shy, kind, gentle face of my cousin—at the faces of the only family I had in America: four adults and a boy. Everyone else—fathers, mothers, sisters, brothers, aunts, uncles, cousins; more than one hundred fifty in number—was still in Europe.

"Hold the candle still, David," my uncle said softly, looking at me through its flame.

I stiffened my hand. The pain behind my eyes had begun to travel upward to the area above the bridge of my nose and downward along the ridge of my cheekbones. I could no longer breathe through my nose.

My uncle raised his cup of wine. They were all looking at the flame. Beyond the warm brief spread of light from the flame were the shadows that spread grotesquely upon the ceiling and walls and the velvet darkness of the night that lay heavily upon the tall wide front window. My uncle chanted in his soft, faintly nasal voice.

"Behold, God is my salvation; I will trust and not be afraid."

The candle sputtered and smoked and flared; they seemed transfixed by its flame. My uncle chanted on, completing the brief introductory prayer. He made the blessing over the wine, then put the wine cup on the table and picked up the exquisitely filigreed silver spice box, made the blessing over spices, and sniffed at its interior through a silver window which he opened. He handed the metal box to my father, who repeated the procedure and handed it to my mother. By the time the box had made its circuit of the family and had come to me, my uncle had completed the blessing over the flame and had once again raised the cup of wine. I could not smell the spices through my clogged nose. I put the box on the table. A sudden single stabbing flame of pain sliced through the area above the bridge of my nose and disappeared. I held the candle stiffly and listened to the beating of my heart.

"Blessed art Thou, O Lord our God, King of the universe," my uncle chanted, "who distinguishes between sacred and profane, between light and darkness, between Israel and the other nations, between the seventh day and the six days of labor. Blessed art Thou, O Lord, who distinguishes between sacred and profane."

"Amen," everyone murmured.

My uncle leaned forward and extended the cup to me. I saw his fingers around the silver wine cup as he tipped it to enable me to drink from its rim. I drank the dark sweet liquid, felt it warm and sweet on my tongue and faintly irritating on my throat. He spilled the remaining wine into a dish on the table, took the candle, and put the flame into the wine. The flame sputtered, fought for life, and died. There was a moment of total darkness. Then someone turned on the lights in the crystal chandelier and the room came starkly alive.

"A good week, a good week," were the murmured wishes.

I blinked in the sudden light and once again felt the pain shoot through the front of my head.

My mother bent and kissed my forehead. "A good week, my darling son," she murmured. I felt her lips hesitate on my forehead. Her lips were dry and I felt them moving against my forehead as she murmured words I could not understand: "Armimas, rmimas, mimas, imas, mas, as." She straightened slowly and gave me a weary look. Then she sought out my father's eyes and nodded briefly in my direction. His gray eyes focused immediately upon my face; then he turned and spoke rapidly in a low voice to my uncle. "Two thousand dollars is enough," I heard my uncle say. "More than enough."

At the far end of the dining room my aunt drew the drapes and shut out the night.

My cousin stood beside me. "Are you getting sick again, Davey?"

"I think so, Saul."

"I'll wish you a good week anyway."

"A good week, Saul."

"I'm sorry the story about Abraham upset you."

"What story was that?" my uncle said. He had come over to us to wish us a good week. "Did my storyteller tell you a new story today?"

"About Abraham and the idols and Abraham breaking all their bodies and heads and their noses and lips and eyes. I didn't like the story, Uncle Meyer."

My voice had come out high and strained. They looked at me. I could feel them all looking at me as I kept my eyes on my uncle's face.

"Why didn't you like the story, David?"

"I didn't like the smashing and the breaking and all the arms and eyes and noses everywhere all over the sidewalks and the streets." I stopped abruptly. The pain had stabbed again through my head and this time had licked downward toward the cheek on the right side of my face.

The room was very quiet. They were all looking at me intently.

My uncle bent down very close to me and gently pulled me to him. He was not so heavy-chested and muscular as my father; still he seemed very strong. I saw his gray eyes—like my father's eyes but clear and without the lines in the corners.

"Don't you think Abraham tried talking to the goyim before he broke the idols? Don't you think he talked and talked to them, David?"

I had not thought of that. Saul had not told me that. I looked up at Saul. He was staring at his father.

"What should Abraham have done when he talked and talked and they didn't listen? And all the time he believed he was right." He held me to him lightly. His thick wavy brown hair lay neatly combed on his head and his face was stubbled, as was my father's, for they did not shave on Shabbat. On the right side of his forehead a vein throbbed slowly as he spoke. I watched its pulsing rise and fall, and asked myself in wonder and dread, How can you smash a head? There are so many precious and beautiful things in a head. Eyes and a nose and lips. Even in a head of stone. Still, if Abraham had talked and talked and talked—"What should he have done, David?" my uncle said. "Sometimes you have to smash." His voice was soft; it was barely audible. He had spoken his last words almost in a whisper. "You have to smash."

I felt a shudder pass through me and was silent.

My uncle bowed his head, as if in sadness. "You're frightened," he murmured. "You needn't be frightened, David."

"Saul, what kind of stories are you telling the child?" I heard my aunt ask with a tone of accusation. "Look how you frightened him."

"But it's about Abraham, Mama." Saul was bewildered by my reaction. "Everyone knows that story about Abraham. I only thought to tell it to Davey because Mr. Bader showed me the story in the midrash this morning in synagogue after the Torah reading. He was teaching me to read it in Aramaic."

They all looked at him. Slowly, my uncle straightened. I inclined my head and gazed up at his face. My eyes and forehead and cheeks hurt. I could not breathe through my clogged nose and my throat was dry and scratchy. The room seemed to expand and contract in front of my eyes, as if it were pulsating, like the vein in my uncle's forehead. A strange silence had crept into the room, dark and cold and vaguely resonant with fear. Through the silence came the clang and clatter of a trolley car on the street.

"I think," my mother began, in her hesitant, uncertain way of talking, "I think the boy is not feeling well."

"Yes," my uncle said gently, gazing down at me. "He has fever."

My father gathered up our coats. We stood at the door.

"I will come by tomorrow night," my father said.

"Tomorrow afternoon would be better for me," my uncle said. "Tomorrow night I have a meeting."

"Tomorrow afternoon is bad—no, it is fine. I can stop by on my way over to the Bader apartment to pick up our umbrella. Fine, Meyer. Tomorrow afternoon."

They were all saying their goodbyes.

"I have better stories than that one," Saul whispered to me. "I'll tell you a happier story next time."

"I liked it, Saul. It just scared me a little. There was a dog on our block that was run over on its body and head."

He patted my arm. "I hope you're better soon, Davey."

We went down the stairs and into the street. I tried to breathe through my nose and could not. Cold night air streamed across my throat and into my chest. I coughed. My father bent over me. I felt his hand on my face. His fingers were icy cold. I shivered. He raised me effortlessly and held me to him tightly. He carried me the long block home.

We found my brother awake and playing happily with the babysitter.

"He's such fun to be with, Mrs. Lurie," the baby-sitter said. She was a thin, pretty-faced girl in her early teens. "He slept two hours and I fed him and changed him. He's smart."

"I need a glass of coffee," my father said, and went into the kitchen.

My mother gave me medicine. I lay in my bed and cried with the pain and fever. "Sha, sha, darling," my mother kept saying. Her voice sounded dim and her face looked hazy, as if I were seeing it through mist. "Mama will tell you a story about the farm in Bobrek." She told of a new calf and the way she had helped feed it and keep it warm one winter during a two-day snowstorm. The pain in my head and face was excruciating and she put her cold hand on my brow. "You'll be all right soon, darling. Mama is right here next to you."

But when I woke in the night sobbing with pain and fever

she was gone. I saw my uncle standing next to my bed with a revolver in his hand and wearing a heavy coat and a Russian-style fur hat. "Sometimes you have to smash," he said in his gentle voice. "But I'm sorry we frightened you, David."

I cried out and my mother came rushing into my room, her robe open, her long hair uncombed and straggly. She held me and murmured words I could not understand. "Ochnotinos, chnotinos," she said in a whisper. "Notinos, otinos, tinos, inos, nos, os." The dark room pulsed slowly to the rhythm of the pain in my face and forehead. My throat was sandpaper dry. I talked through the pain and fever, hearing myself and won-dering who was speaking. It seemed as if a disembodied being had crept inside me, was talking on and on, uncontrolled, the fever severing the reins on his tongue. Slowly I became aware of my mother's strange and distant silence. But the words continued flowing from me. I felt light-headed; everything around me seemed to be expanding and contracting. Vaguely I saw my mother rise from my bed and go hurriedly from my room. I heard heavy rain falling with loud pebble sounds on the trees and pavement and on the panes of my window.

My father stood next to my bed in his pajamas. By the dim shaded light of the lamp on my dresser, I saw his eyes were puffed and weary. His hair was rumpled and his face was tight with strain.

"What photograph?" he asked in a strangely harsh voice.

I talked on and on. I could not stop talking.

He was very quiet. My mother's eyes darted around the room.

I said, "The canary and the dog, Papa. They were also accidents."

"What?" my father asked, startled. His voice shook faintly.

"They were accidents, Papa. I didn't kill them."

My mother sat down quickly beside me. I felt her cold, small fingers on my forehead. "Sha, darling, sha. Who is even thinking of the canary and the dog? No one even remembers it anymore."

"Of course it was an accident," my father said loudly.

"I saw the photograph by accident. It was on the desk and I picked it up. I couldn't see you too good, Papa. Were you behind the sign? But I saw Uncle Meyer with the gun."

"All right, David," my father said. He was tense and dis-traught. "Go back to sleep. Mama will give you your med-icine."

From my parents' bedroom came the sudden high-pitched wailing cry of my brother.

"Master of the Universe," my father breathed. "This will be a bastard of a night."

"I am going to the baby," said my mother. "Give the child his medicine."

"The photograph was on the desk?" asked my father quietly when my mother had gone.

The room had begun to revolve, very slowly, as if a wind were turning it on a tall stick. I thought I heard a rattling, clattering sound on the floor. I shut my eyes in horror. Pieces of shattered heads were rolling back and forth. The crushed head of the dog was there. And yellow feathers, rolling heavily from wall to wall, banging and clattering across the floor. I heard my father say something. The head of the dog made rolling, thumping sounds on the floor. And there was blood.

I cried out and my father held me to him.

"You are having fever dreams," he said. "Let me give you your medicine."

I sat up and drank the sour-tasting liquid and the water, and lay back on the pillow. My throat hurt terribly.

"Go to sleep, David," my father said. He was silent a long moment. Then he said, "There is no such photograph as the one you say you saw. But we will talk more about it tomorrow."

He went quickly from the room.

The rain beat against the window and the trees and the street. There had been snow and a dense forest with ice and snow on the trees. The ice hanging from the branches had looked like the knives in the hands of some of the men: long and pointed and white against the darkness of the trunks. There is no such photograph. How could there be no such photograph? I felt sleep darkening the fringes of thought. My father had not said that. I had heard him incorrectly. How could he have said that?

He said it again the following morning. He came into my room wearing his pajamas and I sensed him by my bed and woke. I saw him through a fog of pain and fever. My window shade was gray with morning light.

"How do you feel, David?"

"Hurts," I said, restraining tears. "Throat."

He gazed at me intently, his squarish features weary. He had forgotten to shave last night. His face was dark with stubble. From his crib in my parents' bedroom my brother cried out in his sleep, then lapsed back into silence. My father frowned and shook his head. His gray eyes stared at me dully. He ran his fingers across his head but his hair remained wild, spiky.

"Can you breathe through your nose?" he asked.

I shook my head, feeling the heaviness in my forehead and along my cheekbones.

"I'll call the doctor to come and examine you." He hesitated, gazing down at me intently. "David, I called Uncle Meyer. There was never any photograph taken of him with a gun."

I did not know what to say. Was that rain on my window? Had it rained through the night?

"In a forest, Papa," I said, feeling dry, searing pain in my throat.

"What?"

"It was in a forest. And there were flags."

My father stared at me. Then he shook his head. I could see his chest through the two top open buttons of his pajamas. He was strong. He exercised every morning before he washed and dressed and prayed the Morning Service. Sometimes he would let me feel the muscles on his arms and stomach and chest. There were muscles in his neck, too. His neck was thicker than my uncle's. No, it had been my uncle's face, not my father's.

"I called Mrs. Bader. She does not know about any such photograph. There is no such photograph, David. When Mr. Bader comes back from Europe we will ask him what you saw. But you could not have seen a photograph of your uncle with a gun. Now let me help you go to the toilet and wash up. Mama will come in soon with some cereal for you."

"There was a photograph," I said later to my mother through my pain.

"Your uncle never played with a gun in his life," she said nervously. "Eat your cereal. Here, let me feed you. In Europe, your uncle went to yeshivas. Gangsters play with guns, not your Uncle Meyer."

I lay in my bed, breathing slowly through my tormented throat. There was sunlight on my window now and on the bare trees outside. Soon Joey Younger would be playing on the street. And Tony Savanola. My brother would be in his carriage, sleeping in the sun. I turned my head to the wall and closed my eyes. I had dreamed it. I had dreamed the photograph. Who had entered the darkened study and removed it from my hands? Yes, there had been a forest and faces and knives and revolvers. Why were they all saying there was no such photograph? But perhaps I had dreamed it.

I heard the door to my room open. I turned my head. My mother came quietly inside. "Dr. Weidman is here," she said, her eyes looking nervously past my head at a point somewhere on my pillow.

He came in cheerfully, pink-faced, smiling, vaguely redolent of outside air. I wondered where my father was. Dr. Weidman chatted amiably, took my temperature, looked in my throat, felt the sides of my neck, tapped my chest and back, listened to my lungs, and wrote a prescription. "It's the same black year," he said cheerfully in Yiddish. "A more severe case. But the same thing. Maybe we should have you bring him into the office for a complete checkup, Ruth. When he is on his feet again. This medicine is three times a day, once after each meal." He pinched my cheek, patted my arm, and left, followed by my mother.

I lay very still in my bed, ill once again from the injury that had not been done to me, and thought of the faces of Uncle Meyer and Dr. Weidman in the photograph everyone was saying I had not seen.

I was out of bed in a week, suffered a relapse, and was in bed for another ten days. Pale, enervated, I sat on a chair in the sunlight on the street and watched my friends at play. Then I looked at the tiny buds that were slowly appearing on the trees, as my mother had promised, and felt vaguely calmed. My brother lay asleep in his carriage. I touched the carriage and felt it sway. My brother stirred. I removed my hand and sat very still in the sunlight. I was exhausted, drained of will and thought.

A few weeks later I heard my father's rage when my mother told him the results of the examination in Dr. Weidman's office.

"Is he crazy? This is how he repays me? To make such a mistake! What kind of a doctor did he turn out to be?"

I shivered in the darkness of my room listening to his raging fury.

"He is a good doctor, Max. Please don't shout. Doctors make mistakes. Everyone makes mistakes."

"It is the job of a doctor *not* to make mistakes!"

"Max—"

"The Bratzlaver was right. A doctor is a messenger of the Angel of Death!"

"Max, please, please!" Her voice was shrill. "Doctors can't help anyway."

"What do you mean?"

"They are after the boy."

"Oh, stop it, Ruth! Women's superstitious nonsense. That too you learned in Bobrek? It is not enough that you try to protect him with those useless incantations?"

And there was silence. I lay in my bed and listened fearfully to that silence. It was broken finally by the voice of a radio announcer.

They did not tell me what Dr. Weidman had discovered. In a vague way I understood that I would be repeatedly ill all my young life. I was very frightened. I would try to forget the photograph that my father, mother, uncle, aunt, Mrs. Bader, and, finally, Mr. Bader himself said I could not have seen.

"You saw Jews at a wedding holding bottles of wine," Mr. Bader had told me softly with a kind smile when he returned from Europe. "No, I don't have it anymore. It wasn't mine and I returned it. There are many pictures of Jews celebrating weddings out of doors. Do you want to see some? No? All right. But gun? Knives? David Lurie, no one told me you had such a strong imagination. Do you enjoy listening to stories? Yes? I thought so. But truth is more important than stories, David. All you saw was a photograph of happy Jews celebrating a wedding in a forest."

There was the zoo and the meadow and the small still pond; there was the clearing in the pine wood and the picnic in the clearing later that spring when my eyes really saw for the first time the scar on my father's face.

The zoo was located one block away from our wide street. In its cages, pavilions, and outdoor pens lived lions, tigers, panthers, elephants, giraffes, llamas, foxes, wolves, bears, and exotic animals whose names remain unknown to me to this day. Seals sunned themselves and swam in an outdoor paradise of water and smoothened stone; hippos bathed and snorted; monkeys leaped about and searched in each other's fur for fleas and lice; tropical birds flashed bright hues through the aviary; lizards and crocodiles lived in primal silence within glass-enclosed terrariums. There were oaks and maples and sycamores and pines; there was grass; there were flower beds that brought wonder to my mother's nervous eyes.

The boulevard side of the zoo was rimmed by a high white stone wall into which was set a wide, ornate wrought-iron gate. All day long people came and went through that gate. Along the other side of the zoo, adjoining the pens and pavilions that housed the lions and tigers and elephants, was a low rolling meadow with a small pond. Beyond the meadow lay a dense pine wood within which was a small clearing. As far back as memory takes me I remember picnics in that clearing with my parents and my little brother and sometimes with my aunt and uncle and Cousin Saul. There we would eat and I would play with my father and he would periodically check the muscles of my arms and appear unimpressed and remind me that brains were important but muscles were important too and when would I stop throwing a ball like a woman. There my father and uncle would have long quiet conversations away from my mother and aunt and the noisy boys. And there, after a while, the nervousness would leave my mother's face and she would sit in the sunlight and smile faintly at memories that seemed to come to her nowhere else but in that clearing.

We went very often to that zoo, accompanied at times by my Cousin Saul. Together we would slowly walk the zoo's meandering paths, and Saul would poke his thin pale face and brown curly hair and clear blue eyes as close as he could to the animals and birds, and murmur in wonder about the endless variety of living things created by God. He was deeply religious. He read a great deal and in a firm voice transmitted without hesitation the pertinent contents of his reading.

He said to me in Yiddish one day as we walked by ourselves through the zoo, "All these animals are alive because there were animals saved by Noah in the Flood."

I knew about Noah and the Flood.

"You know what it was like in the ark? You know what it was like to feed all those animals?"

That aspect of things had never occurred to me.

"It was a noisy mess. There were some animals that had to be fed during the day and other animals that had to be fed during the night."

"Really?"

"That's right. Noah didn't sleep. The noise was terrible. But the lion was quiet. He had a fever but still he was quiet and didn't bother anyone."

I had always looked with awe at the golden power and grace of the lions in the zoo. Now I admired them for the patient thoughtfulness of their ancestor.

We stopped once at the pond in the meadow near the pine wood. Small fish swam smoothly in the still water.

"Did you know that fish weren't killed in the Flood? That's right. Because they didn't have any sins. That's why God sent a flood. So the fish wouldn't die."

"Really?"

"That's right. They just swam around the whole time."

I gazed deep into the water and marveled at these descendants of the only sinless beings in all creation now swimming placidly in the sun-warmed pond of our zoo.

Each walk through that zoo with my cousin brought me new knowledge from his reading.

"Did you know that before the Flood there were more non-kosher animals than kosher animals in the world?"

"No. Really?"

"Noah took seven pairs of each kosher animal into the ark and only two pairs of the nonkosher animals. And now there are more kosher animals in the world than nonkosher ones."

I envied him his ability to read and hungered for the day when words would be more than shapeless squiggles to my eyes.

One day as we walked near the outdoor elephant pen he said, "I read something interesting about Noah last night."

"Yes?"

"There was a giant called Og on top of the ark."

"Really?"

"He was the king of a place called Bashan. He promised that he and his people would be servants to Noah and his family forever. But he couldn't fit into the ark, so Noah let him ride on the roof."

"A giant. With all those animals."

"I read something else. Falsehood tried to come into the ark."

"What?"

"An animal called Falsehood tried to come into the ark. But Noah said he was only admitting animals by pairs. So Falsehood looked for a partner and found Misfortune, and

Noah let them into the ark. Falsehood and Misfortune became partners together forever."

I was about five at the time and did not understand that. My cousin seemed disappointed by my childish inability to grasp this latest truth. He offered me a simpler truth in its place.

"Did you know that elephants can pull trees right out of the ground with their trunks?"

"No," I said, staring in wonder at the gray wrinkled giant beings in the pen. "Really?"

I grew to love that zoo, its curving paths and grassy knolls, the animals in the cages, pavilions, and pens on its sprawling grounds, the wooden benches beneath its trees, and the drinking fountains located precisely at those points where thirst was likely to be most acute. I laughed at the monkeys, gazed with delight at the tropical birds, marveled at the silken movements of the swimming seals, and befriended a young white-haired billy goat to whom I fed peanuts, chocolate, and an occasional ice-cream bar, which he often swallowed together with its wooden stick and paper wrapper. And I stood in awe before the sleek-skinned tawny lions, the restless tigers, and lumbering elephants; they roused in me lurid and exciting visions of the steaming jungles my cousin told me had once been their home.

Early one Sunday afternoon about two and a half months after my accidental encounter with the photograph of happy Jews celebrating a wedding in a forest, I walked with my parents and two-year-old brother through the zoo and the meadow toward the clearing in the pine wood. We were going to the annual picnic of an organization to which my father belonged. I had been taken to this picnic before, and remembered dull speeches and the extraordinary sight of my father expertly engaged in a soccer game and a wrestling match. I regarded with distaste the prospect of sitting through the speeches but looked forward keenly to the games and the wrestling.

It was a sunny, windless day. The air was blue and warm. At the edge of the wood I paused to watch a flock of small, shrill birds wheeling in wide circles against the sky.

In our apartment the new canary sang often. But my father would not let it out of its cage. It was the job of a canary to sing and not to fly, he said. And so our canary sang and did not fly. I was jealous of its lovely voice and the way everyone who came into our apartment would gaze at it in rapture when it sang. It would not hurt it to let it fly. Only after our first canary had flown out of my bedroom window had my father thought to say that it was the job of a canary to sing and not to fly.

"Starlings," I heard my father say now. "It is the job of starlings to make noise and dirt. I do not like starlings."

"How they fly," murmured my mother. "A starling is sometimes a good sign."

"Vultures also fly," said my father with faint derision. "Should the world admire vultures?"

He had said to me after the canary had flown out of my bedroom window, "I told everyone to leave the windows closed. Since when does a four-year-old boy open windows? What did you do, stand on the chair? You could have fallen out."

"I thought it was back in the cage, Papa."

"You thought. It is the job of a child to listen to his father. Now a cat will eat it."

I shuddered.

"Yes. A cat will eat it. All of it, bones and flesh and everything, except the feathers. It is the job of a cat to eat birds. But it does not have to be our bird."

And he smacked my hand. "So you should remember that your job is to listen."

He saw the world as firm and fixed. He said it gave him comfort to know that everything had its place and task; for example, he said, it was his task to provide for his family, and that was why he went away to his real estate business every morning and sometimes returned late in the evening. But he did not have to like everything in the world, he said. Some things had gone wrong of themselves after God had created them. He did not like volcanoes, tidal waves, large flesh-eating birds and animals, anti-Semitic goyim, diseases that killed or crippled people, children who did not obey their parents, and numerous other prevailing evils. These things made the world unsafe and dirty, he said. What he did not like he let us know about, often derisively.

For the picnic he had put on white summer trousers, a striped shirt, a white collar and dark tie, and a light blue jacket. His hard straw hat was tipped back on his head. The large picnic basket he carried in his right hand had been packed to the brim with food earlier in the day by my mother.

He held it as if it were one of the weightless birds wheeling about overhead. In his other hand he carried a blanket.

"I do not like starlings and vultures," my father said. "Starlings are gangsters with wings."

"But they tell us guests are coming," said my mother. "On the farm when we saw starlings Mama would send us out to bring in another chicken."

"They are noisy birds and they dirty the world. That is their job, but I do not have to like them. Are we going to the picnic or shall we stand here all day talking about birds?"

She gave the starlings a final uneasy glance and retreated from the conversation. Often she would wilt like a flower in the cold winds of a disagreement. Her face would dissolve, all the parts of it would melt and flow together under the slightest strain: a diaper pin that pricked her finger; a hot iron that scorched a blouse; a sudden pool of ink from the unpredictable Waterman's pen with which she wrote her letters to her family in Poland. It seemed about to dissolve now under the strain of my brother's efforts to free his hand from her grasp.

"Stop pulling," she entreated. "Alex, please."

I went quickly over to him and grasped his free hand. My mother released him. He looked up at me with delight. He liked me to walk with him.

A moment later the four of us entered the pine wood.

The air changed abruptly from sun-filled warmth to pine-scented shadowy coolness. A narrow dirt path pointed a curving finger through the trees. My father sniffed at the cool air, smiled briefly at a private memory, and led the way, ducking agilely beneath low branches and helping my mother across a fallen tree. I followed behind my mother, holding tightly to my brother's hand. He stopped at the fallen tree and bent to inspect a colony of ants that had made a home in the earth beneath the torn roots. I pulled at his arm and he pulled back at mine. I squeezed his hand hard and he yielded, first giving me a puzzled look as if to ask what right I had to cause him pain. Then his gray eyes and small squarish face flashed with sudden anger and he pulled hard against my arm. He wanted another look at the ants. My mother reached over from the other side of the tree and, straining her short thin arms, lifted him across. I took his hand again. He walked beside me but he was angry now and every so often he gave a tentative pull at my hand to test how strongly I was holding him.

The cool piney air of the wood was delicious. I felt it like cool water on my hands and face and on my bare legs beneath my shorts. I loved places dense with trees and leaves and blue shadows beneath the leaves and moist dead leaves on damp earth; like the forest behind the small white cottage we owned somewhere near tall mountains far away from the city. We went there in August. My father called it going to the country. We went to escape from something called polio that made people very sick and sometimes paralyzed or killed them. "The Angel of Death is doing his job again," my father would say, and he and my mother would pack quickly and we would go off in a car to the white cottage and the forest. I was not permitted to go more than a few feet into the forest. "If you get lost, you will give the police a hard job to do," my father warned me. "Who needs a job like that, eh, my little David? You can go into the forest only until the stream, that is all." The stream lay about ten feet into the trees. "You go beyond the stream, it will be my job to smack your behind. You understand?" I understood. But here I could walk deep into the pine wood and breathe its scented air and listen to the mysterious rustling of its branches when I stood still and closed my eyes.

I followed closely behind my mother. My brother walked docilely beside me. I liked him to walk beside me like that: quiet and obedient. Insects swam lazily in the shade and glittered with brief incandescence as they flitted in and out of the beams of sunlight that penetrated the pine-needle roof of the wood. Here and there along the path, as we walked its beckoning curves into the heart of the wood, a huge gnarled root showed its dark power as it lay pushing up the earth. I really loved this pine wood. I loved its silences and the still sounds of a summer breeze in its branches. I liked things to be quiet. I did not even like it when our new canary sang too long. But I did not open my window to let our first canary fly out. I would not do anything like that. It had really been an accident.

Like the accident with the dog.

The woman in our apartment house who had owned the dog was a middle-aged, thin-chested, flinty widow with a mole on her upper lip and a brassy voice. She let the dog roam through the neighborhood. He was a large dog with long, shaggy brown hair, rheumy eyes, and dirty teeth. He would upset garbage cans, relieve himself against the maple in front of our house, and squat to empty himself right on the sidewalk. The woman's name was Mrs. Horowitz and the dog's name was Shaigitz, a derisive Yiddish colloquialism for a non-Jew. No one on our block liked Mrs. Horowitz, and no one disliked Shaigitz, except our Irish janitor who had to repair the carnage of overturned garbage cans the dog left in his wake. All the kids on the block would pet Shaigitz and feed him candy and cookies. I would pet him when he came over to me while I watched my brother asleep in his carriage. He had a moist, dirty smell about him and his breath was hot and odorous, but I petted him and liked him because everyone else did.

My father came home early from his office one day and saw me with the dog. He shooed the dog away with his Yiddish newspaper and said to me, "Dogs are dirty."

I hung my head. It was two or three weeks after the canary had flown out of my window.

"In Europe dogs were trained by the goyim to bite Jews. I detest dogs. Keep that filthy dog away from the carriage. Do you hear?"

"Yes, Papa."

"And do not put your hands in your mouth or your eyes until you wash them."

"Yes, Papa."

"And do not look so unhappy. It is not the end of the world."

He peered into the carriage, smiled briefly at my sleeping brother, and went into our apartment house. The dog sniffed at a tree near the edge of the sidewalk and went off to join a crowd of kids playing with bottle caps near Mr. Steinberg's candy store.

My mother said to me that night as she put me to bed, "A dog once bit your father." Her eyes blinked nervously. "Sometimes the soldiers had dogs," she added.

"Which soldiers?"

"Soldiers," she murmured. "And Papa would pay them to keep it quiet."

"Papa?"

"My papa," she said. "Your grandfather."

"Keep it quiet?"

"Go to sleep, David." And she shuddered.

The next day I saw the dog urinating on one of the wheels of my brother's carriage. Then he got up on his hind legs and stood there, his forelegs on the carriage, his head poking around inside, his tail wagging. I had moved away from the carriage to join a game of marbles. I rushed back and with my open hand—my father had smacked me that way when the canary had gone through my open window—hit the dog hard on his hindquarters above the wagging tail and shouted, "Go away!" The dog yelped, ran into the street, and was struck by a car.

The front left wheel of the car ran over his head. The rear wheel ran over his back. The car braked to a stop. All up and down the block everyone froze. Heads turned. The dog let out short, ear-piercing, yelping cries, lifted himself from the cobblestone street, his head crushed, his back broken, dragged himself to the curb, and died. There was a lot of blood. His long shaggy brown hair began to turn orange with blood. There was a trail of glistening blood on the street and a pool of blood along the curb. One eye hung from its socket by a bleeding thread of flesh.

A crowd was gathering around the dead Shaigitz. My brother continued to sleep peacefully. I leaned against his carriage, cold and trembling, my legs barely able to support my body. Mrs. Horowitz came rushing out of our apartment house, led by Joey Younger, a thin-faced, unkempt busybody about my age. She looked at Shaigitz and screamed.

I leaned forward away from my brother's carriage and vomited my breakfast onto the sidewalk. My nose began to bleed.

"It was an accident," I kept saying, holding a handkerchief to my nose.

"What did you hit him for?" the kids on the block kept saying.

"He had his head right in the carriage," I kept saying.

"You could have told him to go away," they kept saying. "What did you hit him for?"

"It was an accident," I said to my father.

"Do not worry yourself over it. He was a filthy dog. Who needed him around making dirt on the sidewalk and overturning the garbage cans? Do not look so sad. It is not the end of the world."

"It was an accident," I said to my mother.

She blinked her eyes nervously. "In Europe they made less fuss when a Jew was killed than they are making over this dog."

"I thought he would bite Alex."

"Of course," my mother said. "Why else would you have hit him like that?"

"It was an accident," I said to my cousin.

"Sure," he said, and gave me a pitying look which I did not understand and was afraid to ask him to explain.

"You killed my dog!" Mrs. Horowitz screamed at me one afternoon in the entrance hall of our apartment house. "I'm all alone!"

"It was an accident," I cried, cringing in terror.

"You did me a favor, sonny," said the barrel-chested Irish janitor of our house when I went into the alleyway one day after a ball. "That dog was a pain in my ass."

"But it was an accident, Mr. Ryan."

"Sure it was, sonny. Sure it was. But you did me a big favor."

At night I dreamed of the dog and the blood and the eye dangling from the socket by the single thread of flesh. I cried in the darkness when I woke from my dreams. They had really both been accidents. But I cried bitterly—for the scattering of yellow feathers that had once been our bird and for the crumpled mass of hair and flesh and bones that had once been Mrs. Horowitz's dog. And for the feeling I had that somehow no one really believed me when I said that they had both been accidents. . . .

I stepped very carefully over a root, holding tightly to my brother's hand. He pulled again at my hand but I would not let him go. I felt his small fingers straining against mine. He had short chunky arms and legs. My arms and legs were like sticks. He wore dark brown shorts and a white shirt and diapers beneath the shorts. He had stopped abruptly, attracted by something on the edge of the underbrush alongside the path. I pulled at him but he would not move.

"Bud," he said, pointing. "Bud."

I looked and saw a small gray-feathered bird lying dead on the moist dark floor of the wood. Its black eyes were gaping, its beak was open wide, the feathers stood out starkly from its head—as if death had crept up on it and shouted in its ear before striking. I felt cold and nauseated looking at it. My brother seemed fascinated. He bent closer.

Dead birds were common in this wood. The week before we had seen gray feathers scattered on the path. No bones or flesh; only feathers.

"An owl ate it," my father had said. "Owls eat that way. And cats," he added.

My mother had looked away. I had felt my stomach knot and turn over. The blood beat in my head. I had feared another nosebleed.

My brother bent closer to the dead bird on the dark earth of the wood.

"Bud," he said eagerly.

"Yes, bird," I said, turning away from the decayed and pulpy form. "Come on."

He bent still closer.

"Come on," I said.

He reached out to touch it. I raised my hand to hit him, and stopped. I lowered my hand quickly.

"Look where Mama and Papa are already," I heard myself say. "Look. We'll be lost."

He straightened. His dark eyes gave me a brief frightened glance. I led him away from the dead bird.

The canary had flown in from the small hallway that led from the living room to my bedroom. I heard it before I saw it—the rushing flutter of its wings. It struck the upper closed part of the window and fell onto the sill. In a wild panic I reached for it and held it in my small hands. It struggled and pecked at my fingers. I felt it straining against my fingers. I did not want to crush it. I eased my hold on it and suddenly it was free and out the window and gone. I had been ill again and had opened the window because I could not breathe in the hot airless room. My throat was dry and sore. I was feverish and had opened the window for air and the canary flew out and had ended up only feathers or moldering in death. In my lunge for it after it had gone out the window I had almost fallen out the window myself. But I did not tell that to anyone. I thought my father might hit me again if I told him that.

"Putty bud," my brother said happily.

"Yes," I said. "Pretty bird."

He toddled along beside me, his squarish baby face glowing with delight. Had I been so unknowing at two years of age? Probably. I could not remember. I was almost six and I could not remember having been two. What was my earliest memory? My parents talking softly together in Yiddish in the kitchen or living room of our apartment. I would lie in my bed and listen to them talking together in Yiddish.

"You're sick a lot," Joey Younger, the neighborhood busybody, had once said to me.

"You get sick too, Joey."

"Yeah, but you're sick practically all the time."

"I am not," I said.

"You want to race me to the candy store?"

I could not race. I had been ill and had to sit in the sun and rest. He knew I could not race.

"Why am I sick practically all the time?" I asked my mother that evening as she put me to bed.

"You'll outgrow it," she said, and turned her nervous eyes away from me.

She had gone out of my room and later I heard her talking quietly with my father in the kitchen. Sometimes they would listen to the radio or the Victrola in the living room and then sit there and talk. But listening to them talking at night was not a very sharp early memory. I could not remember my earliest memory.

"Bud bud bud," my brother was saying loudly and joyfully. "Budee budee."

I held him tightly. The path had thinned to a narrow wedge between dense growths of underbrush. I wished he would be still.

"Budee bud bud," he kept saying. "Alek thee budee."

"Yes, Alex saw a bird."

The path widened, its dark earth crisscrossed by snaking roots. Up ahead my mother had stopped for a moment to look back at us.

"Are you all right, David?"

"Yes, Mama."

"Be careful, darling. Watch that Alex doesn't fall."

"Yes, Mama."

"And here we are," I heard my father say loudly around a curve in the path that concealed him behind a dense clump of pines and brush. "Look who's here. Either you are early or we are late." There was a brief pause. "We are late. As usual."

My mother turned and was gone around the curve in the path. I came into the curve in time to see my father step quickly from the bluish shadows beneath the pines into the pool of shimmering opalescence that was the clearing. A moment later my mother followed him, moving quickly into the light. They would both move quickly into the light just like that, walking softly and quickly from my room after they put me to bed and stepping from my darkness into the light of the small hall and the living room. Quickly, as if they were glad another of my days had come to an end and they could be alone to talk together in the kitchen or living room. And I would lie awake and listen to them talk, for sleep would come to me swiftly only when I was feverish and had been given medicine. After a while they would cease talking quietly and use their normal voices. I would hear strange words and strange names from a world that was not my own. I could remember some of them clearly: Warsaw and Lemberg and Lodz and Pilsudski; the names of relatives in a distant place called Poland; the word Cossacks; and two words that seemed resonant with peculiar menace, the words machine gunner. The words and names entered the darkness of my room and echoed softly between my walls. I hungered to understand their meaning but would not ask, for I was afraid my father would hit me if he discovered I lay awake listening to him talk. Sometimes they quarreled. But I could not understand what they said then, for when they raged at one another it was in a language other than Yiddish. I lay in terror listening to their voices. I could not imagine what my mother's pale gaunt face might look like as she screamed at my father; she rarely spoke above a nervous murmur to anyone when she was with me. The quarrels were fierce, loud, and brief. They would end with my mother breaking into tears and often my father's strangely subdued soothing words in Yiddish, "It will be better, Ruth. It will be better. We blame ourselves for what the goyim did." Finally, exhausted, I would hunger for sleep; but it would come only of its own will, sometimes sooner, sometimes later, uncaring of my needs and fears. And always before it came there would be the light and the talk on the other side of my door, just as now there was the milky white light of the clearing beyond the trees and the talk between my parents and my aunt and uncle and Cousin Saul.

"Good afternoon, brother mine. You're late." It was my uncle's voice, gently chiding.

"Of course we are late. When aren't we late?"

"If I were buying a property you would be on time."

"For a customer I am never late. How are you, Sarah? Your back is better?"

"Much better, Max."

"God in heaven, Saul. What happened to your lip?"

"I fell, Uncle Max."

I heard the talk through the trees as I came along the path to the clearing. There was a brief silence. Then I heard my uncle say, "He's all right, Max. It looks worse than it is."

"Yes." It was my father's voice. "Well. Let's get settled."

"You look pretty today, Ruth. I like your dress." It was the musical voice of my aunt.

"Thank you, Sarah." My mother's voice was almost indistinct.

"We will put the blanket here," said my father. "How did you fall, for God's sake?"

"Against an open drawer in my room."

There was another silence.

"Tall?" my brother said suddenly. "Tall?"

"Yes," I said. "It's Saul."

"Tall, Tall, Tall," cried my brother elatedly. "Tall!"

"Who leaves drawers open in a room?" said my father.

"Here, I'll help you with the blanket," my uncle said.

"An open drawer," my father said. "God in heaven."

"Don't make more of it than it is, Max," said my uncle. "Watch where you're stepping. You'll make ash and dust of the chicken."

"You should be more careful, Saul."

"Yes, Uncle Max."

"Pull your corner over to you more," said my uncle. "All right. Fine. Now we forget about lips and other troubles and we have an enjoyable day. Let's settle the details now before the others come."

"Tallee!" my brother cried out again with joy and pulled me from the shade of the wood into the brightness of the clearing. I blinked in the sudden white sunlight that stung my eyes. The ground in the clearing was level and grassy. I released my brother's hand and watched him break into a waddling run toward Saul, who sat in the sunlight on a blanket in the center of the clearing.

"Tallee!" my brother cried joyfully. "Tallee! Tallee!"

"Be careful of the lip," I heard my father say. "It is a boy's job to—"

"Max," my uncle said. "For heaven's sake."

My brother flung himself upon Saul with a cry of delight and they went down together on the blanket.

I stood alone on the edge of the clearing. Through the pine wood came the distant trumpeting of an elephant. The sound sent through me a vague sense of alarm. A bird called softly from the canopy of pine boughs overhead, its song rising and falling and rising again; then a brief flutter of wings, and silence. I felt weary and warm from the walk through the wood and there was a slight pain behind my eyes. That was the signal: I would be sick again soon. The pain, and then the fever and the stuffed nose and the choking sensation of not

being able to breathe, of a mask clamped over my face shutting off the air. I would breathe through my mouth, and my
throat would become parched and the pain of its raw dryness
would reach down into my chest, and I would cry and the pain
would get worse; and my mother would comfort me and sit
with me; and sometimes Saul would come over and tell me
stories about Adam and Noah and Abraham and kings and
battles, stories from the Bible; and sometimes in the night I
would wake inside my fever and think I heard my father in
my room praying softly, his short, thick-shouldered form
vaguely outlined within the darkness; but I was never certain
if he was really there or I dreamed it, and I did not ask. I
could not remember clearly when I had last been ill but it did
not seem to me I had been well a long time.

"Hey, were you sick again, Davey?" Tony Savanola had
asked in a kind voice when I had come out of the apartment
house after my last illness. He lived in the ground-floor apartment directly below us and was my age. He was a little taller
than I and had olive-colored skin, dark hair, and dark eyes.
His father owned a shoe store somewhere in Manhattan. "I
didn't see you for a while," he said.

"Yeah, I was sick, Tony."

"You're sick a lot, Davey."

I did not know what to say and felt a little ashamed.

"You want to play immies?" he asked in a gentle way.

"Hey, Davey!" a woman's voice called. "Davey Lurie!"

I looked and saw Tony's mother leaning out of her ground-
floor window. She was a very fat woman with many chins and
many children. Tony had two older brothers, three older sisters, and one younger brother. She waved a pudgy arm at me
and gave me a big smile.

"How you feel, Davey?"

"Better, thank you, Mrs. Savanola."

"You look thin like a stick," she said loudly. "What your
mother feeding you? Lotsa fettina you should eat, not the
skinny pollo. You look pale like a ghost. I gonna talk to your
mother." She disappeared behind the curtains of the window.

I looked down at the sidewalk. Cars and trucks went by on
the cobbled street. I was vaguely aware of the shouts of playing children and of the clang and clatter of a trolley along the
boulevard that paralleled the zoo a block away. My legs were
weak. But I wanted to play. It had been such a long time now
since I had played with someone my age. The last illness had

seemed interminable: in my bed staring out the window at the
sunlight on the maple; the way it played on the leaves; the
sounds of the street below; the fever; interminable.

"I'll play you immies, Tony."

"You got any?"

"Upstairs."

"Nah, don't go back upstairs, Davey. I'll lend you some.
Come on."

We played a long slow game of marbles and I won a few
and paid him back the ones he had loaned me.

"You're a good player, Davey."

"Thanks, Tony. Thanks for lending me."

"I hope you don't get sick again too soon, Davey."

His wide dark eyes were kind and earnest. I felt buoyed by
his presence. He wanted to play another game but I needed to
rest.

"What're you hanging around with that Tony Savanola
for?" Joey Younger asked me later that morning.

"I like him."

"He's a goy. You got to be careful with goyim."

"But he's nice, Joey."

"Yeah? My brother says they all hate Jews. You going to
play with Eddie Kulanski?"

"I don't know Eddie Kulanski."

"He moved in while you were sick. You going to play with
him?"

"I don't even know him, Joey."

"He's a goy. My brother says he's a Polak and all Polaks
hate Jews."

"What's a Polak?"

He looked at me with disbelief and vague contempt. His
family lived on the fourth floor of our apartment house; his
father sold furniture. He was a few months older than I, and
almost two inches taller. His thick brown hair was in wild
disarray and he was sweaty and dirty from the running games
he had been playing all morning. He explained the word to me
without concealing his disdain at my ignorance. "Boy, you
miss a lot because you're sick so much," he said, and bounded
up the front stoop and into the house.

I sat in the sun next to my brother's carriage. A moment
later, the entrance door to the house opened and Mrs. Horowitz emerged. I cringed in my chair as she passed by giving
me a black raging look.

"I see you're well again," she said in her brassy voice. "Whose dog will you kill today?"

She woke my brother. He began to cry. I rocked his carriage and it was a while before he went back to sleep.

Yes, there was the pain behind my eyes now and I would be ill again soon; perhaps by the end of the day but certainly by tomorrow morning. Should I tell my parents? My father would not let me play the picnic games with him. I stood uncertainly on the edge of the clearing and watched my little brother playing on the blanket with Saul, and my father and uncle talking quietly together, and my mother and aunt setting out the food. The air of the clearing vibrated softly with the insect hum of the wood. Birds sang. The noise of traffic was indistinct. I looked down at the grass and the earth and listened to my brother's laughter.

Again, faintly through the dense pine wood yet still edged with shrillness, came the trumpeting cry of one of the elephants in the zoo. It seemed a cold, frightening sound to me now. Was someone hurting the elephants? Who would dare hurt an animal so huge and powerful?

"They live a long time," Saul had once said. "Hundreds of years."

"Really?"

"And they have very good memories. They never forget anything."

I had difficulty remembering things sometimes: days blurred; time fused into a shapeless gray mass; I could not call back to memory the correct order of events.

"You came to America first, Mama?" I had asked when I was last ill.

"No, darling. Your father came to America first."

"From where did he come, Mama?"

"Lemberg. A city in Poland."

"Before the big war?" Words came from me in an uncontrollable rush when I was ill with fever. I could not stop asking questions and talking. "From Og?" I asked. "From Logz?"

"No, darling. After the war. Your Uncle Meyer also came after the war. Your Aunt Sarah is from Lodz, not Logz."

"Where are Papa's papa and mama?"

"They are still in Lemberg."

"And your papa and mama?"

"Near Lemberg. In Bobrek. You should be quiet now and rest, David."

Bobrek. Mr. Shmuel Bader had recently traveled to Bobrek. With a package of medicine for Mama's mother. He had returned and had come to our apartment to see my parents. They had talked a long time in subdued voices.

"Why are they there?" I heard myself ask.

"They can't come to America yet, darling."

"Where is America?"

"America is here, darling. We are living in America."

"Why did you and Papa come to America?"

"We were running away from goyim who hated Jews."

"Is America far from Poland?"

"Yes," she said, and her voice trembled faintly. "Very far."

"Mama, could I have some more water? My throat is hurting me."

"Yes, darling. Yes. Did you have a dream last night?"

"No."

"No dream? Nothing? You're sure?"

"I can't remember, Mama."

She seemed disappointed.

"Joey isn't sick so much," I said. "Why am I sick so much?"

"Sha," she said. "You'll be all right. You'll outgrow it. Your nose will become all better when you grow up and become a big boy."

It was difficult to remember things clearly. I remembered the canary and the dog clearly. But I could not remember clearly why I had so loosened my hold on the canary as to let it fly off or why I had really hit the dog so hard. But they had been accidents. I remembered them clearly as accidents. I had thought the canary would fly back into the living room and the dog would scamper away along the sidewalk.

"You killed my poor dog, you miserable little boy!" Mrs. Horowitz had screamed at me later that day in the entrance hall of our apartment house. Her words echoed and reechoed between the marble walls.

I had cringed in terror against a stuffed chair.

She put her gray, powdered, wrinkled face close to mine. I saw the mole on her upper lip; small ash-gray hairs grew from it like pygmy vegetation. Her breath was warm and stale and reminded me of the dirty teeth of her dog. She had dry gray hair and wrinkles on her lips.

"You evil little boy!" she screamed in a thin, shrill voice. "If you hate everything because you're sick all the time, why don't you turn the evil eye on your own family? What did you want from my poor dog? Do you know what it is to be all alone?"

I did not understand what she was saying and I cried out in fear and bewilderment. A door opened. Mrs. Savanola stepped into the hall.

"Why you shouting?" she shouted at Mrs. Horowitz.

"Stay out of this, you!" shouted Mrs. Horowitz, her face going crimson with rage beneath the layer of powder.

"Stop you screaming!" Mrs. Savanola screamed.

"He killed my poor dog! He is an evil boy!"

"You crazy, you screaming this way! I call the police!"

I fled upstairs.

"I will give her, that lump of a cow, that stinking witch," my father shouted with rage when he came home and was told by my mother of the incident. "I will go down right now and give her."

"Max, don't make trouble. Please."

"It was an accident. What does she want from the boy?"

"The pain is not easier because something was an accident," my mother said. "Last night I dreamed of Avruml."

I sat at the kitchen table and saw the dark silence that fell across my father. I saw it descend over his raging eyes and his hard-boned face and jutting lower jaw. My mother looked down at the floor, her hands beneath her apron.

"What is there to eat?" my father said finally in a cold, quivering voice. Then he said, "I need a glass of coffee."

The entire house had talked about the dead dog. The entire block had seethed over the dead dog.

"So hard you had to hit him?" Mr. Steinberg, who owned the corner candy store, asked me. "He was such a friendly dog."

"It was an accident."

"And you kicked him yet, too."

"I didn't kick him. Who said I kicked him?" I could not remember having kicked him. I had hit him with my open hand, the way my father had hit me when the canary had flown through my open window. I had no memory at all of having kicked the dog.

"On the street people are saying you kicked him."

"But it's not true."

He blinked his pink-rimmed watery eyes and shook his bald head. "A pity and a shame. Such a nice dog. I used to sometimes give him candy to eat."

I went home and lay on my bed. I would not go outside. I

lay awake in the nights and listened to my parents talking. Sometimes my brother's crying woke me. A few days later I was sick again and I gave myself over gratefully to the darkness of drugged sleep.

I had not kicked the dog. Why had someone said I kicked the dog? I could not remember ever having kicked the dog.

"Does an elephant really remember everything, Saul?"

"That's what people say."

"It must feel good to be able to remember everything. I wish I could remember everything."

"Why?"

"Because I'd be the smartest man in the whole world. No one could fool me."

"You think so? Why?"

"Because I'd always know what the truth is."

"Maybe," he said, smiling. "Hey, you want to feed your billy goat some candy? We have to go home soon."

Each time I came to the zoo now I liked to feed the billy goat. He was young and small with white shaggy hair and a goatee and warm moist lips. Sometimes I could feel his breath on my face. I had fed him again today on the way through the zoo to the meadow and the wood.

"He likes you," my father had announced.

"Be careful he doesn't bite your hand, David," my mother warned, holding tightly to my brother's hand.

The goat's lips left a tickling sensation on my open palm. I laughed with delight.

"Silly billy goat," I said through the wire-mesh fence of the pen. "My nice silly billy goat."

"Dote," my brother said, straining to approach the fence. "Dote."

"No," my mother said, and held him back.

"My nice nice nice silly billy goat," I said, and felt very happy.

"Come," my father said. "We will be late."

And we were. But it had made no difference. They had expected us to be late. They often talked about that, my father and uncle.

"People who arrive late show they don't really want to come at all," my uncle had once said mildly, with a short laugh.

"From what book did that pearl come?" asked my father. His voice was vaguely annoyed.

My uncle named a title and an author.

"A treasury of wisdom," my father said derisively. "For such wisdom you crossed an ocean and came to America?"

"Just coming to America was wisdom enough," said my uncle.

"Yes," said my father quietly after a moment, nodding approval. "That was wisdom."

And over my uncle's gentle features had come a pink flush of pleasure at my father's words. Now I recalled vaguely a similar moment in Mr. Bader's apartment. Where had my father and uncle said that to one another about arriving late and coming to America? In our house? Sometimes they sat in the living room for hours, talking quietly. But I could not remember. For some reason it disturbed me not to be able to remember that.

I bent and touched the grassy earth of the clearing. I skimmed the open palm of my hand back and forth over the low grass. The grass tickled the palm of my hand. My nice nice nice silly billy goat.

"David," I heard my Aunt Sarah call from her blanket. "What are you doing there all alone? Come here and say hello to me."

I moved reluctantly into the clearing and crossed to where my aunt was seated. The sun had gone behind a layer of very thin clouds.

"Come here and give me a kiss," my aunt said, smiling and peering out at me from beneath the very wide brim of a flowery yellow hat. She had on a loose-fitting, pale blue summer dress. Her face was beautiful. She had long dark lashes and dark arching eyebrows. I kissed her cool cheek. She smelled of sweet perfume. Her short hair tickled my neck. I liked her but I did not like to kiss her. It was like kissing a wind: she was there and not there. Even as I kissed her she was poking and prodding me and talking.

"You are all bones," she chided, lowering her eyelids and turning to my mother. "The boy should have tonic. Do you give him tonic?"

"Yes," my mother answered very quietly from the adjoining blanket where Saul and my brother were rolling and laughing. "Tonic, cod-liver oil, sweet cream, everything."

"Then you should take him to a doctor."

"I took him to a doctor."

"What did he say?"

"That we should give him tonic, cod-liver oil, and sweet cream."

"Bones," my aunt said, turning back to me. "Look at you. You should go to the country and rest and eat."

"Soon," my mother said. "Perhaps even in middle or late July. Everything here is"—she hesitated—"ready."

"Yes," my aunt said softly. "We will be going about then also." She gazed at my mother. "It will be good to see them."

"Master of the Universe," my mother said, her eyes blinking. "Yes, it will be good to see them."

"Ouch!" Saul said loudly. "Watch it! You just hit my lip! Are you strong!" He let my brother roll over on top of him.

"This hat was a bargain," my aunt said to my mother. "You need a new hat, Ruth."

"Where are the others?" my mother murmured.

"They'll be here soon. There's a hat store on Fordham Road, Ruth. You really need a new hat."

I moved slowly away from them. They did not notice me. My father and uncle stood beneath a tree at the far end of the clearing, talking quietly. I moved toward the path we had taken through the wood. At the point where the path entered the clearing, I sat down in a patch of shade and waited for the faint throbbing behind my eyes to move into my forehead and become cruel pain. I did not think I would be able to play the picnic games today. If I was quiet and behaved myself during the meeting, my father had promised, then, after the soccer game and the wrestling, he would play with me—some running games and crawling games and hide-and-go-seek. I felt faintly shivery with the dark edge of oncoming fever. I could not remember the last time I had played a running game or a game with a ball. Mostly I played marbles. I would play with Tony Savanola and sometimes even with Joey Younger when he wasn't running around wildly or being a busybody. A while back I had come out of the house with a pocketful of marbles and had found Tony Savanola playing with a boy I did not recognize.

"Hey, Tony," I had said eagerly, coming up to them. It was a bright day. The maples were full and green with leaves. It felt good to be outside. I had been ill a very long time and my legs were weak. I longed to play with a friend.

Tony Savanola had looked up from the game and his olive-skinned features had taken on a look of happy surprise and then, almost immediately, of caution.

"Hey, Davey," he said, and glanced warily at the new boy, who was getting slowly to his feet from a kneeling position over the marbles game. I saw that the new boy's knees were red and pitted from the sidewalk. He was two inches taller than I, had pale blond hair and very pale gray eyes, and was dressed in shorts, a polo shirt, and sneakers. His eyes had a strange, half-closed, sleepy look to them, and his lips were small and thin. He looked to be about six years old.

"Can I play?" I asked eagerly.

"We're in the middle of a game, Davey."

"Can I play when you're finished? I got some good immies, Tony."

"I don't know," Tony Savanola said uncertainly. He looked at the new boy. "This is Eddie Kulanski," he said, as if to explain his wariness.

"I'm Davey Lurie," I said.

"Are you the kid that's always sick?" Eddie Kulanski asked.

"What?" I said.

"Hey, Eddie," Tony said quietly.

"We don't want your germs," Eddie Kulanski said.

"What?" I said again, feeling the weakness in my legs, and my heart suddenly leaping and pounding.

"Come on," Eddie Kulanski said to Tony, and got back down on the sidewalk. "It's my shot."

"I'll play with you later, Davey," Tony said.

They played as if I were not there. After a few minutes I turned and walked away. I went into the house and carried out the tricycle my father had given me a few weeks back after another of my lengthy periods in bed. I rode around slowly for a while. Eddie Kulanski and Tony Savanola finished their game and began another. The street was busy with traffic. Children ran about on the sidewalk; women shopped; an old man sat on a chair near a stoop, his wrinkled face to the sun. A horse and wagon clattered by on the cobblestones. From time to time I checked my little brother, who lay asleep in his carriage near our front stoop. Riding up the block slowly beneath the trees, with the broken sunlight and the late spring air on my face, I forgot Tony Savanola and Eddie Kulanski. I began to love the tricycle; I felt free on it; I could move easily; and there was the wind on my face and in my ears.

Joey Younger turned the corner of the block on a slanting run, saw me on the tricycle, and stopped. He trotted over to me, turned, and kept pace with me as I continued riding. He ran effortlessly, his brown hair wild, his face streaked with dirt and sweat.

"Hey, give me a ride, Davey," he said.

"Soon," I said.

"Come on, Davey."

"To the corner and back," I said. My legs had begun to tire. I rode over to my brother's carriage and dismounted. I saw Joey Younger look at Eddie Kulanski and Tony Savanola. His thin, long-nosed face hardened. He leaned toward me confidentially. I could smell the sweat on him. His thin rangy body seemed to radiate sweat and heat.

"That's Eddie Kulanski," he said in a low voice.

I nodded to indicate he was not telling me anything I did not already know.

"I had a fight with him. He called me a dirty Jew. He beat me up and my mother and his mother screamed at each other. They're Polaks."

I said nothing and watched Tony Savanola lean forward expertly for a marble shot. He struck the marble, pocketed it, and leaned forward again. Eddie Kulanski saw me looking at them. His lips moved briefly but I heard nothing. He turned away from me.

"To the corner and back," Joey Younger said. "You want to race me?"

"You know I can't do that, Joey. Why do you keep asking me to do things you know I can't do?"

He pedaled away on the tricycle, leaning forward into the wind, his hair blowing wildly.

I sat down on the chair next to my brother's carriage and closed my eyes and rested. The sounds and smells of the street moved warmly against me.

"Hey, Davey." It was Joey Younger's voice. "Can I have another ride?"

I nodded without opening my eyes and heard him speed away. Another horse and wagon clattered by. How good it was to be outside on the street!

"Davey?" It was Tony Savanola.

I opened my eyes wide.

He smiled uncertainly. "You want to play now, Davey?"

I looked up and down the block.

"He had to go inside," Tony Savanola said.

"Sure I want to play, Tony."

We played quietly together while Joey Younger rode my tricycle wildly up and down the block. Once he almost ran it into a baby carriage outside the grocery at the far end of the street.

"I don't think I like Eddie Kulanski," I said to Tony Savanola at one point during the game. "He called Joey a dirty Jew. Why did he call him that?"

"He hates Jews. His father says Jews killed Jesus."

"Really? I never heard that."

"Good shot, Davey. My father says Jews didn't kill Jesus. He says Jews never killed people by putting them up on crosses. Only the Romans did that."

"Who are the Romans?"

"The ones who came before the Italians. They once owned the country where the Jews lived."

"Why do you play with him, Tony?"

"That was another good shot. I can't not play with him, Davey. We go to the same church. Next year we'll go to the same Catholic school. Hey, you're cleaning me out, Davey."

"I'll loan you some."

"That was a good game. Boy, you sure cleaned me out."

In the afternoon Eddie Kulanski was back down on the street. Tony Savanola played with him. I rode my tricycle for a while, grew weary, parked it in its place beneath the stairway in the entrance hall of our apartment house, and sat in the sun near my brother's carriage. Weary with the morning and afternoon, my leg muscles still twitching from my brief afternoon of wheeling about on the tricycle, I fell into a light floating half-sleep through which the sounds of the street came to me dimly as if filtered through the sheet I sometimes put over my head while lying in bed. I loved the milky white world beneath the sheet; it was my very private world. I was a lion and a tiger and an elephant in that world. I was the giant Og on Noah's ark in that world, my sheet-covered, milky-white bed world. I sat half asleep and listened dreamily to the street.

I thought I felt something hit my shoulder but knew I was dreaming it and did not open my eyes. Again, something struck my shoulder, hard this time. I sat up and opened my eyes and found myself looking into the pale-blue sleepy eyes of Eddie Kulanski. I sat up very straight.

He stood in front of me. "You get sick all the time," he said. He held his hands on his hips as he spoke. "What're you sick from?"

I felt the dryness in my throat and the quivering in my legs and was quiet.

"You got some kind of Jewish disease or something?"

"No," I heard myself say.

"What're you sick from?"

"I don't know."

"You got a Jewish disease."

"Go away."

"What?"

"Go away. Leave me alone."

"Who're you telling to go away? You think you own the sidewalk? You own all the money, but you don't own this here sidewalk."

"What?"

"You want to try and make me go away?"

"Please," I said. "I don't want to fight."

"Please, I don't want to fight," he mimicked cruelly.

"I didn't do nothing to you. Leave me alone. I'll tell my mother."

"Tell your mother. Tell your father so he'll come yelling to my father and my father will beat him up good." Eddie Kulanski's father was a very tall man with long muscular arms and a hard, ruddy, cruel face. "And listen, you stay away from my friend. Tony is my friend and you stay away from him." He seemed to notice my brother's carriage for the first time. He took a step forward and peered into it, raising himself on his toes.

I got quickly to my feet. "Get away," I said.

He stepped back slowly, taking his time. "That your kid brother?" he said. His sleepy eyes had a strange flat look.

"You get away from him," I said, raising my voice.

He said something I did not understand. Then he said, "Don't tell me what to do, you Jew creep."

I stared at him. The blood was beating in my head. I would have another nosebleed. Right in front of him I would suddenly have a nosebleed. And he would laugh. My legs were shaking and trembling. I could hear the trembling in my voice as I spoke.

"You leave me alone," I said. "I never did nothing to you. I never killed no one."

He seemed vaguely surprised. His sleepy eyes widened a little. Then he said, "Your old man's from Poland?"

"What?"

"Tony says your old man's from Poland."

"From Poland, yes."

"*Anonymowe Panstwo,*" he said harshly, as if mouthing a vile epithet.

"What?"

"*Anonymowe Panstwo*," he repeated. "And keep your Jew face away from my friend Tony."

He turned, went up the stoop of our apartment house, and disappeared inside.

I felt myself sliding back onto the chair. I sat very still, thinking none of it had really happened, I had had a nightmare during a daytime sleep. I had had such daytime dreams before. I sat there and listened to the terrible beating of my heart.

I did not tell my parents. I stayed away from Tony Savanola all that week. I sat on the chair near my brother's carriage or rode on my tricycle. My legs were stronger now than they had been at the start of the week. I really loved the tricycle. When I rode it I did not mind too much watching Tony Savanola and Eddie Kulanski playing together. But when I sat resting on the chair near my brother's carriage I did not like looking at them. I would close my eyes and think I was in the milky world beneath my sheet.

One day that week strange boys came into our block from another street and played rough games with Eddie Kulanski and Tony Savanola. They played in front of our house and woke my brother and I pushed the carriage to the next house and then carried the chair over to the carriage. The chair was very heavy in my quivering arms. They played noisily until Tony Savanola's mother put her head out of her window and shouted, "Hey, you boys, where you think you are, in a jungle? You play quiet or you get away from here, or I call the police!"

They quieted down immediately. After a few minutes they sauntered off. Eddie Kulanski went with them, leaving Tony Savanola alone in front of the house.

I saw Tony Savanola start up the stoop, then stop and turn to look at me. He smiled wanly and waved. Then he went slowly down the stoop and came over to me.

"Hey, Davey," he said, trying another smile.

"Tony," I said quietly.

"How do you feel?"

"I'm okay now."

"You look better, Davey." He hesitated. "You want to play me immies?"

"Eddie Kulanski said—"

"I know what he said. My mother says I shouldn't listen to him. You want to play me immies?"

"Sure, Tony."

"I'll loan you some."

We played three wonderful games. Near the end of the fourth game, Eddie Kulanski came slowly up the street, passed us stiffly with a quick glance, and went into the house. I was sweating and trembling and had difficulty holding my marble in my hand. It slid from my fingers into a wildly careering shot.

"He won't do nothing to you," Tony Savanola said quietly. "He just talks a lot."

I hung my head.

"Why you so scared of him, Davey?"

"I don't know."

"Take that shot over again, Davey. It don't count when it slips like that."

"Saul," I said that Shabbat afternoon after my cousin had finished telling me a story from the midrash, "what does *Anonymowe Panstwo* mean?"

"What does what mean?"

"*Anonymowe Panstwo.*"

"Is it Polish?"

"Yes."

"I don't know Polish. Did you ask your mother or father?"

"I don't want to," I said, and told him about Eddie Kulanski.

We were in his room and the June sun streamed in through his window. But his thin face darkened and his eyes became a little frightened behind their shell-rimmed glasses.

"You ought to tell your father," he said.

"No," I said. "Give me your word you won't tell."

He was silent.

"Give your word," I said. "Please."

"I give my word," he said reluctantly. "But you stay away from him."

"I don't like him," I said. "Why should I go near him?"

But the next day Eddie Kulanski came over to me along with a tall, blond-haired boy who looked about eleven or twelve. I sat on my chair near my brother's carriage and watched them come out of the apartment house, walk down the stoop, and start toward me. They looked like twins except that Eddie Kulanski was shorter and thinner than the other boy. He was imitating the older boy's manner: his springy walk on the balls of his feet, his hands in his pockets, his flat sleepy look, and the small cold smile on his thin lips. I glanced quickly up and down the street. A few children were playing a game of box ball; a horse-drawn wagon was turning into the street from the side street near Mr. Steinberg's candy store; an old man sat on a chair near the store, sunning his shrunken face.

"Hey," Eddie Kulanski said. He put his hands on his hips and gave me a little smile. He had a pointed chin and a straight, sharp pointed nose. His eyes looked sleepy. "You ain't sick again yet with that Jewish disease?"

The other boy looked at him. "He's got a disease?"

"A Jewish disease."

"Yeah? Is it catchy?"

"Yeah, it's catchy. My friend Tony got it."

"Hey, what disease is it, kid?"

I did not know what to say. If they touched me, I would shout and someone would come to help. But the big boy could hit me very hard and then run away and deny he ever hit me. I sat very still, staring at them.

"What's that in there?" the older boy said, pointing to the carriage.

"His kid brother," said Eddie Kulanski.

They sounded like twins. Even their voices were identical, thin, flat, edged with sarcasm and contempt.

"His kid brother," the older boy said. "I got to look." He moved over to the carriage and peered inside.

I looked up and down the street. My arms and legs were trembling. "Go away," I said. "Please. He's a little baby."

The older boy straightened and stepped back from the carriage. "He ain't got them," he said.

Eddie Kulanski looked disappointed.

The older boy turned to me. "When did he lose them?" he asked.

"What?" I said.

"The horns. When do you kikes lose them? He ain't got them. How old is he?"

"Two," I heard myself say through the drumming of the blood in my ears.

"Shit," the older boy said. "We ain't got no kike babies on my block. I thought I would see them." He looked closely at my face and head. "When did you lose yours, kid?"

I did not understand what he was saying.

"We ain't gonna hurt you, kid. What're you shaking like that for? Look at him shaking, Eddie. When did you lose your horns? When you was about one?"

"Yes," I heard myself say desperately in order to tell them what I thought they wanted to hear.

"No wonder they keep those kike kids always bundled up. So we won't be able to see their horns. Right?"

"Yes," I said. My throat was dry. Was I becoming ill again? But there was no pain behind my eyes.

"Sneaky Jew cock," he said. Then he said, "One of these days I got to see a Jew cock."

"Hey," Eddie said eagerly, looking up at the older boy.

The other one ignored him and regarded me intently out of his half-closed eyes. "Listen," he said. "Eddie here is my cousin. I like to take good care of my cousin. You stay away from him and his friends. I don't want him catching none of your Jew germs. Understand?" He put a long bony forefinger against my chest. "Understand?" he said again, and poked me hard with the finger. It felt like a bar of iron. "Understand?"

"Yes." My chest ached where his finger had jabbed me.

"You understand. Okay. We don't like to be too close to Jews, that's all. My old man says you all got a bad smell and now I find out you got a Jewish disease. So stay away from my cousin and his pals."

Inside the carriage my brother stirred. I saw the carriage rock slightly on its springs. My brother cried softly and was quiet.

Eddie Kulanski's cousin looked at the carriage with a sudden sharp return of interest.

I got up off the chair onto my feet and stood alongside the carriage.

Eddie Kulanski looked up at his cousin. "Hey, I want to," he said.

"Yeah," his cousin said. "The kid's up anyway."

I blocked their way.

"We ain't gonna hurt him," Eddie Kulanski's cousin said. "We just want to look."

"Go away," I pleaded. "I'll yell. I'll call the police."

The older boy stiffened. The smile vanished. His eyes narrowed. "You hear that, Eddie?" he said. "He's gonna call the cops."

"Yeah," Eddie Kulanski said.

"You know what we do when someone calls the cops?"

"Keep away from my brother!"

"Look at him," Eddie Kulanski's cousin said. "He's gonna shit right in his pants."

Eddie Kulanski laughed.

"I'm gonna tell you—" Eddie Kulanski's cousin began, and stopped.

Behind him Mrs. Savanola had put her head out of her window. "Hey, you, Eddie Kulanski!" she shouted. "What you doing there?"

The two of them turned to look at her.

"You keep your hands off that Davey Lurie. You want me to tell his papa you making trouble?" I could see Eddie Kulanski's lips curl into the little smile. The smile seemed to incense Mrs. Savanola. Her face reddened beneath its olive coloring and her chins trembled. "What you laughing at me for? You take your cousin away from that Davey or I tell his mama to call the police."

The two of them stared at her. Eddie Kulanski's cousin rubbed his hands along the sides of his shorts. Without a word he turned, went up the front steps and into the house. Eddie Kulanski gave me a cold, malevolent look and followed him.

Mrs. Savanola looked at me. She had dark shiny hair and dark eyes. "That's a mean boy, that Eddie's cousin. How you feel, Davey?"

I opened my mouth but no sound came out. I swallowed hard and felt I was downing sand.

"I'm okay," I said to her in a hoarse dry voice.

"You look like a stick, like a, whatchamacallit, a scarecrow. You got to eat more, Davey. My Tony, he sick in bed today. Why you no sit more in the sun? You pale like a sheet."

She pulled her head inside. The lace curtains stirred and were still.

I sat down on the chair next to my brother's carriage and felt the trembling move through me. After a moment I began to cry. I sat there, trembling and crying. My brother stirred again in his carriage and was quiet. Near Mr. Steinberg's candy store, the old man rose slowly and moved his chair out of the shade that had crept over him and sat down once again, his face to the sun, his palsied hands shaking as they rested on his knees. A few minutes later, I went into the house and brought out my tricycle and rode around for a while.

Joey Younger came out of the house and watched me.

"Davey," he called.

Inside his carriage, my brother began to cry.

"What did you have to yell for?" I said, and got off the tricycle.

"Can I get a ride, Davey?"

I let him take the tricycle and stood there rocking my

brother back to sleep. I sat down in the chair and put my face to the sun.

"Hey, Davey," Tony Savanola said behind me.

I turned in the chair and saw him in the window. His dark hair was uncombed and he wore red pajamas. He smiled at me and I was happy to see him. I got down off the chair and went over to the window and looked up at him.

"How're you feeling, Tony?" It was a strange sensation to be asking someone else how he was feeling. I felt almost a little happy to be able to ask that, to be seeing someone else who was ill.

"I got fever, Davey. Don't come too close to me. The doctor said it might be measles. My mama said Eddie Kulanski and his cousin were bothering you."

I looked down at the sidewalk.

"Did they hurt you, Davey?"

"No."

"His cousin is mean, Davey. I don't like him. He hurts things. I saw him hurt a cat once. Hey, you haven't been sick since last time. That's good isn't it, Davey?"

"He says I got to stay away from you, Tony."

Tony Savanola looked uncomfortable.

"I don't want no trouble, Tony."

"What you doing at the window, you crazy!" I heard Mrs. Savanola's loud voice from inside the apartment.

Tony's dark eyes looked momentarily startled.

"You sick and you standing by the open window!"

He waved at me and vanished behind the lace curtains.

Joey Younger rode by at high speed, his hair wild, his body bent forward over the handlebars, his legs pumping.

I sat down on the chair. Near Mr. Steinberg's candy store, the old man had fallen asleep. The sun had moved and his face was in shade. His gnarled arthritic hands continued to tremble faintly as he slept. I sat in the sun and watched Joey Younger riding my tricycle up and down the block. I was tired. After a while I closed my eyes.

My cousin said to me in my room that Shabbat, "It means 'Anonymous Empire,' Davey."

He and his parents had come over to join us for Shabbat dinner in the early afternoon. Now we were together in my room and our parents were talking quietly in the living room. Saul sat next to me on my bed, looking troubled.

"I asked one of my teachers in school," he said. "He wanted to know where I heard it and I told him one of the goyim on my block yelled it at me. He said goyim think there's a group of Jews who keep meeting secretly somewhere and planning ways to take over the whole world. They're called Elders of Zion. This group is supposed to be able to make all kinds of problems for the goyim because it owns most of the banks and newspapers in the world. These old Jews can do almost anything because they have so much money and control the news and what people say and think. They have plans for all the goyishe governments to get into such bad trouble that they'll fail—and then these Jews can take over the world. My teacher said that in Poland they call this secret organization *Anonymowe Panstwo*. It's even in the Polish dictionary, he said. Almost everyone in Poland believes it."

"What do 'anonymous' and 'empire' mean, Saul?"

He explained the words to me.

"Is it true, Saul?"

"No, it's not true, Davey."

"The goyim really believe that?"

"A lot of goyim believe it."

"But so many Jews are poor. And Mama said she was in a place in Poland once where Jews were hurt and killed by goyim. How could that happen if we're so strong?"

"My teacher says the goyim think we let some Jews stay poor and get hurt and killed so the goyim shouldn't know how strong we really are."

"Goyim really believe that, Saul?"

"That's what my teacher said."

"They believe that we killed Jesus and own all the banks and things and want to take over the whole world and we let some Jews stay poor and get killed so the world should think we're really not strong?"

He nodded soberly, his eyes dark.

"Saul?"

"Yes, Davey."

"I have to tell you about something that almost happened with Alex." Very quickly, fearfully, I recounted the incident with Eddie Kulanski and his cousin.

Saul was very upset; he seemed frightened. "You should tell your father," he said.

"They didn't touch him, Saul. I would tell if they touched him."

"You should tell anyway."

"I don't want them to fight, Saul. Eddie Kulanski's father is so big."

My cousin chewed his lip and was quiet.

"What does it mean, horns and things, Saul?"

"Some goyim think Jews have horns."

I stared at him.

"They think we're like Satan or the Angel of Death or something. They think we kill goyishe babies and use their blood in matzos for Pesach. They think we're like devils or demons. Every terrible thing that happens in the world they blame on us."

"Why?"

"Because they hate us."

"But why do they hate us?"

"Because they think we do all those terrible things."

"I don't understand it, Saul."

"Neither do I," he said. "If Jews owned all the money and banks why would your father and my father have to work so hard to make money to bring all the rest of our families to America? It's a way goyim have of telling lies about us and getting everyone to hate us."

"Does everyone hate us, Saul?"

"My father says most goyim hate us."

I could not understand what it was like to be hated by so many people. I could not remember ever having hated anyone and so I did not understand the feeling—unless it was something like the way I felt about being ill so often. Yes, that must be a little of what it must be like to hate.

"It's a scary feeling, Saul, so many goyim hating us."

He nodded again, slowly. His eyes were dark behind their glasses.

"Is Papa bringing all the families to America?"

"In a few months. He has money to give them and places for them to live and work. Yes, in a few months. When your mother's mother is all well."

"Is she sick, too, a lot of the time?"

He looked at me uncertainly, started to say something, and stopped. "She'll be all well soon, Davey. You want to hear a new midrash I read this morning about the giants in the time of Noah? Mr. Bader showed it to me. Then we'll go to the zoo, if your papa and mama say it's okay."

He told me the midrash and, later, we walked the long narrow side street to the wide boulevard and crossed over and came into the zoo. For the first time, I found myself frightened of the tawny-skinned lions. Saul held my hand as we circled their outdoor pen. Inside the tiger pen, a huge tiger rose suddenly on its legs from a reclining position, and roared. I cried out. Saul took me quickly away from there to my billy goat.

I petted his warm wet nose and let his hard lips and wet tongue tickle the palm of my hand.

"You ought to tell your father about Eddie Kulanski and his cousin," Saul said quietly, watching me.

"You gave your word, Saul. You gave me your word."

He looked away and was silent.

The billy goat licked my hand and after a little while I was able to laugh with delight—as I had laughed this afternoon when we had stopped to feed the billy goat on the way through the zoo to the pine wood and the clearing where I now sat watching my father and uncle talking earnestly together near a tree at the opposite end of the clearing, and my mother and aunt sitting and talking on the blankets, and Saul and my little brother Alex playing happily together on the grass. I sat near the path that had taken us through the wood and kept skimming the palm of my right hand lightly over the low grass. The tickling sensation was delicious. Overhead the sun cleared the thin layer of clouds and sent a stream of golden light onto the clearing.

From somewhere in the wood behind me came the sudden sharp sound of a cracking branch and the soft murmur of voices. I turned and saw a straw hat moving across the top of a clump of tall brush alongside the path. Then the brush fell away and a man and woman stepped into the curve of the path. They were followed by two more couples, then, a moment later, by three more couples. The men carried blankets and picnic baskets. I recognized them all: they prayed in the same little synagogue near our house as did my parents and aunt and uncle. I had not been in that synagogue more than four or five times during the past few months because of illness and because my father sometimes went very early and would not wake me. The last time I had been in the synagogue was about a week ago during the Festival of Shavuoth. I had not liked being there. I had not liked sitting in the same small room with some of the men whose faces had been in the photograph everyone said I had not seen.

They were all about the same age as my parents, somewhere in their thirties. They were smartly dressed in light-colored summer clothes. The men wore straw hats or fisher-men's caps; the women had on wide-brimmed flowery hats. They greeted me as they went by; some asked how I felt; one man, a tall man with small eyes and a large nose, bent down and pinched my cheek. "Good to see you, little David," he said cheerfully in Yiddish. "A very beautiful day today, yes? Good to see you." He had held a gun and a knife in the photograph.

A moment later Mr. and Mrs. Bader came up the path, passed me with a smile, and entered the clearing. Mr. Bader did not carry a blanket or a picnic basket. He looked tall and trim and dapper in a light blue summer suit, a red bow tie, and a hard straw hat.

My father and uncle had broken off their conversation when the first couples had entered the clearing. They came forward to greet them. There was loud happy chatter; blankets were spread out on the grass; the silent wood filled with the sounds of voices speaking Yiddish.

I sat on the grass near the path at the edge of the clearing and watched the men and women on the blankets. They spoke to one another in their bantering Galician Yiddish, the way they did in our little synagogue or when they met on the street. They had all been friends in another land, it seemed to me, darker land and time; nothing of what they said meant anything to me. As I sat watching, four more couples came through the wood and entered the clearing. They did not pray in our synagogue but came to the house from time to time for an evening. All four of the men were in the photo-graph I had accidentally not seen. Not all the men who had been in the photograph were now in the clearing but all the men in the clearing had been in the photograph, except Mr. Shmuel Bader.

The vague pain behind my eyes had disappeared for a while; now it returned and began slowly to move into my forehead above the bridge of my nose. Yes, I would be ill again soon. I sat there skimming my hand slowly back and forth across the low grass.

The women were removing food from the picnic baskets and laying it out on serving dishes and paper plates on the blankets. My brother and I were the only very young chil-dren there; some people had seemed surprised to see us. Our blanket was in the center of the rough semicircle formed by the blankets, and I saw one of the men talking earnestly to my father and pointing to me and my brother. I looked quickly away and scanned the food appearing in awesome quantities from the apparently bottomless picnic baskets. There was smoked meat, delicatessen, fish, Kaiser rolls, rye bread, sour pickles, sauerkraut, salads, fruit, soda water. From the bowels of a basket a woman produced and held high a bottle filled with amber liquid. There was a burst of laughter and scattered hand-clapping. Startled by the noise, a bird rose from a branch over my head and flew deep into the wood with a swiftly vanishing flutter of wings. The pine wood returned the noise faintly to the clearing as it caught and echoed the sudden laughter and applause.

While the women busied themselves setting out the food, the men gathered around my father and Mr. Bader near the far edge of the clearing. They stood in a small tight circle listening intently to my father, then to Mr. Bader, then once again to my father. I was too far away to hear anything of what was being said. Nor was I interested. The thought of the coming week had begun to fill me with despair. Wasn't there any kind of medicine they could give me to keep me from being ill over and over again? No, Dr. Weidman had said without his usual cheer. There was no medicine that could cure the grippe; medicine could only relieve the symptoms and bring down the fever. A mustard plaster could help if my chest became congested; Argyrol could be swabbed or brushed onto my raw throat; there were nose drops for my clogged nose and ear drops if my ears became infected. But there was no way to prevent my becoming ill and no way to cure me once I came down with the illness; there was only bed rest until my fever returned to normal and remained normal for twenty-four hours. I would be spending the remainder of this beautiful late June week in my bed. I looked into the dark cavern of the coming days and shivered with dread.

Seated on the blanket my father had carried and spread on the grass, my mother was changing my brother's diaper and talking hesitantly, timidly, with two women who had sat down near her. She kept glancing around as she spoke; once she had looked in my direction but her eyes swept past me and scanned the bluish depths of the wood through which everyone had come. My brother kept squirming beneath her hands and she was finding it difficult to pin one side of the diaper. Her face was pale and taut and I thought she would cry; but one of the women took the pin from her and completed the diapering. My mother smiled nervously and held my brother on her lap. He kept reaching out for Saul, who lay on the grass with a hand over his eyes, his thin face and battered lip turned to the sun.

No one seemed to be taking any notice of me. I felt as if I were invisible. I rose slowly, feeling the dull pain in my forehead; but the earth remained firm beneath my feet. I walked unseen around some of the women in the clearing and sat down on the grass next to Saul. He looked to be asleep. I stared at his lip; a queer shivery feeling came into the calves of my legs. The edge of the open drawer had struck the center of his delicately bowed upper lip and had split the skin. The lip was purple and blue and swollen to about twice its normal size. The swollen lip distorted his features and I thought what if he had fallen on one of his eyes or his nose.

"They were accidents!" I had screamed hoarsely through fever and pain during my last illness. The dog and the bird had appeared bloated and monstrous. Mrs. Horowitz had shrieked in my ear.

"Of course, darling," my mother had soothed. "Of course. Did you have a dream?"

"Again with the bird and dog," my father muttered.

I felt myself soaked with sweat. I lay in the bed, exhausted.

"The fever is breaking," my mother said, wiping my forehead gently with a towel. "Ochnotinos, chnotinos, notinos, otinos, tinos, inos, nos, os."

My father stood near the bed. "What isn't an accident?" he asked suddenly in a raging voice. "When is there ever a time without accidents? The stinking war was an accident, the train robbery was an accident, what happened in the forest was an accident, the pogrom was an accident, your mother catching pneumonia was an accident. Being born a Jew is the biggest accident of all. A man plans and God laughs. God in heaven, if there is a God in this world, how He must laugh! He is not doing His job, Ruth!"

"Max, the boy is awake."

"None of them will come, you know that. Without your mother not a single one of them will come. All or no one, they wrote. All or no one. If her lungs are scarred and weak, the doctors there may not pass her through. You know that. Why did she have to go out into a snowstorm? To deliver a baby! It is a joke. The whole world is a joke!"

"Papa," I cried hoarsely, and opened my eyes.

They looked at me.

"I'm scared, Papa."

They were silent. A trolley car rushed vaguely along the distant boulevard.

"Max, it is not a father's job to frighten his son," said my mother very quietly. She made a motion with her hand and a strange sound with her lips.

My father sat down on my bed. He smelled of coffee.

"I frightened you," he said brusquely. "I am sorry. Sometimes when I feel very upset I say things that are not nice to hear." His lower jaw jutted out sharply as he spoke. "Your mama is right. Sometimes I do a bad job as a father."

"I don't want to have accidents anymore, Papa. I don't want to be sick anymore, Papa. Please, Papa. I don't—"

"You don't," he said. "You don't. And do you know anyone who does? About accidents we do not have many choices. Our job is to make better the world God gave us. We are partners with God. One day you will understand. We have to work hard to make it a good world. But it is not an impossible job."

I lay very still, feeling the heavy pounding of my heart. After a moment he put his lips briefly to my sweaty forehead; then he got to his feet.

"Good night, David."

"My throat hurts, Papa."

"Mama will give you medicine to make it feel better. I am going to take myself another glass of coffee, Ruth. Then I have to go over and talk to Bader."

He went from my room.

My mother sighed softly and wiped my forehead with the towel. "You are a little cooler now," she said. "The fever is going down."

But I did not feel that the fever was going down. There was a buzzing sensation in my ears and a throbbing weight against my forehead and cheeks. I felt my tongue light and uncontrollable.

"Is Mr. Bader back, Mama?"

"Yes, darling."

"Wasn't he away a long time?"

"Yes."

"Did he see all your friends and Papa's friends?"

She hesitated. "Some of them. You should not talk so much, darling. You will hurt your throat."

"He could recognize them all from the photograph?"

"What?" She stiffened perceptibly and drew away from me. "What photograph?"

"With the guns and the knives and Uncle Meyer and Papa and the men in the synagogue."

"There is no photograph like that, David," she said in a tense, strained voice. "Once and for all, there is no photograph like that."

"It was an accident that I saw it, Mama. People are always angry at me that I have an accident."

She was silent.

I felt the tightness of oncoming tears in my throat, and closed my eyes. The blood beat in my head and the room had begun to spin. I took the medicine my mother gave me and then lay back on the pillow and listened to my parents talking quietly in the kitchen. Then I pulled the sheet over my head and lay with my lips gently touching the cool smooth cottony material. I licked at it with my tongue and opened my eyes. The dresser lamp had been left on. I saw its light milky whiteness through the sheet. This was my quiet world. I had made this world. There were no accidents in this world. I could not understand the world outside. I did not understand what my father had said. It seemed a terrible world, God's world, and I liked my cool white sheet world where dogs were not killed by cars and canaries flew back through open windows—we had left our windows open for hours that day, hoping, hoping— and where the giant Og, who had promised to serve Noah, would slap Eddie Kulanski and his cousin and keep them away from me; my silent, peaceful, lovely white world where I could travel to the zoo and feed my billy goat and watch the small fish in the pond near the pine wood. Why did I need my father's world when I had my own world?

I had slept and woke in the night. The light had been turned off. In the darkness of the room a dark form had sat by my bed chanting softly. I knew it was a fever dream and tried to get the form to go away. But it had been a long time before it dissolved and I was able to slide into deep and dreamless sleep, the kind of sleep that Saul seemed now to be enjoying despite the people all around him who were arranging themselves on the blankets before the food.

My aunt glanced at Saul and decided to let him sleep. I sat on the grass and looked at his bruised lip. No, I did not like this accident world; I felt alone and frightened in it. I did not know whom I might hurt the next minute or who might hurt me. I did not like people to be angry at me for things God did. If God made accidents happen, why did my father hit me? Maybe he was angry at me. But what had I done?

Maybe he was angry at God or at the world. Was that what people meant by hate, being angry at something or somebody so much that you needed to hit somebody? I had never had that feeling, not even about being ill. I did not want to hit anybody because I was ill all the time.

I sat next to my cousin and skimmed my hand lightly over the grass and closed my eyes and put my face to the sun. Yes. The clearing was almost like my opalescent sheet world. I held its pure and silent whiteness untouched for a long moment. Then I opened my eyes.

A loud intrusive cheer had hurled itself against my white world. I saw Saul come awake and sit up dazedly. He looked at me, smiled, and winced with the pain from his lip. His eyes looked glassy, as if he too would soon be ill with fever.

"It hurts," he said to me.

"You could have hurt yourself really bad, Saul."

"I hurt myself bad enough."

"Didn't you see the drawer?"

"I tripped. It was an accident."

"Let's make a l'chaim," someone said.

The bottle of amber liquid was being passed around and tipped briefly over the rims of waiting glasses.

"For ritual purposes," someone said breezily.

"Of course," someone else said.

"For medical purposes."

"Of course."

"One bottle for all of us and there's still plenty left. If goyim drank like this, bootleggers would be out of business in a month."

"In that case, I'll drink a little more. God forbid we should make the gangsters into anti-Semites."

"I read this book about the Golem of Prague," Saul said. "Yesterday I read it. I had it in my mind when I tripped."

My father stood up in front of the group, holding his glass. There were now about twenty-five men and women seated on the blankets in the clearing, all gazing at my father.

"What's the Golem of Prague, Saul?" I asked.

"L'chaim," my father said, raising his glass. "To the families and dear friends who will, God willing, soon be with us."

"To the friends who went to Eretz Yisroel," someone said.

"To our organization," someone else said.

"To our organization!" came the loud response.

"To the forest."

"To the forest!"

"To Shmuel Bader."

"To Shmuel Bader!"

"To Max Lurie."

"To Max Lurie!"

"I will drink to Max only if he shows us some sharpshooting."

"Here? You're in the Bronx, not Lemberg. To Max, our leader."

"To Max! To Max!"

They drank from their glasses, my father first sniffing at his. Even my mother drank. My father remained standing in front of the group. His hard straw hat was tipped back on his head; his face was flushed. He seemed very content. He raised himself on the balls of his feet and smiled briefly at the people seated in a ragged semicircle in front of him.

"You know I do not make speeches," he said. "I let the politicians make the speeches. Ten years ago I said we needed an organization to fight against the pogroms. Otherwise we would be like someone plowing a field with his nose, and nothing would get done. We created the Am Kedoshim Society. We planned, we succeeded, and we came to America. Today we are celebrating our tenth anniversary. We have learned never to forget the harm our enemies inflict upon us. We have learned that when we work together we can defeat our enemies. We will not stand by with our arms folded when our enemies attack us; nor will we do as some of our families did almost three hundred years ago in Tulchin when they decided not to attack the Poles in that city because they feared what Poles in other cities might do to Jews. We leave such righteousness to other Jews, to the Hasidim, to Jews whose pure souls make them unable to shed goyishe blood. We are not so pure. When our enemies come to attack us, we will fight them. Not we but our enemies will crawl up smooth walls. That is my entire speech."

"Strength!" someone shouted. "You should have strength!"

"Strength he has plenty," someone else said.

"We should remember those who fell," someone said querulously. "A minute to remember David and Gershon and Avruml and the others."

A darkness came upon the group. My father closed his eyes, then opened them immediately, his face gone rigid.

In complete silence, everyone rose to his feet. I stood next to Saul. My mother held my brother. The skin had tightened over her features; her eyes seemed to sink into their sockets and become dark grayish pools. I watched her as she held my brother. Her face was turned downward toward the grassy earth of the clearing. She raised her hand absently to brush a strand of stray hair from her eyes, and I saw the smear of ink from her Waterman's pen on one of her fingers; she had written letters that morning before packing the picnic basket. Her thin shoulders sagged; she seemed to be cringing at some fear or memory concealed within her. I saw my uncle reach over and put his hand on her arm. His face was stiff.

In the silence, a breeze whispered silkenly through the pine wood and a distant bird trilled a brief song.

Quietly, my father cleared his throat. Everyone sat down. As I once again took my place near Saul, I noticed Dr. Weidman come from the wood and enter the clearing. He was greeted by a number of people and a place was found for him on a blanket.

"What's Tulchin?" I asked Saul in a whisper.

He shrugged. "I'll ask my teacher."

"What's the Golem of Prague?"

"Later," he said.

"Mama, Papa dawtin," my brother said loudly.

"Yes, darling. Papa's talking. Sha."

Faintly, as if borne on a wind through the dense wood, came the trumpeting cry of an elephant. It was difficult to remember we were in a zoo in the Bronx in New York in America. I had thought for a long moment that we were in the forest bordering my mother's parents' farm outside Bobrek. Was it as green there now as it was here? Did it have a stream like the one that ran clear and narrow over smooth pebbles in the forest behind our cottage in the mountains? Was there a meadow nearby with a pond full of fish? I envisioned the forest and the farm and saw cows chewing placidly on the grass of a rolling meadow and my mother's parents and brothers and sisters—she had two brothers and three sisters, all younger than she; I saw the farm and the surrounding countryside and my mother's family, all as she had often described it to me; like something out of a book of lovely tales. I did not understand why my mother told me only good memories of her childhood when all my father seemed able to talk about regarding his European past was hate, enemies, and pogroms.

"We have today," my father was saying, "assets amounting to considerably more than I was able to report to you at our last board meeting." And he named a sum of money.

I saw smiles, nods, and heard a murmur of approval.

"A sharpshooter and a financial wizard," one of the women said. "Max, you are a wonder."

My father did not react. He stood stiffly on the grass in front of the group, looking at the piece of paper he had taken from the inside pocket of his jacket.

"Of this, half remains in the Free Loan Fund, ten thousand dollars has just been distributed by our good friend, and the remainder is in real estate and stocks and bonds. The dues we have been paying to the organization have been repaying us many times over. Apartments have been obtained for the people who will be arriving after the holidays; jobs await the men, good jobs, not filthy jobs in sweatshops. It is enough some of us had to work in sweatshops. Meyer has completed all the necessary legal work on their papers, and they have all received visas, with the exception of Ruth's mother, who is still not well. I am at present in the process of acquiring jobs and apartments for the group that is to come early next year. That is my report."

He folded the sheet of paper and replaced it in the inside pocket of his jacket.

"A good report!" one of the men said loudly.

"If there are no questions or comments, we will hear from our friend," my father said.

"A cheer for Max the sharpshooter," someone called out.

"I do not need it," said my father quickly. But they cheered anyway, in a language I did not understand, and the noise rang through the clearing. I wondered if the trumpeting elephant would hear it. Do they really remember everything, those elephants?

My father acknowledged the cheer with a curt nod. He seemed uncomfortable in the presence of praise. My mother's eyes had darkened once again at the mention of her mother. Alex sat quietly on her lap, chewing a Kaiser roll into moist oblivion.

"A word from our good friend," my father said. "He has brief messages for the organization and I have asked him to deliver them to all of us here. Then we will eat."

Mr. Shmuel Bader rose slowly from the blanket on which he had been sitting and came over to stand next to my father. He touched his bow tie, buttoned his jacket, and smiled. From an inside pocket he produced a long slender leather wallet which he opened, revealing a writing pad and a small gold pencil. He spoke in a quiet voice.

"Nissan asked to be remembered to the organization and is grateful for its help. He hopes in two or three years to be able to come to America. There is a difficulty with his father. Business is bad now in Bobrek, he says, because of competition from Lemberg, and new people want to join the organization. I have informed Max of this and it will be discussed by the membership committee. In Lodz, Yonah Brenner and Levi Bromberg have expanded their textile business successfully, despite the tariff problems and the small Polish market, and next year they will be able to make a substantial contribution to the Free Loan Fund as a mark of gratitude for the help given them by the organization. Levi's brother hopes to come to America in two years and Yonah's sister, Tziporah, is going to Eretz Yisroel in November. There are other messages from Lodz, but they are of a private nature and I will communicate them in the course of the day. In Warsaw, Aaron Schnitzer asked me to inform the organization that he is now in diamonds and is eager to be of help to the organization in any way it sees fit. He has also asked me to inform the organization that he now has connections in Amsterdam, Rotterdam, Paris, Tel Aviv, Johannesburg, and Capetown. He expresses his deepest gratitude to the Am Kedoshim Society for the help it rendered him concerning his brother's problems. He is especially grateful to Meyer." He paused, looked up from the pad, and said quietly, in Hebrew, "He who understands will understand," then continued reading from the pad.

I looked away from him and gazed slowly around at the people seated in the clearing. They were listening intently, hungry for each word he spoke. The food, covered with paper napkins, lay untouched on the blankets. An occasional fly settled on the napkins. My mother listened with her eyes closed, a sad, wistful, longing smile on her thin lips. Alex sat quietly on her lap, apparently awed by the silence of the group, chewing wetly at his Kaiser roll. Wispy clouds sailed lazily below the sun. A flock of small birds raced across the sky in the direction of the zoo.

Mr. Bader went on speaking in his placid businesslike manner. My father stood beside him, looking somewhat dwarfed by Mr. Bader's tall sparse form. My father stood with his legs spread slightly apart, his hands clasped behind him. Once in a movie I had seen soldiers stand like that. My father liked to see movies about soldiers. He had once taken my mother and me to a movie and there had been many soldiers running and falling and shells exploding and long charges across broken smoking earth and men firing rifles and machine guns and hand-to-hand fighting with bayonets and rifles in trenches, all in absolute silence save for the piano that gave tinny life to the movement on the huge screen. My mother had come out of the movie looking very pale. She walked leaning heavily on my father's arm. "I was sure you would be over it," my father kept saying. "I apologize, Ruth. It was a stupid mistake and I take full blame." When had that been? I could not remember. My father never took us again to movies about soldiers. He went alone.

My forehead ached and I felt the first faint chills of the approaching fever. A sudden burst of laughter followed by a heavy stirring sound came from the group. I looked around: faces had turned strangely hard. He had said something just then about Polish anti-Semites. What had it been? I should have listened. It had been something about Poles and drunkenness and a man falling off a wagon. They had all laughed, even my mother; then had come the tense rustling movement, as if everyone there had crossed together from the satisfaction of achievement to the expectation of further menace and challenge. I could not remember when I had last seen my mother laugh. She never laughed. Laughter was as much a stranger to her as sleep was to me. Yet she had laughed. I would have to listen and keep my mind from wandering back and forth through memories. But my head was beginning to hurt badly now. Still I would try hard to listen. What was Mr. Bader saying about Pilsudski? I could barely hear him, his voice was so calm and quiet.

"Max can tell you more about Marshal Pilsudski than I. He was in Pilsudski's army killing Russians while I was first getting used to wearing United States Army puttees. But almost everyone I met informed me that life for Jews in Poland under Pilsudski remains very difficult. Max once mentioned to me that Pilsudski was the kind of anti-Semite who did not want the Jews in his army harmed by Poles. That is an accomplishment in Poland. But the peasants are hungry and angry. The crop failure has aggravated the situation. The peasants and townspeople blame the Jews for everything, and Pilsudski does very little to protect the Jews because he does not want to antagonize the Poles. That is the picture, in case some of you here are not entirely up to date. Did you hear that there were ritual murder stories this year in Lublin and Vilna? I see some of you did not. Yes, Jews were accused of killing Christian children and using their blood in the baking of matzos. In Eastern Europe we are still agents of Satan and the Angel of Death." I glanced quickly at Saul. His eyes were wide behind their shell-rimmed glasses. "Little has changed since you all left. There was a serious anti-Semitic riot in Lemberg recently. You know that. Yes. About Lemberg you all know everything. Fine. In any event, though life is somewhat more stable now than it was a few years back, there is still considerable unemployment, especially in Warsaw, and Jews have not yet recovered from the devastation of the war and the revolution and the epidemic. I need not tell you the details. You all receive letters from your relatives and friends. You know what is happening. Your friends and families are grateful for the help given them by your organization. I am happy to be able to be of service to you and continue to be grateful for the accident that brought me into contact with your founder, Max Lurie. Since everyone here is a board member of the organization, I don't mind telling in absolute confidence —and I am certain that young Saul Lurie understands what that means. Yes? Good—I don't mind telling you that the ARA and the State Department are not helping Jews too much and if it were not for the JOAC, Jews would be starving. That is my report. Thank you."

Again, the group stirred heavily. There were whispers and nods. Mr. Bader went back to his blanket, hitched up his trousers with a deft motion of his wrists, and sat down.

My father stood alone in front of the group. He cleared his throat.

"I thank Mr. Bader for his report. Ten years ago when the Am Kedoshim Society was founded in the forest outside Bobrek, did anyone dream we would be as active and as rich an organization as we are now? God has been good to us. I am sure that David, my dear brother, may he rest in peace, has been a good interceder for us. The forty of us who were there, who had served with Pilsudski for the sake of Poland and had returned to Lemberg and Bobrek and Polish anti-Semites, decided it was time for us to help ourselves. To hell with the Poles and their filthy anti-Semitism. Jews would help Jews. Why should we help a people that wants to kill us? Let the stinking Poles take care of their own problems. You remember I said it would take only a little money from each of us to get ourselves started. I learned that in the trenches from a clever goy whose father was in banking and who used to make money from the watches and wallets he stripped off the dead bodies of the Russians I killed. I am giving this little speech now because I want you all to know that we are not in the business of making money but using money to help our members. I have prepared a full report of our stock transactions over the past few months and you will receive it in the mail soon. At the next meeting of our finance committee I will request the right to sell off stocks as I see fit in order to increase the availability of liquid capital. Our good friend is returning to Europe for a quick trip in three weeks. I want him to go with a lot of our money and to help a lot of our members, both old and new, the new ones our membership committee will accept at its meeting tomorrow night. And, please, I do not need your cheers. I do this because I see it as my job. If we are truly am kedoshim, a nation of holy people, then each of us has a job to do, and he should do it without the silliness of public praise. I have completed my remarks. Let us wash our hands and enjoy our picnic. And I challenge any of the men here to a wrestling match afterward."

There was a burst of laughter and loud cheers. People began to rise to their feet, when my father suddenly clapped his hands sharply together and said, "I forgot something. I am sorry. Forgive me. I asked Dr. Weidman to come and speak to us very briefly about a serious matter that has to do with health."

Dr. Weidman, short, pink-faced, red-haired, wearing his pince-nez and smiling cheerfully, talked briefly in Yiddish about the various kinds of paralysis that could result from poliomyelitis; he stated that the usual epidemic would probably break out this year some time in August; he talked of precautions, danger signs, urged everyone to be conscious of the need for cleanliness, to avoid fatigue, and to go to the country for August if that was possible. "Do not let your children become chilled. Do not swim for too long. Do not become overheated and then jump right in for a swim. Try to avoid crowded areas. If there is a sore throat with a high fever, call a doctor immediately."

He left behind him an apprehensive silence when he returned to his blanket.

My father said, "Now we can wash and eat."

He joined us on our blanket. "Nu, Ruth. We lived to see it. Ten years. Where is the water bottle?"

He washed his hands, spilling the water onto the grass. All around us people were washing their hands in similar fashion. He said very quickly the prayer for washing the hands and for bread. He broke a piece off a slice of rye, sniffed it, chewed it, and swallowed.

"How are you feeling, David?"

"I'm all right, Papa."

"Did you understand what went on here before?"

"I think so, Papa. I understood a little bit."

"It is not a topic for street talk, David. It is like the things we keep only in the family. That you understand?"

"Yes, Papa."

"Good."

"Papa?"

"Yes, David."

"What is JOAC?"

"It stands for Jewish Overseas Aid Committee. J is Jewish. O is overseas. And so on. You understand? It is an organization of American Jews who help Jews in Europe."

"What is ARA?"

"You remember all those letters like that?"

"I told you, Max," my mother murmured from behind a smoked meat sandwich.

"Yes, I know you told me. ARA stands for American Relief Administration. It is an American government organization set up to help very poor people in Europe."

"Why does America help Europe?"

"Because America is a rich country and it feels it has a job to help people who are poor."

"The way Jews help Jews?"

"Yes. But America helps mostly goyim in Poland. The American money is given to Polish organizations, and they give it to goyim. Why don't you eat your sandwich, David? Meat gives you muscles. Afterward we will play some games, yes?"

"Yes, Papa." I could feel he was happy; he never showed happiness on his face, but you felt it when it was there. His movements were slower and gentler and he answered questions patiently rather than brusquely. I did not want to spoil his happiness by telling him I had begun to feel ill. Perhaps I would play anyway despite the pain in my head. But if the pain reached my face I would not be able to play. I would have to be very still then and perhaps even need to be carried home.

"God makes such coincidences," Saul said. He was chewing cautiously on a piece of meat, trying to hold his upper lip still. "I just read about the way it happened in Prague."

I did not understand what he was saying.

"Where the Maharal created the Golem. In a city called Prague in Czechoslovakia hundreds of years ago."

"What does Maharal mean, Šaul?"

"It's short for Morenu harav Loew. Our master, Rabbi Loew. Mem is morenu. Hara is from harav, rabbi. You understand?"

JOAC. ARA. Maharal. How people played with letters and words.

"He was the Rabbi of Prague. He lived about four hundred years ago. And he was almost a hundred years old when he died."

"Really?"

"Ouch, my lip. I hurt my lip." He was silent a moment. "Stupid accident," he said. "The book I read said the goyim in that city kept accusing Jews of killing children and using the blood for matzos. The Maharal made a tall strong man out of clay—a golem—and he would go around and see what the goyim were doing, and if a goy made plans to harm the Jews the Golem would report it to the Maharal, who would tell the police. Sometimes he was invisible."

"Really? Was he a giant?"

"I don't know if he was a giant. But the book said he was very tall and big and strong."

"How did he become invisible?"

"The Maharal gave him some kind of lucky charm, and whenever he wore it around his neck it would make him invisible."

"He made the Golem out of clay?"

"Near the Moldau River in Prague there are places where you can find clay. The Maharal went down with two people from his synagogue in the middle of the night and made this shape out of clay and said some special prayers and it came to life."

"Really? It came to life? And it helped the Jews against the goyim? And it was invisible? That's a good story, Saul. I like it better than the story about Abraham smashing all those heads."

"Isn't it strange how Mr. Bader heard about the same thing just now in Europe when he was there?"

"It's just an accident that you read the book now, Saul."

My parents were talking quietly together. Alex had finished his roll and was attacking a slice of rye bread, unperturbed by the talk and laughter and movement around him. Most of the people were speaking Yiddish; some were speaking in a language I did not understand; I heard no English. A man began to sing and the song was quickly picked up by others around us. It was a Yiddish lullaby about a fire burning in a hearth and the house warm and schoolchildren being taught the Hebrew alphabet. They had stopped eating and were all singing together, including Mr. and Mrs. Bader. I noticed that Dr. Weidman was gone.

The song ended; the eating resumed. My brother became disenchanted with his slice of rye bread and tossed its soggy remnants onto the grass. He got up on his feet, began to explore the blanket, and stepped into a paper plate of sauerkraut. My mother put him on her lap and gave him a bottle of juice. He put the nipple to his lips, let out a gurgle, and sucked greedily.

One of the men on a nearby blanket called out, "Max, are you going back this year?" He was a dark-haired man in his thirties who came often to our house in the evenings. "You've never gone back."

"No," my father said. "I am not crazy."

"I may go over," said the man, lowering his voice.

"Don't be a fool, Aaron."

"They have no memories for old crimes."

"Do what you want. But you are a fool."

"I'm considering it."

"Better they should come here."

"That's it. That's where the dog lies buried. They won't come. My father is like your father. He says his job is to stay there."

I saw my father's face go stiff.

"What should I do, Max?"

"Whatever you do," my father said in a flat, cold voice, "do not go."

"You always see the dark side of the world, Max."

"Yes. And I am rarely surprised. Who is that? Sonia?"

A woman's rich contralto voice had suddenly burst into a lively song. The talk ceased immediately; heads turned. The woman sat near the side of the clearing that was across from the path we had taken through the wood. She was small and slight of build, but her voice filled the clearing and echoed within the silent branches of the trees. She was singing a song in a language I did not understand; it sounded like Polish, the language my parents spoke on occasion when they were alone or with friends or when they did not want me to understand what they were saying. After a moment some of the people began to hum the melody and then sing the words. Soon everyone was singing except me, my brother, and Saul. My mother sang with her eyes closed, her body swaying slightly from side to side. I saw she had taken my father's hand in hers. He was singing very quietly, his face wearing a stiff look. I felt like that sometimes when I wanted to cry but for some reason would fight back the tears: all stiff and hard and stone-like in my face and chest and fingers.

As I watched my father, I saw my brother take the bottle out of his mouth. I thought he was about to toss it on the grass alongside his discarded piece of bread, and I reached out for it. But he put it back into his mouth. Then I looked across his shoulder and along the front of the group and saw Eddie Kulanski standing very still just inside the pine wood near the edge of the clearing. Behind him stood a tall man and woman in their late twenties or early thirties. The man was flaxen-haired and wore a tight polo shirt and tight trousers. The woman had very full breasts and a round face with high cheekbones and long blond hair. They stood behind Eddie Kulanski and looked around the clearing and listened to the song. Some of the men had removed their straw hats and were wearing skullcaps. I saw Eddie Kulanski and his parents standing there and looking at us. I did not know how long they had been standing there. Eddie Kulanski's father carried a picnic basket and his mother carried a blanket. Eddie Kulanski held a baseball bat, a glove, and a softball. On his head he wore a baseball hat. I felt cold seeing him there suddenly on the edge of the clearing like a ghost in one of Saul's stories, the ones that were not from the midrash but were just plain stories that no one believed but were exciting to hear. As I sat there staring at them, Eddie Kulanski turned his head slightly and his eyes met mine. His thin pointed face and half-closed eyes remained expressionless and cold. He did not seem surprised to see me; he must have noticed me earlier. There had been no one near the edge of the woods during the speeches. They must have come just a short while ago. What were they thinking as they stood there watching and listening to a group of Jews singing a Polish song? They would talk about it afterward when they left. The Golem might know what they said if he followed them. Invisible, he could follow them and listen to everything they said about Jews. What did goyim say about Jews when they were only among themselves?

The song ended. There was a burst of applause. My brother, startled, took the bottle from his mouth and let out a small cry. I saw Eddie Kulanski's father turn his head and say something to the woman. She threw back her head and laughed. Then her hands moved swiftly across the front of her body, describing the shape of a cross.

"Saul." I tugged at his shirt and spoke in a very low voice.

He looked at me over the piece of meat he was carefully putting into his mouth.

"That's Eddie Kulanski." I felt frightened just saying his name.

He stared.

"And his mother and father. See how big his father is."

Saul sat very still and looked and said nothing. At that moment Eddie Kulanski and his mother and father turned and went back up the path and disappeared into the wood.

"Why were they here, Saul?"

"For a picnic," Saul said.

"Isn't he big?"

"Yes."

"You see what I meant? About fighting?"

He nodded and gave me a dark look. His glasses had slipped down along the bridge of his nose.

"There are so many places in the zoo and the meadow they could go for a picnic. Why did they come here?"

"I don't know. Take it easy, Davey."

"You see? It was an accident. You see?"

"I see."

"I hate accidents. Why does God make accidents?"

"Take it easy, Davey. Keep your voice down."

"He scares me, Saul. I'm very scared seeing him like that. Suddenly, like a ghost. I wish Abraham would break his head."

"Davey—"

"You think the Golem could follow them and find out what they're saying?"

He looked at me. Slowly, he pushed his glasses back up along the bridge of his nose.

"I don't like him, Saul. He's not a nice person. Are all goyim like that?"

"Your friend Tony isn't like that."

"No. You're right. He isn't like that. You're right, Saul. But Eddie Kulanski really scares me, Saul. He makes me feel more terrible than Tony Savanola makes me feel good."

Saul looked at me and said nothing.

My father, who had been talking quietly to my mother, now turned to me. After a moment he said, "Why aren't you eating? You have not touched your sandwich. You will have muscles like a woman when you grow up."

I ate slowly. My eyes hurt. Someone was talking to me. I raised my head. It was Mr. Bader.

"Hello," he said. "You're so busy eating and thinking you don't even hear me."

I tried to smile at him.

"I haven't seen you in a long time, David. How are you feeling? Have you grown since I saw you last? I think you have."

I shrugged. He frightened me a little now. The calm voice and the smooth gentlemanly manner and the small black skull-cap and the brown hair meticulously parted in the middle and the very dark, penetrating eyes; and all that traveling to strange places where Jews were hated; and all those people he had talked to; and the photograph.

"It was a nice surprise seeing you here," he said in his soft calm voice. He had bent down to speak to me. Now he hitched up his sharply pressed trousers and sat on his haunches and rested his manicured hands on his knees. His craggy face was deeply tanned. "Your father told me you've been ill. I was sorry to hear that."

I hung my head and was quiet. Out of the corner of my eye I saw Saul lying on his blanket. His eyes were partly open and he was watching me.

"I saw your grandmother," Mr. Bader said. "She is very eager to meet her American grandsons. She sends you very special love."

I acknowledged the words with a nod. I never thought too much about my relatives in Europe. They were simply there, like the teachers I was supposed to have when I started attending yeshiva after the summer, dim unformed presences I might meet in a future I could barely perceive or understand.

"Is my grandmother sick?" I asked.

"She is better," he said.

"Will she come to America?"

"We all hope so."

"Did you see my father's parents?"

"Yes. In Lemberg. They are well."

"Were you able to recognize my father's friends from the photograph?"

He looked at me. His eyes widened momentarily, then became very narrow. He brushed a speck of dust from his jacket sleeve and put his fingers to his bow tie. He looked around casually. Then he looked at me.

"How old are you, David?" he asked in a very low, calm voice.

"Almost six."

"Well, you're a big boy. And a very bright boy." He paused. "Are you big and bright enough to believe that you never saw the photograph you say you saw?"

"I saw it," I said. "Why do you all say I didn't see it?"

"David, you have to be very big and bright to believe me when I say that you did not see it."

I looked away from him. He was really frightening me now. His eyes had a sharp glittering darkness and the bones in his face seemed to have hardened perceptibly as he spoke. How could I be big enough and old enough not to have seen a photograph everyone knew I had seen? I did not understand what he was saying. I saw Saul gazing at me from his prone position on the blanket. Most of the people seemed to have finished their lunch and were walking about, talking loudly and laughing. My parents and aunt and uncle were surrounded by friends, all of them listening intently to what a short, thin-faced, dark-haired man was saying about stocks and bonds and something called futures and margin. I saw another strange couple come from the wood into the clearing. They looked around, turned, and went back into the wood. From somewhere in the crowd the woman with the contralto voice began to sing a soft, sad Polish song. Her voice drifted through the clearing and mingled with the laughter and the noise and the excited talk about stocks and bonds and futures and margin.

I felt Mr. Bader put his hand on my arm. "You weren't listening, David. You have a habit of not listening. Did your father ever tell you that you have such a habit?"

I nodded slowly.

"It's not a good habit, David."

I was quiet. I wished he would go away. I could only breathe through my mouth now and my throat had begun to feel dry and tight. I wished he would go away and leave me alone. I wanted to go home and lie in my bed beneath my sheet and look into my quiet white world. I would brush my eyelids against the sheet. That was a good feeling.

Instead of going away, Mr. Bader sat down.

"That's an uncomfortable position. There are people in the world who can squat like that for hours. Did you know that? I saw an Arab woodcarver sit like that for half a day once. Amazing. But it's not for me. Listen, David. I am going to find out just how big a boy you really are. Since it was my fault that you accidentally saw that photograph, I am going to have to explain something to you. We'll keep it to ourselves, all right?"

He was speaking in a very low, urgent tone. I could barely hear him. From somewhere in the clearing came a shout and a burst of laughter.

"I don't think your father would like me to tell you this. He prefers—how shall I phrase it?—secrecy to openness, even with his own family, especially with a six-year-old boy. Let me see if I can explain it to you in a way that will help you to understand it. Lemberg was captured by Russians in the second year of the war. Then the army of Pilsudski captured it back from the Russians. The part of Poland where your mother and father lived, the part called Eastern Galicia, had been under the control of Austria. The Austrian army gave the Jews weapons to protect themselves in case of pogroms by Poles. Then the Austrians left Poland. And there were pogroms. Your father had been a very good soldier in Pilsudski's army. He organized his friends in and around Lemberg and they fought back. They saved Jewish lives and killed Polish hooligans. Then the Polish government ordered all the people to turn in their weapons. When that photograph was taken it was illegal for anyone who wasn't a policeman or a soldier to possess a weapon. The Jews in that photograph were breaking Polish law. There could be problems. Do you understand? Is all this too much for a six-year-old head?"

"Why did they take the photograph, Mr. Bader?"

"Do you understand what I just said to you?"

"Some of it. The part about the Austrian army and the weapons. Yes."

"That is all you need to understand. It is better if no one knows about that photograph."

"But why did—"

"You weren't listening to me, David."

"I was, Mr. Bader."

"Good. Then you understand that you never saw such a photograph."

I was quiet.

"I hope you understand that clearly, David."

Some people in the group were clapping in rhythm to a song. Along a stretch of grass near the far edge of the clearing six or seven men had begun to kick around a soccer ball. My father was there. He had removed his jacket and shirt and straw hat and had on his white undershirt and trousers. I saw the muscles in his chest and arms. He ran lightly and effortlessly back and forth across the grass, kicking the soccer ball, passing it, taking passes from others. He seemed to glide over the ground with the kind of ease I often saw in the zoo animals as they moved about in their pens and cages: smooth silken gliding movements that met no resistance from earth or air. Eddie Kulanski moved like that. I wondered what it must feel like to be able to move easily and freely. I almost never had that feeling now for more than a few days at a time. And even then I did not fully have it because I always knew I would soon be losing it. Yes, I had it when I was on my tricycle. That must be the feeling: smooth and at ease and the wind caressing your face, often even tickling it a little the way my billy goat tickled the palm of my hand. But I tired easily on my tricycle. No, I never really had that free smooth feeling when my feet were on the ground.

"People tell me your father was an excellent soccer player in Poland," Mr. Bader said quietly. "He led a team in Lemberg. They say he would play fiercely." He was gazing at my father with the same expression of admiration that I had noticed on his face during the wet April day I had seen the photograph. "Those are his very good friends, the men he is playing with. They played as children in the courtyards of their homes in Lemberg and in the fields and forests. He helped them come to America. He has strong loyalties, your father. They all have strong loyalties. Do you understand that word, David?"

I nodded hesitantly.

"Your father has a habit of referring to it as his job. I call it loyalties. Duties and loyalties." He looked away from the game at the sky. A mass of dark cloud had covered the sun. The air in the clearing was suddenly cool. He gazed down at me and touched his fingers to his bow tie. "Sometimes I have the feeling you understand a great deal more than you let everyone think you understand. Is that true, David?"

I did not know what to say.

"I suppose that is not a wise question to have asked. Is there anything you want to tell me?"

"Was the photograph really taken at a wedding, Mr. Bader?"

"I don't want to talk any more about that photograph. I will answer your question and that will be all. The answer to your question is yes, the photograph was taken at a wedding."

"Did you grow up with my father?"

"No. I grew up in a very big city. Warsaw. I came to America when I was fourteen. Look at him. Look at your father. How he moves! He was the fastest runner in his neighborhood when he was young. So your uncle tells me."

"Was he frightened by goyim?"

He looked surprised. "What do you mean?"

"Did he have to run away from goyim?"

"Ah, I see. No, your father didn't run from goyim. They would run from him. I think your father is the only Jew I know who is truly not afraid of goyim. He hates them and is not afraid of them. He said to me once the only way to live with goyim is to know them thoroughly and once you know them you cannot help but hate them. Have you ever heard him say that?"

"Yes."

"I was certain you had. He does not keep it a secret."

"Do you hate goyim, Mr. Bader?"

"I don't hate anyone, David, because no one has ever really hurt me. I am a fortunate Jew." He spoke in an intimate manner. "I was fortunate to have been in America and not in Europe during the war. Sometimes I feel guilty about that. Do you understand what I mean? No, I suppose not."

I gazed at the small group of players. Most of the people in the clearing had moved off their blankets and had gathered near the game. Eight men were playing now. My father seemed to be everywhere at once on the length of grass that had become the soccer field. The sun had burned through the clouds and I could see it glistening on the sweat that covered his face. As he raced and kicked he shouted instructions to his teammates in Yiddish; once he shouted in the language I thought was Polish. I heard the thud of his shoe against the ball. He ran with it, dodging and sliding through opponents, doing little dances around it, sidestepping neatly the charge of the tall man with the small eyes and the large nose who had held both a knife and a gun in the photograph. Then, near the blanket that served as a makeshift goal, he feinted to the left, twirled like a dancer around the ball, and sent it off to the right with a swift, clean, expertly aimed kick that shot it past the head of the goalie, the thin-faced, dark-haired little man of bonds and futures, and off into the trees beyond the clearing. There was a loud cheer and hand-clapping.

"David?"

I turned away from the game. I was beginning to feel strangely disturbed by the frenetic activity of the players. My aunt and uncle had moved off their blanket to a point closer to the game. My brother had fallen asleep and my mother sat near him on the blanket, a dreamy smile on her face. She seemed in another time and place. That almost always happened to her when we came to this clearing; she closed her eyes and drifted off on a journey through distant memories. Saul lay very still, watching me through slitted eyes. From the playing field came a shout and a cheer. But I did not turn to it; my head hurt badly now—from the noise of the game, the confusing words of Mr. Bader, the taut sensation I had in my arms and chest from watching my father, and from the illness I knew would soon come upon me.

"David, you aren't listening to me. People talk to you and you drift away into your own world. That's a bad habit."

I murmured an apology.

"How are you teaching yourself to read?" he asked.

I stared at him.

"Your mother tells me you have begun to read Hebrew and Yiddish though no one is teaching you. How are you doing that?"

I shrugged a shoulder.

"What's that, David?" He imitated my motion.

I was quiet.

"You have no answer?"

"I don't know."

"That's better. 'I don't know' is an answer. It interests me very much that you are learning to read without a teacher. Are you reading English too?"

I shrugged a shoulder. Then I said, "Yes."

His dark eyes glittered and I thought I saw a smile play briefly on his lips.

There was another shout and cheer from the field. I looked down at the blanket, feeling surfeited with talk and noise and pain. I wanted Mr. Bader to leave. Then I heard myself say abruptly, "Do you ever have accidents, Mr. Bader?" I listened to myself ask the question and I could not remember having wanted to ask it. I had no memory at all of any intent to ask that question. The question had appeared suddenly as if it had existed secretly within me all along and had decided now to make its own search for an answer.

"Of course I've had accidents, David."

"All the time?"

"What do you mean?"

"Do you do something and think there's nothing bad in it, and you hurt people and kill animals and birds?"

He did not answer. But he was peering at me very closely.

"I have accidents all the time. I killed a canary and a dog by accident. And I fall and hurt myself. And I almost started a fire once in our kitchen. And I almost fell out of my window. And I tripped climbing into a trolley car and cut my lip. And I fell over backward in my chair in the kitchen and cut my tongue. There was a lot of blood."

"You do have accidents," he murmured. "You ought to be careful."

"I'm very careful, Mr. Bader."

"People have accidents all the time, David."

"So many accidents?"

"No, not so many."

"I dream about it a lot, Mr. Bader."

"Yes?"

"Every night I dream about having accidents. I have terrible dreams."

"Every night?"

"Almost every night, Mr. Bader."

"Indeed? So many dreams?"

"Sometimes I think there's something wrong with me."

"Now, now," he murmured.

"It's very scary to have that feeling, Mr. Bader."

He gazed at me, then nodded slowly. He seemed preoccupied for a moment, as if a memory had suddenly surfaced and overshadowed his awareness of the clearing and the conversation he was having. Then he said something but I was no longer listening. The question had receded and taken refuge once again deep within me. I could actually feel it darting into folds of darkness and disappearing into the comforting oblivion where I had wanted it to remain. Mr. Bader was talking to me but I could not listen. I saw my cousin raise his head slightly off his blanket, then put his head back down and close his eyes. From the soccer field came the sound of shoes against the leather ball, a sharp thud, and

another cheer. "Good shot, Max!" someone shouted. "You're
a killer with those feet."

"You play like a goy, Max," someone else shouted.

"Why not?" another voice shouted back. "Who do you
think taught him to play, his teachers in the yeshiva?"

"David," Mr. Bader said, insistently.

"I saw the photograph but I won't tell anyone or ever talk
about it again with anyone."

He smiled faintly. "Thank you," he said. "I must say that
you are a bright young man. When you know to read Hebrew
well, you may want to learn Bible with me. I learned Bible in
Europe with a great teacher. It is more than thirty-five years
since I have learned with him, but I remember everything.
That will be my way of repaying your—how shall I put it?—
your forgetfulness regarding a certain photograph." He leaned
forward and patted my arm. "It was good talking to you,
David. And you should tell your mother you are not feeling
well. A child should never conceal such matters from his
parents. Goodbye, David. Shall I give your grandmother your
love? I will be seeing her again soon, God willing."

I nodded.

He rose quickly from the blanket, looked down at me,
gave me a smile, and went off toward the people near the
game. He had a light tread and he walked erect and seemed
to glide across the grass, as he had glided out of the shadows
and crossed his study to take from my hands the photograph
I had now promised never to tell anyone I had seen. I lay
back on the blanket near my brother. My mother seemed to
have fallen asleep in a sitting position at the other end of
the blanket. Her eyes were closed and her head lay to one
side. The brim of her white flowery straw hat was bent
against her shoulder. Asleep, the taut skin of her face had
slackened, and she looked strangely old.

A few feet away from me, Saul stirred and sat up.

"Davey," he whispered.

I looked at him.

"Are you all right?"

I nodded.

"You talked a long time."

I was quiet.

He waited. "I couldn't hear anything you said, Davey."

I remained quiet. He put his head back down on the
blanket. "As long as you feel all right," he said.

I closed my eyes and lay very still and began to go over

the entire conversation from the beginning. I could hear the conversation inside my ears. I could slow it down or speed it up or stop it, as I wished. When I was done going over it, I waited a moment, and then began to go over it again. I fell asleep.

Through my sleep I heard the thudding of shoes against the leather ball. At times the people watching the game seemed very still. In the warm air of the clearing, the sounds of the shoes striking the ball moved piercingly toward the trees. Very clearly, as if my eyes were open and my head were thrust close upon the swift-moving legs of the players, I saw their shoes striking the ball. Then the ball became a dog's head. A wave of nausea moved through me. I opened my eyes and sat up.

There was no soccer game going on at all. The length of the grass that had been the soccer field was now a wrestling ring. My father lay on the grass wrestling the tall man with the small eyes who had held both a knife and a gun in the photograph. I looked at the bulging muscles on my father's arms and chest and back. The crowd was quiet. I could hear the tall man's heavy grunting breaths. My brother and Saul lay asleep. My mother was not on our blanket. I looked carefully and saw her standing alongside my uncle. I saw again the muscles on my father's arms. He was intertwined with the tall man, rolling with him on the grass, now holding him about the head, now locking his arms about his shoulders. Sweat poured from both their faces. The sun shone brightly but there were dark clouds now in a distant corner of the sky.

I lay back down on the blanket and closed my eyes. I did not want to sleep, for I was fearful of dreaming once again. I fell asleep.

A voice woke me. It was a strange soft musical voice, sweet, almost whispered. I had never heard it before and knew it was a dream and slid into deeper sleep.

Raindrops woke me. But I thought it odd that there would be rain while I could still see the sun through my closed eyelids. The clearing was still; the wood vibrated softly with insect life. I lay very still and opened my eyes and saw my father and mother.

They stood beneath the branches of a tall pine with their arms around each other. My father had his shirt and straw hat on once again. His hair was combed and his face was dry. He stood gently caressing my mother's face and head, running a finger across her cheek and chin and nose and eyes and forehead. I felt his finger moving and caressing; he moved it across the bridge of her nose and along the wings of her nostrils and slowly over her lips. And she kissed his finger and the palm of his hand and bent her head. And he cupped her head in his hand and kissed her cheek and forehead and eyes and lips. And she held him; her short, thin, fragile body locked tightly to his strong frame, his arms around her. "How good you are to me," she was saying. "How I don't deserve this," she was saying. "I love you, my husband," she was saying. "I do, I do. No matter what you may think, I do. David was beautiful, David I loved, David I worshipped, David was from a world of dreams, David was the Garden of Eden, David was like the wind that is the bodies of angels. It is you I love now, my husband. Though I do not deserve it. I am a woman with nothing but fears and superstitions and a sick child and memories. But I do love you. Yes. Yes. Very much. Yes. Hold me and love me. Yes. And what they did to you, the goyim. What they did to David and to you and to all of us, the goyim. What they did to you, to you, oh what they did to you." With her hand she caressed his cheek and with a finger she traced the outlines of his bony features, the sharp bony jut of his jaw, his firm lips, his straight nose, his high, lined forehead, his small eyes, his cheekbones; and with a finger she gently, slowly, tremulously, it seemed to me, caressed the scar that lay across his right cheek.

The scar was a dry white line that began a little below the cheekbone and ran the length of the cheek almost parallel to the straight line of the nose. It terminated above the jawbone near the dip of flesh that marked the end point of the lips on the right side of the face. It was narrow at its end and wide and clearly ridged with healed tissue at its center. It was a little less than two inches in length. It lay upon his thick squarish features like a miniature road marker and had, until that moment when I saw my mother's finger move across it gently and with love, been regarded by me as possessing an invisibility similar to that attributed to the color of one's eyes or to a birthmark or freckles. Then I saw my father take my mother in his arms and kiss her lips. I lay very still on the blanket and listened to the pounding of my heart.

From somewhere nearby came the rumbling sound of thunder. My brother woke and cried. I sat up. The sky was a mass of dark, boiling clouds. My parents came quickly from beneath the pine tree. Covered by the dense canopy of branches and absorbed in one another, they had not sensed the coming of the thunderstorm. Gathering up the blanket and the picnic basket, my father looked quickly around the clearing. It was deserted and clean. There was not a piece of paper on the grass. I had dreamed it. There had been no one there save ourselves. I had dreamed all of it. We went quickly through the wood and the meadow and along the path between the deer and llamas and camels. There was my silly billy goat. The air was very still and dark. The leaves on the trees seemed paralyzed. Half a block out of the zoo, the rain hit us with a sudden dense slanting rush of thick drops. Then it became a waterfall. My father lifted me and carried me beneath his jacket. The picnic basket bumped against my legs. My mother carried my brother. They ran with us through the rain to our apartment house. The street smelled of hot wet pavement and the excrement of horses. Was my billy goat out in the rain? And what would happen to the Golem in the rain? Would his clay body melt?

I stood at the window in my room and watched the rain falling into the maples. The leaves shuddered. I felt the fever in my eyes and the pain in my forehead and cheeks. Soon I would tell my parents I was ill. There was no hurry. They were busy now with other matters. The pain in my face was not yet unbearably severe. Standing at the window, I saw Eddie Kulanski and his parents walking along the street, laughing and holding their faces to the rain just as the old man on our block would hold his face to the sun. They were drenched. I could see the outlines of their bodies beneath their summer clothes. They passed beneath a maple and were gone from view. I turned away from the window and lay down on my bed. The high fever and the facial pain came swiftly then, and I cried out for my mother.

She came in quickly and undressed me and helped me wash and put me to bed. I could not associate her with the woman who had spoken with such love beneath the tree on the edge of the clearing. Now she seemed, as always, dry, brittle, frightened, her eyes darting about, her face gaunt and pale, her fingers cold and moist on my body. She spoke in her nervous, harried, high-pitched voice. Then who had been the woman with my father? There had been no such woman. It had all been a dream. The entire afternoon had been a fever dream. Nothing connected the afternoon to the bed in which I now lay as I waited for my mother to leave so I could create with my sheet the white world of tranquillity which I loved. Nothing, it seemed, except the scar on my father's face.

My mother gave me my medicine and went from the room. My father came in to say good night. He stood stiffly at my bedside, a short rigid man whose strong arms I imagined I could see through the long-sleeved striped shirt he wore. I looked at the white line of the scar. No, I had not dreamed the scar. Perhaps I had dreamed the picnic. But not the scar.

"How are you feeling, David?"

"It's my nose and eyes and throat, Papa."

"The same black year again."

"Was there a picnic today, Papa?"

"What?"

"Did we go to a picnic?"

"Of course we went to a picnic." His voice shook.

"I don't think I liked it, Papa. I don't think I want to go again next year."

He stood near the bed and looked at me and was silent.

"You made that organization, Papa?"

"Yes."

"Is it a big organization?"

"It is big enough."

"You made it to help Jews?"

"To help my friends and their families."

"Goyim don't help us, Papa?"

"Goyim? It is a world that hates Jews. Why should goyim help us?"

"Maybe I'm glad I went, Papa."

We were silent a moment. The distant clang of a trolley car came dimly through the sound of the rain.

"I wish it could be a better world," I said.

He stirred faintly and was still.

"Yes," I heard myself say. "I'm glad I went. But I wish God would make the world clean."

"David," he said softly and was silent.

"Papa. The cut on your face. Was it an accident?"

I thought I heard him draw in breath very sharply. The rain drummed on my window.

"Papa?"

"Yes," he said in a strange, quiet voice. "One can say that it was an accident."

My eyes were half-closed. I felt the cool smooth sheets on my legs and hands. The lamp on the dresser burned brightly. It would be white beneath my sheet. Soon, soon.

"You fell, Papa? When you were a little boy?"

"No." I could barely hear his voice for the noise of the rain.

"Did someone cut you, Papa?"

"Yes."

Someone had cut him. Someone had cut my father's face.
There would have been a lot of blood.

"Who hurt you, Papa?"

"A goy. A Polak."

His voice, thin and expressionless, had come as if from very
far away. Slowly he sat down on my bed. His hands dangled
between his slightly spread thighs.

"In Lemberg, Papa?"

"No. In a troop train on the way back from the war
against the Bolsheviks. The train was held up in a forest by
Polish bandits." He spoke quietly above the noise of the rain,
looking strangely small on my bed, as if his words were
diminishing his size. "They came through the train stealing
only from Jews. They only wanted the Jews, they kept saying."

"How did they know who were the Jews, Papa?"

"They knew," he said after a moment, and seemed to become smaller still.

"Papa?"

"I think you should go to sleep now, David." His voice was
very soft.

"Why did the goy cut your face?"

"He wanted to steal my tallis and tefillin. I would not give
them to him. I would not let him take my tallis and tefillin.
He cut my face with his bayonet and took them. None of the
goyishe soldiers said a word. I had served with them for
years. They did not lift a finger to help. The job of a Jew is
to suffer, they think, the stinking Polaks. With that job they
are ready to help us. So. Now you know. Your mother and I
wondered when you would ask about the scar."

"Was Mama hurt by goyim?"

"What? No." He rose abruptly from the bed. I felt the
mattress move upward. The rain beat loudly upon my window. "It is late," he said. "I have a customer I must see early
tomorrow morning. Aren't you tired? I am tired. Playing ball
and wrestling. I am very tired. I need a bath and then I am
going to bed."

"I like when we talk, Papa."

"Yes? Well." He seemed embarrassed. "We talk. Don't we
talk?"

"Am I named after your brother David?"

"What? Yes."

"He was killed by goyim?"

"Yes." His voice was very small.

"Were many Jews killed?"

"Yes."

"Did you kill many goyim, Papa?"

"Not enough," he said. "Good night, David."

"Good night, Papa."

He went quietly from the room.

I slid beneath my sheet. Now I was safe. I could hear the pounding of the rain on my window. The world outside was dark with horror. It hurt Jews and I was always having accidents and getting sick in it. But I knew I was safe inside the clean white world I had created for myself. Nothing could touch me inside that world. It was cool and white and the Angel of Death never entered it with his arsenal of accidents. The rain was loud upon my window. I listened to the rain. It fell steadily and strongly upon the earth. It fell from the clouds through the dark night and the trees and the yellow ghostly arcs of the street lights. It beat like fingers upon my window. Perhaps it was another flood. No. God had promised there would be no more floods. But God could change His mind. God could do anything. I lay in my white world and listened to the summer rain and knew it was another flood. Like the first Flood. A flood that would cover the earth and the trees and the buildings and the valleys and the mountains. A flood that would cover the Bronx and Bobrek and Lemberg and Warsaw and Lodz. A flood that would cleanse and not kill. And Og would ride the waves carrying the zoo animals and my little billy goat, and the clay golem would not melt, and Eddie Kulanski and his cousin would turn their faces to the rain and laugh and float cleansed on the surface of the water and talk to me without hate. And afterward, when the water receded and the world outside was as clean and white as my white world inside, my mother would smile often, and my father and I would talk often, and Mr. Bader would explain to me why that photograph had not yet been destroyed if it was so dangerous to so many people.

I lay in my white world listening to the rain and feeling the slow inward curling of sleep and knew in my heart that when I woke in the morning everything outside would be clean and white and the Angel of Death would have less of a job to do because goyim would not kill Jews and the entire world would be free of accidents. Perhaps the Angel of Death himself would die in the flood; the only one to die.

The rain woke me in the night. My head was on the pillow outside the sheet. The light in my room had been turned off. A small dark form stood near my bed. "Ochnotinos, chnotinos, notinos," it murmured. "Otinos, tinos, inos, nos, os." But I knew it was a fever dream and did not cry out. The form remained near my bed, murmuring. I slid under my sheet.

Three days later I was well enough to go outside. I ran over Eddie Kulanski's hand with my tricycle.

TWO

It was an accident.

I had been ill only two days. All of the second day I was free of fever. During breakfast the following morning, my mother said quietly to my father, "Two days, Max. I must thank Mrs. Horowitz."

"Women's nonsense," he said, looking up from his Yiddish newspaper.

"But two days, Max."

"You want me to believe in that witch? She hates the child."

"But she gave me the words out of pity," my mother said, and added, "She has a new dog."

"Mazel tov," said my father. "More dirt on the sidewalk."

"What did Mrs. Horowitz give you?" I asked.

"A special prayer, darling. Against your fever."

I stared at her.

"Eat your cereal," my father said. "You'll go outside and play in the fresh air. That is the best protection against sickness. I need another glass of coffee. Ruth."

A few minutes later he murmured the Grace After Meals and went out of the kitchen.

"Can I ride my bike, Mama?"

"Yes, darling."

"Can we go to the zoo?"

"Today? I must write letters. Finish your cereal, darling. Look how Alex has finished all his cereal."

I finished my cereal. I did not feel weak. I could not remember when I had felt so rested after an illness.

Later that morning I came slowly through the glass entrance door of the house, dragging my tricycle. It was a warm sunny day. The street was busy with traffic. Children played all up and down the sidewalk. At the far end of the street the old man sat on a chair, his face to the sun.

A little to the right of the stoop, Tony Savanola and Eddie Kulanski were playing a game of marbles. Tony gave me a smile.

"How do you feel, Davey?"

I told him I felt very good and mounted the tricycle.

Eddie Kulanski was on his hands and knees, gauging an intricate shot. He ignored me.

"Did you have a good time at the picnic, Davey?" Tony Savanola asked.

I looked at Eddie Kulanski. "It was a good picnic, Tony. My father belongs to an organization that has a picnic once a year. They have games and wrestling and things. Do Catholics have picnics?"

"Sure Catholics have picnics." He gave me a queer look. Eddie Kulanski raised his head slightly and fixed his half-closed eyes on my face.

I pumped the pedals of my tricycle back and forth in short thrusting motions. It was shady beneath the maples on the street. But the air was very warm and I felt strange strength in my arms and legs.

"My father told me we got permission from the zoo for the picnic," I said. "He had to write a letter and everything. They have to tell the zoo a long time in advance or they can't have it."

Eddie Kulanski looked back down at the game of marbles on the sidewalk.

I rode off and spent the morning on the tricycle and was not weary when I had to go in for lunch. I parked the tricycle under the stairway in the entrance hall and went upstairs. It was strange that my legs were not shaking and trembling after all that time on the tricycle.

I came downstairs immediately after lunch. The door to the right of the stairway opened quietly. Mrs. Horowitz stepped into the entrance hall.

I was dragging my tricycle through the hallway. I stopped and looked at her and was a little frightened. She was skinny and wrinkled; her large eyes and thin neck gave her the appearance of a bird.

"You're all better," she said, smiling.

I did not know what to say. I nodded. Her breath was sour.

"I have other special things to give your mother. She's a smart woman, your mother. Smart. She knows whom to ask for help. Against fever I found something from the Bible—Numbers, chapter twelve, verse thirteen, and Deuteronomy, chapter seven, verse fifteen. There's nothing more powerful than a verse from the Bible. Nothing. It says so in the holy books I have. We'll be friends, yes? You don't want to hurt an old lady."

I could not grasp what she was saying.

"There are verses against enemies and demons and the evil eye. But sometimes the evil eye is too strong." She gazed at me out of her large eyes as if I were supposed to understand what she was saying.

I began to edge away from her, pulling my tricycle.

"I found a special prayer for a good memory. I gave it to your mother. You say it after Havdalah. It's in the holy books."

"What?" I said, bewildered.

"Promise you'll stay away from my dog," she said abruptly.

I stared at her.

"He's a new dog. Promise."

I could smell her sour breath and see the tiny cracks in the powder on her cheeks.

"Promise," she said again. "Promise."

I did not know what she was talking about. Inside the apartment I heard a dog bark briefly.

"I promise," I heard myself tell her because I wanted to get away from there and be outside on my tricycle.

Her powdered, wrinkled face broke into a smile. "You won't be sorry," she said. "My father's uncle was the Rhiziner Rebbe. He made miracles. I'll pray for you. I have books with prayers and charms for everything. You won't be sorry. But take away the evil eye."

She stepped back into the apartment and closed the door. The entrance hall echoed faintly with her words. I stared at the door. Then I decided she was a little crazy and it was too nice a day to spend any part of it thinking about Mrs. Horowitz. I brought my tricycle down the stoop and mounted it.

Joey Younger appeared as if out of the air, dirty, sweaty, greedy. "Can I have a ride, Davey?"

"Sure, Joey. Later. When my mother brings my brother out."

"But that's a long time, Davey."

Near the stoop, Tony Savanola and Eddie Kulanski were engaged in a game of bottle caps.

"I'll race you to the corner, Joey. Can you beat my tricycle?"

For more than an hour I rode back and forth on my tricycle. I went up the side street with it to the wide boulevard that ran alongside the zoo. I rode it back to my street, quickly, feeling the exhilaration of new strength and the wild flush of giddy joy from the sense of power and freedom I now had. I did not know where it had all come from and I did not care. I had it; it was in my arms and legs. I had been sick in bed and some strange thing had happened to me in that time and now I was absolutely and truly well and I could enjoy it, love it, feel the wind of it and the sun of it on my face, watch the swift sliding of the sidewalk beneath my wheels and the dark green of the branches over my head. I rode with that happiness for a long time, pumping my wheels and looking at the underside of the leaves on the maples and at Joey Younger's sad face each time I passed him by and at the sunken features of the old man asleep on his chair in the sunlight. I rode joyously and wildly and I rode over Eddie Kulanski's hand.

I felt it as a slight bump. It made no sound. It was the faintest of obstacles. It was Eddie Kulanski's hand.

The tricycle did not weigh very much and I did not add to its weight to any great degree. But the grooves of my narrow right rear tire had picked up pebbles somewhere and the pebbles went over Eddie Kulanski's hand as it rested on the sidewalk supporting his lanky form while he steadied himself for an attack upon one of Tony Savanola's bottle caps. The pebbles inflicted pain and broke the skin of the hand a little above the knuckles.

Eddie Kulanski shouted and jumped to his feet, staring at his hand. I rode on and heard him shouting. It was a moment before I realized that the bump I had felt was more than a sidewalk indentation. I wheeled around and rode quickly back.

Eddie Kulanski was staring at the blood coming from the small cut on the top of his hand. He looked at me and said, "You fucking son of a bitch."

"Hey," Tony Savanola said. "It was an accident, Eddie."

Eddie Kulanski stared at his bleeding hand. I looked at the hand and down at the tire. It was then that I saw the pebbles.

"You son of a bitch. Look what you did to my hand," Eddie Kulanski said.

"The pebbles did it," I said.

They stared at the tire.

"It's not bad," Tony Savanola said, looking closely at Eddie Kulanski's hand. "My mom can fix it for you."

"It hurts like hell," Eddie Kulanski said.

"I'm sorry," I said.

"You're sorry," Eddie Kulanski said. "You ride around like you own the sidewalk."

"I was only—"

"It really hurts," Eddie Kulanski said.

"Come on inside," Tony Savanola said. "I'll ask my mom to—"

"You Jew fuck," Eddie Kulanski said.

"Hey, come on, Eddie," Tony Savanola said. "It was just an accident."

"He did it on purpose," Eddie Kulanski said.

"What?" I said.

"You did it on purpose, you fuck," Eddie Kulanski said, and he took a step forward, put both his hands on the handlebar of my tricycle, and pushed with all his weight, sending me backward toward the curb of the sidewalk.

My legs had been off the pedals. I put the heels of my sneakers on the ground and stopped the tricycle before it reached the curb.

"What did you do that for?" I said.

"Get out of here," Eddie Kulanski said.

"You could've hurt me," I said.

"What's this?" Eddie Kulanski said, holding up his bruised hand. Again he took a step forward. His eyes were half-closed. "What do you call this?"

I sat on my tricycle and looked at him. No. I would not let him darken my clean new white world. Not for a stupid accident.

"I didn't mean to do that," I said. "I'm really sorry."

"I'm really sorry," he mimicked my high voice. "I'm really sorry. Listen to the creep, Tony. He talks like a baby. I'm really sorry. I don't believe you, you Jew creep."

Again, he put his hands on the handlebar of the tricycle and pushed me backward very hard.

"Hey, cut it out, Eddie," Tony Savanola said.

Behind me was the afternoon traffic that traveled our cobblestone street.

I turned the wheel of my tricycle and pedaled forward to get away from the curb and his pushing hands. I thought I would get down off the tricycle; but I feared he would send it into the street beneath the wheels of a car. He would say I had deliberately run over his hand and he was only getting back at me. What was wrong with him anyway? He seemed a little crazy to me. He was trying to hurt me badly and I had not hurt him badly at all; and besides it had been an accident.

He moved in front of the tricycle and blocked my way.

Joey Younger, who had been sitting on the stoop, now rose slowly to his feet. He stood about ten feet away, watching, his thin greedy face suddenly fearful.

"Get out of my way, Eddie," I said. "I don't want no trouble with you."

Tony Savanola went quickly up the stoop and into the house.

"I don't want no trouble with you," Eddie Kulanski mimicked. "You think you own the sidewalk and all the money and the picnic places and everything." He was pushing me backward toward the curb. "You fucking kike. My father says you stink up the world." He kept leaning on the handlebar and forcing the tricycle backward. I held my feet down hard on the pavement but I could not match his weight.

"Hey, you, Eddie Kulanski!" Mrs. Savanola shouted, appearing suddenly in her window. "Are you crazy? What you doing?"

Eddie Kulanski released the handlebar. Mrs. Savanola quickly withdrew her head from the window. The curb was a foot or so behind me. Cars went by, going quickly over the cobblestones. He stood there, looking at me and at the tricycle and back again at me. There was a queer smile on his lips. His thin features seemed made of points and edges: pointed nose and chin, high cheekbones planing down from sharp ridges of bone. His face had changed as he had pushed me backward; it had become stony and old. But I knew I was imagining it. Hate could not make anyone old. He had forgotten completely the cut in his hand.

He stood there, looking at me, breathing heavily, and hating me. He seemed more a force than a person. I did not believe anyone capable of such hatred. I had never seen such hatred. The clean white world had lasted half a day. The weakness had returned to my legs. The Angel of Death and his accidents had survived the second flood. I bowed my head and wanted to cry.

Eddie Kulanski put his hands on the handlebar of my tricycle.

The entrance door to the apartment house was thrown open and Mrs. Savanola came quickly down the stoop, her fat form and many chins quivering with anger. She pointed a stubby finger at Eddie Kulanski.

"Hey, you, what you doing?" she shouted. "You leave that boy alone."

Eddie Kulanski looked at her with malevolence. Then he looked past her at Tony Savanola who had come outside and was standing on the top step of the stoop. I glanced quickly up and down the street. Two boys who had been playing a marbles game in front of the building to the right now broke off their game and looked at us. A curtain stirred in the window to the left of the entrance door where Tony Savanola stood.

"Shame on you, you fighting a sick boy!" Mrs. Savanola shouted. "Leave him alone, you!"

She towered over him like a raging whale. Eddie Kulanski released the handlebar and backed away slowly from her finger.

"You crazy?" she shouted. "You push him in the street, you make a accident."

He glared at her sullenly out of his sleepy-looking eyes. Then he said something to her in the language I did not understand, ran past her, bounded up the stoop, brushed Tony Savanola aside, and disappeared into the house.

Mrs. Savanola looked at the entrance door. "That's a bad boy sometimes," she said. Then she looked at me. "You be careful how you ride your bike, Davey."

"Yes," I heard myself say in a dry, quivering voice.

"You all right, Davey?"

I nodded.

"You go upstairs and rest. You white like a ghost."

The curtain in the window to the left of the entrance door stirred again and I saw, dimly through the white gauzy material, the birdlike face of Mrs. Horowitz.

I climbed down from the tricycle and brought it over to the stoop. Tony Savanola came down the three steps and helped me drag it up. Joey Younger stood by, watching.

Inside the doorway, Tony Savanola said, "You were riding wild, Davey. But he shouldn't have done that. He could've made a bad accident."

"I was having fun, Tony. I was feeling very good. I don't feel very good too many times."

He looked down at the floor.

"It was a good feeling, Tony. I can't remember when I felt that feeling before. I didn't mean to make the accident."

He seemed embarrassed to hear me talking that way.

"I hope he won't get angry at you, Tony. I hope he won't stop being your friend."

"Nah, he won't stop. He gets angry easy but he stops quick."

"He hates me because I'm a Jew."

Tony Savanola said nothing.

"I don't hate him because he's a Catholic."

Still Tony Savanola said nothing.

The entrance door opened. Mrs. Savanola came into the hall.

"You go upstairs and rest, Davey Lurie. You tell your mama I said you should rest a little bit."

She went into her apartment to the left of the stairway. Tony Savanola went back outside.

I dragged the tricycle beneath the stairway and bent to peer at the rear right wheel. I felt the pebbles. There were three of them, wedged tightly in the tire. I could not get them out.

Somewhere in the hall a door opened and a dog barked. I heard soft footsteps and straightened quickly and stared up into the powdered wrinkles that lay across the features of Mrs. Horowitz.

"I saw and heard," she said in a cautious whisper. "That boy is evil. He is a hater of Jews."

"I have to go upstairs," I said.

"Certainly," she said. "I understand. But there are things that can be done. We are not helpless."

I stared at her.

"There is a charm with names," she said eagerly.

I moved around her toward the stairs.

"Can you read yet?" she asked in a sudden shrill voice.

I stopped. "A little."

"Good," she said, dropping her voice to a thin whisper. "Very good. I have books. Many books. My father, may his soul rest in the Garden of Eden and may he be a good interceder for me, left me two walls of books. Most of them I cannot understand. My son cannot read any of them. You understand me?"

I did not understand and wanted to get away from her.

"I have charms for your reading and your memory. I will make a charm to take care of that Polak. Don't worry yourself. Keep away the evil eye. We will be partners."

I fled upstairs, her thin shrill voice echoing inside my head.

He met me on the stairway the next morning. I was going down, he was going up.

"I'm really sorry," I said. "About the accident."

"Shit on you," he said, his pointed features stiffening, and continued on up the stairs.

Outside I sat in my chair in the sun. The entrance door to the apartment house was opened and a large, black, long-haired dog raced down the stoop. It went immediately to the maple in front of the house and lifted a hind leg. It squatted on the sidewalk and emitted coils of black feces. Then it ambled along the street sniffing at tree trunks, turned the corner, and was gone.

Joey Younger rode up on my tricycle.

"I just saw Eddie Kulanski and his cousin on the boulevard."

I said nothing.

He gave me a pitying look. Then he said, "Can I have one more ride around the block?"

"I'm going inside," I said.

"One more ride, Davey."

I stood up. "Get off," I said.

He looked at me. Then he dismounted.

"You didn't ask me to race you today," I said. "How come you didn't ask me to race you?"

He did not say anything.

"Why didn't you help yesterday?" I asked. "I could've been hurt."

He shrugged.

"You just stood there," I said.

"It wasn't my business," he said. "I don't want no trouble from that crazy Polak."

"But I could've been hurt."

"I didn't want no trouble. Especially from his cousin. It

was your accident, Davey. You were riding all day too fast."

"I was having a good time. For the first time in I can't remember when, I was enjoying myself."

He shrugged again.

"I'm going upstairs," I said.

"Can I ride the bike tomorrow?"

I looked at him. "No," I said.

I struggled up the stoop with the tricycle, got it through the door, and put it under the stairway.

I heard the front door open. There was the sound of animal legs on the marble floor. I came out from beneath the stairway and saw Mrs. Horowitz standing in her doorway. She had on a dark blue bathrobe. Her hair was dry and gray. There was no powder on her face. She looked very old and weary.

"David," she said. "How are you feeling?"

I told her I was feeling all right.

"Yes? I am glad to hear it. The charm is working." She sounded tired. Her voice was hoarse. She peered at me through watery eyes. I saw her eyelids were inflamed. "I am having one of my bad days. Nothing works. If I could understand the books I would find something that works. But most of them I cannot understand. One day you will come in and see the books, yes?"

I nodded slowly and said nothing.

"You saw my new dog?" she asked eagerly.

I nodded again.

"A lovely animal. A comfort. You will be good to him, yes? His name is Bilam. You gave your word. I have prepared a charm to help you in your study of Bible when you begin school. A special charm. What is greater than studying the Bible to protect oneself, ah? Nothing. Nothing is greater. The charm is yours." She shivered suddenly and pulled the robe closer to herself. "A cold wind on such a hot day?" she muttered. "There are strange beings about. I will give the charm to your mother. Your mother informs me that you dream. One day you must tell me one of your dreams. I have many dream books, some by Joseph and Daniel. I have the famous dream book by Solomon Almoli. You will tell me your dreams, yes?" She peered at me intently out of her inflamed, watery eyes. From within the apartment came the barking of the dog. She smiled. "He is hungry. He eats like two men. But he is a comfort. Dogs know when the Angel of Death comes to a neighborhood with his poisoned sword.

They won't move. You didn't know that? Oh, yes. That's the truth. You will come in to see the books? My son never comes. Never. Goodbye."

She closed the door softly.

I stood there for a moment, staring at the closed door. Then I went wearily up the stairs to our first-floor apartment. My mother was at the kitchen table, writing letters. I lay down on my bed.

Later my father came home exhilarated over a sale he had made that day. We ate dinner and he talked about the sale. "And do you know what went on in the market today, Ruth?" He heaped sour cream on his baked potato, dug at the potato with his fork, sniffed, and ate.

My mother stared down at the food on her plate. She seemed not to have heard anything he had said. "I was thinking of the beech trees and the boxwood in the forest behind the farm," she murmured. "Can you remember them at this time of the year?"

He stopped chewing. "Yes." His voice was low.

"Will Bader be able to go to Lemberg?" she asked after a pause.

"Bader is on his way to Switzerland. It depends on what happens at the conference."

My mother looked down at her plate.

"What conference, Papa?"

He glanced at me, annoyed that I had interrupted his conversation with my mother. "A Zionist conference. Eat your fish, David. Fish gives brains. You have not touched your fish."

"The beech trees are especially beautiful now," my mother said. "The color of the bark in the sunlight. I remember."

Afterward she sat in the living room and listened to the canary singing. And in the night I lay awake and heard them speaking in Yiddish of summers in Lemberg and Bobrek, of forests and rivers, of Poles and Cossacks, and of my father's dead brother. I had dreams that night but could remember none of them when I woke with a sore throat in the morning.

It was a mild sore throat. There was no pain behind my eyes. My mother sat at the kitchen table, writing letters. I looked at the envelopes she had addressed and saw the word Poland. I said the word inside my head, imitating her pronunciation of the letters. My brother played quietly on the kitchen floor. I went downstairs to get my tricycle and discovered that the front tire had been cut clean through to the rim.

I stared at the tire. Part of it lay on the floor of the hall, a black ribbon of dead rubber; the rest of it was still on the wheel. As I rolled the tricycle backward with my hand on the handlebar, the rest of the tire came off and lay twisted and vaguely reminiscent of the excrement left behind on the sidewalk yesterday by Mrs. Horowitz's dog.

I went back upstairs.

My mother came downstairs with me and looked at the tire. She seemed weary.

"Why should anyone do that?"

I told her about Eddie Kulanski's hand. "It was an accident, Mama."

She regarded me with a strange dark look in her eyes. "We will tell your father when he comes home," she said. "I must finish my letters and make Shabbos." She brought the tricycle upstairs to my room. It stood in the corner near my dresser, looking crippled. And yesterday it had been so alive. What I had done to Eddie Kulanski had been an accident; but this had not been an accident. Someone had deliberately cut it. Eddie Kulanski and his cousin had wanted to hurt me; I had not wanted to hurt Eddie Kulanski. But I had not expected anyone to cut it. When you didn't expect something to happen and it happened, that was also an accident. My Cousin Saul had said that to me once. Whoever cut the tire of my tricycle had caused me to have an accident. I hated the dry, cold, helpless anger I felt.

I came outside into the morning and sat down on the stoop. It was a warm day. Tony Savanola and Eddie Kulanski were playing marbles. Leaning against the tree near the curb was Eddie Kulanski's cousin. He just stood there, leaning his shoulder against the tree and looking at me. There was a little smile on his small lips. He kept looking at me and smiling. After a while I got up and walked along the street to Mr. Steinberg's candy store. I stood at the newsstand for a few minutes, searching out familiar letters and words on the front pages of the Yiddish newspapers. Then I walked along the narrow side street toward the boulevard and the zoo. I stopped in front of the window of a bakery shop and stared at a chocolate cake. As I turned my head, I noticed Eddie Kulanski's cousin coming slowly up the block toward me.

I stood very still near the window of the bakery shop.
Eddie Kulanski's cousin passed very close to me; he seemed
about to push me against the window of the shop. But he did
not touch me. He went by me and on down the street. At the
corner he turned into the boulevard. A moment later, he
turned back into the side street and started toward me once
again. I walked quickly back along the street, into my own
block. My legs were trembling. I sat down on the stoop. He
came up to the tree in front of the house and stood there,
leaning against the maple and smiling vaguely. Eddie Kulanski
and Tony Savanola were playing quietly together. Joey
Younger was not on the street. After a moment Eddie
Kulanski's cousin withdrew a pocketknife from his trousers.
He opened the blade. It was a small knife with a red handle.
At the base of the maple were large, gnarled protrusions of
roots. He proceeded to toss the knife into one of these roots.
The knife would enter the root and remain upright, quivering. I watched him handling the knife. After a while I went
upstairs and lay down on my bed.

My mother said nothing about the tricycle during lunch.
She moved about the kitchen feeding me and my brother, but
from the drawn and dreamy look on her face and in her eyes
I knew she was elsewhere. I ate quickly. I did not like to be
with her when she was near me and not near me at the same
time.

After lunch I went back to my room. There was a vague
scratchy sensation in my throat. I lay down on my bed and
covered my eyes with my hands. The doorbell rang. I heard
my mother's footsteps in the hallway. The door was opened.
A moment later it was closed. I heard a voice and my mother's
quiet response. I could not make out the words. Outside my
open window a horse and wagon clattered by on the cobblestones. I heard the voices of children playing on the sidewalk.
I thought I would go downstairs and sit in the sun. But I
could not move from the bed; I had no will to move. The
whispered conversation continued for a while in the hallway
of our apartment. Then the door opened and closed again. I
lay on my bed wondering what my mother and Mrs. Horowitz
had talked about.

I got down off the bed and went through the dining room
into my parents' bedroom. It was a large sunny room, with
twin beds, a dark mahogany bureau with a huge mirror, a
tall dark chifforobe, and drapes over the two windows. The

drapes had been opened and sunlight filled the room. I went to the little bookcase near my father's bed and removed his prayer book. On the wall opposite the beds hung my parents' wedding picture. It was a large, oval-shaped, sepia photograph framed in dark wood. My father wore a tuxedo, my mother had on a white gown. A crown of lace topped by a veil covered her hair. She looked very beautiful, and my father looked filled with softness and warmth. The photograph was a three-quarter view of their faces, and they were both staring off at something distant from them, their eyes limpid, dreamy. They seemed lost in private memories. It occurred to me that I did not even know how long they had been married. I stared at the photograph and tried to read their eyes. It's like freezing someone, I thought. People do things and think thoughts before and after a picture is taken; but the picture freezes them and we have to try to know what they thought about and did before and after the picture. My parents did not look so nice now as they did in the picture. My mother was always tired; my father was always stiff and often angry. What had they been like before the picture? I took the prayer book to my room and spent the rest of the afternoon looking at it on my bed, finding letters and words that were familiar to me. When my father came home I went quickly into my parents' bedroom and slipped it back into his bookcase.

"How do you know it was Eddie Kulanski who did it?" he asked me brusquely after my mother had spoken to him. "You saw him do it?"

"No, Papa."

"Then you may not say that he did it. A hooligan may have done it. I will have the tire repaired next week. We will keep it in the apartment from now on. I will bring it down in the morning and take it upstairs when I come home."

I was quiet.

"And be careful how you ride it. If you ran over my hand, I would not like it too much myself. I need to start getting ready for Shabbos. Was there any mail today, Ruth?"

There had been a letter from a cousin in Lodz and a friend in Lemberg. No mail had come from anyone in my mother's family that day.

My father frowned and went off to the bedroom.

"Is my grandmother still sick, Mama?"

"I don't know, darling. We're waiting to hear."

"But the medicine was supposed to help her, Mama."

"It did help her. But she's old and very tired."

"Will she be able to come to America?"

"I don't know, darling. We hope so. We'll know in one or two months."

"Will you ask Mrs. Horowitz to make a special prayer for your mama to come to America?"

"I don't know what to do," she murmured. "I don't know. I don't know." Then she said, "Why don't you go with Papa to synagogue for Kabbolas Shabbos?"

"I don't want to go outside anymore today, Mama."

She sighed and went into the kitchen.

I went back to my room and lay on my bed and watched the afternoon wane. I looked through my window at the tree and the sky and kept seeing the knife striking and entering the maple and remaining upright, the blade in the root, all of the knife quivering. If someone took a photograph of the knife, it would not show the knife quivering. It would freeze the knife. But it was the quivering that I remembered most about it. I closed my eyes and lay very still on my bed and watched the quivering movements of Eddie Kulanski's cousin's knife.

As always, we ate our Shabbat meal that evening in the dining room off the kitchen. As always, I sat quietly listening to my parents talk about their friends, their plans, their lives in Poland. And, as always, it was as if I were not there much of the time.

I sat to my father's right and across from my little brother, who was dribbling soup on the wooden table of his high chair and disintegrating the large piece of braided bread my mother had given him to render him silent after my father had chanted the Kiddush and made the blessing over the challah. My father, wearing a suit and collar and tie, had begun to eat hungrily, peppering his soup and finishing it off quickly. He was working on the chicken foot that had accompanied the noodles as part of the furniture of the soup when my mother, who had been eating slowly and moodily, said, "Perhaps we could give the doctor a gift."

My father stripped the meat off another finger of the foot, sucked on the small bones, spat them into his plate. "With Americans you do not play games. They are not like Polaks. All the families would be here already if Americans were like Polaks. Everyone says to me never to dare play games with American immigration. So we will wait. They will come,

Ruth. She will be cured soon, and they will all come. I promise you."

"From your mouth into God's ears," she said, and rose, gathered up the soup plates, and went into the kitchen.

"They will be here for the new year," he said to her, speaking in the direction of the open doorway that led to the kitchen. "They will certainly be here for Pesach." He hesitated, and added, "If she does not deliver any more babies in the snow."

"It was a matter of saving a life, Max."

"That life is now preventing Jews from leaving Poland."

"And it was a goy. If she had refused and the woman had died, there would have been trouble."

"That I can understand," he muttered. "Tulchin I understand. I despise that mentality. But I understand it."

"It was her bad luck, Max." She came back into the dining room with a chicken platter in one hand and a serving dish of sweet potatoes in the other. "The stars were bad for her that month."

"An old woman in a snowstorm would get sick even with good stars, Ruth. Why are you talking nonsense?"

"No, Max. I know a little about such things."

"All right. Let it be that way."

"I looked into it with Mrs. Horowitz."

He made a face.

"If it had not been the snowstorm, something else would have happened. It was not a good month for my mother, Max."

"All right, Ruth. I heard the first time. The chicken needs salt."

"Alex, darling, don't throw your challah all over the floor. Here is some chicken. Eat some chicken for Mama."

My father was stripping the meat off a drumstick with his knife and fork. "All week long people are telling me it was a good meeting last Sunday. The closest to the old meetings."

"Nothing can be like the old meetings," my mother said.

"The closest, they said. Not exactly like them. The closest."

"It was a good meeting, Max. But the trees were different."

"The Bronx is not Galicia. You discovered America."

"Please don't be sarcastic, Max. I didn't mean anything bad."

He put down his knife and fork and looked at her. There was a moment of brittle silence. Then, slowly, he picked up his fork and continued eating. I saw the muscles working in his jaws and neck.

My mother bent over her plate, her elbows on the table, eating without appetite. The down of hairs on her forearms seemed darker than usual below the white lacy edging on the sleeves of her pale blue dress. A film of perspiration lay across her forehead and beneath the faint dark hairs on her upper lip. There was a gray pallor to her face. Sunday she had appeared well and happy; now she seemed ill. She was with her father and mother on the farm outside Bobrek. Her moods were the barometer of their distant state of being. I tried to imagine what her mother might look like. I saw a wrinkled old lady in a long dress and a shawl. I could not imagine her face. There were no photographs of either my father's or mother's parents in our house: they had never let themselves be photographed.

The flames burned steadily on the four white candles that stood in tall silver candlesticks in the center of the cloth-covered table. I loved looking at the flames. They burned blue and yellow around the wicks and sometimes they burned white. Now they were very pale blue and light golden yellow, edging faintly into red whenever a breeze from the evening street came through the open window. The Havdalah candle had a different flame. What did my mother murmur as she kissed my forehead after Havdalah? A special prayer for a good memory that had been given her by Mrs. Horowitz? I shuddered. I felt vaguely unclean thinking that a special prayer by that woman was being spoken upon my forehead by my mother. Why did my mother need prayers from her? Weren't there enough prayers in the prayer book? And there was the small flame that burned in a tall glass filled with white wax; all through the ten days between Rosh Hashanah and Yom Kippur it burned, on the shelf in a corner of the kitchen above the icebox, away from the window and sudden draughts of air. My mother seemed to need the flames of candles; shadows frightened her. On Shabbat especially she tried to avoid stepping into the shadows that collected in some of the corners of our apartment as the day paled and evening came on.

Someone was speaking to me but I could not remove my eyes from the flames. Finally my father's voice penetrated the warm brightness.

"Why don't you eat?" I heard him say. "Why do you sit there like a golem?"

I took my eyes from the flames and looked at him. His squarish features and thick shoulders and neck, together with his dark suit, white collar, and dark tie, gave him a stark appearance. He seemed carved of wood rather than made of flesh. That Shabbat evening I realized that I did not truly know who he was, and I remembered that in some of the dreams I had been having he had appeared as a darkly red apparition, gargantuan, terrifying; that in the recesses of my memory lay horrors I could dimly sense but not see; and I shuddered.

"Eat," my father said. "Your eyes will fall out of your head, the way you stare at the candles."

"Some believe it strengthens the eyes," my mother said meekly.

"What strengthens the eyes?"

"To stare at candles."

"Who believes?"

"I heard it somewhere."

"Eat," my father said to me. "You are so skinny soon the wind will blow you away."

"She has a library," my mother said.

"What?"

"Two walls of books. Left by her father."

"What books?"

She told him.

He sat very stiffly in his chair and looked at her. "You saw those books?"

"No. She herself told me about them. I have not been inside her apartment."

"Books against the goyim," he muttered. "Books of magic? Is that what she said?"

"Yes."

"God in heaven, Ruth. Why do you have anything to do with her?"

"She is a lonely old woman. Her only son refuses to see her."

"The son is doing a wrong. He is violating a commandment of the Torah. But we do not need such books to help us."

"What can it hurt, Max?"

"It violates the Torah."

"In Bobrek there were Hasidim who did what she is doing."

"Hasidim." He spoke the word with contempt. "They have the souls of day-old sheep."

"Sometimes the rabbi in Bobrek made a charm."

"The rabbi in Bobrek was a superstitious fool. Better a man like Bader who is a man of the world and can also learn than a bearded shut-in with the brain of a genius and the soul of a calf. Are we done eating? Is there dessert? Finish already, David. Do you think I want to sit here all night watching you eat a piece of boiled chicken that would leave the canary hungry?"

Dessert was a compote. We ate in silence. My mother brought in tea and cake. Then she went off with my brother to put him to sleep.

I sat at the table with my father, nibbling at a piece of cake and staring at the flames of the candles. One had burned out; three continued burning on low wicks, dancing in a warm breeze that blew in gently from the open window behind my father. An occasional car or horse-driven wagon went by on the street outside.

"What is Tulchin?" I heard someone ask. I looked away from the flames and glanced quickly around. No one except me and my father were in the room. My father was staring at me.

"Tulchin," he said.

I had only thought the question. I had not meant to ask it. The same thing had happened to me with Mr. Bader: a question had risen by itself to my lips. How did that happen to a person? I held my breath and stared down fixedly at my piece of cake.

"Tulchin was a catastrophe," I heard my father say with dense anger in his voice. "I despise it and am contemptuous of it. When a goy comes to kill you, kill him first. Let other Jews learn to take care of themselves, and you take care of yourself."

I looked up at him and did not understand what he was saying. His face was dark. His fingers were tight around his fork.

"Was Tulchin a person?" I heard myself continue to ask.

"Not a person. A city in Russia. There were in it Jews and Poles. Cossacks attacked it. The Jews fought well. The Poles wanted to surrender. The Jews could have taken over the city from the Poles and continued fighting. But their rabbi would not let them do it. He was afraid that Poles all over Poland would take revenge on all the Jews in Poland. So the Jews of Tulchin gave all their possessions to the Poles to give to the Cossacks. They hoped the Cossacks would take the money and jewels and gold and not destroy the city. The Cossacks took it all from the Poles and then asked the Poles to hand over the Jews. They handed over the Jews, the same Jews who had fought with them to defend the city. The bastard Poles. The Cossacks slaughtered the Jews. Out of fifteen hundred Jews, three hundred half-dead Jews managed to flee from the city. Then the Cossacks turned around and slaughtered the Poles. A nice story, yes? The courageous Jews! What martyrdom! They could have lived if they had converted to Christianity. Not one of them accepted the offer. What was there in Christianity? It is the idolatry of butchers and murderers. So they were slaughtered by the bastard Cossacks. A disgusting story! I remember hearing it when I was a child your age. No, younger than you. It came down through the generations in our family. One of our family was among the three hundred who managed to survive. My father would become enraged when anyone tried to defend the rabbi of Tulchin. He struck a man once, very hard, during a quarrel about that rabbi. He knocked him unconscious. There was trouble with the police. My father has a temper. And he is very strong. Fifteen hours a day working in the flour mill the family owns just outside Lemberg. He has the strength of two oxen. I can still feel his hand on my face when he—"

One of the remaining three candles sputtered loudly. The flame smoked and spiraled and leaped high, as if gasping for air. Then, abruptly, it died. Bluish gray smoke drifted slowly upward toward the chandelier and the ceiling. My father's nostrils twitched.

—"when he struck me because I had said something to him that was disrespectful. It is a father's job to teach a child respect, he said. How did I get to this? You asked about Tulchin."

"Did it happen before the war, Papa?"

"What war?" he asked brusquely.

"The big war. The war where you were a machine gunner."

"Yes, it happened before that war. It happened about three hundred years ago."

Three hundred years. I could not grasp it. But three hundred was less than five hundred. And Saul had said that the Golem of Prague had been created five hundred years ago. That meant the Jews of Tulchin had been killed between the time of the Golem and the big war.

"If someone comes to kill you, kill him first," my father said. "Do not become a saint and do not worry about anyone else. Kill him." He leaned forward against the edge of the table. "Kill him," he repeated. "Enough Jewish blood has been spilled in this world. The last war was a Jewish bloodbath. I read an article somewhere that said there would be thirty million Jews in the world today if it had not been for the way goyim have slaughtered us for the past two thousand years. But the last war was a special horror. Everyone butchered Polish Jews. Russians, Ukrainians, Poles. Everyone. The Austrians were civilized. The others were all murderers. Especially the Russians and Poles. First the Russians came and made a slaughter; then the Poles made a slaughter."

"You joined the Polish army to fight against the Russians, Papa?"

He regarded me intently out of narrowed eyes. "Yes."

"Were you afraid to be a soldier, Papa?"

His eyes seemed to close. But he was still looking at me. I could feel him looking at me. "I did not want to be killed," he said. "But I wanted even less to live as a coward and tremble before goyim all my life."

"It is a world full of goyim, Papa."

"Yes. And it is our job to live in it as Jews. If they let us live, fine. If not, we must find ways to live."

"I'm afraid of killing, Papa."

"What?"

"I don't want to have to kill anyone in order to live. I hate killing and dying."

"Here you will not have to kill. We are hated everywhere. But not everyone who hates us kills us. America is not Poland. No place is Poland. Except perhaps Russia. That is why I am here."

"But there are very bad goyim here, Papa."

"Then it is our job to decide how to deal with them."

My mother returned to the room and slipped quietly into her chair. She looked tired.

"Are you having tea and cake, Ruth?" my father asked.

She shook her head.

"Then let us finish the meal and David will go to sleep."

My mother said to me later, as she helped me prepare for bed, "What were you and Papa talking about?"

I told her.

She nodded wearily. "It's like a bone in his throat," she murmured. "The first time I met him he told me that story. I am tired of it. There are other ways to fight goyim besides killing and killing. How many goyim can you kill? The whole world is full of goyim."

"What other ways, Mama?"

"One looks around, one finds an idea. Your father has his ideas, I have my ideas. I do not have your father's strength."

"I don't like Mrs. Horowitz, Mama."

She made a vague, weary gesture with her hands. "I want you to go to sleep now," she said.

But I could not sleep. My room was dark; it was a waste to let my light burn through all of Shabbat, my father had said before my mother had lighted the candles. It was time I grew up, he had said. The candles had been lit and my lights did not burn at all. I had no white world beneath my sheet. I lay awake a long time listening to my parents talking in the living room and, later, to the strange noises that came from their bedroom. Sometime during the night I pushed aside the curtain that covered my open window and peered out into the dark street. I saw the lights of the lampposts and the shadows they made on the leaves of the trees. Above the roofs of the apartment houses across the street the sky was filled with tranquil stars. The street was very still. The trees were silent. In all the world I seemed the only one awake. Goyim were resting from killing Jews and Jews were resting from defending themselves. It was a good hour to be awake, the streets deserted, the air cool, the night calm, Shabbat everywhere in a dark and secret corner of time. After a while I returned to my bed and was finally able to fall asleep.

That Shabbat morning a new man appeared in our little synagogue. He was of average height but solidly built. His features were angular and there was a mole under his right eye. He was given the honor of being called up to make a blessing over the Torah during the reading of the portion of the week. He chanted the blessing loudly in Galician-accented Hebrew. In the absence of Mr. Bader, my father read aloud from the Torah. He always read from the Torah when Mr. Bader was away. In Europe the men in his family had been Torah readers for many generations. When the man was about to leave the podium, he turned, embraced my father, and kissed his scarred cheek. No one in the synagogue appeared surprised. I recognized him as another of the men in the photograph.

The synagogue in which we prayed was a rented room inside a very large synagogue that stood on the boulevard near the zoo two blocks from where we lived. More than five hundred people prayed in the main sanctuary of that large synagogue. The room in which we prayed could contain about a hundred people.

Everyone in that little synagogue, except Mr. and Mrs. Bader and the children who had been born in America, had come from the area of Lemberg. They had wanted to pray in their own style, in the informal Galician manner they had known all their lives. My father had approached the big synagogue with the request that they rent one of their rooms to the Lemberg group. The request had been coldly turned down: the Lemberg Jews could pray with all the other Jews in the main sanctuary. Since when were Lemberg Jews better than Warsaw Jews and Vilna Jews and Kiev Jews? My father then had a private conversation with the president of the synagogue. The next week the board of the synagogue met and granted my father's request. Saul told me the story. He did not tell me what my father had said to the synagogue president because he did not know.

The synagogue stood on a corner of the boulevard. Directly across from the synagogue, on the side street that led to the boulevard, was a Catholic church, a tall white stone building with stained glass windows, a huge cross on its angled roof, and on its small front lawn the stone statue of a woman in robes which my mother had once called an idol. The woman wore a long robed garment. A cowl covered her head. Her face was serene and very beautiful. There was a sad sweet smile on her lips; her arms were raised in a tender, warmly beckoning gesture. I sat near a window in our little synagogue and looked out at the large church and wondered how a statue whose face was so full of love could be worshiped by someone whose heart was so full of hate.

As I sat looking at the statue, the huge carved wooden front doors of the church were opened and a small crowd of people drifted slowly outside, walked down the dozen or so front steps to the street, and began to disperse. I saw Eddie Kulanski and his parents. Eddie Kulanski wore a dark suit with short pants, a white shirt, and a dark tie. His parents were neatly dressed. They were joined by a man and woman who looked to be their age and by Eddie Kulanski's cousin. Together they started up the side street in the direction of my apartment house.

I looked at the statue. For a long moment I saw it lying in

fragments upon the sidewalk, bits and pieces of it scattered about, smashed, stone splinters of its eyes and nose and mouth littering the street like refuse.

I looked away and continued listening to my father chanting from the scroll of the Torah that lay before him on the podium near the center of the room. The congregants were silent. My father's loud voice filled the small room. Saul, sitting next to me, his injured lip almost healed, was following the Torah reading with his finger on the page of the Bible he held on his lap. I looked at my own Bible. I was able to make out only the short, simple words. How I hungered to read and understand! Saul understood. He followed the reading with ease. I gazed intently at the worn Hebrew Bible on my lap and sensed it as a warm refuge against the hateful, raging world outside.

After the service the men crowded around my father and the newcomer. The women, who sat by themselves behind a gauzy curtain off to the left of the room, began to leave. I went outside and stood on the sidewalk staring at the statue across the street.

Saul came over to me. "Where did you disappear to?"

"It was hot inside."

"I found out about Tulchin."

I told him I knew about Tulchin. "From my father." Then I asked, "Who is the new man?"

He shrugged. "Did your father tell you that the Ukrainians ended up killing the Poles anyway?"

"He told me."

"Did he tell you that in Lemberg the Poles wouldn't turn over the Jews to the Ukrainians?"

"He didn't tell me that."

"In Lemberg, Brody, and two other places I can't pronounce."

"Your teacher told you that?"

"Yes."

"I don't understand it. I don't understand the goyim."

"Neither does my teacher."

He shrugged again. His eyes were somber and brooding. The scab on his upper lip was like a blackish mole. "My teacher says the best thing is to stay as far away from them as possible."

"How can we stay away from them, Saul?"

"He says to study Torah and to have nothing to do with them."

"I don't understand." I gazed across the street at the church.

Then I felt myself suddenly weary of talking about it, and asked, "Are we going to the zoo today, Saul?"

"Sure," he said. "Of course. You don't want your billy goat to think you're not his friend anymore. I got to go now. My father is calling me. Have a good Shabbos."

Later, I walked with my father past the busy shops on the side street.

"Who was the new man, Papa?"

"A friend."

"From Lemberg?"

"Yes."

"Did he just come to America?"

"On Wednesday."

"Is his whole family in America?"

"Yes. They all came with him."

We turned the corner into our street and walked beneath the maples. It was a hot day. I could feel the heat even in the shade of the trees.

"Did you bring him from Europe, Papa?"

"Me? No. We loaned him money and got him a job and a place to live."

"We?"

"The Am Kedoshim Society. You remember the picnic last Sunday?"

"Yes." But it seemed a long memory away. Had it only been last Sunday? "Did you know him in the war, Papa?"

"Yes. He was in the unit I led."

I looked up at him. "You led? What does it mean, Papa?"

"I was an officer. A lieutenant. A kind of leader."

"But you were a machine gunner, Papa."

"I was many things," he said. "It was a long war."

My mother was standing alongside my brother's carriage in the shade of the maple in front of our house. Half a dozen children were playing in front of Mr. Steinberg's candy store. The old man sat in the sun near the store, his palsied hands on his lap. As I came up to the house with my father, the curtain in Mrs. Horowitz's window stirred.

"He just fell asleep," my mother said tiredly. It was not yet noon and she was already weary with the day. "I wanted to see Lezer."

"He will come to the house this afternoon," my father said.

"How is he? How does he look?"

"The same. A little older. Otherwise the same."

"I wish Avruml were here. I wish that search had never happened. I wish—"

"Ruth," my father said.

She turned her pale face to the sidewalk and was silent.

"Who is Avruml?" I heard myself ask suddenly.

My father gave me a sharp look. "Avruml is dead," he said harshly. "We will not talk about Avruml. I am going into the house. When you are ready to come inside we will make Kiddush and eat."

He went quickly up the stairs and into the house. His anger resonated faintly on the quiet street.

I looked at my mother. She sighed and shook her head. "It is his nature to be hard. He was always hard. And stubborn. You get used to it. There are things your father does not like to talk about too often. They remind him of failure. So we do not talk about them, especially on Shabbos." She hesitated. "It's hot today. Suddenly it has become too hot. I do not remember such sudden heat in Bobrek. And yesterday was such a nice day. It was a pleasure to make Shabbos yesterday. Avruml was the new man's brother, the man who just came from Poland. He was killed. We talked about it once, David."

"How was he killed?"

"Goyim shot him."

"In the war?"

"After the war."

"They shot him? They just shot him?"

"It was a very bad time. The goyim were killing each other, too. But they killed many Jews. They said the Jews were Russian spies."

I had never heard the word spies before. She explained it to me.

"Was Avruml a spy, Mama?"

"Avruml was a good soldier in the Polish army. He had been with your father and was wounded. They were all with your father, all of them."

"Who?"

"His friends, the ones you see in the synagogue and in the house. They fought together under your father in the war. He is a hero to them."

"Was Papa's brother also in the Polish army, Mama?"

She turned her sad eyes upon me. "David?" She said it with the same inexpressible tenderness I had heard in her voice when I had awakened after the picnic last Sunday. "David?"

It was a queer sensation hearing my name and knowing she meant a David long dead.

"David was not in the army," she said. "No, no, David could not be a soldier. David was a dreamer, not a soldier. David was frightened of the army. David was a—" She stopped abruptly. Her eyes had filled with tears. She stood there, her head bowed, crying silently.

"Mama?" I heard myself say, my throat suddenly choking.

She said nothing. She was not there. She was crying in front of my eyes on a street in the Bronx, but she was somewhere else, crying for another time, over a death carved cruelly into her memory. I could not comprehend her grief and I did not know what to do.

"Should I go inside, Mama?"

She nodded.

I left her there, weeping beside my brother's carriage beneath the maple in front of our house, and went upstairs and lay on my bed. The canary began to sing but I could barely hear it over the beating of my heart.

Later that afternoon the apartment filled with my father's friends. They came with their wives and children. The adults sat in the living room and I brought the very little children, nine of them, into my bedroom. I told them stories about Noah and the animals in the ark; about Og clinging to the roof of the ark and promising to serve Noah for saving his life; about Abraham and the idols. They sat on the bed and on the floor, listening attentively. I wondered if I should tell them the story about the Golem of Prague but I thought it might frighten them to hear it and in the end I did not tell it.

When my throat began to hurt with all the storytelling, I took out some of my simple games and let them play by themselves. Then I came out of my bedroom and stood in the small corridor near the doorway to the living room. I poked my head out from behind the portiere and had a clear view of the room. It made no difference that my head could be easily seen by everyone in the room; it was as if I were not there.

The room was jammed with people, men and women my parents' age. My aunt and uncle were there, as were Saul and some of his friends. I could barely see the rug and the parquet floor for the people. Chairs had been brought in from the kitchen and the dining room. A dozen conversations were going on simultaneously, most of them in Yiddish, some in accented English. Occasionally I heard what sounded like a

Polish word. The conversations were animated, loud, people speaking at the tops of their voices. Words were accompanied by lively gesticulations. The windows were open but the room was very hot. The men sat in their jackets and collars and ties; all had on skullcaps. The women sat in their summer dresses and wide-brimmed flowery hats. In the easy chair to the left of the sofa sat my father; that was my father's chair; no one else ever sat in it, just as no one else sat in his dining room and kitchen chairs. He wore his dark suit, white shirt, and dark tie. To his right sat the man who had arrived this past week from Poland; next to him sat a thin, dark-haired, nervous woman who kept glancing around with a look of fatigue and disbelief in her eyes. The two of them were seated on the large sofa with my aunt and uncle. My mother sat in the easy chair across from my father. On the coffee table and the end tables were bowls of fruit and nuts and candies and cakes. The sounds of nutcrackers punctuated the loud conversations. Through it all my father sat in his chair, his gray eyes occasionally moving across the faces of the people in the room. The scar on his cheek was a dull thick whitish furrow in the afternoon stubble that covered his face. Sometimes he would abruptly join a conversation in this or that section of the room, speaking from his chair in his loud voice to agree or disagree with a point that had just been made. From time to time the newcomer would lean forward and say something to my father, and my father would nod and smile and pat his arm. Once a man came over and whispered into my father's ear, and my father rose and went with him into another room. A few minutes later they returned and my father resumed his seat. He ate an apple; he cracked open and consumed a walnut; he regarded for a long moment the woman sitting next to the newcomer, then he leaned over and spoke softly to the newcomer and once again patted his arm. The newcomer smiled, gave my father a look of gratitude. I stood there, listening and watching. You never saw anything like it, I heard someone say. Wall Street goes up and up without end. In Warsaw we could already hear the Bolshevik artillery, I heard someone say. Max was clever, I heard someone say. He pivoted at the marsh and hit the flank and that was the beginning of the end for those Cossack bastards. It's a golden land if you have brains and luck, I heard someone say. General Electric, someone said. I prefer radio, someone else said. They wanted to water their horses in the Dnieper, those crazy Poles, someone said. So the Bolsheviks kicked their behinds back to Warsaw. Without Pilsudski the Muscovites would be in Warsaw today, someone said. Pilsudski had help, someone said. Don't forget Weygand and the French officers. What heat, someone said. When did we ever have such heat in Lemberg? What doctor do you use? someone said. No, besides Weidman; for the eyes, I mean. Were you with Max when we trapped those Cossacks? someone said. Sure, you were there. I remember. You brought up the mules with the ammunition. Did you ever see such a look of surprise on a Cossack's stinking face before? Clever, that Max, someone said. Very clever. There were more than a hundred of those bastards. We counted the bodies. A small payment for what they did in Lemberg. These apples are delicious, someone said. Ruth, where do you buy your apples? How long can it continue to go up? someone said. Forever, someone said. Why not? It's America.

I moved back from the doorway and returned to my room. I lay down on my bed and watched the little children play.

Later, I walked with Saul to the zoo. A few minutes before sunset he brought me back to the corner of my street. "Have a good trip tomorrow, Saul." He and his parents were leaving early tomorrow morning for their place in the mountains. They had a cottage near ours, and they sometimes went on summer vacation earlier than we did.

He gave me a hug. I felt his long thin arms embrace me. "Take care of yourself, Davey. Don't get sick."

"I'll miss you, Saul."

"It'll only be one or two weeks. That's nothing, Davey. I'll see you in one or two weeks. Maybe your father will let you go horseback riding."

I watched him walk away along the side street toward the boulevard, thin and gangly and walking quickly so he could make it to the synagogue in time to pray the Afternoon Service before the setting of the sun. After a moment I turned and walked home.

The door to the right of the stairway opened silently as I passed it. Mrs. Horowitz stepped out. She glanced around the entrance hall. Then she put cold bony fingers on my arm and leaned toward me.

"Be careful, David," she said in a whisper. "I heard them talking. The two creatures."

I stared at her and felt the sudden loud beating of my heart.

"They want to hurt you. But we are not without defenses.

There are things that can be done. Spittle is a possibility. But we must find a man who is fasting. Also your name can be changed. That deceives them sometimes."

Her breath was foul. I wanted to get away from her. She clutched my arm.

"I will help you," she breathed. "But watch yourself."

Within the shadows inside her apartment something huge and dark moved suddenly and I saw it was her dog. He moved toward the door and stood behind her, peering up at me, breathing heavily in the heat.

"Good Shabbos, David," she said. "Do not worry. They are powerful, but we will defeat them. Isn't this heat terrible? If it is this hot on the thirteenth, we will have hot weather all of Tammuz, Av, Elul, and Tishri. Yes. That's the truth. Good Shabbos." She squeezed my arm, stepped back, and silently closed the door.

I ran upstairs.

Later, I listened to my father chant the Havdalah Service. The candle trembled in my hand. The huge flame danced and gyrated and curled upward toward the kitchen ceiling. "The Lord of hosts is with us," my father chanted in his loud voice. "The God of Jacob is our refuge. The Jews had light and joy and gladness and honor. So may it be with us." My brother stood alongside my mother, staring at the flame of the candle. I looked through the flame at my father's face. He concluded the service and gave me and then my brother to drink from the cup of wine. He poured what was left of the wine into a dish and doused the flame in it. Acrid smoke filled the air.

"A good week," my father said in a loud voice.

"A good week," my mother said. She kissed my brother. I felt her dry lips on my forehead. "A good week, my son," she said. Then, her lips still upon my forehead, she murmured almost inaudibly, "Armimas, rmimas, mimas, imas, mas, as."

"I have to see Meyer yet tonight," my father said. "I need a glass of coffee, Ruth."

"I wish we could leave with them tomorrow," my mother said.

"Go alone with the children."

"No."

"I have two more jobs to find. For Sender's brother and brother-in-law. It will take a few days. A week."

My mother said nothing.

"They depend on me," my father said.

Still my mother said nothing.

"They are like little sheep," my father said. "Didn't you see them?"

My mother sighed.

"It is my responsibility to do it," my father said. "A man cannot ignore the job given him by his life. I am not to blame if goyim kill Jews. I can only be blamed if I do not do my best to help my friends who have been hurt. God in heaven, Ruth, I really need a glass of coffee."

I lay awake a long time in my bed that night, staring through the darkness at my crippled tricycle. I thought of Eddie Kulanski and his cousin and the statue in front of the Catholic church. I wondered what the Golem of Prague might have done to Eddie Kulanski's cousin.

He brushed by me the following Monday morning as I sat on the chair near my brother's carriage, and whispered an obscenity. Then he went over and stood leaning against the tree watching Eddie Kulanski and Tony Savanola playing a game of marbles near the stoop. He did not play with his knife; he merely leaned against the tree. From time to time he would look at me. Then he would look back at the marbles game.

I closed my eyes and sat very still, feeling the warm morning sun on my face. On my lap were the comics from Sunday's newspapers which the janitor of our building had picked out of the trash cans for me.

"Here you are, sonny," he had said when I had gone down to the basement earlier that morning. "We got them all."

"Thank you, Mr. Ryan."

"You wouldn't be thinking of an accident with that new dog now, would you?" he asked, and a cornflower-blue eye winked in his pink face.

"Oh, no."

"That dog's a real pain in the ass, sonny. Okay. You got any hard words, you come and ask me. Hot as hell today, ain't it."

I thanked him again.

"Pain in the ass dog," he had muttered. "Where does the old witch find them?"

The comics lay on my lap. I was using them to teach myself to read English. They lay unread. I did not want to have to look at Eddie Kulanski's cousin. I sat with my eyes closed and my face to the sun. After a while I opened my eyes and raised the comics so that they blocked my view of Eddie Kulanski's cousin. I saw him slide out from behind the newspaper to my left and lean against the apartment house near Mrs. Savanola's window. He stood there, leaning against the house and watching me.

I put the comics on my lap and closed my eyes. A moment later I opened my eyes and saw him standing near me, peering into my brother's carriage. He moved smoothly away and went over to the tree. I felt my legs trembling.

After lunch I walked to Mr. Steinberg's candy store to buy a shoe leather. Outside I stood at the newsstand for a while, looking at words in the Yiddish and English newspapers and sucking at the pressed apricot candy. Then I moved away from the newsstand toward my house. Something very hard struck my left shoulder, spun me completely around, and sent me to the pavement. I threw out my hands to shield my fall and felt the skin of my palms scrape against the ground.

"Jesus Christ!" I heard Eddie Kulanski's cousin say in a very loud voice, loud enough for him to be heard by Mr. Steinberg and the old man on the chair and the nearby children. "I'm really sorry, kid. I didn't see you. I was just running up the block here. It was an accident."

He even helped me to my feet, his pointed features piously solicitous and concerned.

"You okay?" he said. His pale gray eyes regarded me.

There was a small cut in my left palm. My right palm and both knees were scraped. My apricot candy lay on the sidewalk.

"Sorry, kid," Eddie Kulanski's cousin said. "Really sorry. You want me to buy you another shoe leather?" His cold eyes clearly warned against my taking his offer seriously.

I shook my head. He turned and ran lightly up the block and stopped beneath the maple in front of the house.

I went upstairs. My mother washed the scrapes and bandaged the cut.

"On purpose?" she said. "How do you know it was on purpose?"

"He's bothering me, Mama. I think it was on purpose."

"I'll talk to your father."

"I'll have a talk with the Kulanski boy's father," my father said when he came home that evening. He left the apartment. I went into my room and lay down on my bed. The tricycle was gone; my father had taken it to be repaired. It was very hot inside my room. The air seemed fetid, as if Mrs. Horowitz's odor had somehow risen to our apartment. I was afraid my father and Mr. Kulanski would fight. I heard the front door open. I came quickly into the kitchen.

"The boy denies everything," my father said. "Are you sure, David?"

"Mrs. Horowitz said she heard them talking and thinking of ways to bother me."

"Mrs. Horowitz! Don't bring me evidence from that lump of cow! Why didn't you tell me sooner? It would have saved me a trip upstairs."

The next morning Eddie Kulanski came over to me. "You have an accident yesterday?" His gray eyes were cold.

I said nothing.

"Too bad," he said. He brushed pale blond hair from his eyes. A little smile formed on his lips. "My father says accidents happen all the time."

He walked on up the block, imitating the light bouncy step of his cousin, and disappeared around the corner.

I sat on my chair near my brother's carriage. Tony Savanola came outside and offered to play a game of marbles with me. I shook my head. He shrugged and went off to join a group of children down the street.

Joey Younger ran by, ignored me, and went into the house.

I closed my eyes and peered into the white-gold world the sun made upon my eyelids. The air was hot.

That afternoon I walked along the side street to the boulevard, asked a middle-aged woman to help me across to the other side, and entered the zoo. I fed my billy goat and caressed his moist nose and silky head. I came home and went upstairs and played alone in my room. Then I went downstairs and sat next to my brother's carriage.

"*Zhid*," Eddie Kulanski said quietly, coming up to me. "*Zhid*."

I did not understand what he was saying. I closed my eyes to shut him out. When I opened my eyes I saw his cousin standing near the tree, watching me. I kept my eyes open until my mother came down to bring my brother upstairs.

"You see, Mama?" I said, and nodded my head at Eddie Kulanski's cousin.

She gazed at him. "I'll tell your father."

"He stands there and looks?" my father said later that day. "That is all? You want me to tell him he cannot stand in the street?"

"He's bothering me."

"How is he bothering you?"

"He keeps staring at me. Sometimes he tosses the pocket-knife at the tree."

"There is no law against carrying a pocketknife."

"He scares me, Papa."

"Yes," he said. "I see that. So tell yourself not to be scared. Let him stand there and waste his time, the idiot. What does it matter to you?"

The next morning Eddie Kulanski's cousin began tossing a Spalding ball against the wall of the house. In one of his throws the hard pink ball narrowly missed my head. "Sorry, kid," he said. "An accident." He went on tossing the ball. I got up, moved my chair and my brother's carriage a few feet away from him, and sat down. He moved over toward me and continued tossing the ball.

"Get away," I said.

"Shit on you, kid," he said in a quiet voice. "You stupid kike."

"I'll call my mother."

"Go ahead, kid." He eyed the carriage. "Go ahead."

I got up and moved the carriage beneath our front windows and called up to my mother. Tony Savanola and Eddie Kulanski had stopped their bottle-cap game and were looking at me. My mother came to the window. I turned my head in time to see Eddie Kulanski's cousin round the corner near Mr. Steinberg's candy store and disappear.

He was back after lunch, leaning against the tree, waiting, the little smile on his lips. I went on up the block and along the side street. A man helped me across the boulevard. I entered the zoo. I fed my little billy goat. I walked along the meadow, past the pond, and into the wood. The air was cool and shadowy. I sat on the fallen tree that lay across the path near which my brother had seen the dead bird on the Sunday of the picnic. There was a humming in the air: the pulsing of insect life, the soft whispers of the trees. I sat on the trunk with my eyes closed and listened to the wood and sensed within myself a strange, quivering sensation. I wondered if that was what you felt when you experienced the feeling called hate.

The heat was stifling. On the sidewalk later that morning I played a marbles game with some boys my age who lived in the house near Mr. Steinberg's store. Eddie Kulanski's cousin edged over to the game and kept looking at me. Later, I sat in the chair near my brother's carriage and saw him near the tree. I closed my eyes and prayed he would disappear. I opened my eyes and he was still there leaning against the tree, that little smile on his lips, looking at me out of his half-closed eyes.

Mrs. Horowitz came out of her apartment as I entered the hall. Her dog walked behind her, panting in the heat. She opened the front door and he slipped outside. Then she peered at me.

"You will have no more trouble from them," she said. "I have found it. Erase them from your mind."

I was tired and wanted to go upstairs.

"Perhaps one day you will come into my house and let me give you a glass of milk and a cookie," she said. "I have good cookies. A recipe from my mother. Sugar cookies. Do you think you would like that?"

I nodded vaguely.

"No one comes into my house," she said. "Do you know what it's like when no one comes into your house? It's like living with the Angel of Death. My son loves more the goyim than he does his own mother. You will come in one day, yes? For milk and cookies."

I nodded again.

"And do not worry yourself anymore about those two. I have taken care of the matter."

I went upstairs.

That afternoon I walked up the side street to the boulevard. An old man helped me through the heavy traffic. I entered the zoo. It was very hot in the sun. I stood in the sunlight and fed my little billy goat. He licked my hand and I laughed. I wished I could climb over the fence and hug him to me. After a while I took the curving path that led between pens of camels and bucks and sheep and deer to the meadow. For a moment I stopped at the pond in the meadow and stared at the fish swimming smoothly in the dark still water. How I envied them their cool silken life! I left the meadow and entered the wood and came to the dead pine that lay across the path. I sat down on it and rested.

The air in the wood was warm and silent and filled with bluish shadows. I closed my eyes and smelled the pines. Why don't we use pine needles for spices during Havdalah? I thought. It would remind me of the wood and the clearing and the silences I loved. I wondered why I was so sleepy. There was a small clear area in the shadows near some undergrowth a few feet from the fallen pine. It lay not far from where my brother had seen the dead bird on the Sunday of the picnic.

When had that been? Two Sundays ago? Only two Sundays? It seemed an age since that picnic. I had not yet run over Eddie Kulanski's hand then. They had used that as an excuse to begin bothering me. Why were they bothering me? How could someone enjoy threatening and giving no peace to another human being? It was because they were goyim and I was a Jew. I could not understand it and I decided I was too tired to sit any longer on that dead pine. I rose and went over to the tiny clearing and lay down on a bed of pine needles. I lay on my stomach and saw, very near my eyes, an exquisite network of fallen needles, some brown, some blue-green, covering dark moist earth.

There was a noise somewhere in the wood toward the meadow. I lay very still. An animal had broken loose and was in the wood! A lion or a tiger! I felt my heart thudding upon the earth. A low shield of brush lay between me and the path. Looking between the thin leaves and branches, I saw, coming carefully up the path, Eddie Kulanski's cousin, followed by Eddie Kulanski, and heard, faintly, Eddie Kulanski say, "He went in here, Mike. I saw him."

"Keep quiet!" the older one hissed.

They came to the dead tree and stopped. A dragonfly moved like a winged dart through the warm shadows. I closed my eyes. They'll go away if I don't see them. My eyes will attract them. I breathed through my mouth, soundlessly.

"He's where they all had that picnic," Eddie Kulanski said. "They had a whole gang of them there."

"Quiet, for Christ's sake!"

They moved on up the path. I waited. They walked on, then stopped again. I heard them whispering. I could not see them but was certain they were coming back. I jumped to my feet as Eddie Kulanski's cousin turned in my direction. There was a shout and a heavy scrambling through the brush. I was on the path and running and I fell across the dead tree and they were both on top of me.

I remember the words they used and their breath on my face. One of them smelled as if he had just eaten a pressed apricot candy. They were not hitting me but their hands were all over my body and one of them was doing something with my shorts. I lay pinned down by the enormous weight of a body on my chest and stomach, and there were hands tugging at my shorts and underwear. Out of a corner of an eye I saw a face and I brought up a foot and the face went away. There was a shout and I was suddenly free and I ran, holding up my shorts to keep them from falling. I could not hear anything behind me for the noise I made rushing through the trees. I broke from the wood and ran past the pond to the other side of the meadow. I looked behind me. They had not yet come from the wood. I buttoned my pants and tucked in my shirt. They had still not come from the wood. I had hurt one of them. I was frightened I might have hurt him badly. I turned and ran along the path. I went past the billy goat. Outside the zoo I asked a woman to help me cross the boulevard. I waited a moment on the corner. They were still inside the zoo. I walked hurriedly home, feeling inside myself the trembling of panic. I must have hurt one of them very badly. I must have hurt his eye or his nose or his mouth. I must have hurt his head. Joey Younger was on the stoop. I saw him watching me as I went past him into the house. Inside the apartment my brother was crying. My mother let me in and went back to my brother. I lay down on my bed. I could not stop trembling. My head hurt and there was the pain again behind my eyes. I saw smashed eyes and noses and mouths and when I closed my eyes I saw them still. My brother went on crying. I heard my mother's weary, soothing voice. "Sha, sha, little Alex. What's the matter, darling? What? Is it too hot? Yes, the heat is terrible. Terrible." He grew quiet. A few minutes later she came into my room.

"What's the matter, darling?" She put her hand on my forehead. "You have no fever. Are you tired from the heat? Rest, darling. Your brother's asleep in his bed." She looked at me closely. "Are you all right, David? How did you make yourself so dirty? Look at you." When I said nothing, she sighed, and went from my room.

I lay in bed with my eyes closed and waited. But no one came to the door. The hours of the afternoon went by. Still no one came to the door. It was in the night, after long hours of lying awake, that I began to understand that I probably had not seriously hurt anyone after all and that they had not come after me because they had already seen what they had set out to see.

The heat lay like a flame over the neighborhood. Leaves drooped on the trees. Eddie Kulanski and Tony Savanola were playing a game of marbles near the stoop when I came outside. Tony Savanola acknowledged my presence with a vague smile in my direction. Eddie Kulanski grinned to himself and ignored me. I joined a group of boys in a bottle-cap game near Mr. Steinberg's store. A few minutes later I saw Eddie Kulanski and Tony Savanola run down the street together and turn the corner.

Mrs. Horowitz's dog came out of the house. He walked slowly, salivating in the heat. I saw him moving along the block, sniffing at trees and lampposts. I waited until the end of the game, pocketed my winnings, and went into the house.

Mrs. Horowitz answered my faint tap at her door almost immediately. She tilted her small head on her birdlike neck and gazed at me eagerly out of her bulging eyes. Her wrinkled lips formed a smile. She looked so thin and withered and lonely. A parchmentlike hand made a faint beckoning gesture. I had the impression she had been expecting me and wondered if she had been using any of her special prayers to get me to her door. It made no difference. Her magic had not worked on Eddie Kulanski and his cousin. She was as helpless as I. We were kindred souls. I went inside.

The apartment was small and dimly lighted. There was a musty odor in the air and the vague smell of camphor. Damask and dark-wood furniture from another age crowded the living room. The drapes were drawn but she would not turn on the light. Her eyes were sensitive to light, she murmured. She hoped I would understand. Did I want a glass of milk and some cookies?

In a tiny kitchen I watched her putter around near her icebox and sink. Her hands trembled faintly as she put the glass of milk and the plate of cookies on the table in front of me. Then she sat down and watched me eat and her withered face took on a look of quiet joy. She closed her eyes for a moment, and when she opened them I saw they were moist. She blew her nose daintily into a lace-edged handkerchief, which she tucked back into the long sleeve of her prim, high-necked, dark-blue dress. The apartment was strangely cool and still as if by shutting out the light she had shut out heat and tumult as well. I liked the stillness. It surprised me how much I really liked the cool calm of this tiny musty apartment.

Then, in a halting voice, she began to tell me how kind I was to be paying a visit to a lonely old lady. Her only companion was the Angel of Death, she said, and when I had come in the door she had seen him slip out of the apartment through the outside wall. The Angel of Death never spoke, she said. He just sat there, waiting, his poison-steeped sword still sheathed, for it was not yet her time. But now he was gone. For the first time in as long as she could remember, he was gone. She was grateful, very grateful. Did I want another glass of milk and some more cookies?

Sitting there in the dim tiny kitchen, listening to her soft querulous voice, I began to sense her loneliness. I felt deep remorse for the pain I had caused her by bringing about the death of her first dog. To sit alone with the Angel of Death. I could not imagine it. That would be like having Eddie Kulanski and his cousin inside my apartment. I felt a trembling nausea begin to rise within me and I fought it back.

"Are you all right?" she asked, peering at me.

I nodded hesitantly.

"Are you frightened of me?"

I shook my head.

"Sometimes I think people are frightened of me. Such a thought fills me with despair. I am only an old woman. But often I see a frightened look in your eyes. You are frightened of those creatures? Don't be. You will overpower them when the time comes. I have seen to it."

I said nothing. The sugar cookies had turned to dust in my mouth.

"I have given you weapons," she said, lowering her voice to a conspiratorial whisper. "You need no longer be frightened."

I did not like it when she talked like that.

"My father, may he rest in peace, said they contained the strongest weapons. He knew about such matters even though he was not learned. I have no school education. I know only what I learned from my grandmother and mother. I cannot read them. But when you learn to read well, you will come here and read them. Finish your cookies, David. How good it is to sit and talk to you. Finish your cookies and I will show you the books."

But I did not see the books that day. I heard a loud coughing bark that sounded as if it had come from inside the apartment. "Ah," Mrs. Horowitz said, rising. "I must let Bilam inside. Please do not go away." But I told her I had to go upstairs or my mother would begin to worry about me. Outside in the hall I thanked her for the milk and cookies.

"Visit me again, David. Please."

I nodded and went upstairs. The pain behind my eyes was severe but not yet difficult to bear. The illness seemed to be coming on very slowly this time, as if it were encountering opposition.

That afternoon, as I sat on a chair next to my brother's

carriage, Tony Savanola came over to me and said, "Hey, are you okay, Davey?"

I nodded vaguely.

He said quietly, not looking directly at my eyes, "That stupid Eddie Kulanski told me. He bragged."

I turned away from him, my face burning.

He said, "I don't like what he did, Davey."

I said nothing.

After a moment he said, "You want to play me a game of immies?"

I shook my head. I was frightened.

"You don't have to be scared, Davey."

But he could not take away the fright merely with his words.

He regarded me in silence for a moment. Then he turned and went slowly into the house. I did not see him again until the middle of the following week when I lay seriously ill with fever and pain and a calm willingness never to leave my bed again.

That was a strange Shabbat. My father returned from his office Friday afternoon and I knew immediately from the look on his face not to do anything that might upset him. He was distraught. I moved quietly about the house trying to be unseen and unheard. Our Friday evening meal was dense with silence. My mother's eyes roamed and darted nervously about and seemed unable to focus upon anything. The skin of her face was drawn tight; she looked to be a bloodless mask of herself. My father's squarish, scowling face retreated deeper and deeper into solitary moodiness. At one point in the meal he even spoke briefly to himself in the language I did not understand, though I thought I heard the name Avruml among his words. My mother stared down at the white tablecloth and seemed close to panic and tears.

Later, as I lay in my bed, I heard them speaking together. But they were talking very quietly and I could not make out their words.

I said during our Shabbat afternoon dinner, "Will we go to the country soon, Papa?" I had only thought the words; I had not meant to speak them.

But he seemed not to have heard me. My mother gave me a swift warning glance. I was glad he had not heard me and did not repeat the question.

Later that afternoon I went downstairs and tapped lightly on Mrs. Horowitz's door. It was opened immediately. I went inside and heard her close it behind me. The lock clicked softly.

Just off the small narrow hallway was the living room, deep in shadows. Out of the shadows a huge dark form rose and came slowly toward me. I heard his heavy breathing and smelled his foul breath and felt his cold wet nose upon my face. He sniffed at my feet. Then he turned slowly, ambled back into the living room, and melted into the shadows.

"I am so glad you came again to see me, David. Come, sit with me in the kitchen. I leave a little light burning there for all of Shabbos. Would you like some tea and cookies?"

I sat in the kitchen and drank tea and nibbled at her sugar cookies. The tiny table was covered with a white cloth and had on it two tall silver candlesticks. She wore a gray dress with a lace trim at the high neckline. The folds and wrinkles of her neck disappeared inside the dress. She kept looking at me with an eager smile and putting cookies on the table. I was a good boy, she said repeatedly. I kept my promises. I had come to see her again as I had said I would. Yes, I was a good boy. Not like other boys she knew. I was a fine son.

"Please take another cookie, David. Then I will show you the books."

A huge shadow suddenly appeared in the doorway to the kitchen. It glided across the floor and drank noisily from a water dish near the icebox. It raised its head and peered at me out of reddish eyes. I saw Mrs. Horowitz looking intently at it. After a moment it lowered its head and went silently from the kitchen.

"A good sign," I heard her say. "Bilam has given us a good sign." I did not ask her what she meant. I did not want to know.

She pattered eagerly about the kitchen, giving me a second glass of tea and a third dish of cookies. I could drink and eat no more. She brought me into a small dark room and pointed a bony finger at two of its walls.

We were in her bedroom. A fourposter bed stood in the center of the room opposite a heavily draped window. The carpet was thick. Dark furniture stood near the bed and against the walls. Against the wall to the right of the door stood a narrow dark-wood bookcase. Another narrow bookcase stood against the wall opposite the door. They were jammed with books. The air of the room was dense with the odor of moldy carpeting and dusty bindings.

"A wandering bookseller would come by our house every

year and my father, may he rest in peace, would buy from him. They would bring good luck, the bookseller said. They were weapons against the goyim."

They had lived in a village in the part of Poland that had been annexed to Russia. Her father had been a dairyman and his reading skills had extended only as far as the prayer book and the Book of Psalms. But the bookseller was a link to a Jewish world he hungered to believe in; that world somehow made his misery tolerable. So he bought books. Special books. Powerful books. One day his son or grandson would read them. He had no son and only one daughter. In America, to which they fled during the bloodbath that followed the unsuccessful 1905 revolution, her father ran a grocery store with his son-in-law, a Russian Jew with a walleye and a stutter. The father died. Her husband died. Her son became wealthy in furs and stocks and put her into this apartment with books neither of them could read. She lived alone with her books and her dog and her memories. And now I had come into her life and she would take care of me and protect me from the creatures and the menace they brought to the world. And one day I would read the books and tell her the secrets they contained. All she was able to read were some books in Yiddish which told her what to do in certain cases and how to behave and not behave because of the danger. It was important to know what to do in order to overcome the danger. She kept talking about the danger. I had not understood some of what she had said at first and was barely listening to her now. I had gone over to the bookcase near the door. Some of the books had titles in Hebrew letters; others were in a strange spiky alphabet I had never seen before: peculiar dark letters with hooks and sharp daggerlike ends and saberlike curves. I removed one of the books from its shelf. A faint cloud of dust rose to my nostrils. I felt my nose begin to burn. The pages were old and yellow and crowded with the strange dark jagged letters. I put the book back and felt on my hands the dust that enveloped it. I wiped my hands against my shorts. But the dry sensation of grime remained on my fingers. I would be going to school soon, yes? Mrs. Horowitz was saying. How long would it take me to learn to read? When would I be able to come in and read the books to her? That was all she had left, these books. Would it take long?

She peered at me wistfully. I told her I did not know how long it would take but that I would read the books as soon as I could; that seemed a safe and honest thing to say. Then I needed to get out of that dim and dusty room. My nose was beginning to hurt and there was pain now in my forehead.

She went with me to the door.

"Please visit me again, David."

I nodded and thanked her for the tea and cookies.

She reached over and patted my cheek with a dry bony hand. I was surprised that I did not mind her doing that to me. In a vague way I understood that I had made her happy and somehow that was important to me.

I went upstairs. Eddie Kulanski passed me as I reached my floor and went by as if I were not there, his eyes looking straight ahead; but a little smile formed on his lips and as he went out of sight beyond the turn in the stairs I thought I heard him laugh.

Inside the apartment my father was asleep. My mother, who had opened the door for me, returned to the living room and sat listening to the canary sing. I lay on my bed and thought of Mrs. Horowitz and wondered why it was taking so long for the sickness to come this time. Falling into a restless sleep, I dreamed strong bony hands were stripping me naked and touching me everywhere. Over and again, coarse knobby fingers poked and prodded and squeezed. I woke bathed in sweat and feeling faintly nauseated, and was frightened of returning to sleep. I lay in my bed until my mother called me into the kitchen for supper.

I lay awake for hours that night, listening to my parents talking together in the living room. When they had gone to their bedroom and the apartment was silent, I could not sleep. The night had cooled; its silence was exquisite. Through the open window came the faint rustling sounds of the maple as it responded to an occasional breeze. Somewhere within the darkness of my room there was a vague stirring, a slow coming to life of benign force. I smiled deeply to myself. Not yet, I thought. But I'm glad you're here.

When I came out of my room the following morning, my father was not home.

"He went to see your Uncle Meyer," my mother replied to my question.

"To the country?"

"It is important business."

"When are we going to the country, Mama?"

"Soon."

"I want to go to the country, Mama. The city is hot. I hate the city. I want to see Saul."

My mother passed her hand wearily over her face. "We will go as soon as we can. Get dressed, David."

The brief coolness of the night had vanished with the coming of day. The sun expanded to encompass all the arc of the heaven. The sky burned. On the radio there was talk of an outbreak of infantile paralysis in a distant part of the city.

The street was deserted when I came outside later that morning. Even the old man who always sat on a chair in the sunlight near Mr. Steinberg's candy store was not there today. There was no traffic. I seemed the only one alive in all the silent city.

I had thought to spend a little time with Mrs. Horowitz that day. But the illness finally came on during the early afternoon and my mother put me to bed and gave me medicine. I was in my bed the following morning when the investigator from the State Department came to the apartment.

It was his voice and the way he spoke English that woke me. At first I thought it was a fever dream, for we heard English spoken that way only on the radio and occasionally by Mr. Bader, and Mr. Bader was in Europe. But the voice did not have a radio resonance to it. I heard it coming from the door, then from the kitchen, then from the living room. I heard my father responding in his accented English. That was strange; my father almost never spoke English in the house. Weak and shivery with the illness, I slipped from my room and went through the small corridor to the portiere.

"At the request of the consul," the voice was saying. "A routine investigation. May I sit down?"

"Yes, yes," my mother said. "I am sorry. Please. Sit down. Here."

But he misread the motion of my mother's arm. Through the minute space between the portiere and the frame of the doorway, I saw him take my father's chair.

My parents sat down on the sofa.

The man was tall and lanky and looked to be in his late thirties. He removed papers from a briefcase, sat back, and crossed his knees. His manner was relaxed and cordial. He took a black fountain pen from the inside pocket of his jacket, unscrewed the cap, and placed the cap on the back of the pen. It was a Waterman's, the same kind of pen with which my mother wrote her letters to her family in Europe. He studied one of the papers on his lap, then looked at my parents. He had a pleasant voice. I listened to the music of his English.

He thanked my parents for seeing him. It was a bit unusual

for him to be coming to their home, he said. But sometimes people felt more comfortable answering questions in their home than in an office. He paused. Did my father know a Morris Kaplan, a resident of Lemberg in Poland? he asked.

My father, sitting stiffly on the sofa, nodded.

Did my mother know Morris Kaplan?

My mother blinked her eyes and nodded.

Quickly, the man searched through the papers on his lap and held up a photograph. Was this the Morris Kaplan my parents knew?

My parents looked at the photograph and nodded.

From where I stood I had a clear view of the face of the man in the photograph when the State Department investigator held it up to show it to my mother.

He put the photograph away and noted down something on the paper with his Waterman's pen. Then he looked up.

The American consul in Poland had requested that an inquiry be made into the visa application of Morris Kaplan, he said. Mr. Kaplan had listed my parents as American citizens who would vouch for his character and reputation.

The canary chirped briefly and was silent. The man glanced up at the canary. He looked around the room. Then he asked my father how long he had known Morris Kaplan.

They had grown up together in Lemberg, my father said. They had gone to school together and had served together in the Polish army under Pilsudski.

What schools had Morris Kaplan attended?

The local Jewish elementary school, then the yeshiva and the gymnasium, said my father. Gymnasium meant high school, he added.

The man nodded, smiled, and turned to my mother. How long had she known Morris Kaplan?

She had met him only after she had met my father, around the time of the end of the war, my mother said.

He turned back to my father. In what capacity had he known Morris Kaplan in the Polish army?

They had served together in the same machine-gun unit during the offensive that had pushed the Russians out of Galicia, my father said. When my father became a noncommissioned officer, Morris Kaplan remained with him and continued to serve in his unit. Later, when my father had transferred to a cavalry unit, Morris Kaplan had transferred with him.

When had that been? the man asked.

"In the war against the Bolsheviks," my father said. They had fought together in the flanking maneuver against the Bolshevik Seventeenth Division near the town of Kozin, my father continued. Morris Kaplan had been a noncommissioned officer; my father had received a field promotion to the rank of lieutenant. They had also fought together against the Bolsheviks near Lublin. Did the gentleman want to know all the details of their army experience? Morris Kaplan had been a brave soldier and had been wounded in the Lublin engagement.

The man wrote for what seemed to me to be a long time.

Did either my father or mother have any reason to believe the potential immigrant was likely to seek to overthrow the United States government by violence or in conspiracy or combination with others of like mind? the man asked.

My parents shook their heads.

Was the potential immigrant an anarchist?

Again, my parents shook their heads.

Did either my father or my mother have any knowledge of the potential immigrant's political leanings?

My mother shook her head. My father said, "He hates the Bolsheviks. That is his whole politics."

Did either my mother or my father have any reason to suspect that the potential immigrant had ever been in serious violation of the laws of Poland?

My mother said, "No."

My father asked if he might respectfully inquire as to whether or not a police record was still a necessary part of a visa application.

It was, the man said. But in certain cases they liked to go beyond the mere record. For example, they also had the military record of Morris Kaplan. Nevertheless it was useful to have certain things confirmed. Was my father able to answer the question?

Yes, my father was able to answer the question. "The answer is no," my father said, his face impassive, his lower jaw protruding.

"But, Papa, the man is holding a gun in the photograph," I heard someone say in a high voice.

My blood froze. I shut my eyes. I had not meant to say it. I had only thought it. I could feel the beating of the blood inside my head. I listened with my eyes still shut and could not hear anything from the living room, no exclamations of

surprise or rage, no footsteps, nothing. Had I said it with
my mouth? Perhaps I had only thought it very loudly and
had not said it at all. My knees trembling, a cold sweat running down my back, I opened my eyes and peered into the
living room. They were not looking in my direction. The man's
pen was making scratching sounds as he wrote. The apartment
was very still. My parents looked directly at the man, watching
him. He glanced through some of his papers, then screwed the
cap back over the tip of the pen, and put the pen into his
jacket pocket. He returned the papers to the briefcase and got
to his feet.

My parents stood. My father seemed strangely short next
to the man. He did not seem so short next to Mr. Bader, who
was an inch or two taller than this man.

The man thanked them for their cooperation and wondered
if he might call on them again should the need arise.

My father said, "Yes." He and my mother accompanied the
man to the door. I heard the door open and close. There was a
brief silence.

"I need a glass of coffee, Ruth," my father said in a small,
tremulous voice.

I slipped back into my room and climbed into bed. The sun
was bright on my window. I heard the trees and the passing
cars and the voices of children on the street. After a while I
slid down beneath my sheet and looked into my silent white
world and realized that it had been the repeated warnings of
the nonexistence of that photograph, together with Mr.
Bader's explanation during the picnic, that had restrained the
words in my head and prevented them from coming out of
my mouth. I tried to imagine what might have happened had
the words actually been spoken. I lay in my white world,
shivering with fear and fever, and thought how nice it would
be if I did not ever have to leave my bed again. The street
reeked with the odor of malevolence; the zoo and the meadow
and the pine wood were deadly with menace and horror. Yes,
it would be nice to stay here. Very nice. How smooth and cool
the sheet was. I rubbed my eyelashes against it; I licked it
with my tongue. Cool and white and smooth and silent. I lay
very still and gave myself over willingly to fever and pain.

The room was dark. I was on fire. A figure sat in the darkness, murmuring Hebrew words. I thought it was my father,

but I knew it was a dream and I closed my eyes. My head throbbed. Pain traveled back and forth across my face. Through the silence of the night came the murmured Hebrew words. I wanted the words to go away; I wanted to be alone with my fever and pain. Go away! I shouted at the words. There was an abrupt silence. Go away! I shouted again. Then I screamed. Then a flood of words poured from me and I no longer knew what I was saying. There were voices and lights and sudden patches of darkness and someone weeping in the distance. A branch of the maple reached across the window-sill and slid along the floor to my bed. I felt it knifelike upon my throat and I screamed a name and its leaves flew off like yellow birds through the open window and I could see them beating their wings and wheeling about against the sky like starlings. Hey, Davey, a voice said. Here I am, Davey. My mother says to tell you hello from the family. But it did not make any difference: the Angel of Death remained perched on the quivering pocketknife, waiting, his jeweled sheath glinting in the sunlight. Hey, sure I'm your friend, Davey. But I can't squeal on no one. You don't want me to be no squealer, Davey. The wall was white and smooth and cool. I lay with my face to it. If I put my face very close to it the whole world became white. My white sheet world and white wall world. What else did I need? Why was I crying? I could not stop crying. I was so frightened. Dr. Weidman was in the room. And my mother and father. Yes, yes, as soon as the fever goes away, Dr. Weidman was saying. Yes. The best thing to do. Why are you crying, David? What's wrong? You've been sick before. Why is he crying, Max? Sha, darling, my mother kept saying. Sha, my David, my soul. Why are you crying? Your bike is fixed, my father said. You can ride it again. Stop crying. What happened that's making him cry this way, Max? Dr. Weidman kept saying. It's bad for his throat to have him crying this way.

My fever subsided on Friday. Two days later my parents packed, closed up the apartment, and drove with me away from the city and the Angel of Death.

The cottage stood on a small hill that sloped gently down to the beach and the lake. Beyond the low smooth grass of the beach was a narrow ribbon of yellow sand that shone like gold in the sun. Sometimes when I looked at the grass I thought of the clearing in the pine wood beyond the meadow, and when I looked at the sand I thought of the powdered earth in the pens of the zoo. But there was nothing near the cottage that could remind me of my street, and I was grateful for that.

Behind the cottage was a brief stretch of lawn and beyond the lawn was the forest. It rose like a wall out of the earth, dank, sunless, vaguely foreboding. I did not go near the forest that July. I played in the sunlight in front of the cottage.

There were about a half-dozen cottages spread out on our side of the lake, all of them owned or rented by members of the Am Kedoshim Society. Some boys my age were there that summer and I played with them. But I could not run and often I was alone. Sometimes I played with my brother. We built castles on the moist sandy fringe of the beach; we dug holes in the sand to a distant place called China; we tumbled about on the grass.

One morning he wandered away from the beach and I found him sitting in the tall grass digging a hole in the moist earth. I asked him what he thought he was doing.

"Digging to China," he said.

"I'll help you."

"No!" He pushed my hand away. "I do alone."

His small square face shone with fierce determination. I almost thought he would add the words, "It's my job." I stood guard over him as he dug at the earth with his toy spade. He left behind a good-sized hole when he finally wearied of it and ran back to the beach.

"I do alone here, too," he said, getting down on his haunches and scraping at the sand.

Often I would glance up from my games with my brother and look at my mother sitting in a wicker chair beneath the elm in front of the cottage, reading a book. She never read books in the city. It gave me pleasure to see her so at ease away from our street.

One morning my brother spotted a salamander on the beach and before I could shout a warning he had stepped on its head. He picked up the salamander and shook it by the tail. It dangled limply from his fingers. He dropped it to the sand and poked it with a toe. Trembling, I took his spade and dug a deep hole. He watched me curiously. I put the dead salamander into the hole. In an instant my brother was beside me, pushing away my hand and getting down on his knees.

"I do it," he said loudly. "Not Davey. Alek do it."

I watched him working frenziedly to fill in the hole. When he was done he patted the smooth sand and said triumphantly, "Not dead. No more dead."

For a long moment I stared at him, feeling a rage I could not understand. Then I turned and walked quickly away and did not go near him all that day.

My Cousin Saul and his parents lived in the cottage down the road from us, near the mailbox to which my mother would bring the letters she wrote to her family in Europe. I would see her walking along the dirt road to the mailbox, holding my brother's hand so he would not go racing down the slope to the beach and the lake. Saul would be on the screened-in porch of his cottage or outside on a blanket on the grass, busy with the summer reading assigned to him by his teachers in the yeshiva. At the mailbox, my mother would check the address and postage on the envelopes and place the letters inside. Then she would walk back to the cottage, and sometimes she would stop and talk to my aunt and I would be alone for a while on our beach. The water was clear and clean and dark blue and sometimes dark green near the shore line. There were often rowboats and sailboats on the lake from the summer camp on the opposite shore, but they never came near us. The camp was owned by a member of the Am Kedoshim Society and everyone there knew that my father and his family wanted privacy during our weeks away from the city.

I said to my mother one morning, "Why do you read here and not in the city, Mama?"

"I have no patience for reading in the city. I don't like the city."

"Because you grew up on a farm?"

"I suppose." She gazed at me inquiringly.

"The Angel of Death lives in the city."

Her eyes widened.

"Will you teach me the names of the trees, Mama?" She had promised to do that when I had been ill once in the spring and now I remembered.

She taught me the names of trees, the shapes of their leaves and trunks and crowns. In a week I was able to distinguish the different kinds of spruce and pines that grew near the cottage. I learned the pyramidal shape of the larch, the scraggly divided shape of the walnut, the drooping shape of the willow, the spreading bushy shape of the dogwood. I liked especially the slender grace of the birches with their chalky bark marked with dark triangular patches and their thin twigs. There were some aspen near us too but I did not like to look at them; the endless trembling of their leaves disturbed me.

She knew all the names in English; and she knew too the English names of the shrubs and berries and vines and flowers that grew wild along the sides of the road. She almost never used English at home; and whenever she did it was with a hesitation that sharply reflected her insecurity over her adopted language.

I asked her about that one day, and she answered, "When your father bought this property I bought a book and learned the names. I know them better in Polish. But I could not live here and not know the names of the trees in English. On the farm I knew every tree and every bush by name. I knew when their leaves would come and which of them would lose their leaves first and which last after the summer. What tree is that, David?"

I told her.

"And that?"

I told her.

"You have a good memory." She smiled. "Mrs. Horowitz may be a silly old woman, but it can't hurt."

I did not ask her what she meant. I did not want to think of Mrs. Horowitz. I did not want to think of anyone who lived on our street.

But Mrs. Horowitz returned to our conversation that week when I looked at the book my mother was reading and was startled by the shapes of the letters.

"What book is that, Mama?"

She smiled shyly; her face—the skin no longer drawn tight now, the eyes no longer dark—her face flushed a bright pink. "A book of silly stories for women, David."

"What are the letters, Mama?"

"I don't understand."

"What language?"

"German," she said.

"Mrs. Horowitz has books like that, Mama."

"What?"

"In her house. She let me see them."

Her eyes went wide.

"Is it your book, Mama?"

She nodded slowly.

"But I never saw it in the house."

"I have books in my closet, David. From the years I went to school in Vienna."

"What is Vienna?"

She told me.

"Did you go to school in Vienna after the war?"

"Before and during the war."

"Did you meet Papa's brother David in Vienna?"

The question sent a tremor through her. She put the book on her lap and gazed at me. Her wide dark eyes were suddenly brimming with tears. I had touched the secret pool of sorrow within her. She nodded and turned her head away from me. I went down to the lake, wondering where in our apartment she kept the photograph I had seen in Mr. Bader's study and which of the faces in the photograph belonged to my father's dead brother.

After lunch I would rest for a while in my room. Through my window I would hear the scratching sounds of my mother's pen as she sat on the porch writing more letters. I rested every day that summer after lunch, on the orders of Dr. Weidman. Later, if the day was sunny and windless, Saul would come over and we would splash around in the water for a while. I could not remain in the water too long for I chilled easily. Then he would take me out on the lake in the rowboat. On most afternoons my mother and aunt would go swimming together in the lake. My aunt was an excellent swimmer; my mother swam too, but not well. They would dry themselves and sit on the beach in the sun, talking quietly together until it was time to prepare supper. From the boat on the lake I would watch them swimming and talking. Saul told me they talked a great deal about their families in Europe.

I loved the lake. It was fairly large and vaguely elliptical in shape, with quiet coves and inlets and a shoreline dense with tall grasses and trees and an occasional grotesquely shaped fallen trunk and sudden boulders and schools of small fish that darted about in the clear shallow sunlit water.

"Look, look!" I cried out one day as I peered into the teeming water along the shoreline far from the cottage. "Look at the fish, Saul!"

He peered over the gunwale and smiled and almost dropped an oar into the water.

"There are hundreds of them, Saul! All over! Can you see them?"

He nodded and continued rowing slowly across the shallow water along the shoreline. I saw shiny pebbles and rippled sand and underwater plants, and everywhere the schools of small, dark darting fish. I was reminded of the fish that swam in the pond in the meadow of our zoo. I drifted away from the lake, but only for a moment; Saul's quiet voice called me back. He had said something about the fish.

"Really?" I said, and looked down again over the gunwale into the water.

"That's right. It's in the midrash. They're the only creatures who didn't sin. God destroyed everything in the Flood, but the fish just swam around."

Then I reminded him that he had told me that once before.

"Really?" he said. "I don't remember."

He rowed slowly, lazily, stopping every few moments to push his glasses back up on the bridge of his nose. The sun shone on his thin face and brown curly hair. His blue eyes were very pale in the sunlight; at times the sun would strike the discs of his glasses at an angle that would transform them into opaque pools of burning gold, and I would be unable to see his eyes at all.

I fell one morning down the two front steps of our cottage and bruised my upper lip. Later, on the beach, a mosquito bit me near the bruise. I ached and itched simultaneously. In the boat with Saul that afternoon I complained about the mosquitoes and flies that sometimes made living in the country uncomfortable. And I wondered why God had created them.

"There was a reason," Saul said firmly.

"What reason?"

"I don't know." He rowed cautiously near the blackened trunk of a dead tree that lay partly submerged in the water. "But everything God created has a reason."

"Even bugs?"

"Yes."

"What good are bugs?"

"Everything has some good, Davey." He had read about that and talked about it with his teacher, he said. Snails are supposed to be a cure for certain infections. Gnats are used against the poison of a viper. The viper cures other kinds of infections and the lizard is used when someone has been bitten by a scorpion.

I regarded him with wonder and awe.

"That's right," he said, rowing us away from the tree and skirting a dense patch of water lilies. "Everything was created to help man and to praise God." We can learn a lot from insects and animals, he said. For example, when a cat makes

dirt it always covers it up afterward. That teaches us something about cleanliness. A grasshopper sings all through the
summer until it bursts and dies. It knows that it will die. Still
it sings and sings. Because that is its duty. And that teaches
us that man should do his duty toward God, no matter what
might happen to him.

"But what if a bug is going to bite you, Saul?"

"Then brush it away or kill it. But that doesn't mean that
bugs can't do something good somewhere else."

I found it deeply comforting to know that everything in all
the world was useful and good. And in the nights, lying awake
in my bed, I would listen to the loud rhythmic sounds of insect
life that came from the lake and the forest and imagine that
I could see grasshoppers singing.

Saul was studying very hard that summer. I asked him
once, "Do you have to do all that reading, Saul?"

"I want to do it. I like it."

"Does everyone have to do it?"

"In the higher grades. But most of the kids joke about it
and don't do it."

"I wish I could read."

"You're beginning to read very nicely, Davey. You're not
even in school yet."

"I wish I could read like you."

"You will," he said. Then he asked, "Did your father say
we're going to the movies tonight?"

"Yes. We're going to the movies."

My father and my uncle would leave for the city every
weekday morning on an early train and be back by late afternoon, often in time for a swim. At the train station, my
father always checked the movie placards. After supper that
night a big car came for us, and our two families climbed in
and were driven to a movie house in the nearby town. We
saw a Charlie Chaplin film, in which a poor cleaning man
in a bank dreams he has foiled a robbery and is embraced
and gently kissed by the woman teller he loves, then wakes to
find himself kissing a mop. I thought the movie was funny
and sad. It was strange how something could be both funny
and sad. No one thing seemed to be the same thing always.
My father was stiff and stern; but in the movie he had laughed
with delight, as I had. And when we came outside he took my
hand and held it gently. He had on the fisherman's cap he
liked to wear when he was away from the city. It gave him a
happy, jaunty look. He was so relaxed here, so much at ease,

as was my mother, as were my aunt and uncle. Why did we have to go back to that city and that street?

The sky blazed with stars. There was a warm light breeze. We ate ice cream in a nearby candy store. I gazed through the window. The town seemed asleep, its white houses and clean walks and embowering trees tranquil in the early night.

The car came for us. My brother had fallen asleep in my mother's arms. I curled up in my father's lap and he held me to him. He cupped my face in his hands and put his lips to my brow. Why did we have to go back to that street? For the first time in as long as I could remember I fell asleep in my father's arms.

Every evening after supper he would go for a walk. Often I would accompany him. We would walk down the dirt road past my cousin's cottage and the mailbox and out onto the paved road that we had taken to the town with the movie house. The grasshoppers would be singing in the scrub brush by the side of the road.

"Do we have to go back to the city, Papa?" I asked one day as we walked along the paved road.

He smiled indulgently.

"I like it here," I said. "I don't like the city."

"Who likes the city?" he asked. "You think I like the city? Or your mother, who grew up on a big farm, you think she likes the city? But we have jobs to do. Your job will soon be to go to school and be a very good student. How will you go to a yeshiva here?"

I was quiet.

"Yes," he said. "It would be nice to stay here. It would be a pleasure. But where is it written we are born to pleasure?"

He held my hand, lightly, warmly. We continued along together.

"Papa?"

"Yes, David?"

"Did you come to America together with Mama?"

He seemed mildly surprised. "I came first and after a few months I sent for your mother and she came."

"Where did you have the money to come?"

"Friends in Europe loaned it to us. I paid them back and helped them to come. And they helped others to come."

"The friends in your Am Kedoshim Society?"

"Yes."

"Is it your idea, Papa, the Am Kedoshim Society?"

"Yes," he answered quietly. "My idea and the idea of my brother David, may he rest in peace."

"Mama said goyim killed him."

His fingers tightened slightly around my hand. He said nothing.

"Is America better for Jews, Papa?"

"Yes."

"But there are goyim here who hate us."

"The government does not hate us. That is the difference. The government was made by good Christians. A good Christian is better than an evil high priest. Your Uncle Meyer says that. Remember? Why are you asking so many questions, David?"

"I like to know things about my mama and papa."

"Yes? That's very nice. But now let's walk quietly for a while and listen to the birds doing their job."

"I wish we could stay here. I wish we didn't have to go back to our street. Isn't God here more than He is in our street?"

He narrowed his eyes. "God is wherever we bring Him. That is our job, David. I am sending you to the yeshiva so that you will understand that and not ask impossible things." He was silent a moment, looking at me thoughtfully. Then his squarish features softened with a faint smile. "I know how you feel. I sometimes get tired and say the same thing to myself. But I remind myself that if I had felt that way years ago I would still be in Europe today. Then I am suddenly no longer tired."

He held my hand. We walked quietly together. The grasshoppers sang loudly in the scraggly brush along the sides of the road.

I lay awake a long time that night, listening to the sounds of the lake and the forest. In the morning I stood at my window and saw my father come out of the cottage onto the screened-in porch. My mother was with him. He kissed her. Then he went down the steps and along the dirt road. My uncle came out of his cottage. I saw them walking together in their straw hats and light summer suits to the road juncture near the mailbox where the bus picked them up to take them to their train. They walked quickly, keeping in step together, my father treading somewhat stiffly, the way a soldier might march. After breakfast that morning, I sat on a chair in the screened-in porch and looked at the Yiddish newspaper my father had brought in with him from the city the day before.

My mother's German book lay on the small round table and I ignored it.

On Shabbat mornings my father would pray quietly on the porch, and then read aloud the Torah portion to himself. His voice rang out in the stillness and I wondered sometimes if it traveled across the mirror surface of the early morning lake and was heard in the summer camp on the other side.

The Shabbat midday meal would be eaten with my uncle's family in their cottage, and they would eat their Friday evening meal with us in our cottage. Around the table, my parents and aunt and uncle would talk about events of the day. From time to time I heard Mr. Bader's name mentioned; he was at the Zionist Congress in Zurich. Earlier in the summer he had been to Rome and Geneva. After the Congress he would be going to Vienna, Berlin, and Hamburg. I could not determine from what I was hearing if he was traveling for his export-import business or for matters having to do with Jews or for both.

During dinner in my uncle's cottage one Shabbat afternoon, I asked, "Where did you meet Mr. Bader, Papa?"

"In my office," he said as he chewed his meat.

I did not understand.

"He was looking for an apartment."

"How did you and Mr. Bader become such good friends?"

"I discovered that his father had come from Lemberg and had grown up with my father."

"A delightful coincidence," said my aunt urbanely by way of a commentary to my father's words. "He is a charming man."

"A useful coincidence," my uncle murmured with a smile. "Helped into existence by my clever brother."

"God sent him to help us," said my mother.

Saul nodded his silent affirmation of my mother's view of things.

During one of those meals there was a heated conversation between my father and uncle about a man they called Jabotinsky. They seemed to be taking sides together against those who disliked him. It had something to do with Zionist politics and I did not pay much attention to what they were saying. I was thinking that July was over and in a month we would all be returning to the city.

I heard the name Jabotinsky often that summer. Every Shabbat afternoon my father and uncle and all their friends in the cottages along the dirt road would get together for an hour or so under a tree or on a grassy beach. There were only eight men in the group, not enough to constitute a quorum for prayer, but more than enough to enable them to engage in very noisy debates. They seemed all to be followers of this man called Jabotinsky and they were loud in their denunciation of his opponents. Saul would be present at those meetings, listening attentively. I went once, understood almost nothing, and never went again.

On the grass beach one Shabbat afternoon, when both families were lounging in canvas chairs, I said to my father, "Who is Jabotinsky, Papa?"

He put down his Yiddish newspaper. "A Jewish leader," he said. "A great man."

"There are people who don't like him?"

"There are people who hate him. He is not a coward. He could have been a great Russian writer. But he chose to help Jews. He said his job was to help Jews, not write stories. He is a very great man, David."

Later, I went over to my uncle. "Did you know Mr. Bader before he met Papa?"

He turned to me his gentle younger replica of my father's squarish face and seemed momentarily surprised. Then he said, "Yes. One of my law partners helps Mr. Bader in his business and told me he was looking for a new apartment."

"Did you know Mr. Bader's father came from Lemberg?"

"No. Your father found that out. He is the question-asker in the family." He peered at me and smiled. "He and his son."

"Uncle Meyer?"

"Yes, question-asker?"

"Is it hard to become a lawyer?"

"Yes."

"Did you study a long time?"

"Yes."

"In America?"

"Yes. And in Poland. But when I came to America I had to start all over again. In Poland I spent a year studying law in the University of Jan Casimir in Lemberg before I decided a Jew had to be out of his mind to want to become a Polish lawyer. So I wrote to your father and he sent me and your Aunt Sarah the money to come to America."

"Do you like America, Uncle Meyer?"

"Yes," he said quietly. "I like America, David."

"But there are so many goyim here. And sometimes they hate us."

"As long as they don't hurt you. Their hate won't kill me."

"But what if they hurt you?"

"Get witnesses and take them to court and the court will punish them." He looked at me closely. "What's the matter, David?"

I was quiet.

Down on the strip of sand beach my cousin was chasing my brother. They were laughing loudly and delightedly. There were sailboats on the lake. I saw people swimming off the beaches that fronted some of the nearby cottages: not all of my father's friends heeded the very orthodox injunction against swimming on Shabbat.

"You don't have to break heads here, David," my uncle said. "This isn't Poland."

I looked down at the grass. He returned to his book. I sat there, skimming the palm of my hand back and forth slowly over the grass and looking at the sailboats on the lake.

Very early on the first Sunday morning we were there, I was awakened by the sound of the front porch screen door being opened and closed. I peered out of my window and saw my father, wearing a light sweater and dark trousers and his fisherman's cap, walk down the dirt road and turn into the paved road beyond the mailbox. The sky was pale white; drops of dew glistened on the grass and gossamer webs lay like fine crystal across the lower branches of the elm. The wicker chair in which my mother sat had been left outside and was drenched with dew. I remained at the window, watching and waiting. The minutes passed. Then, from the paved road, a horse ridden by my father came into view. It was a black stallion with a large white mark like a four-pointed star across its head just above the eyes. My father rode at a light trot, sitting easily in the saddle, rolling with the smooth gait of the horse. He came up the dirt road and went a few yards past our cottage. Then he wheeled the horse about and sent it in a sudden wide curving gallop across our beach and into the tall grass. Then he was out of sight. A few minutes later I saw my father come crashing back through the tall grass, the stallion galloping in a sharp, abrupt manner. My father reined in the horse near our cottage, patted its neck, and seemed to be speaking to it. The horse raised its head in response and shook it heavily; tiny waves rippled across its wet black flanks. Then my father leaned forward and raised his right arm, swinging it in a circle over his head, and again the horse went dashing down the beach and into the tall grass. Three times my father made that circuit with the horse: the road in front of our cottage, the beach, the grass, and back across the beach to the road. Then he cantered down the dirt road and was gone. A while later he came walking back to the house. I heard him making coffee for himself in the kitchen.

Every Sunday morning he rode that horse. I never ceased marveling at the sight of him riding.

I asked him once, "Where did you learn to ride, Papa?"

"In Poland."

"From a Jew?"

"No. From a Cossack."

I stared at him.

"A deserter. He ran away from his army and we captured him."

"Can I ride with you, Papa?"

"I will ask Dr. Weidman."

But I never found out if he asked Dr. Weidman for he did not speak to me again about riding. I watched him from my window and that seemed wonder enough for me that summer.

The days passed slowly, quiet summer days that seemed to linger and expand until, by the middle of August, I began to feel that all the world was sun and warmth and a singing of grasshoppers in the night. Sometimes it rained and a mist would come up from the lake and cover the beach and the dirt road. A hush would fall upon the world and through that hush I would hear the soft pattering of the rain and the call of a bird. Early one morning a deer came out of the forest in the rain. I felt a fever of excitement watching it through my window. It was a young, tawny, light-antlered buck. It crossed our back lawn and came up to our screened-in rear porch. I saw its head held high, its ears up, its nose twitching. I wanted to touch its nose and caress its head and feel its antlers. Then it must have heard a noise, for it pivoted suddenly, plunged back across the lawn, and vanished into the mist and bluish darkness of the forest. That was the day one of our neighbors came over with the news of the massacre in Hebron.

She was the wife of the man who had wrestled with my father during the picnic of the Am Kedoshim Society. She lived in the cottage on the other side of the tall grass. She was a short, thin, excitable woman and she came over in the rain, carrying an umbrella, and asked if we had heard the news on the radio. We did not have a radio in the cottage. My father disliked having the world trail after us while we were on vacation. It was enough to read the Yiddish papers. On the radio there had been news of a terrible massacre of Jews in Hebron a few days ago. Jews had also been killed in Jerusalem, Safed, Tel Aviv, and Haifa. But Hebron had been terrible. Yeshiva students had been slaughtered. She had a nephew in the yeshiva in Hebron, the son of one of her brothers who lived in Chicago. Could my father find out what had happened to her nephew? She had just called her brother and he did not know and was frantic with dread. Her brother was not a well man. He had had a heart attack three months ago. Could my father help her?

It was the first week of the two-week vacation my father and and uncle had reserved for themselves that year. My father had been sitting in the kitchen over a glass of coffee. He got up, took an umbrella, and went out into the rain. We saw him go into my uncle's cottage where there was a telephone. My mother put a glass of coffee and a piece of cake in front of the woman, who had sat down at the kitchen table, murmuring to herself in Yiddish. My mother's hands trembled. The drawn look had returned to her face. She responded soothingly to the woman in Yiddish. Then they sat in silence at the kitchen table. The coffee and cake remained untouched.

I went into my room and stared out the front window at the mist on the lake. Then I gazed out my rear window at the dripping trees of the forest. I saw my brother playing one of his favorite games on the screened-in back porch. He was lining up his toy soldiers and knocking them down with his toy cars. I watched him for a while, then lay down on my bed and covered my eyes with my hands.

Sometime later my father returned and I heard him talking very quietly to the woman. He could find out nothing more than what she had heard on the radio. The people he had telephoned had no additional information. Yes, there had been a pogrom in Hebron. Yes, yeshiva students had been killed, dozens of people had been killed. That was all he knew at the present time.

My mother went out with the woman and walked with her in the rain back to her cottage. Our cottage was very still. The rain fell softly on the roof and against the screens of the porch. Then I heard a sudden crashing sound and my father's voice. "The murdering bastards!" He choked back the rage, but the words were clear. "Where was the protection? Were they blind?" I lay very still on my bed. My mother came back to the cottage. I heard them talking together but their words were indistinguishable. They went into their bedroom and continued talking. There was a noise outside. I got off my bed. Through the front window I saw a car come down the road and stop in front of our cottage. My uncle came out of his cottage, wearing a suit and a raincoat and rain hat, and carrying a small dark valise. He climbed into the back of the car. I heard my father's heavy tread and saw him come out onto the porch, followed by my mother. They spoke quietly together for a moment near the screen door. Then my father went down the steps. He too wore a suit and a raincoat and rain hat, and carried a small valise. He walked quickly, ignoring the puddles that had accumulated in the ruts and dips of the road, and climbed into the car next to my uncle. The driver, the same man who had taken us to the movie house to see the Charlie Chaplin film, carefully turned the car around, leaving tire tracks on the wet grassy slope beyond the dirt road, turned into the paved road, and was gone.

The house echoed with silence.

My Aunt Sarah and Cousin Saul came over and had supper with us that evening. The meal was dense with my mother's fearful darting glances and my aunt's apprehension.

I went out to the front porch with Saul after the meal. The rain fell steadily through the dark grayness of the early evening. I could hear it on the grass and in the elm. I glanced around the porch. The wicker chair was outside; no one had thought to bring it in. I could not see the lake for the mist and the rain.

Saul stood with his face very close to the screen, staring out at the rain and the encroaching darkness of the night. He had been strangely silent all through supper, staring at his plate, picking at the food and eating very little. He had helped my mother feed my brother but with a grim silence that had brought a puzzled look to my brother's eyes. Now he kicked moodily at the wood frame of the porch screening, his face pallid, his eyes wide and dark.

"Saul?" I heard myself say.

He said nothing.

"I thought pogroms were only in Europe, Saul. How could there be a pogrom in Eretz Yisroel?"

Still he said nothing.

"Did they really kill yeshiva boys, Saul?"

He nodded faintly.

"How old were they, Saul?"

"Older than you," he murmured. "The Hebron Yeshiva is for older students, I think."

"Older than you, Saul?"

He shrugged.

I hesitated a moment. Then I said, "If you were going to that yeshiva, you might have been killed, Saul."

He turned his head slightly and gazed down at me. Then he looked back through the screening. "How could I be going to that yeshiva? I'm here, not there."

"But if you were there, Saul. If."

He was quiet.

I gazed out through the screening at the rain and the slow coming of the night.

My mother and aunt had been talking quietly inside the cottage. They stood on the other side of the front door and I could hear them through the open window.

"Will you be all right, Ruth?"

"Yes."

"Maybe I should sleep here with you tonight."

"No, darling. Thank you."

"Are you sure, Ruth?"

"Yes."

"How will I know if you need me during the night?"

"I'll be all right. I won't need you."

The door opened and they came out onto the porch. My aunt's face looked gray beneath her dark tan.

"Good night, Ruth. Be a good boy, David."

They went out into the rain.

It rained all that night. I lay awake and listened to it falling. Across the room from me my brother slept silently in his crib. I slid down beneath my sheet and closed my eyes and suddenly heard a voice chanting softly in Hebrew. I dared not move. It was my mother's voice. How had my mother come into the room without my seeing or hearing her? Unless I had fallen asleep without knowing it and now my mother was in the room, chanting in Hebrew. The darkness was impenetrable. My mother's soft chanting voice floated toward me eerily out of the chilling blackness.

"Mama."

The voice ceased abruptly. There was silence.

"I'm not sick, Mama."

I heard nothing.

"Is it you, Mama? I can't see. Is it you?"

"Yes, darling."

"Are you all right?"

"Yes, darling." There was a queer tremulous hesitation to her voice. I could barely hear her.

"I'm all right too, Mama. We don't need Mrs. Horowitz."

"I know, darling. Go to sleep, my David. You need rest. You'll be all better soon and we'll leave."

"But I'm not sick, Mama."

"Of course. Don't I know? And I love you. Your mother loves you. Go to sleep, my David. I'll watch and keep them away. The soldiers with the dogs won't find us."

But I could not sleep. I lay with my eyes closed beneath my sheet and listened to her soft chanting. Finally it ceased.

My father and uncle returned by car late the next afternoon. That evening all the people who lived in the cottages along the dirt road crowded into our parlor. The owner of the camp across the lake came too. He was a tall thin man in a white suit. He reminded me vaguely of Mr. Bader: his manner was gracious and suave. Had my father found the machine and driver useful? Yes, my father had found them very useful, and he wanted Mr. Shenker to know how grateful he was. Mr. Shenker nodded cordially. Any time he could be of help. Any time.

We sat around—seventeen men and women, Saul, myself, and a few boys and girls my age; my father had insisted that all the children, except my brother, be present—and my father reported to them the information he had gathered from his own sources regarding the Hebron pogrom. He spoke in a soft, urgent voice. The summer of sun was all gone from him now. He was as he had been before, tight, rigid, but smoldering with new rage. He would be brief, he said. He did not like to make speeches. But he did not want to repeat the story to each of us separately, so he had called us together. He especially wanted the children to hear it, he said, though he was certain it would give them nightmares. Sometimes it was important to have nightmares, he said. One could learn from a nightmare. He asked the children to pay attention and sit quietly until he was done. On the fifteenth of August, Tisha B'av, there had been Arab disturbances in Jerusalem. The British said these had been in reaction to the demonstration staged by the followers of Jabotinsky at the Western Wall protesting new British regulations that interfered with Jewish religious services at the Wall. But we knew all about the British, he said. Our dear friends, the British. They announced that they washed their hands of the Jews as a result of this demonstration, and the Arabs took the hint. The day after the demonstration, on Tisha B'av, a group of Arabs beat up Jews gathered at the Wall for prayers, and then burned copies of the Book of Psalms which were left lying nearby. Then the Mufti of Jerusalem spread the rumor that the Jews were ready to capture and desecrate the holy mosques on the Temple Mount in Jerusalem. The Arabs began coming into Jerusalem from all over the country. In Hebron, Arabs who were friends of the Jews reported that messengers of the Mufti had been in the city and had preached in the mosque near the Cave of Machpelah that the Jews had attacked Arabs in Jerusalem and desecrated their mosques.

"Now listen to this," my father said. "And if anyone understands it, please explain it to me. I challenge anyone to explain it to me. The leaders of the Jewish community of Hebron met secretly. They were informed that the Jewish self-defense organization had sent a message from its headquarters in Jerusalem that it was prepared to dispatch a group of armed young men to defend the Jews at Hebron. At the same time, the leaders were informed that the British district commander had guaranteed the safety of the Jews of Hebron on condition that the Jews do nothing to provoke the Arabs and that no one who was not a resident of the city should enter it. Arab leaders had promised to do all in their power to help preserve the peace of the city. The Jews decided to reject the offer of the self-defense organization. They believed the goyim. They were possessed by the mentality of Tulchin. Explain it to me. They could not bring those boys in secretly? They could not hide them and their weapons somewhere? I do not understand it. On Friday, the twenty-third of August, a band of Arabs returned to Hebron from a mass meeting led by the Mufti and his followers in Jerusalem. They ran through the city attacking Jews. They killed a student they found in the yeshiva. They stabbed him to death with their knives and swords. On Shabbos morning, very early, Arabs began coming into the city from all over. They carried rifles and revolvers and knives and swords. The Jews locked themselves in their houses. The police warned the Jews to remain inside. Like sheep, they remained inside. And like sheep, they were slaughtered. They were shot and stabbed and chopped to pieces.

They had their eyes pierced and their hands cut off. They were burned to death inside their homes and inside the Hadassah Hospital in Hebron. They were—"

A woman gasped. The group stirred. A child began to cry. "Max!" my mother broke in sharply. "The children!"

"Let the children hear," he said. "Let them hear. Let them know what a pogrom is so they will not shrug their shoulders when they hear the word in the future."

"Max, Max," said my uncle gently. "Think a moment."

My father was quiet. He closed his eyes. His face, which had turned dark with his accumulating rage, slowly lightened. He took a deep breath, then shook his head. "I am sorry," he said. "Forgive me. I was talking of Hebron, but I had in mind—someplace else. It is all the same. No matter where it is, it is the same horror, the same heartbreak, the same helplessness. It is even the same story of one or two good goyim who risk their lives to save Jews. I am sorry. It is the killing of the yeshiva students that is the horror in this pogrom. It was a yeshiva that moved from Slobodka to be in Hebron. There were geniuses in that yeshiva. They came from Europe to die in a pogrom in Hebron. The irony. Do you understand it? I do not understand it. Three American boys who went to study in the Hebron Yeshiva were killed." I saw heads turn toward the woman who had come to our cottage yesterday; she and her husband sat together, staring down at the floor. "The Genius of Shklov was killed. Twenty-four yeshiva boys were killed; another thirteen were injured. I do not know how many of the injured are expected to live. I also do not know yet the exact toll of all the dead. It is somewhere around sixty. What else can I tell you? I have the list of names here if any of you want it. Meyer had copies made. We wired a large sum of Am Kedoshim Society money to our person in Jerusalem to use as he sees fit to help the survivors. We have also contacted Jabotinsky. But I will tell you more about that later. There is something else we must do now."

He went on talking. I looked around the room. Saul was listening avidly to my father, who was saying something about public opinion and the JOAC and Mr. Bader. Then I was no longer listening. I did not want to hear any more talk. I slipped from my chair, went past the kitchen and through the small hallway to my room. I stood at the back window, staring out into the darkness. The night was clear and filled with stars. I could make out the sudden blackness that was the tall wall of the forest. Through the open window I felt the cool dry air of the mountain night and heard the sounds of the forest. Grasshoppers were doing their job: they were singing even though they knew their hearts would burst. I undressed and washed and climbed into my bed. Tomorrow, I thought. We pay you back tomorrow. David Lurie son of Max Lurie will pay you back tomorrow. For everything. Tomorrow. Master of the Universe, why do they do this to us? But tomorrow we will do our job and pay them back.

The morning was warm and brilliant with sunlight. After breakfast I crossed the back lawn and came up to the forest. I stood in the warm sunshine a long time, gazing deep into the forest, looking at its gray and blue-green shadows, at the slender fingers of golden light that probed through the dense foliage and shone upon the fallen leaves and branches that were the ragged carpet of the forest floor. A narrow boundary of shade separated the sunlight of the lawn from the darkness of the forest. Slowly I stepped through the shade and came inside the line of trees.

The air was cool, almost cold, and pungent with the odor of decaying leaves. I walked in the chill shadows of the trees and felt the moist black earth and the slippery wet-paper texture of the leaves beneath my feet. The leaves were yellow and brown and stained with death. Twigs and branches littered the earth, some brittle with age, others delicate and young, knocked down by the weight of the recent rain, with leaves the color of green apples still clinging to them. A vast stillness covered the forest. Even the breeze from the lake did not penetrate beyond the first line of trees. And the stream, full though it was and running swiftly, moved in utter silence over its shallow bed of black earth. I stopped at the stream and waited, listening. The stream was a little over a foot wide and about six inches deep. Roots and pebbles lay across its bed, yet the stream ran on soundlessly, carrying along in its current an occasional twig or leaf that bobbed and swayed and whirled around at the mercy of the swift current. I bent and put my hand into the water and felt its icy coldness. As I straightened, a bird called from somewhere deep inside the forest, one long piercing raucous call that terminated abruptly. There were no echoes. Then someone screamed.

The forest was alive. Shadowy figures flitted in and behind the trees. Overhead the dense ceiling of branches creaked and swayed. A pall of yellow smoke rose from a burning

tree and blew across my face. I stepped through the smoke
and jumped lightly across the stream. Listen, I said. Listen to
me. It cannot go on this way. They are all slaughtering us.
Each side kills us as if we were bugs. We have to do something! Look what the stinking bastard Cossacks have left
behind in Lemberg. Look! Look what they have left behind
in Galicia. You are going to sit here reciting Psalms? When
did a Psalm prevent a throat from being torn open? Are you
listening, Meyer? Are you listening, David? We have to do
something. All right, stay with your books. I have to do something. I have to stop them. I have to break their heads. I have
to take revenge for my friends the Cossacks killed. Did you
see how they died? We must do something! Avruml, are you
with me? And the rest of you? We will go in together. The
stinking Cossacks. We will sing Yiddish songs as they come
charging at us before we turn Pilsudski's guns on them. Yes,
all of us together. You can kill a lot of Cossacks very quickly
with a machine gun. This is a Torah I want to learn. Set it
up here, Avruml. Near these trees. And you, set yours over
there. That's right. With the sun behind our backs. They will
stop to let their horses drink. Look at them. The bastards. In
their red tunics and fancy pants and riding boots. The stinking Cossack bastards. And the ribbons on their horses. And
their fancy saddles. And the Jewish blood on their sabers.
And the Jewish flesh on their whips. Wait. A moment longer.
Wait. Wait. Through the bare winter trees a pale sun shone
like an uncaring eye. I sighted along the machine gun I had
fashioned out of a large damp fallen branch. Now! Now! Kill
them! The forest floor shuddered. Horses reared and crashed
to the earth. The stream turned red. Glinting sabers fell in
the grass. The cold morning wind blew through the trees and
the chopped-up cavalry brigade turned and rode wildly away.
The earth of the forest rippled and broke into waves. The
wind whipped the branches. Trees burned fiercely. The crack-
ling of leaves and the spitting snap of roaring wood thun-
dered in my ears. There was a sudden total silence.

A solitary bird trilled.

I got up, brushed off my clothes, and walked back to the
cottage for lunch, leaving my machine gun near a tree beside
the stream.

"Where were you all morning, David?"

"I told you, Mama. I went to play in the back."

"All morning?"

"I like it now in the back."

"How did you make yourself so dirty? Look at you."

"Where's Papa?"

"Talking to your Uncle Meyer."

"Is there any more news, Mama?"

"Yes. The Angel of Death worked hard last week. Please eat your lunch, darling, and don't wait for your father. He will be late."

The sun burned red in the pale early afternoon sky. Deep inside the forest I rode a black stallion, holding in my right hand the long slender curving branch that was my saber. Around the marsh, Nathan, I yelled. We will meet them on their left when they come out. Ride, all of you! Ride! I want to see their faces when they spot us. Ride! Here we are. Now! Now! For Avruml! Now! I circled around a thicket of gray birch. The drooping branch of an oak scratched the side of my head. Wounded! I was wounded! I wheeled the stallion about and slashed away with my saber. Metal rang against metal in the fetid stillness of the marsh. The red sun dipped low in the sky and brushed the earth, leaving in its wake boiling rivulets of blood.

The sky darkened. The air turned gray. A dull yellow sun shone wearily overhead. Dense white clouds came from the mountains and covered the sun and dropped snow upon the silent fields and trenches, upon the still forests and frozen streams, upon the brightly lighted cafes and dark shuttered shops. No, I said. No. It will be in the open. I did not fight all these years so my brother should have a wedding in a cellar. It will be in the forest, under the stars. You hear me, David? You hear me, Ruth? And you too, Meyer. In the forest under the stars. I want the stars to see my brother David take a wife. I want the trees to hear the blessings. And we will be there with the Am Kedoshim boys to make sure there is no trouble. If the bastards come, we will break their bones. Hey, Nathan, it is a good feeling to hold your own weapon and be able to defend yourself against those Poles. Search the trees. What is that, Yitzchok? You brought the flags? And your camera? For what? We are never together for a picture? All right. Fall in, everyone, for a picture. Better for a picture than for a march. Right? Stop pushing! What kind of soldiers are you? The Jews of Lemberg depend on you for their lives and you play games. Yitzchok, take the picture already. These clowns are impossible. My brother's bride will be here soon. Am I right, David? The guests will be here soon. What are you doing there, Yitzchok? How long can this bunch of heroes and this groom wait for a photograph to be taken?

The camera clicked loudly, freezing the group in memory. All the years of their lives, all their whispered dreams, all their hopes and passions, all the horror they had witnessed and the comradeship they had forged, all of everything they had been since childhood was in that rectangle of frozen memory called a photograph. You could not unfreeze it, you could not make the people in the photograph meaningful, unless you asked questions and listened and caught their words and glances in the nets of your silence. The camera clicked and the photograph within the forest stirred as the men stepped from the rectangle and continued about their tasks.

Nathan, search the area and post a guard. Yitzchok, pack up that camera and come with me. Did you bring the torches? We will make a surprise for the pogrom boys if they come near us tonight. No one will disturb my brother David's wedding. How many brains like David do you think there are in this stinking world?

The night came. Stars burned icily in the black ink of the sky. I rode my stallion through the darkness. Green-uniformed infantry followed on foot. Now Bolsheviks, Yitzchok. It will never end. There will not be many of us left after this war. Between the Polak anti-Semites and the Bolshevik Cossacks our blood is being thinned to water. Where is Yankel? Go tell Yankel the platoon on the left is falling behind. That is all we need—for some Cossack bastards to drive a wedge into us now.

Villages were burning in the night. The heavens glowed a dull red. All along the horizon flames leaped into the charred sky. The train, winding its way tortuously through the bare winter forest, was halted at a curve in the tracks and boarded by a gang of armed bandits, shouting, Where are the Jews? We only want the Jews. We won't touch a hair of any of our patriots. Who are the kosher-eaters? You, soldier, tell me quick who are the Jews or you get it in the belly. All right, you patriots, all of you, off with the pants, off, off, now! Is that what you want? Take your hands off me, you swine. I am an officer. Parden me, officer, sir. What did you say, soldier? A Jew? An officer who is a Jew? You bastard Jew. Where did you steal the uniform? Hey, you guys, this Jew is wearing the uniform of an officer in the glorious cavalry of the Marshal. And you called me a swine, you bastard. You're lucky

I don't cut your heart out. Give me that pack. You get your hands off my pack. Hey, you guys, this Jew is tough. You want to see how tough he is? I'll show you how tough he is. There! Now you got a cut on top to match the cut on bottom. Everyone finished? Any more Jews? Off! Off! Get the train out of here and keep it moving!

There was blood everywhere. On the tunic and trousers. On the seat and windows. The floor was slippery with blood. The soldier who had pointed to the Jewish officer moved to another car. In Lemberg. David was dead in a pogrom. Two days dead. All right, Ruth. We know what to do, Ruth. We will bring everyone together and make plans. We will not be destroyed, Ruth. We know what our job is, Ruth. Mama. Listen to me, Ruth. Mama. Mama!

Afternoon shadows drifted slowly into the forest. There was a long faintly resonating silence. And in that silence I thought I could hear the dark anguish of secret weeping. Sha, Ruth. Sha. We will do what is right. The weeping continued, chilling the shadows that filled the forest.

Then I heard a branch snap and low urgent voices, and there they were, coming slowly from the direction of the stream, walking stealthily, searching. I put down my saber and picked up my machine gun. Crouching beside a tree, I sighted carefully and waited until they were only a few yards away. Then I shot them both. They fell and lay very still. Their eyes were closed. I would never again have to see their sleepy eyes and the little smiles on their narrow high-cheeked faces. I had to kill them. Master of the Universe, how they hurt us. I felt the jumping and leaping of my heart. My hands and feet tingled with cold. I stood very still inside the dark forest, looking down at the bodies of Eddie Kulanski and his cousin and listening to the wild beating of my heart.

After a while I put the machine gun down on the forest floor next to the saber and came out of the trees into the slanting afternoon sunlight on the back lawn. Tomorrow I would play it all over again. Maybe tomorrow I would be Uncle Meyer or David. Yes. Tomorrow I would be my dead Uncle David. I bent down and skimmed my hand over the grass of the back lawn. I still could not grasp that my mother had once been married to my dead Uncle David. I would play again the way they took the photograph in the forest before the wedding. I would play my Uncle Meyer and my Uncle David. But the best was to play my father. He was the strongest and bravest of them all. I would play him again. Mostly I would play when he was a machine gunner and a cavalryman and then came back to Lemberg and organized the Am Kedoshim Society to fight against the Poles who were killing Jews and then returned to the cavalry of Pilsudski to fight the Bolsheviks. And I would play the way his face was cut on the train. And maybe I would play the way he married my mother after Uncle David was killed and then came to America.

Over and over again throughout the few remaining days of that summer I played inside the forest. Sometimes, at the insistence of my parents, I had to be on the beach in the sun. But whenever I could be alone I was in the forest, riding, swinging my saber, and firing my machine gun.

They won't kill David again, I kept thinking. We have to smash their heads. There isn't any other way. But always when I came out of the forest there would be the strange wild leaping of my heart and the cold tingling in my hands and feet. And one day I stood silently beside my father as he waited and joked with his brothers and friends, and Yitzchok's camera clicked loudly and added a new face to the photograph.

We left the cottage in the first week of September. As we drove into the city, I realized with astonishment that I had not been ill during all the weeks we had been away and that I had had only one minor accident. When we pulled up in front of the house, Mrs. Savanola came out of her apartment, greeted us effusively, and informed us that Mrs. Horowitz had died three days before and her funeral had been yesterday. The dog had been taken away by her son.

Three

Mrs. Horowitz was dead, but for days her voice and face remained fixed inside my head. I would be playing in the street or eating in the kitchen or lying in my bed and my eyes would fall upon an object—a leaf, a glass, a light bulb—and the object would blur and then become sharply focused, and I would see her face and hear her telling me about the dangers and the Angel of Death and the books in her musty bedroom. She would come to me at the oddest times and places, in light or dark, in the shade of the maples that had begun to turn now on our street or in the strong sunlight of the zoo as I fed and petted my billy goat, during a Shabbat morning in our synagogue as Mr. Bader talked about the Torah reading, during a walk along the boulevard with my Cousin Saul. Once I sat in the kitchen watching my mother write a letter to her parents in Europe, who had received their visas but had decided they were not yet ready to leave for America, and I looked up from the moving point of the Waterman's pen and my mother's flowing curvy handwriting, and saw Mrs. Horowitz. I closed my eyes and opened them, and the face was again my mother's It was a while before I could no longer hear the beating of my heart.

Often I wondered how the Angel of Death had finally claimed her. Had he shouted in her ear before piercing her with his poisoned sword? Had she looked in death as bulging-eyed and starkly surprised as the dead bird I had once seen in the pine wood? Her dog had whined and moaned in the night

and all through the morning and the janitor had opened the
door with his passkey and had gone inside, first putting a
handkerchief across his face to ward off the stench. It took an
entire day to find her son.

Two weeks after we returned from the cottage a van drove
up and two burly men removed the furniture from her apartment and drove off. Painters came. At the end of the month
a quiet elderly couple moved into the apartment. They did
not own a dog. Mrs. Horowitz dissolved into the sharp
autumnal air of our street and was gone. I could no longer
see her face or hear her voice. But I wondered often what
had happened to her dog.

Eddie Kulanski did not dissolve; nor did his cousin of the
quivering knife and the Spalding ball and the malevolence as
poisonous as the Angel of Death. I was ill for a few days
during the week we returned to the city. But it was not too
enervating an illness this time, and when I came back outside
I was able to play. I stayed away from Eddie Kulanski and
played with others on the block. Once Tony Savanola asked
me to play a bottle-cap game with him. I refused.

His dark eyes looked hurt. "Why, Davey?"

"You play with Eddie Kulanski."

"He won't bother you."

"I'm afraid of him, Tony."

"He just talks a lot, Davey. He's got a big mouth."

"He scares me a lot, Tony. People like him grow up and
kill Jews."

A look of astonishment came over his face. "What are you
talking about, Davey? What killing?"

"I'm afraid to play with you, Tony," I said, and walked
away from him to join a marbles game near Mr. Steinberg's
candy store. Afterward I rode my tricycle up and down the
block for a long time, leading my men in cavalry charges
through exploding shells and whining bullets.

Often I would pass Eddie Kulanski inside the apartment
house as I went up or down the stairs. He seemed not to
notice I was alive. He looked past me or through me. One
morning I was going down the stairs and saw his cousin
coming toward me two steps at a time. A shock of cold fear
coursed through me and, for the briefest of seconds, I felt
myself frozen to paralysis on the stairway. But he ran right
past me without saying a word; only the swift raking glance
of his eyes gave me any indication that he had in any way
noticed my presence.

I did not know if they hated me or loathed me or were simply indifferent to my existence. At times I had the cold raging impression that what they had done to me in the pine wood had simply been for them a lazy summer day's amusement, a prank, the offhand taunting of a stray dog or cat that carries with it quickly forgotten savagery. Slowly, I began to counter their indifference toward me with a comforting sense of contempt toward them. I despised them for the brutes I thought them to be. Then, in the second week of September, I began to see very little of Eddie Kulanski and his cousin. I was going to school.

My father had bought me a briefcase. It was black and shiny and the bone handle was smooth and cool and dark gray. The leather creaked. It smelled like new shoes. Into the briefcase I put my Hebrew notebook, with its alternating wide and narrow lines, my English notebook, my pencil case, and a soft eraser. For days I walked around inside the apartment, carrying that briefcase and waiting for my first day of school.

The night before my first day of school the Hebron pogrom reappeared in a conversation between my parents. I had not heard any mention of Hebron since we had left the cottage. My father had returned to his real estate business. My uncle had returned to his law firm. My mother wrote interminably to her parents in Europe, pleading with them to come to America. She wrote to her brothers and sisters, to her aunts and uncles and cousins. Yes, her parents had the money to come, she said in answer to my question. Yes, her mother was now entirely cured of her sickness. Yes, they could be on the boat now to America. Yes, we could be meeting them in a few weeks near the Statue of Liberty. But suddenly they had grown fearful of building a new life for themselves in a strange land. Life was difficult in Poland under Marshal Pilsudski but better than it had been after the war. Ridding themselves of the farm had become a complicated affair. Papers had been lost in the war; new surveys had to be made of the land; bureaucrats shunted them from one office to another; in the land registry office someone had wondered aloud how it was that Jews could have been sold a piece of the holy soil of Poland. There had been sidelong glances; furrowed brows had been raised; narrowed eyes had given them dark scowling looks. And so they were having second thoughts. Visas finally in hand, the faceless elderly people who were my mother's parents and whose separation from her had become almost unendurable to her over the years—this elderly couple had

gazed across western Poland and Germany and the vast
waters of the Atlantic and been chilled by the sudden keen
awareness of the looming physical and cultural crossing that
lay before them. They would stay a while longer. They would
see. They had their visas. They could leave any time they
wished. They hoped their daughter would forgive them. Please
understand our feelings, dear daughter, wrote her mother.
To uproot a life at our age—it is like parting the Red Sea.
Papa and I send you and Max and our dear grandchildren
our love on the New Year. It should be a year of health and
happiness and peace and prosperity. It should be a good year
for Jews and for all the world, because if it isn't good for the
world it won't be good for the Jews. Have an easy fast on
Yom Kippur, dear daughter, and if God wills it we will see
one another again soon. Amen. My mother read the letter
to me and tears overflowed her haunted eyes. I did not like to
see my mother cry.

My father would grow angry when she would plead with
him to do something that might break the impasse. I lay in
bed and listened to them talking about her parents.

"Do what, Ruth? What do you want me to do? You want
me to go over to Poland and drag them to America by the
hair? What do you want from me?"

"Talk to Bader. Maybe he can give you an idea."

"What do you want from Bader? He has his own headaches.
God in heaven, Ruth, you cannot make a person come to
America. A person has to want to come. You said when they
had the visas they would come."

"They wrote me that, Max. You saw the letters."

"They never believed they would get the visas. That is what
it was. They never really wanted to come. All the prepara-
tions. All the weeks and weeks of running around filling out
papers. All the money they got. They never really thought
the day would come when they would hold the visas in their
hands."

"They aren't running off with the money, Max."

"Your parents and my parents. A perfect match. Stubborn
and blind. Where did you put the coffee, Ruth? They need a
pogrom. They need a Hebron in Bobrek. Then they would
come."

"God forbid, Max. What are you saying? God forbid." She
made dry spitting sounds with her lips.

"They never believed they would ever have the visas. That
is the reason they agreed to apply."

"Max, they're old. They don't know what to do."

"And your sisters and brothers? They are also old?"

I heard no response from my mother.

"Another Hebron," my father said with bitterness in his voice. He was angry. My mother's parents had wasted his time and, in a way, had defeated him. It would have been an achievement of sorts for him to have brought them from Bobrek to America: everyone knew how ill his mother-in-law had been. But indecision had been the true obstacle, not illness. He could not combat distant indecision. And so he loathed it and was angry at my mother's parents and bitter over the way his firm and fixed and rigidly organized way of doing things had been upset. He added sarcastically, "A few dozen dead Jews in Bobrek would bring them to the Bronx in a wink." He was quiet for a moment. Then he said in a softer voice, "Anyway, Bader will be in Lemberg after Simchas Torah. I will ask him to go to Bobrek."

She murmured words of gratitude. They sat in silence. The radio was turned on.

Early the next morning I came out of the house with my father and walked with him to the boulevard adjoining the zoo. He rode with me on the trolley to another part of the Bronx and accompanied me through alien streets to the yellow corner building that was the yeshiva. There, on the sidewalk, in a noisy crowd of students and parents, he bent down and held me to him and I heard him murmur a blessing. I felt the bony jut of his jaw against my face and saw, out of the side of my eye, the white dry line of his scar. Then he said, still holding me to him, "Be a good student, David. Do a good job and make us all proud." I nodded. He led me up the stone staircase and through the wooden double door of the entrance and along the corridor to the classroom. At the door to the classroom he kissed me again, then turned and went away.

Late in the afternoon I came out of the school building, pushed and jostled by older students whose shouts and strident laughter rang disturbingly in my ears, and saw my father waiting for me at the foot of the stone stairway. He was talking to the man with whom he had wrestled during the picnic; the man he had ridden with in Europe; the man called Nathan Ackerman, whose nephew had been killed in Hebron. They were talking about something called warrants. I stood next to my father while he continued his conversation. The sidewalk in front of the school was thick with parents and children. The noise raised by the children mingled with

the sounds of the heavy traffic on the street and thickened
the dusty afternoon air. I clung to my father's hand. The
students seemed so wild, running through the crowd, chasing
one another, racing up and down the stone steps. I saw my
Hebrew teacher, Mrs. Rubinson, a tall, slim, middle-aged
woman with graying hair which she wore in a bun and with
wide warm eyes and a patient smile that would come slowly
to her lips when she seemed annoyed. I noticed Joey Younger
in the crowd; he charged through a knot of parents to get at
a classmate he was chasing. He was in my class. I had said
nothing to him all day. I waited patiently on the sidewalk
next to my father and looked at the worn five-story reddish
brick apartment houses that lined both sides of the wide paved
main street onto which the yeshiva faced; at the dirt and soot
on the sidewalks; at the large-windowed building that was the
public school directly across the narrow side street from the
yeshiva; at the high chain-link fence that enclosed the play
yard behind the yeshiva building; at the tall crucifix on the
roof of the church next to the Catholic school a block away
from the yard down the side street; at the looming trestle of
the elevated train that ran along a wide dark avenue one long
interminable block from our yellow building in the opposite
direction from the church; at the stark treelessness of all the
neighborhood; I looked at the world in which was set the
school I would be attending for what then seemed to me to be
all the years of my life—and I felt cold and a little frightened.
I tugged gently at my father's hand. I wanted to go home to
my own street and its trees. Maybe Saul would come over
tonight. Maybe he would tell me a story. I thought I might
like to hear the Golem of Prague story again. I had seen Saul
only briefly during the day; his class was in the rear of the
building on the fourth floor; mine was in the rear of the
building on the first floor. He had told me he would be staying
in late today to help his teacher organize the classroom. I
hoped he would not stay late too often. I hoped I would see
more of him during the day. And why had my teacher given
me that curious smile when I had told her I already knew the
Hebrew alphabet after she had showed us the letter *bet* on a
card and asked us to pronounce it? And why had the class
tittered? And why had the boy named Larry Grossman come
over to me during mid-morning recess and called me a name?

"Shmucky show-off," he had said. He was tall and wore
shiny knickers and a yellow long-sleeved shirt frayed at the

wrists and worn thin at the elbows. He had a round face and small eyes.

"What?" I had said.

Some of the classmates gathered around us. I saw Joey Younger. Their young faces, crowded together, looked like painted balloons. Students from other classes sauntered by; a few stopped to watch.

"I don't like show-offs," he said. He was playing to the faces around us. "You going to spend all year showing off?"

I looked at him in astonishment.

"I know the whole alphabet already, Mrs. Rubinson," he mimicked. Some of the others laughed. A few stood by silently, watching.

I felt my face burning.

All around us swirled the wildness and noise of two hundred children at play.

"You know the English alphabet, too?" Larry Grossman taunted. His round face was damp with sweat. He had fat stubby fingers. "How about Chinese? You know Chinese?"

I said nothing. Someone laughed loudly.

"Ass-licker," Larry Grossman said contemptuously in Yiddish, and stalked off, followed by Joey Younger and some of the other classmates who had stood around us.

I looked about to see if I could find Saul. But the play yard was wild with racing games and knotted with pockets of static games and with students who just stood around talking to one another.

Two of the boys who had stood by watching Larry Grossman taunt me came over to me.

"He's a jerk," one of them said. "He's dumb. Don't let him worry you."

"Your father is Max Lurie," the other said.

They were both taller than I. The one who had spoken first was fair-skinned with pale blond hair and dark eyes. The other was dark-skinned and had black hair and a small mole on his left cheek.

"Yes," I said.

"I'm Yosef Ackerman. Nathan Ackerman is my father. This is Yaakov Bader. Mr. Shmuel Bader is his uncle. We were over at your house once or twice. You don't remember?"

I remembered vaguely.

"We're in second grade. You got any baseball cards? How about a game of baseball cards?"

I had plenty of baseball cards. We played all through the recess. I played with them during the midday recess, too. Toward the end of that recess, I walked over to the chain-link fence and gazed out at the street and the crucifix on the church a block away. Then I turned around and looked at the frenzied play inside the paved yard. I was tired. My eyes throbbed. I sat down on the floor of the yard and leaned back against the chain-link fence. At the foot of the fence the thick wires culminated in twists with two sharp jutting ends pointing downward from each twist about an inch or so above the ground. I sat very quietly watching the activity inside the yard until the shrill sound of the whistle terminated the recess.

When the English teacher, a young, pretty, brown-haired woman in her twenties named Mrs. Bernstein, held up the card with the letter *B*, I raised my hand and informed her that I knew the entire English alphabet. She looked at me. The class was very quiet. She said in a soft voice, "Do you really? What is your name again? David Lurie. Yes. Well, that's fine, David. Everyone will soon know all the letters and we'll be able to go on together."

My father said to me later when he came out of the trolley car, "Now listen to me, David. Are you listening? You will be going to school with Saul from now on."

I stared at him and my heart leaped with joy.

"I thought it might be possible for me to bring you and take you home. But I came too late to my office this morning and had to leave too early. I will call your uncle and ask if Saul can wait for you on this corner in the morning. Then you can take the trolley car together."

"Yes, Papa."

"In the afternoon, either you will come home with Saul or I will come for you. I do not know when Saul gets out of school."

The following morning I met Saul on the street corner in front of the church. His old, frayed, misshapen briefcase bulged with books. I felt a little shamed by the emptiness of the new briefcase I held in my hand.

"Hello, Cousin," he said. "That's a nice briefcase. Use it well. Or I should say tear it well, since it's made of leather. Is it leather? How was your first day in school?"

We were standing on the sidewalk in a large crowd of adults and other schoolchildren. Across the street from us was the zoo. I saw our trolley coming up along the boulevard.

We found two seats together. I told him about Larry Grossman.

"Stay away from him," he advised solemnly. "In every class there are one or two or three guys like him. Stay far away from them. They're a bunch of time-killers and stuffed heads. How did you like Ruby?"

I said I liked Mrs. Rubinson.

"She's nice," Saul said, and a dreamy look came into his eyes. "I liked her."

We rode in silence for a while. It was a cloudy day. The air was bleak and chilled. I saw a dead gray cat lying like garbage along the curb of a cobblestone street.

The trolley stopped and we got off and walked along the treeless street to the yeshiva. The apartment houses were of grimy reddish brick. Around the windows and wide entrance doors were rectangles of white stone stained dark gray with dirt and age. The stoops were smooth and worn.

"What is Washington?" I asked as we hurried along the street.

"The capital of America. You don't know that?"

"Oh, I know that, Saul. But is the street named after the capital or after the president?"

"They're both named after the president."

"And who was Paul?" I asked as we came to the side street.

He looked up at the street sign. "He was a very important Catholic."

"A Catholic? Really? What do the letters in front of his name mean?"

"That's short for saint. It means he was one of their very great people. He helped start the Catholic Church."

"Really? What did he do?"

"I don't know, Davey. I don't interest myself in such matters."

We crossed St. Paul's Place. The public school, with its enormous enclosed paved yard, stood on our right. The play yard and the school building took up an entire block of Washington Avenue. Across the next side street stood the yellow brick building of the yeshiva. The streets were filled with students walking toward both schools. There were students in both play yards. As I crossed the side street with Saul, I looked toward the Catholic school and church and saw that the street in front of it was deserted.

"What time do they start school?" I asked Saul, indicating the Catholic school.

"They start early. Around eight thirty or quarter to nine. Come on, Davey. We'll be late."

We went up the stone stairway with other students. Inside the hallway, Saul stopped at the side of the wooden staircase and said, "I'll meet you in front right after school and we'll go home together. Right after school. Okay? Did your father tell you that on Wednesdays he'll meet you and bring you home?"

I nodded. "Where will you be Wednesdays, Saul?"

"I'm studying Torah reading with Mr. Bader. Every Shabbos and Wednesday afternoon. Except when he has to go to Europe. He's also going to teach me grammar. I'm going to read the Torah for my bar mitzvah. And then I'll read it afterward too in the synagogue, for Shabbosim and holidays."

I stared at him. "We won't be able to go to the zoo anymore, Saul."

"Sure we'll go," he said. "We'll find time, Davey."

A group of students surged past us, jostling me heavily. I almost dropped my briefcase.

"That big one in the blue shirt is Larry Grossman," I said.

"Well, stay away from him, Davey."

"What sidrah will you be reading, Saul?"

"For my bar mitzvah?"

"Yes."

"Noah," he said.

"I'm going to miss not going to the zoo with you, Saul."

"We'll go, Davey. Besides, soon you'll be reading books and you won't even be interested in the zoo."

He went to his class, and I went to mine. I sat and listened to Mrs. Rubinson talk about letters I had learned to recognize and read months ago. She wrote the letters on the blackboard, printing them slowly with a long stick of white chalk that occasionally let out a nerve-chilling squeak. She told us to copy the letters, and I wrote them down in my notebook. She asked me to read a line of letters in the book she had given us the day before. I read quickly. She asked me to continue. I read on to the foot of the page. She asked me to stop and called on someone else to start again from the first line of that page. I sat very still with my eyes on the page, vaguely listening to the student read and feeling very bored and thinking with sadness that the beautiful Shabbat afternoons Saul and I had spent in the zoo were now at an end. I tried to remember some of the walks we had taken together but it was like seeing them through rain and mist. I closed my eyes. It was easier to see things you thought about if your eyes were closed. I listened to the boy reading from the book and saw myself walking with Saul beneath the trees of the zoo. There were the lions and the elephants and the tigers. The sun was on the leaves of the trees and the lions lounged in the shade of outcroppings. As we passed by, a lion raised his maned head, gazed at us out of slitted yellow eyes, and yawned. His mouth opened wide and I saw the huge, stained, pointed teeth. The dog's teeth had been stained and dirty and pointed. He had lain against the curb like the dead cat. Did the Angel of Death carry a pointed sword? The billy goat rubbed his hot moist sandy tongue on my palm. I stroked his goatee; soft silken white hair. It curled and blew in the wind when he ran about. His hooves raised little clouds of powdered yellow earth; I could hear their soft quick sounds. But the horse my father rode had galloped soundlessly on the dew-moistened grass. And why was Saul starting so early on his bar mitzvah studies? Did it take so long to study how to read the Torah? And what did grammar mean? "Dikduk Hamikra," he had said in Hebrew. The grammar of the Bible. What did that mean? I wished I could have a seat near one of the windows. But I had been placed by Mrs. Rubinson in the third row slightly to the left of her desk. I could look at the uncombed black head of hair in front of me, or at my worn, scarred desk top with its slots for pens and pencils and its empty inkwell, or at the faded yellow-green walls, or at the streaked blackboard, or at the flaking white ceiling, or at the wood floor with the color pounded out of it by the feet of students, or at Mrs. Rubinson. Or I could close my eyes and listen vaguely to the class and see things I could conjure up at will.

Mrs. Rubinson had called my name. "David Lurie, please read the next line," she had said and in the instant it took me to open my eyes, I remembered that her voice had sounded almost exactly like the contralto voice of the woman who had sung Polish songs during the picnic of the Am Kedoshim Society. I glanced over to the boy on my right and saw that the class had moved on to the following page. His finger was on the third line. I turned the page, read the line, and stopped. Mrs. Rubinson asked me to continue reading. I read to the foot of the page, and stopped. She called on another boy and asked him to read the first line of the page. He read the vowel and letter combinations haltingly. I closed my eyes, and wondered if Eddie Kulanski and Tony Savanola were

in the Catholic parochial school down the block. I would
have to ask Saul or my father if there was a Catholic school
in our neighborhood. I spent the rest of the early morning,
until recess, with my eyes closed, riding a black stallion
through burning forests and firing my machine gun at charging Cossacks.

I found Saul in the yard during the recess. He was standing
with a group of his friends, talking quietly. He introduced me
as his cousin Davey Lurie.

"Max Lurie's your father?" one of the boys said.

I nodded.

There were four of them. They stood around looking at me.
They appeared simultaneously awed and uncomfortable.

"Saul, is there a Catholic school in our neighborhood?"

He stared at me through his glasses. "I don't think so," he
said after a moment.

"They're building a big school over on Tremont Avenue,"
one of the boys said,

"This is the only Catholic elementary school and high
school in the whole area," one of the boys said. "I got a
friend goes to that school."

"What's the matter, Davey?" Saul said.

I told him nothing was the matter.

"Hey, is it true your father killed more than a hundred
Cossacks in the war?" another of the boys said.

I looked at him.

"What's the matter with you?" I heard Saul's sudden angry
voice.

Behind me there was a sudden increase in the volume of
noise as prisoners in a game of ringaleveeo were freed and
went racing wildly through the yard.

"Never mind," someone said.

"Is that Tremont and Webster, opposite the telephone building?" someone else asked.

"Yeah."

"That's gonna be a church. A Protestant church."

"My janitor said it was for the Catholics."

"There's a sign in front that says 'Our Lady of the Sacred
Heart Church.' Something like that."

"It's the Catholics."

"What's a sacred heart?"

"I don't know. I don't interest myself in such matters."

I edged away from them and went over to the chain-link
fence. The public school play yard was deserted. By putting

my face flush up against the fence, I could see the gray stone front of the church and, immediately beyond it, the gray stone school building. The crucifix on the angled tile roof of the church jutted starkly into the gray sky. The church and the school stood directly on the street, without an intervening lawn. I could not see any statues. As I stood there against the chain-link fence, one of the tall front doors of the church opened and a man stepped out and went quickly down the half-dozen front steps and started on up the block. He was coatless and wore a dark suit and hat. Halfway up the block, I saw he was a priest. He had a smooth pink face and pale eyebrows and gray-blond hair. He was of medium height and heavy-shouldered. I stood there watching him go by on the street outside the chain-link fence. The street was deserted. He was walking quickly and seemed to be hugging the fence. He passed within two feet of where I stood inside the fence, and I felt a strange chill of dread seeing him so close to me. He stopped near the mailbox on the corner of Washington Avenue, checked the traffic, crossed the street, and went on along the side street toward the elevated train. A few moments later the whistle blew and the recess was over. The yard began to empty out immediately.

On my way through the metal double door that led into the building from the yard, someone pinched my left buttock very hard. I turned quickly to the left and saw no one near me, then turned to the right and saw Larry Grossman rushing along a few feet ahead of me; then he turned to the right and went into our classroom.

I felt a choking sensation in my throat. I waited in the corridor for a moment. Mrs. Rubinson was calling the class to attention. I slipped inside and took my seat. Larry Grossman was busily turning the pages of his notebook and did not look at me.

I stared across the rows of seats to my left at the reddish brick apartment house that bordered the school yard. Above the apartment house dark gray clouds lay like dirty milk across the sky. Inside the classroom the air was hot and stale. I itched with heat and discomfort. Mrs. Rubinson stood at the blackboard in a long-sleeved, high-necked dark blue dress and pronounced letters and vowels. The class imitated her pronunciation. Again, she wrote letters and vowels on the blackboard and we copied them into our notebooks. Then she called on someone to read. I turned to the last page in the textbook, read it through quickly to myself, and turned back to the page the class was reading. I had read the entire book the day before, soon after I had returned home. It had not taken me too long to do that. I listened to the students read. After a while I closed my eyes and went into the zoo and fed my billy goat. Then I walked about in the meadow and stopped to watch the fish in the pond. They swam slowly and smoothly in the dark water. Then I went to the movie house in the town near our cottage and saw the Charlie Chaplin film about the cleaning man in the bank. I was watching another Charlie Chaplin movie we had seen the past summer about a floorwalker in a department store when I heard Mrs. Rubinson call on me to read. I opened my eyes, took a quick look at the finger of the boy sitting next to me, turned the page, and read. When the bell rang for lunch and the end of the Hebrew studies segment of the day, Mrs. Rubinson asked me to stay behind for a moment.

The classroom emptied quickly. I stood next to Mrs. Rubinson's desk. She was gathering up her notebooks and attendance book. The textbook we studied from was open on her desk to the last letter we had learned. She looked tired. Strands of graying hair had come loose from the bun that sat like a cupola on the back of her head.

"Well," she said, sitting back in her chair and smiling wearily. "What are we going to do with you, David Lurie?"

I stood near her and did not understand what she was saying. She smelled vaguely of sweat. Her eyes were brown and there were tiny wrinkles in their corners. She closed her eyes for a moment and I saw tiny winding rivulets of veins on her eyelids. Then she opened her eyes, turned to the last page of the book, and asked me to read. I read swiftly to the foot of the page. She nodded and shut the book.

"Parents do not do their children a favor when they teach them to read too early," she said.

I looked at her nervously. "My papa and mama didn't teach me to read. I teached myself to read."

"I taught myself to read," she corrected automatically.

"Yes, Mrs. Rubinson. I taught myself to read."

A group of students went running through the corridor outside the classroom. The floor trembled.

Mrs. Rubinson shook her head and put the textbook on top of the pile of books and notebooks. She leaned sideways, opened a bottom drawer in her desk, and pulled out a thin book with a pale blue cover. She shut the drawer. "Let's do each other a favor, David. I'll give you books to take home and read, and you'll sit at your desk and not go to sleep. All right?"

"I wasn't sleeping, Mrs. Rubinson."

"You won't sit at your desk with your eyes closed, then. It disturbs me to see one of my students sitting at his desk with his eyes closed."

"Can I read these books in class, too, Mrs. Rubinson?"

She hesitated. "We'll see," she said tiredly. "Read this book at home first and when you've finished with it bring it back to me and we'll sit and discuss it. Now go have your lunch before there's nothing left for you to eat. If you get any skinnier than you are now you may become a shadow. Go ahead, David."

I read the book at home that night and brought it up to her at the start of the mid-morning recess the next day. She stared at me. She had long bony fingers and they fluttered for a moment in the air over her attendance book, which lay closed in a corner on top of the desk.

"Sit down, David."

I sat at the desk directly in front of her.

"Tell me what the book is about, David."

I told her.

"Read the last page of the book, David."

I read the last page of the book.

"Did you like the book, David?"

I shrugged.

There was a brief silence. She daubed at her long upper lip with a lace-edged handkerchief. I thought I heard a faint sigh escape from her, but I was not certain. The windows were open. The din of the recess in the school yard came into the classroom like the sounds made by heavy rains and winds when they lashed the forest in back of our cottage.

She reached into the bottom drawer of her desk and gave me another book to read. Then she sent me outside to the yard.

During the period after the recess, she asked me to sit with one of the students in the back of the room and help him review his reading. I sat and listened to him read quietly. He wore thick glasses and seemed to have difficulty recognizing the vowel notations. I wondered if he was able to see them. He had irregular teeth and sour breath. We sat together at one of the desks and he droned his way haltingly through the letters.

On the way to the lunchroom later that morning, Larry Grossman shouldered past me in the corridor, hissed into my

ear, "Shmucky teacher's pet," and sent me heavily into a wall.
I dropped my briefcase. The fall jarred it open and my notebooks and pencils spilled out onto the linoleum floor of the
corridor. I leaned against the wall, catching my breath and
trying to keep my quivering legs straight and firm. Some of
my classmates were picking up the notebooks and pencils and
putting them back into my briefcase.

"It's all back inside, Davey," one of them said, and handed
me the briefcase. He spoke in Yiddish.

"That's a wild animal," another said, also in Yiddish. "You
ought to tell Mrs. Rubinson."

"How will that help?" the first one said. "He'll say it was
an accident."

"He's a wild animal," the other said. "A dumb wild animal."

"I heard he has an older sister that's deaf and dumb," the
first one said.

"We'd better go eat before there's nothing left," said the
other.

"What do you carry your briefcase to lunch for?" the first
one asked me. "We go back to the same room."

"I like to keep it with me."

They looked at each other.

We went down together to the lunchroom, washed our
hands at one of the sinks outside the doors, said the blessing,
and went inside. I found an empty place on a bench and sat
down. A woman brought me a bowl of reddish soup in which
pale green and dull yellow vegetables floated like dead fish.

"This is the second time you are late for lunch," the woman
said. She was middle-aged and wore an apron. "The way you
look, you should be here first not last."

In the trolley car I said to Saul, "I didn't see you in the
yard at recess."

"I was inside helping my teacher." He was quiet for a moment. I stared out the window at the smoke and the traffic and
the crowded sidewalks. I could feel him looking at me. "You
ought to find your own friends, Davey. It's not good for you
to be with me all the time."

I did not say anything. But I felt cold. The school had
begun to change everything. I did not like the school. It had
taken me away from my world and given me nothing in
return. It was not even really teaching me anything. The
trolley stopped. I looked out the window at a passing horse
and wagon. People were pushing through the crowded trolley
to get to the doors. We would be getting off at the next stop.

The doors closed and the trolley started up again. It made the wide sweeping turn and there was the zoo to our right. It rolled on for a block and came to a stop.

Saul helped me off and walked with me quickly across the boulevard to the sidewalk in front of the church. We crossed the side street.

"Tomorrow morning," he said, went back across the side street and on toward his house.

I stood on the street corner, waiting. Eddie Kulanski had not been on our car. I waited until two more trolleys had stopped and disgorged their passengers. Then I went home.

My father had gone directly from his office to a meeting of the Am Kedoshim Society somewhere downtown. I ate with my mother and brother. How was school? my mother wanted to know. I shrugged. She sighed and moved quietly about the kitchen.

"Davey go to school," my brother said from his high chair.

I looked at him. He was making white mud pies out of his mashed potatoes, taking little globs and arranging them on the tray of his chair.

"Davey read books," he said happily, his face beaming.

I said nothing.

"Books books books," my brother said. "Alex wants books."

I ignored him. My father had told me they would be moving him into my room soon; he was getting too old to be sleeping in the same room with my parents. I did not understand that; but the look on my father's face when he had told me made it clear that it was not the kind of decision I should question. I ate quickly and went into my room and read the book my Hebrew teacher had given me. When I was finished with it I closed it and stared out my window at the leaves of the maple. Some of the leaves had begun to turn. A few had fallen. The sky was taking on the slate coloring of the coming night. Why weren't any of the books she gave me as exciting as the stories Saul used to tell me about Noah and Abraham or the Golem of Prague? I sat at the window, looking down at the street.

My mother came into my room later that evening. I lay in my bed, staring up at the ceiling. She sat down on the edge of my bed and kissed my forehead and cheek. She smelled of the soap she had used to wash the supper dishes.

"I have the feeling," she said slowly, "that my little David is not very happy."

I shrugged my shoulders under the blanket and sheet.

"David," she said. "What's the matter?"

"Nothing's the matter, Mama."

"Of course nothing is the matter. And the sun will not rise tomorrow. And it will not be Rosh Hashanah in two weeks and Yom Kippur ten days later. You walk around with your nose to the ground like one of the elephants in the zoo."

I closed my eyes and was quiet.

There was a long silence. A horse and wagon clattered by on the street below. Warm humid air blew in through my open window.

I heard her sigh softly and felt her stir on my bed. "I am sure of one thing," she said. "I am sure that after one week in school my little David has forgotten the names of the trees he learned in the summer."

My eyes flew open. "No," I said, and sat up in the bed.

"No? I do not believe it."

"Test me, Mama."

"It's impossible that my David would remember the trees."

"Test me, test me!"

"All right, darling. Mama will give you a test. Is this your first test since you began school? A strange test. What tree is shaped like a cone, has branches that go up, and needles that are flat?"

"A fir tree!" I said. "A fir tree, Mama!"

"Not so loudly. You'll wake your brother and I'll give you the pleasure of putting him back to sleep. What tree is shaped like a pyramid—you remember I told you about the Children of Israel in Egypt and the pyramids they built?—and has short needles that it loses in the winter?"

"A larch, Mama."

"Yes. Very good. A larch. And what tree has a short stem and a head that is shaped like an egg?"

"An elm, Mama. An elm tree. The elm where you read books in the summer."

She gazed at me and was quiet a moment. "Yes," she said finally. "An elm tree. And what tree has twigs and leaves and branches that droop toward the ground like my David these past few days and makes you think that it is crying?"

"A willow," I said in a low voice.

"Yes," she said. "A willow. And why does my David look like a willow? Will he tell me?"

"Mama?"

"Yes, darling."

"I don't like school too much."

She was quiet.

"I don't learn anything and I don't have any friends and there is a boy who picks on me."

She sat very still on my bed, her tired face pale beneath the dark combed-back straight hair.

"And I miss you, Mama. And the trees. And the zoo."

She stirred. "Trees?" she murmured.

"There are no trees anywhere near the yeshiva, Mama. How can they make streets without trees?"

She was staring at me. I saw her eyes very wide and staring at me. Her frail form stiffened.

"And Saul will be studying for his bar mitzvah and I won't see the zoo with him anymore."

She said nothing.

"I don't like the feeling of missing you and the trees and the zoo, Mama. It's not a good feeling."

"No," I heard her say in a very small voice. Then she said, "But you will have to get used to it, David."

"I hate it, Mama."

"Yes. Yes. Hate it. Of course. Hate it. It's a terrible feeling. But get used to it. You will get used to it soon. Didn't you get used to it soon? No. Not soon. But you got used to it. Otherwise it would still all be tears and what difference would it make what shape the trees were?" She broke off suddenly and took a deep tremulous breath. Then she sat very still and was silent.

When her silence had gone on a long time, I said quietly, "Mama?"

She sighed. "Yes, darling. Yes. You'll get used to it, darling. And you will be a wonderful student and make us proud of you. Won't you, darling?"

"Yes, Mama," I heard myself say.

"When I started in the gymnasium in Vienna I was also very lonely. I missed my father and mother. I even missed my brothers and sisters, even though I used to fight with them all the time. They never liked it that I would always be reading. I used to sit under a tree and read. No one thought a girl should read so much. But I missed them when I started the gymnasium. David once told me he also missed—" She stopped, blinked her eyes rapidly, and took another deep quivering breath. Then she sat very quietly on the bed, gazing down at me. "Have I ever told you how much you look like David? Yes, of course I have. It is so hard to hold back the memories, darling. Impossible, sometimes. But we shouldn't remember too much. That is as bad as not remembering at all. Well," she said brightly. "Well. You remembered the trees. That was wonderful. And soon you will find a friend and you will begin to learn good things. You taught yourself the alphabets and that's why you are bored now. Wait a week or two. Be patient. Do you want me to talk to your teacher about the boy who is picking on you?"

"No, Mama."

"Good. Because I cannot come running to your school for all your problems, darling. You will get used to going to school and it will become a better school soon and your memories of your trees will not make you so sad anymore. Give me a kiss good night and say your Krias Shema quietly and go to sleep. Children who want to have good memories should get plenty of sleep."

"Mama?"

"Yes, darling."

"Why is Saul studying three years with Mr. Bader for his bar mitzvah?"

"There is a lot to learn. But ask your father."

"Three years, Mama?"

"Ask your father, David."

"I'm sleepy, Mama."

"Good. It's about time you were sleepy."

"What books did you read when you were young, Mama?"

"All kinds of books. Storybooks."

"Where did you get them?"

"From Lemberg. Sometimes a man would come by the farm with a wagon full of books. My father would buy from him."

"Were they in German, Mama?"

"They were in German and Yiddish and Polish and Russian."

"You can read all those languages, Mama?"

"Yes," she said. "Once I even knew to read French. But I have forgotten by now."

"So many languages," I said. I was light-headed and beginning to float with the dark soft coming of sleep. "How will I ever learn all those things, Mama? I'm not learning anything in my school."

"Sha, darling. Sha. You will learn. This is only your fourth day in school. Even God needed a week to create the world. Sha, my darling. Go to sleep."

Through the embracing folds of sleep I murmured the

Kriat Shema. I felt her kiss me and I reached up through my sleep and kissed her cheek. I heard her go from the room. The last thing I saw before I fell into deep sleep was a sudden sharp picture of my mother as a child, with a frilly dress and dark eyes and long braids, sitting under the elm tree in front of our cottage reading a storybook written in the black spiky letters of the German alphabet.

I sat in our little synagogue and listened to Mr. Bader read the Torah.

To my left sat Saul and his father; to my right sat my father. The synagogue had filled rapidly and by the time the main portion of the Morning Service had begun, almost all the seats had been occupied. Additional chairs were brought in from somewhere in the building and placed in the aisle. These, too, filled quickly. The room had resonated with the loud praying of the Morning Service. Now the room was silent. The first aliyah had been called to the Torah: one of the men in the photograph. He chanted the blessing, the congregants responded with "Amen," and Mr. Bader had begun to read.

Saul and my uncle and father followed the reading carefully in their large-sized Hebrew Bibles. Saul sat bent over his Bible, his small mouth partly open, his head moving back and forth as his eyes scanned the lines. We sat in the front row near the window to the left of the lectern where Mr. Bader stood. My father sat very still, wrapped in his large tallit. I turned my head to the left and gazed across Saul and my uncle to the street outside and the statue of the robed woman in front of the Catholic church. Then I looked back at the Bible I held on my lap. I could not follow Mr. Bader's swift reading of the text. I squirmed with frustration. Abruptly my father, together with some other men in the room, called out a Hebrew word. Mr. Bader had misread a vowel. He stopped, read the word again correctly, and went on reading. I was bored listening to him and felt relieved when the Torah reading finally ended. It was only when the entire congregation stood up for the raising of the Torah scroll from the podium prior to its being rewrapped and replaced in the Ark —it was only then that I realized something out of the ordinary was about to happen: the synagogue had never been this crowded before in as long as I could remember, except for

the High Holidays and for Memorial Services. Then I saw my
father rise from his chair. He went to the podium and stood
there for a moment, the center of the silence that lay thickly
upon the room. Then he chanted, "Yikum purkon min
shemayo," and the congregation repeated the words and continued loudly in separate voices the chanting of the prayers
that were the introduction to the Additional Service.

I leaned over toward Saul. "What's special about today?"

"Everyone is here," he replied.

"What?"

But he put a finger to his lips. My father's strong voice rang
out in the hushed room. His short stocky figure swayed
slightly; his face, raised and tilted to the left, revealed to me
clearly the white line of the scar on his cheek. He prayed
slowly, intensely, and it was easy for me to follow him in my
prayer book.

When the Torah had been replaced in the Ark, there was
a momentary silence. Everyone remained standing quietly, as
if for the briefest of seconds flesh had turned to stone. The air
was charged with a sense of deep expectation. Instead of going
to the podium to continue the service, my father returned to
his seat next to me. Mr. Bader came up to the podium. There
was a brief scraping of chairs and a rustling noise as people
sat down. On the boulevard a trolley car pulled up in front of
the church, discharged passengers, then started up again with a
swiftly receding clatter of wheels. In the silence that followed
I saw my father put his head forward and cover his eyes with
his right hand. His bony chin jutted out sharply and his lips
were set in a hard firm line. I sat next to him, stunned. In the
brief second before his hand had covered his eyes I had
noticed that he was crying.

Mr. Bader cleared his throat gently and brushed a thumb
and forefinger across the knot of his tie. He looked tall and
trim. His brown hair and deeply tanned features contrasted
delicately and warmly with the white tallit that lay draped
across his shoulders. He spoke in a soft voice.

"My father, may he rest in peace, who as you all know was
a close friend of the father of Max Lurie—my father once told
me a few years after we arrived in America that it is human
nature for a person to make all kinds of promises when he is
in difficulty, and promptly to forget them when the difficulty
passes. He quoted to me Abba bar Kahana in the midrash:
'When in trouble, I vow; when relieved, I forget it.' He made
those remarks to me in answer to a question I had put to him

about his coming to America. He told me that the father of Max Lurie had helped him to come to America. Simon Lurie had promised to help my father in return for a small favor, and he had kept his promise. Our good friend Max Lurie has learned well from his father. He has kept his promise. He made to all of you a promise in return for the funds you gave him and Ruth to enable them to begin new lives in America. The Rambam wrote, 'Let not your legal contract or the presence of witnesses be more binding than your verbal promise made privately.' Only your own ears heard that promise the night you all met in Lemberg and Max asked for your trust and swore you would all meet again one day in America. It is written, 'A pledge unpaid is like thunder without rain.' Max has paid his pledge. We can say of the Am Kedoshim Society that it is thunder with rain. For the first time all the members of the original Am Kedoshim Society who are still among the living are together under one roof in one room, and in America. We read in the Book of Psalms, 'Who shall sojourn in Thy Tabernacle? . . . He who swears to his own hurt, and does not change.' After the war and the pogroms not a single one of you had enough money to get you to America, but all of you together had more than enough money to send two people and give them something to live on until they could find work. You sent Max and his wife. I do not have to tell you the work Max Lurie put into making good on his pledge to you. You trusted him. Your trust has helped all of you. I express the gratitude of my father to the father of Max Lurie, and the gratitude of all of you to Max Lurie himself for making possible this Shabbos and all the good years ahead which, with the help of God, we will enjoy in this land."

In the stir that followed, my father rose and went to the podium. Mr. Bader shook his hand. My father began to chant the Kaddish that precedes the Silent Devotion. Chairs scraped softly as the congregants got to their feet. My father's voice broke. He paused for a moment. The congregation grew very still. He continued chanting, his voice low and quavering. I looked at my uncle. He was staring intently at the floor, his eyes fixed—unseeing, it seemed to me—on the black-and-red-checkered design of the linoleum. A dense hush fell across the synagogue. The Silent Devotion had begun.

After the service, there was wine and whiskey and cake and herring and peppery chickpeas, and a tumult of noise and joy. We had gone down the wide stone staircase of the synagogue to the downstairs social hall, and my uncle, standing behind a long table at the far end of the hall, had chanted the blessing over the wine. Then the noise broke over the crowded room like a boom of thunder. There were almost two hundred people in the room—my father's friends, all from that photograph, and some of their families—and they all seemed to make a sudden rush toward my father. The crowd enveloped him in their forward surge and I could no longer see him. I stood next to my mother and brother a few feet from the long table on which the food had been placed. Someone had put a piece of spongecake in my hand and had remembered to give my brother a cookie. My mother stood talking quietly with the woman who had come to America together with her husband just before we had left for the cottage. They were talking in Polish. I saw Mrs. Bader somewhere in the crowd, looking elegant in a pale blue dress and wide-brimmed flowery hat. I looked around and could not find Saul. Then I noticed him standing against the wall opposite the long table. He was talking to Mr. Bader, who was bending down, listening intently to Saul's words and nodding from time to time. Alex was pulling at my mother's hand. He wanted to go home. "Yes, darling," my mother kept saying. "In a minute. Soon. Soon. David, get Alex another cookie." I went over to the table. The food had almost entirely disappeared; the table seemed to have been visited by locusts. I found a cookie and brought it to my brother. He looked at it, took a tentative bite, and tossed it on the floor. He pulled again at my mother's hand. "Home," he said. "Mama, home." "All right," she said wearily. "Soon. Very soon." She looked at the crowd around my father and shook her head slowly. Beneath the wide brim of her hat, her eyes lay like dark ponds in the slanting fringe of shadow that fell across her face.

My uncle came out of the crowd and walked over to us. His face was flushed and his eyes shone behind their gold-rimmed circles of glass. "What a Shabbos, David. Your father deserves it. How he worked!"

"Papa brought all these people to America?" I could not quite grasp what it was my father had really done.

"He helped," my uncle said. "And how he helped. Without your father most of these people would not be here."

I did not understand it. But the noise made it difficult to talk. And I did not want to shout because I had awakened with a vaguely scratchy throat and the dull pain I had felt on Thursday and Friday was still present behind my eyes.

"Home, home, home," my brother said loudly. "Home, Mama!"

I agreed with him. I too wanted to go home and lie down and let the laughter and the shouting, the jostling and the dense crush of the crowd drain off me.

I heard a voice alongside me and looked up and saw it was Mr. Bader. He spoke in a very soft voice and I could not hear him. I strained my head upward, feeling as I did a sudden intensification of the pain behind my eyes. Mr. Bader bent down toward me and put his tanned craggy face very close to mine.

"You've started school," he said.

I nodded.

He smiled. "Congratulations, David. I am delighted. How have you been feeling?"

I shrugged.

"Saul tells me you had a fine summer."

"Were you in Hebron, Mr. Bader?" I heard myself ask suddenly. I could not remember when I had even thought to ask him that question. I had asked a question without even thinking to do it.

He answered very quietly, "Yes." I saw his mouth move and understood the answer though I could not hear it for the noise all around us. Then I heard him say, "Afterward."

"Was it very bad, Mr. Bader?"

He looked at me and nodded slowly but said nothing. He patted my arm. "You read and read and read," he said. "And I'll make you a promise. I promise that you will not be sorry."

He patted my arm again and stood up straight. I looked up at him uncomprehendingly. He spoke with my mother and uncle for a while and then went away.

Through the slowly thinning crowd I could now see my father behind the table, talking, shaking hands, being embraced repeatedly by his friends. One of them, a tall beanpole of a man, came over and saluted him smartly; instinctively, my father began to return the salute, then stopped. His hand in mid-air, he burst into laughter. The tall man laughed and threw his long thin arms around my father. Mr. Ackerman was there, laughing and talking. The room seemed to swell with the noise. It was like the noise in my school yard during recess, an ocean of voices rolling on huge waves within a small bounded space. I witnessed the shaking of hands and the rapid thinning of the crowd. Then the hall was empty and my father was saying, "All the years, all the years," and my mother said nothing but nodded slowly and looked down at the floor.

On the way back from the synagogue, I said to my father, "How did you bring all those people to America, Papa?"

"By working very hard, David."

"But how, Papa?"

"I told you, David. Hard work. Years and years of hard work." His face glowed beneath the bluish stubble. "I kept my word. To every one of them who gave me his trust. I kept my word. That was a job. Right, Ruth? *That* was a job!"

"Yes," my mother said softly.

"All your friends are now in America?" I asked. "The friends you grew up with?"

"The ones who are still alive, yes. And who did not go to Eretz Yisroel."

"Then the photograph is now in America."

"What?" he said, staring at me.

"Everyone is here. The people in the photograph. All the ones with—"

My mother slipped quietly between us. "Max," she said. "Max." Then she said, "David, walk on ahead with your brother. Don't let him go into the street."

"I didn't tell the man about the guns and the knives, Mama. The man, when he came from the government, I didn't tell him anything."

They stopped walking and stood very still in the middle of the street beneath a maple tree. Their faces went dead white.

"I understood, Mama. I didn't let my tongue talk that time. I was a big boy."

They looked at each other. Then they looked at me.

"Sometimes we have to lie to the goyim to stay alive, Papa. I understand that. I'm not a baby."

Late Saturday morning traffic cruised idly up and down our cobblestone street. Near Mr. Steinberg's candy store, some boys my age were playing with baseball cards.

"I'm not a baby," I kept saying. "I understand, Papa. And I'll read, and I'll like my school, and Mr. Bader will teach me the way he's teaching Saul. I'm a big boy now, Papa."

He bent and picked me up and held me tightly.

"I'm not a baby anymore," I kept saying as he carried me through the street and into the apartment house, holding me to him and not letting me see—though I could feel on my cheek—the tears that were streaming down his face.

I went to school. I was ill, but not too often. I suffered an occasional accident, but they were not serious. The world had become firm and fixed and I was comfortable in it. My teachers gave me books to read at home and let me daydream through my classes. Larry Grossman continued to bait me and I continued to bear him silently. Occasionally I met Eddie Kulanski or Tony Savanola on the street or inside the apartment house. I had nothing to do with Eddie Kulanski. Sometimes I would talk briefly with Tony Savanola.

Shortly after Succot, in the closing days of October, three large cartons of books arrived at our apartment by special messenger. A lawyer had written some weeks earlier and my mother, over my father's mild objection, had written back accepting the books left to me by Mrs. Horowitz in her will. My mother looked at them and was puzzled. They were in German and Hebrew; some of them seemed to deal with the Bible. They were difficult to understand, she said. Besides, she had no patience to look at them carefully now, she said. She would ask Mr. Bader when he returned from Europe. My father did not even bother to look at them. The stock market had crashed and he had more important things on his mind than the moldy books of a half-mad old woman. The books were placed in the rear of the lower two shelves of the linen closet in the corridor near my room and were forgotten.

Four

My brother and I were forgotten, too; or so it seemed to me in the months that followed.

Suddenly my parents were away often in the evenings and Saul would come over and stay with us. At first, only my father left, rising from the table after supper, putting on his wide-brimmed hat and camel's hair coat, murmuring good night, and going out the door. During the first week, he would shave before leaving. But his face became irritated from the twice-a-day shaves; red welts appeared on his neck below his jutting chin. Sometimes he cut himself; dark spots of blood stained the rim of his shirt collars. Then he stopped shaving and went out directly after the meal, his features darkened by the stubble of his beard. His eyes too seemed strangely dark.

"Where does Papa go?" I asked my mother one night in November.

"To meetings," she said, bending over my brother, who was resisting her efforts to get him into his pajamas.

"With the Am Kedoshim Society?"

"Yes, darling. And with friends."

"So many meetings?"

"There is a lot to talk about."

"What?"

"David, you have homework?"

"Yes, Mama."

"Take your books into the kitchen and sit down and do your work. I want to put your brother to sleep."

"No!" my brother shouted. "Don't want to sleep!"

"You don't know how lucky you are that you can get a good night's sleep," my mother said.

She raised the side of the crib. He stood up, his stocky figure looking bulky and shapeless in his heavy winter pajamas.

"Lie down and go to sleep," my mother said.

"Sleep in Davey's bed," my brother said. "Big bed! Big bed!"

My mother passed her hand wearily over her eyes. I took up my books and went from the room.

In the kitchen, I sat at the table and did my writing assignments and then read from a new book my Hebrew teacher had given me. A gusting wind rattled the panes in the window over the sink. Weeks ago there had been a gale. The rain had fallen in a slant; for a while it blew sideways through the street. The wind had stripped the leaves from the trees. The wet, suddenly naked branches had looked peculiarly stunted and helpless. Darkness had begun to descend earlier upon the gray face of each day. Now the night pressed solidly against the window; I almost had the feeling the glass would crack and break and the darkness would come flooding into the apartment. Off in the distance I heard the clang and clatter of a trolley car.

Later that winter my mother began to accompany my father. They would go out two or three times a week. She would clean up quickly after supper and put Alex to bed. My father would sit in the living room, reading his newspaper. Often the canary would sing but he did not seem to hear it. Sometimes he put the newspaper down and sat with his hands dangling loosely between his thighs, his eyes fixed on the floor. He seemed weary and bewildered.

There would be a ring at the door and I would go to open it and Saul would be standing there with his books.

My parents would put on their hats and coats and leave.

Sometimes if it rained heavily during supper my mother would say, "Max, you should call Nathan and ask him to bring the machine."

My father would look at the window.

"It's a flood, Max."

He would go into the living room and talk quietly into the

telephone. Then he would return to the kitchen and finish his food in silence.

One night during a snowstorm, I said to him, "Are you and Mama going out tonight, Papa?"

He looked up from his food, which he had been eating listlessly. "Yes," he said.

"It's snowing, Papa."

"Nathan should bring the machine," my mother said from the stove.

"The machine will not run in this snow."

"Papa?"

He had developed the habit in recent weeks of lowering his head and looking at people out of the tops of his eyes. It seemed to me the lines in the corners of his eyes and along his forehead had deepened. The scar was starkly white in the stubble on his face. He peered at me now and was still.

"Why are there so many meetings, Papa? There never used to be so many meetings."

"There were never so many problems," he said.

"What problems, Papa?"

He seemed not to have heard me. "We have to sit and think together. We have to work together. Then we will see results. When we work together there is nothing we cannot do."

"Papa?"

"It is a catastrophe. But it can be solved with hard work and thinking together. Our job is to solve it." He looked away from me and down at the food on his plate. My mother came over from the stove and slipped soundlessly into her seat. In his high chair, Alex was chewing steadily at the soggy piece of rye bread he held in his stubby fingers. "Not for one second do I think we cannot do this job," my father went on, staring at his food. "But we will have to work hard. Isn't that right, Ruth?"

"Yes," my mother said in a very low voice.

He sat very still, staring at his food.

"Papa?"

He did not look at me.

"What does catastrophe mean?"

He turned his head and gave me a sudden sharp look. There was a strange glitter in his dark eyes.

"A catastrophe?" he said. He knitted his brows and rubbed the heel of his palm against the side of his face with the scar. "A catastrophe is a big accident. A terrible accident. It is a way God has of laughing at us. We make plans and God all of a sudden—"

"Max," my mother broke in. Then she said something briefly in Polish.

My father looked at his food and was quiet. After a moment, he said, "But we will make new plans. Won't we, Ruth?"

"Yes, Max."

"The goyim are ruining everything. But we will defeat them. When is the meeting, Ruth?"

"The same time as always. Half past seven."

"The stinking goyim. Who would ever have believed there could be such gangsterism in Wall Street? Is it still snowing, Ruth?"

"Yes."

"We will go anyway."

The snow stopped falling shortly after supper and Saul came and they went out.

Alex was asleep. I sat with Saul at the kitchen table. Outside the bare winter trees creaked in the icy black air. The kitchen window rattled. Saul sat bent over his books, writing intently. He was left-handed and he wrote with the pencil held above his writing rather than below it, the curve of his wrist lying across the head of his notebook. He used a fountain pen and was writing very quickly in Hebrew, the scratching sounds quite loud in the stillness of the apartment. The lights were out in all the rooms save the kitchen. We had never concerned ourselves with electricity before this winter. Now my mother insisted that lights be turned off whenever we left a room. We were eating less meat. My father had not yet bought himself a new winter suit. My winter jacket was tight; my thin wrists stuck out of the sleeves. But it would have to be worn one more winter. "We have enough put away for a long time, Ruth," I had heard my father say one night. "But what if your parents come? And my parents? What then? We have to be careful, Ruth. I am not becoming a frightened miser all of a sudden. But we must be careful." I did not understand what was happening; neither did Saul. It had to do with money, he had told me once.

"We have no more money?" I had asked, vaguely frightened, though I could not understand the reason for my fear.

"We have money."

"Then what?"

"Other people lost money."

"People in the Am Kedoshim Society?"

"Yes."

"Papa and Mama are helping them?"

"They all meet to see what they can do."

"Do your father and mother meet too?"

"Of course."

"Did your father lose all his money, Saul?"

"No. He listened to your father. He didn't lose much."

"I don't understand. How did people lose their money?"

"I don't understand either," he said.

"All of a sudden? Just like that they lost their money?"

"All of a sudden," he said.

All of a sudden, I had thought. Like an accident. All of a sudden. I could not understand it. But it frightened me and made darker the dark cold nights of that year.

Often Saul would help me with my reading. I was reading Hebrew on a third-grade level and English on a second-grade level. My teachers did not seem to know what to do with me in the classroom. Sometimes they asked me to help a faltering student. Most of the time they left me to my daydreams. In a reshuffling of seats that had taken place in the middle of December when two boys had suddenly left the school, I was given a seat in the third row near a window. It was easy to daydream near a window.

When I was done with my homework, I would have a glass of milk and go to bed. Once asleep, Alex slept deeply. We could turn on my light. Lying in bed, I would ask Saul for a story.

"Tell me the Golem of Prague story, Saul."

"Again?"

"I like it, Saul."

And he would tell it to me. And, later, I would lie awake in the dark and see the story inside my eyes. He told it to me again the night of the snowstorm. It was easy to envision the monstrous clay figure moving through the winter night looking for goyim who wanted to hurt Jews. But what had my father meant about goyim ruining everything? Had only Jews lost money? Had there been a pogrom somewhere? They would not talk to me about it.

"Your job is to study!" my father had once shouted in response to my questions. "Never mind money. You study. I will worry about money."

"Max, Max," my mother had soothed.

"Enough questions about money!" he had shouted. "Enough!"

I did not ask him again about money. I had the feeling the questions wounded him terribly.

I lay awake in the winter night and listened to the wind blow the powdery fallen snow against my window. The snow made little ticking noises like a sword tapping softly on glass. From the kitchen came the sound of Saul's thin voice as he intoned aloud the notes of the Torah reading he had been taught by Mr. Bader.

"It's called trup," he had said earlier that night.

"What is?" I asked.

"These notes on top of and under the words in the Bible."

"Really?" I was not very interested.

But he was eager to share the knowledge acquired by him during the weeks he had studied with Mr. Bader, who was now away somewhere on another trip to Europe. On this trip he was traveling with his wife.

"This is called a mahapach and this is a pashto," Saul had said. "It goes like this." And he had chanted the notes. "If you learn these notes by heart, you can read any part of the Torah by yourself without help. But you also have to know the grammar of the Torah."

His eyes gleamed with eagerness. They had once had that same eagerness when we had walked through the zoo and he had told me stories about Noah and the animals in the ark. We had not been to the zoo together since school had begun.

"I'm going to know the whole Torah by heart," he said.

I stared at him in awe. "How are you going to do that, Saul?"

"By reading it every Shabbos in the synagogue. You have to go over it again and again to prepare for the reading, and that way you learn it by heart. My father says it's the best way."

It seemed to me an incredible task. To know the entire Chumash, all the Five Books of Moses, the most sacred books, to know them by heart! My estimate of Saul's journeys to Mr. Bader rose.

I lay in my bed and listened to his voice float through the darkness of the apartment to my room. I could see him sitting in the kitchen with the large tikkun open in front of him, the double-columned pages of dark print lying like a challenge on the table. He would read a verse in the column of normal type, chanting it loudly. He would chant it again. I would hear a pause. Then he would repeat the verse, often haltingly, and I knew he was reading it from the second column, the one which duplicated exactly the scribal writing found in the actual Torah scroll itself, which was read on Shabbat and holidays and which was without vowels, punctuation, or musical notations. I did not envy him his leaps from the first column to the second. The narrow ribbon of white space that separated those columns in the tikkun felt to me like the yawning gaps between the apartment houses on our street.

A trolley went by on the boulevard, its wheels muffled by the snow. I knew I would not sleep until my parents returned home. They never stayed out too late; Saul had to be back home by nine thirty or ten o'clock. My father would walk him home through the cold streets.

"I'm doing it for you, Davey," Saul had said to me one night when we were together in the kitchen.

I had nodded my head in gratitude.

"It's hard for me. Why don't you let your mother get a woman or someone you like?"

"I don't want to be here with a stranger. I'm afraid, Saul. I can't be here with anyone else. I don't—"

"Take it easy, Davey. All right. I'm here."

But I needed to know my parents were back before I could lie at ease in my bed.

I listened to Saul a while longer, then slipped from my bed and padded on bare feet to the window. My brother's crib was to the right of the window. He lay on his back beneath his blanket, snoring softly.

Beneath the glow of the lamps, the snow seemed to be burning with an eerie blue-white flame. The trees, laden with snow, but with trunks and the undersides of heavy branches stark black against the smooth mantle of blue-white snow that lay upon the street, appeared hoary and vaguely grotesque as they jerked and swayed in the wind. I looked up and down the street. It was deserted. I put my forehead to the window and felt the sting of its icy touch. Saul's voice droned on from the kitchen. He read, repeated, paused, read again, hesitantly. Then he stopped and reread the entire passage he had tried to commit to memory. He paused often, repeated a passage numerous times, then went on. I kept hearing the name Noah. But I could not understand what he was reading. I returned to my bed and lay very still, listening.

My parents came back a while later and my father walked

Saul home. When he returned, they sat in the kitchen and listened to the radio. They listened to the radio a lot now. They had ceased entirely to talk about their Polish past.

The snow froze to ice on the street and the ice turned black with the grime of the city. Cinders pockmarked the sidewalk. Cars went by slowly, tire chains rattling. Sometimes in the night I would wake to the sound of a whining tire spinning helplessly in fresh-fallen snow. It snowed often that winter. The maples drooped with snow; peering at them from my window, I often had the feeling they were turning into willows.

Sometimes in the evening people came to the house, friends from the synagogue and the Am Kedoshim Society, and my aunt and uncle—anywhere from ten to thirty to forty of them at one time. They sat in the living room talking and I lay in my bed listening. I heard words in Yiddish and English that I did not understand. How could it happen? someone would say. Who could have foreseen it? There were those who predicted it, someone else would say. No one listened. What good is it to complain? my father would say. We have to think what to do. Tell us, they would say. What should we do? It's lost, a despairing voice would say. There is nothing to be done. That is not a helpful attitude, my aunt would say. But it's the truth, the despairing voice would say. There is nothing to be done. Nonsense, my father would say. We must stay together and we will plan what to do. They would talk back and forth in low voices. Sometimes a voice would suddenly be raised in anger. Once I heard a man cry out, "How long can I go on, Max? They are tearing pieces from me!" And they quieted and soothed him, and I heard my mother say she would bring him a glass of tea. Often there were sudden silences, dense chasms in the uneven contour of their speech, and I imagined I could hear the darkness of the night seeping into the room through the minute crevices in our windows. I thought often of the picnic in the clearing. When had that been? Before the summer? I could barely remember. I thought of the way my father had sounded the shofar on Rosh Hashanah, had prayed the Afternoon Service on Yom Kippur, had danced with the Torah on Simchat Torah. The joy of his friends, the ringing happiness that had filled the little synagogue. Now they sat as if it were the start of a war and they needed to make plans to flee from the Angel of Death. Had they met this way in Lemberg during the big war? I listened and was very tired and wished I could sleep. But sleep remained a cool and distant stranger. I wondered if there were some kind of special prayer one could offer for sleep. Mrs. Horowitz would have known. I stayed awake late into the nights, and slept and daydreamed in my classes during the days. My teachers left me alone.

All through the winter and into the spring those meetings continued. They brought strange dread into the house. With the coming of the warm weather, I began to have the feeling that my father and his friends were having all those meetings not so much for the purpose of making plans as for the simple need to be together and support one another, to drink glasses of tea in each other's homes, to offer one another words of encouragement, to keep away despair. I did not know what they feared, and I was afraid to ask. I lay awake in the night and listened to the meetings, or to Saul practicing his Torah reading, or to my parents talking very quietly in the kitchen and then listening to the radio—I lay awake and felt alone and filled with dread.

I was ill often in the spring, once with a raging fever that kept me in bed more than ten days. They met at our apartment during that time. One night I heard their voices distorted through fever; they seemed the cries of dark and fearful birds. The pain in my face and forehead was almost unendurable. The light stung my eyes. I slid down beneath my sheet and blanket. In the living room I heard my uncle's voice raised in a hoarse shout. There were loud, angry responses. I began to cry. The voices continued, subdued once again, a rushing, murmuring, voice-interrupting-voice multiple conversation of frightened people. I lay beneath my sheet and blanket, crying silently in pain and fever, waiting for the darkness to invade my impregnable sheet world.

It seemed to be everywhere, that darkness; and it grew darker still with the passing weeks. I was ill for the first two days of Passover. But I was in our synagogue for the final two days of the festival and it seemed a weary congregation. There were many empty seats. There was no picnic in the pine wood that June. On the final day of school I was told by my teachers that it had been decided to skip me an entire year. In September I would begin third grade.

I went gratefully to our cottage that summer and had a

restful time rowing and swimming and lying in the sun. My
father and uncle were rarely with us the first three weeks.
They remained in the city and came up for the weekends.

Then in August, my father abruptly stopped going to the
city. "There is nothing happening in the city," I heard him
tell my mother early one morning in the last week of July.
"The city is like a cemetery. Its dead sell apples instead of
lying still. It depresses me. Who needs a real estate broker
now? I will stay here for August."

He would wake late and come out of the cottage unshaven
and stare across the beach at the sun on the lake. He would
sit hunched forward on a wicker chair in the shade of the elm
and stare down at the grass, his veined muscular arms dangling loosely between his thighs. He grew silent. I feared going
near him. His dark eyes burned fiercely and his square bony
face seemed a block of carved stone. Long into the nights I
would hear my mother talking to him, softly, imploringly. It
seemed she did most of the talking now; he was silent.

One Shabbat afternoon he went into the forest and was
gone so long that my mother grew afraid. She was about to
ask my uncle to search for him when he emerged from its
bluish depths and, without a word, went into the cottage. I
saw my aunt and uncle look at each other forlornly. My
mother went inside and came back out a few moments later
and sat down in the wicker chair. She tried reading one of
the German storybooks she had brought with her that summer, but in the end she put it aside and sat gazing at the
afternoon sun on the lake. After a while she rose and returned
to the cottage and did not come out until it was time to call
Alex and me in for supper.

Far into the night my mother and father and aunt and
uncle sat on our screened-in front porch and talked. I lay
awake and listened but they were speaking in such subdued
tones that I could make out nothing of what they were saying.
On occasion one of their voices would rise above the surface
of their conversation, but the others would immediately make
mention of the children, and the loud voice would sink into a
level of sound inaudible to my ears. I was at my window when
they left and I saw my uncle embrace my father. He held him
in the embrace for what seemed to me to be a very long time
while my mother and aunt looked on and, finally, looked
away. Then my aunt and uncle went to their cottage and my
parents went to bed.

But they did not sleep. Through the darkness and the thin

wall that separated our bedrooms, I heard whispers and my
mother's soothing words and my father's strained, subdued
voice. "I cannot understand it, Ruth. There is nothing we can
do. I have never been in a situation like this before. In Lemberg we could do something and see results. Why did I bring
them here?"

"You did nothing wrong, Max. You advised them. That
was all you did."

"But I told them it would be better here. Do you see how
some of them look at me? I feel like a criminal."

"It isn't only here, Max. It's the whole world. Is it better
where they were?"

"But I brought them *here*, Ruth. I worked like a slave—to
bring them *here*. Now it is a catastrophe and nothing we can
do will help. God in heaven, what have I done to my friends?"

And there were more whispers and it all went on a long
time until I fell asleep numb with weariness and dread.

My father did not go horseback riding that summer, though
he took us often to the movies. Sometimes he went to the
movies alone, and I knew it was a war film. We returned to
the city in the first week of September and my father and
uncle sold the cottages and we never saw them again.

The meetings continued, less frequently now but with
greater rancor than before. Often I heard the gentle voice of
my uncle raised in defense of my father. Who hadn't put
money into the market? he would shout. Who hadn't invested
in real estate? They were lucky he had pulled out as much as
he had or there would be no money now to maintain the
cemetery, to keep up the death benefits, to maintain the sick
fund. No, there was no money for travel loans to get families
from Europe to America. Not now. Not until times were
better. But what were they complaining about? Why were
they shouting at Max? Didn't they read the newspapers? People were jumping out of windows. At least there was still
enough money in the treasury to keep the Am Kedoshim
Society from bankruptcy.

I would lie in my bed and listen to his voice and imagine
his gentle face red with anger, his eyes flaring behind their
lenses, and I would remember how he had once said to me,
"What should we have done, David? Sometimes you have to
smash." His voice had been soft then, but I thought I could
remember some of the anger that had been embedded within

it. His eyes had flashed for the briefest of seconds; the face had gone rigid. It was strange how a gentle person could turn so suddenly raging.

There were more empty seats in the synagogue now; people were moving from the neighborhood. Often on my way to meet Saul on the boulevard where we waited for our trolley car, I would see moving vans parked on the curb and brawny men carrying furniture out of houses.

"Why are so many people moving, Saul?" I asked him one morning when we had taken seats in the trolley car.

"They can't pay the high rent. They move to a less expensive neighborhood."

"Will we have to move, Saul?"

"No, we won't have to move, Davey."

"What does the word suicide mean, Saul?"

"Where did you see that?"

"Yesterday in a newspaper in Mr. Steinberg's candy store." He explained it to me.

I sat in the clattering car and stared at him. "Because they don't have money?" I heard myself say.

He nodded. His hair had gone uncut a long time. Brown strands curled out from beneath his winter cap and lay across his narrow forehead. A dark blur clouded his blue eyes as if water had been splashed upon his glasses. For a moment I wondered if he knew of someone in the Am Kedoshim Society who had done that. I was too frightened to ask him.

"I don't understand it," I said. "People kill themselves because of that?"

"Without money you can't live," Saul said. He hunched his thin shoulders and pulled his heavy jacket more tightly around him. It was cold in the trolley car. People rode in silence, reading newspapers or staring at the slatted floor or out the windows at the gray morning. I gazed out my window a moment, then opened my Chumash and reviewed some passages on which we were to be tested that morning. I closed the Chumash and went over the passages again inside my eyes. Then I sat looking out the window.

I counted four moving vans that morning parked along the streets, their backs open like black mouths. One morning in January, as the trolley car turned into the street beyond the small park, I saw men moving furniture onto the sidewalk and leaving it there. I did not see any moving van. The next day, Yaakov Bader came over to me during the mid-morning recess and said, "Come on and have a game with us, Davey."

I shrugged and continued looking through the chain-link fence at the street.

"Come on, Davey. My uncle told me to make sure and take good care of you. I don't want my uncle to be angry at me."

I turned to him. A red wool cap framed his fair-skinned features which were flushed pink by the cold.

"The guys want you to play with us," he said. "Come on." His breath vaporized as he spoke. Slate-gray clouds covered the sky. The air burned with cold.

He led me to a sheltered corner of the yard where, in a basement doorway beneath the outdoor fire stairs, I joined a game of baseball cards. The boys played with their gloves off. They blew into their hands and stamped their feet. I played seriously against the background noise of the recess and lost all my cards.

"Boy, Davey, you may be a big brain, but you're lousy at this. Look at all these Babe Ruths," one of them said.

"You ought to take your gloves off when you play, Davey," another said.

"It hurts my fingers to do that."

"Look at these hands," a third said. He thrust a pair of chapped and reddened hands in front of my eyes. "My mother will kill me. What did I spend money on gloves for if you don't wear them? She'll absolutely kill me. How can you play with gloves on, Davey?"

I shrugged and moved away from them. Yaakov Bader walked with me through the noisy yard back to the chain-link fence.

"They were only kidding you, Davey. Don't be so serious."

We looked out at the deserted winter street.

"Is your uncle still in Europe?" I asked.

"He'll be there until the summer."

"What does he do?"

"He's living in Switzerland this year."

"Is he still in business?"

"Yes."

"So many people went out of business. My father doesn't have much business now. He's home a lot."

We were quiet, staring through the fence at the street.

"And so many people are moving. One of the boys in my house moved the other day. Monday, I think it was. Joey Younger. He's in second grade. Do you know him?"

He shook his head.

"I never liked him too much. But I was sorry he had to move."

"Two of my friends moved last month."

"It's a scary feeling. It gives me bad dreams sometimes."

He nodded.

"You remember what we learned the other day in Chumash? Where Abraham says to God, when he's talking about Sodom and Amorrah, 'Will You destroy the good people and the evil people?' Doesn't it look like it makes no difference now if a person is good or bad? God is just destroying everyone."

"Hey, Davey," he murmured, stiffening and looking quickly about. "Don't talk like that."

"I have that feeling, Yaakov. It's a funny feeling. I don't understand it. What difference does it make if you're good or bad? Can you explain it to me?"

How can it make a difference? I thought. Was that old lady evil, the one Saul and I had seen sitting in a chair on the sidewalk yesterday afternoon surrounded by her furniture? I had dreamed about her. When the trolley car took me and Saul past her house again this morning, she was gone. Evil. It had a queer sound to it in English. It seemed a wet slimy word. The Hebrew word was harsher. *Rasha*. An evil man. *Rishus*. Evil. How could it possibly make a difference? I kept asking myself. Later, in class, I raised my hand and said, "I think there's something not clear in verse twenty-two." My anger did not come through in my words.

The teacher, a young man with a smooth-shaven face and rimless glasses, peered at me from across his desk and said, "Yes? What is not clear?"

"The verse says 'Abraham still stood before God.' But it was God who came to Abraham. The verse should have said, 'God still stood before Abraham.'"

The teacher looked down at his Chumash for a moment, then looked up, cleared his throat softly, and said, "Are you able to read Rashi, David?"

I shook my head. I had taught myself the letters of the strangely shaped Hebrew alphabet in which the commentary by Rashi was printed in the lower half of our Bible texts. But I was not yet able to read the commentary with ease.

"Rashi asks your question. He tells us that Torah should indeed have said, 'But God still stood before Abraham.'"

She had worn an old brown coat and a green scarf over her head and had placed her hands beneath her armpits for warmth. Stand before her and keep her warm, I thought, feeling the rage. How long had she sat in the cold? What happens to you when they put you out like that on the sidewalk?

"No, she will not freeze to death," my mother had said. "Friends or neighbors will take her in. Relatives will come for her."

"She was an old lady, Mama. What is God doing to the world? He's making accidents everywhere."

"Please do not talk that way, David," she had said fearfully. "A Jew must have faith in God."

Everywhere people were moving. In the darkness at night I imagined I could hear the hum and clatter of wheels and the tremor of the earth. Even the earth itself was moving; deep fissures appeared in it in my dreams.

"But the Rabbis did not want it to appear as if God could really have been standing, as it were, before Abraham," said the teacher, "and so the text was changed to what we have now. It is called a tikkun soferim, David. A scribal emendation." He hesitated, then cleared his throat. "All right, David? Do you understand?"

I did not understand. But I nodded my head anyway. I was no longer interested in the question.

I went home in the snow with Saul and was ill in bed for five days. Early in the morning of the second day a rumbling noise woke me from a nightmare-choked sleep and I went to my window. A moving van stood at the curb in front of our house. I turned cold with dread. Two heavyset men got out, trudged through the remnants of the snow, and opened the back gate of the van. Then they went into the house. I looked around wildly. My brother was asleep. The apartment was still. A few minutes later Tony Savanola came out of the house carrying his schoolbag. He stood near the maple and looked at the long black moving van. His shoulders were bowed. Suddenly I had my window open and I was screaming, "Tony! Hey, Tony! Are you moving, Tony?" I saw him turn, his eyes wide. Staring up at me through the winter branches of the maple, he nodded his head and rubbed gloved knuckles into his eyes. I leaned further out the window and the freezing air stung my face and whipped through my pajamas. "It's not fair you should be moving, Tony. That Eddie, he should be moving. I'm sorry, Tony. I'm sorry." I was shouting but I no longer knew what I was saying. I heard a shout behind me. It was my mother's voice. She was pushing me away from the

window. I fought her and kept shouting at Tony. My mother's
face was dead white. Then my father was in the room and
the window was slid shut and I was in bed beneath my covers
shivering not from cold but from a dark horror that had no
face to it but pierced with a poisoned sword good people and
evil people alike. I stared at the glinting tip of the sword and
did not know what to do. After a moment I slid deep beneath
my covers and lay very still, dimly aware that in the dark
world outside my brother had wakened and was crying. I
closed my eyes and did not move and listened to my brother
crying. Then my mother took him out and the room was
silent. In the silence I thought I could hear furniture being
moved and the voice of Mrs. Savanola somewhere in our
apartment. Then she was inside my room and I came out
from beneath my covers and looked at the fat and round
woman dark with sadness now. Tony was with her. They
were saying goodbye. Good luck. You be a good boy to your
mama. She a very good mama. And you listen to your papa.
He a good honest man. Goodbye, Tony, I heard myself say
hoarsely. I'm sorry. I'm sorry. Hey, he said. Hey. Don't get
excited, Davey. You'll get more sick. We played some nice
games, Davey. I'm sorry that crazy Eddie broke it all up.
Goodbye, Davey. Goodbye. I lay beneath my covers and
looked up at my sheet and brushed my lips across its smooth
surface. We have to do something, I thought. Something.
Something.

I was able to go to our little synagogue that Shabbat. My
father read slowly from the Torah scroll, his voice peculiarly
tremulous. He had lost some weight. There were vague hollows now in his cheeks. The scar curved faintly inward within
the darkness of his Shabbat stubble.

There were fewer people every month in our synagogue
now. On the first day of Passover it was almost filled again,
for the weather was lovely and people walked long distances
to be together once more; no one in our group violated the
prohibition against riding on Shabbat or festivals. But that
Rosh Hashanah the little synagogue had many empty seats.
My uncle led the Morning Service. Mr. Bader, back from
Europe, read the Torah. My father sounded the shofar, the
strident blasts rasping loudly through the small room. On the
second day of Rosh Hashanah he faltered over the teruah
blast during the repetition of the Silent Devotion. He stood
at the podium in the white knee-length cotton garment that he
wore over his dark suit and in his tall white skullcap and tried

to complete the series of staccato blasts from the ram's horn, and for the third time the attempt ended in a hoarse spitting wheeze before he was halfway done. His face was dark red; the veins and muscles bulged in his neck. The congregants were very still. He had never had any difficulty sounding the shofar before. He waited a moment, cleared the spittle from the shofar by blowing into it, then tried once again and was able to complete the blast. The congregants stirred with relief and the service continued. My father came back to his seat next to me and out of the corner of my eye I could see his flushed face and the faint trembling of his hands. I turned my head away and gazed out the window at the Catholic church. It seemed to me that in recent weeks its attendance too had decreased. Small sparse groups would straggle from it now rather than the brisk and lively crowds I had once seen. Sometimes I saw Eddie Kulanski and his parents come out of the church. They would go slowly past the statue of the woman in flowing robes and she would gaze down at them, her arms outstretched. They rarely looked at her. I would see Eddie Kulanski and think about Tony Savanola and wonder where he was. People came and went in your life and you never knew what happened to them. And sometimes I found myself thinking too of Mrs. Horowitz and her dog.

At the end of the Afternoon Service that day my father walked home from the synagogue in a dark silence.

I raised my hand in class that week and said to my teacher, "I don't understand something in verse one."

The teacher was a short, pudgy middle-aged man with a smooth-shaven, fleshy face, cold gray eyes, and a sharp tongue. We were in the second chapter of Exodus. He looked up from his Bible text.

"Yes? You waited until the fourth verse before you realized you did not understand the first verse? Where's the brain all your previous teachers told me you have? What don't you understand?"

"It says in the first verse that a man from the house of Levi married a daughter of Levi."

"Yes, it says that."

"And in the next verse it says she had a baby."

Some of the boys turned their heads and looked at me. The teacher sat behind his desk and said nothing.

"In verse four it says that his sister watched him when he was in the river. But if he was the first child born how did he have a sister?"

Yaakov Bader, who sat in the front row, glanced down at his Chumash, then looked back at me in astonishment.

"Moses was not the first child," said the teacher.

"But it says in the verse—"

"They were married before but they separated because of the decree of Pharaoh. Then he took her back as his wife and Moses was born."

"Where does it say that?"

"Can you read the commentary of Rashi?"

I shook my head. I could read the letters and words now but the smallness of the print hurt my eyes and set the letters swimming after a few minutes.

"You will find it in Rashi."

I wondered how Rashi had discovered an important bit of information like that when it was not even written in the Torah.

A few minutes later I raised my hand again. I did not understand verse five, I said.

"Yes?" asked the teacher. "What don't you understand?"

"The verse says, 'And the daughter of Pharaoh came down to bathe at the river.' It should really have said, 'And the daughter of Pharaoh came down to the river to bathe.'"

He stared at me. A block away an elevated train rumbled by on the trestle. We could hear it distinctly through the closed window of our room. One of the students coughed.

"You will find your question in Rashi," said the teacher finally. "You are sure you cannot read Rashi?"

I shook my head.

"Rashi tells us to turn around the verse and explain it as follows: 'And the daughter of Pharaoh came to the river to bathe in it.'"

"Turn around?" I heard myself say. "Rashi means to change around the words?"

"Rashi means exactly what Rashi says. To turn it around." He used the word *sorais*, "transpose." "It is written one way, but when we explain it we turn around the verse." He paused ominously. "Is it clear to you?"

I told him it was clear to me. Across the street, the public school mid-morning recess was beginning. Waves of students rolled onto the vast yard through the outside double doors of the building. I saw a touch football game form up. Some handball games had already begun, one of them with a small black ball. It was a new flood and no one seemed to know it. Everything was about to be swept away and no one believed it. Couldn't they feel the earth trembling and the ground moving? I looked away from the window and closed my eyes and immediately saw my father seated at the kitchen table, unshaven in a collarless shirt. "What is there to go to, Ruth? The office is a tomb."

"Go anyway, Max."

"Go anyway, go anyway. You want me out of the house? Is that what you want?"

"Max."

"I am in your way? What is it? To David you would also have spoken like this?"

"Max, listen to what you are saying. Please."

"I will go. Of course I will go. But it is like a tomb in that office now."

And he had sat staring down at the kitchen table, his eyes puffy with lack of sleep, his shoulders sagging. He had still been sitting like that when I left for school.

I opened my eyes. The teacher was explaining the verse that told of Moses being pulled from the river. I could not understand what Rashi had meant by transpose the verse. How can you change the order of words in a verse in the Torah?

My father came home with a bad cold one day in late December and two days later it became bronchitis. I could never remember his being ill before. Now he was in bed with a cough that racked his body. He was out of bed in two weeks and returned to his office. But he would come home in the early afternoon now and I would find him in the apartment when I came back from school. He sat around the house in his maroon robe and tall black skullcap, reading the newspaper or staring down at the floor. One evening he was in the living room when the canary began to sing. He looked up from his paper, startled. Then he rose and went into the kitchen. A moment later I heard the smooth voice of a news announcer. The canary continued to sing, an eerie counterpoint to what was being said on the radio.

I said to my mother that night when she came into my room, "Is Papa all right?"

"No. He is unhappy because business is very bad. But we will all help him. He helped others, now others will help him."

"I hate to see Papa this way."

"Yes," she murmured. "It's not a pleasant thing to see."

"My nose hurts a little, Mama."

"Go to sleep," she said. "And please try not to get sick, David. I have enough with your father on my hands."

But two days later I came home from school with a very high fever. My mother called Dr. Weidman. He sat on the edge of my bed, looking pink and cheerful, tapped my chest and back, listened to my lungs, and put some kind of instrument with a light into my nostrils. He patted my shoulder and went out of the room with my mother. I lay very still in my bed and settled into my familiar world of pain and fever. I almost welcomed that now. Outside it was dark and cold and the Angel of Death thrust about mercilessly and his huge wings beat the air and sent icy gusts through the streets. I closed my eyes. A moment later I sensed someone entering my room and coming slowly toward me and I opened my eyes and it was my father. He stood for a long moment near my bed and gazed down at me. He had on his maroon robe and tall black skullcap.

"Papa."

He said nothing. His eyes were dark.

"I'm sick again, Papa. I'm sorry to be sick again now. I tried to stay well."

He sat down slowly at the edge of my bed. I felt the mattress tip sideways as his full weight settled into it.

"No one blames you for being sick, David. Not for a minute should you ever think we blame you for that."

"Are you still sick, Papa?"

He was silent a moment. "The bronchitis is gone," he said finally.

"Is it like Lemberg now in the war?" I said, and I did not know why I had said it; I had not even thought to say it.

"What?" he said.

"Is it like everything moving and changing every day and we can't stop and fix anything and keep it from going away from us?"

He was staring at me.

"I hate it, Papa. There are so many dead people everywhere. How can God do such a thing? I see them from the trolley, Papa. Dead people on the street corners. Don't become a dead person, Papa."

"What are you saying, David? What do you mean?"

I saw my mother and Dr. Weidman, standing now in the doorway to my room.

"It's in Rashi, Papa. I saw it in Rashi."

"What Rashi? What are you talking about? You are study-ing Rashi?"

"I taught it to myself, Papa. But it hurts my eyes to read the small letters. Rashi says Dathan and Abiram didn't really die but they became poor and a poor man is just like a dead person. I read it, Papa." I wished I could stop talking. It was the fever. I could not control my tongue. "Rashi says things I don't understand sometimes, Papa. I feel angry at Rashi sometimes. The teacher says Rashi is holy, but I feel angry at him. He puts things into the Torah which aren't there. But why does it have to be Lemberg all over again here, Papa? Wasn't it enough once?"

My voice broke. In his bed, Alex stirred, sighed, turned over, and was quiet. My father bent toward me and kissed my forehead. He smelled strongly of coffee. "My Rashi-reader," he murmured. "And I did not even know. You taught yourself Rashi?"

My mother came over to the bed. "You should rest now, David. I will bring you medicine in a little while."

"You'll be back in school in a few days, David," said Dr. Weidman cheerfully.

"Is it the same black year?" my father asked him.

Dr. Weidman nodded.

They went from the room. I slid beneath my covers. The dead won't get me here, I thought.

Later that night I thought I heard the voices of my aunt and uncle in the living room. Then they stood around my bed, the four of them, but I would not open my eyes.

"The child is burning with fever," I heard my aunt say.

"It's like looking at David," my uncle said.

"Yes," my mother said. "Yes."

"I told you about Rashi?" said my father.

"You told me," my uncle said.

"I have never seen him so hot," said my aunt.

"How many times have you seen him sick?" asked my mother. "In a few days he will be in school."

"The nose will grow crooked from now on?" asked my uncle.

"Yes."

"I see it already," said my aunt.

"It is David," said my uncle. "It is like the resurrection of the dead."

That January my father gave up his real estate business and took a job in a wholesale stationery store run by one of the members of the Am Kedoshim Society. He would return home in the evenings exhausted. He left that job and went to work in a candy store in the West Bronx. He worked late into the nights. After a few weeks he took another job. He had many jobs in succession that year and I do not remember any of the others. Suddenly, in the summer, he was not working at all, though he would leave the house every morning searching for a job. There were no more meetings of the Am Kedoshim Society.

I spent the summer reading in my room and reveling in my newfound sight. A trip to an eye clinic, at the recommendation of Dr. Weidman, had solved my problem with the small letters of the commentary of Rashi. I wore steel-rimmed glasses now. I read in my room at night and in the sunlight outside the house during the day. And I watched my brother, whose wild wanderings through the street had become subject matter for the gossip of neighbors. There was the summer day he disappeared and the janitor found him in the basement playing with the valves of the furnace. He ran into the street after a ball and escaped the wheels of a car by inches. The old man with palsied hands was on his chair in the sunlight that day. There was a sudden shriek of brakes and the scream of a neighbor. The old man slid from his chair in a dead faint as my brother returned triumphantly to the sidewalk, his brown hair wild, his face beaming, for he had successfully retrieved his ball. He ran wild, he chased cats, he fought with boys his age, he raced about on my old tricycle as if propelled by an engine, he was in constant motion. He seemed immune to accidents. He reminded me of Joey Younger.

One afternoon my mother brought a chair outside and sat in the sun near our stoop reading a book. After a while she put it down and closed her eyes. I saw a weight of sadness on her thin face. I had been sitting nearby with a Chumash. I moved my chair over to her and asked her to read to me from her book.

She opened her eyes and slowly shook her head.

"Are you too tired, Mama?"

"The book is in German, David."

"Please read it to me, Mama."

She gave me a queer startled look as if she had suddenly remembered a long forgotten event of the past.

"I will read a page or two, David. It makes no sense to read something you do not understand."

"And you'll show me the letters, Mama."

"Yes, David. I'll show you the letters."

She read to me often after that. I could not really understand most of what she was reading. But I liked listening to the words. It was always exciting to hear new words. It was what I had instead of good friends.

One morning as she sat reading to me in the sunlight I closed my eyes. And there, suddenly, was the cottage and the beach and the lake and my mother under the elm and my father galloping on the stallion through the tall grass. I sat in my chair listening to her and tasted the sharp, clear, tangible reality of our cottage summers. And when I opened my eyes and saw the street and the traffic and Alex playing on the sidewalk and my mother reading to me on her chair near the stoop, I had a sense of sudden cold overwhelming loss and dread. I never closed my eyes again when she read to me that summer. And one afternoon, when she dozed off while reading, I took the book from her hands and opened it and began, painstakingly, to read it to myself.

Early in September a moving van pulled up to our house and men began to empty out Eddie Kulanski's apartment. We heard them over our heads and saw them coming down the stairway with the barrels and the heavy furniture. The van had come very early in the morning. I saw my parents glance at each other each time the men went down the stairs. We could hear them giving one another instructions. After breakfast I came outside with my schoolbag and saw Eddie Kulanski standing on the sidewalk next to the van. He held his schoolbag in his hand. He was bareheaded. His light blond hair blew in the wind. I stood on the sidewalk and felt relieved that I would finally be rid of him. He was watching the two men load a small dresser and parts of a small bed into the back of the van. Then he must have sensed someone looking at him for he turned and saw me standing near the stoop. The pointed features, the small mouth, the sleepy gray eyes had not changed in the years since that summer of sunlight and nightmare. Now the eyes, always expressionless in the past, seemed glazed with sadness. His shoulders drooped. He looked away from me and watched the men place the last pieces of the bed inside the van.

Then I found myself standing beside him. "Hey, Eddie."

He looked at me again, vaguely startled.

"I'm sorry you have to move away. I know you don't like me because I'm a Jew and you think I killed Jesus and we have a strong organization that wants to run the world. That's all lies, Eddie. But even if you believe it, still I'm sorry you have to move and I hope you don't have a bad time in your new place. Goodbye, Eddie."

He looked at me and said nothing. His mouth opened slightly, but his eyes did not alter their sleepy gaze.

I walked quickly away, my heart beating loudly. I could feel him looking at me. I turned the corner and halfway along the block saw my cousin waiting for me at the trolley car stop.

That afternoon I sat in my English class and noticed a moving van come down Washington Avenue and stop in front of one of the five-story, red-brick apartment houses across the street from the public school. Two men climbed out. One of them went into the apartment house and came out a few minutes later with a short barrel-chested man in overalls. The three of them talked for a few minutes on the sidewalk. Then the man in the overalls did something to the entrance doors that left them permanently open. He went back inside and the two men began to move the furniture from the van into the apartment house. They were not nearly done unloading the van when the students from the Catholic school came up the block. I saw Eddie Kulanski go along Washington Avenue, cross the street in the middle of the block, stop near the van. He gazed at the men unloading the van. Then he went into the apartment house. At that point my English teacher, a small, intense, elderly woman with a rouged face and a brassy voice that reminded me of Mrs. Horowitz, inquired whether or not I believed the education I was receiving by staring out the window was superior to what I might be receiving by paying attention to her, and would I please be so kind as to give the class the benefit of my unusual mind and do the problem in fractions which she had written on the blackboard. I went up to the blackboard, did the problem, rubbed my hands together to rid my fingers of the gritty feel of the chalk, sat back down in my chair, and stared out the window at the moving van. Later that afternoon I climbed the stairs to my apartment, feeling light-headed with the knowledge that I would no longer be encountering Eddie Kulanski. I did not think I would have any difficulty at all forgetting Eddie Kulanski and the fear and shame in which I had lived for so many years.

Mr. Bader returned from Europe the week before Rosh Hashanah, looking tired and strangely grim. My father and uncle went to see him a number of times and he came over to our house once. On Yom Kippur I sat in our little synagogue during the Additional Service, listening to the mournful chanting of "Eleh Ezkerah," the liturgical poem that depicts the martyrdom of ten great sages at the hands of the Romans in punishment for their defiance of the ban against teaching the Torah. Mr. Bader was leading the service. He stood in front of the podium, his back to the congregation, chanting softly the words of the poem. I heard him chant, "And they took out Rabbi Akiva, who had expounded upon every letter of the Torah. And they tore his flesh with metal combs." Then he faltered and stopped. The thirty or so congregants in the room continued to the end of the poem, and waited. Mr. Bader stood very stiffly at the podium, his eyes closed. Earlier in the day, before the Memorial Service, he had stood facing the congregation and had told us of an occurrence he had witnessed in Europe. From the window of a passing cab he had seen, on a dark Berlin street, three uniformed Nazis beating a man with their fists and boots; the driver, fearful of involvement, had refused to stop, and the man, a Jew, was found dead the next morning in an alley near a bookstore. The incident typified for him, he had said, what was now beginning to take place in Germany. He had spoken in his usual calm and controlled manner. But now, suddenly, he could not continue the service. Sensing the cause of his inability to go on, the group of worshipers grew very still and waited. I had never before witnessed a display of deep feeling by Mr. Bader; he had always seemed to me the essence of controlled urbanity. But somewhere on a Berlin street a Jew he had not known had been beaten to death by followers of the man whose name I heard often in the news now, and the poem about the death of the Sages had brought the death of that lone Jew sharply to mind; and now Mr. Bader stood in silence before the podium, his shoulders slightly bowed, his craggy face reflecting his efforts to control his emotions. The silence inside the room deepened. To my left, Saul sat in his chair, looking fixedly at his prayer book. I could not see my father's face; he always covered his head with his tallit when he chanted this poem.

Mr. Bader straightened. His tall form seemed to expand as he took a deep breath. After a moment he resumed his chanting of the service.

I asked Saul later that day if he had been able to see Mr. Bader since his return from Europe.

"Twice," he said proudly.

Had he studied with Mr. Bader?

"Of course."

Had Mr. Bader said anything about his trip to Europe?

"We never talk about his work in Europe, Davey. That's not why I go to him."

"Are you still studying Torah reading? You know all of Noah by heart."

"We're studying grammar."

"All the time you just study grammar? What grammar are you going to have left to study in the yeshiva high school?"

"You don't study grammar in that high school, Davey. You study Talmud. That's what I really want to study. Talmud and midrash."

"Where did Mr. Bader learn grammar?"

He did not know. He had never thought to ask him.

"Is he really in the export-import business, Saul?"

He regarded me solemnly through his shell-rimmed glasses. "That's what everyone says he's in." Then he said, as if deliberately moving the conversation away from Mr. Bader, "How are your glasses, Davey? Do they fit all right?"

"They hurt my ears sometimes."

"Mine kill my ears. But if I loosen them they slide down my nose."

"I don't like wearing glasses."

"Can you see without them?"

"No. I see blurs and shadows and I get scared. I don't like it when I can't see things very sharp."

"Sharply," he said. "You could stand learning some English grammar, too."

"Saul, how many mistakes do you think you'll make when you read Noah on your bar mitzvah?"

"None," he said. "With God's help."

God helped. He made not a single error the Shabbat morning he stood before the podium in our little synagogue and read the Torah. He read slowly, with meticulous care. I followed him in my Chumash. The crowded synagogue—more than one hundred of the people who were there had walked on that brisk fall day from distant parts of the city out of regard for my uncle and my father—the synagogue was silent as his thin voice chanted the account of the Flood and its aftermath. My uncle and my father sat together to my right. They followed the reading intently. At the sides of the podium stood two congregants who also followed the reading. Next to Saul stood Mr. Bader, who had just been called to the Torah; and next to Mr. Bader stood Nathan Ackerman, ruddy-faced and mustached, who had been the previous person called to the Torah. Dwarfed by the adults around him, Saul's thin figure swayed slowly back and forth over the open scroll on the podium. He was reading the words of God that had been given to Moses on Mount Sinai: the Torah, the most sacred teaching, dictated by the Master of the Universe to His servant during the awesome time of the Revelation. The words had to be read without errors.

He read flawlessly. And when he was done a murmur of approval swept through the congregation. My uncle bowed his head for a moment; then I saw my father lean over and embrace him. Their faces tightly together as they held that embrace for a long moment while still in their chairs, they seemed startlingly alike, for now there were lines too on my uncle's features, and it seemed one face could with ease be substituted for the other. They seemed alike in their pride in my cousin's singular achievement and, later, they were alike in their laughing reaction to the bags of candy that suddenly came hurtling from the section of the room behind the gauzy curtain where the women prayed. Children scrambled for the candy. Saul ducked his head. There was laughter. Then my uncle went up to the podium to lead us in the Additional Service and Saul sat down next to me after receiving a kiss from my father.

His face was flushed. There were tiny beads of sweat on his upper lip, which was covered now by a soft down of pale blond hair. His forehead was damp. He glowed with pride.

I leaned over toward him. "Not one mistake, Saul!"

He gave me a warm, grateful smile.

He rose again from his seat before the Silent Devotion and stood behind the podium and spoke briefly to the congregation in Hebrew. He cited a verse from the Torah reading and used it to make a point about how important it was for mankind not to lose hope. He thanked his parents and relatives and friends. He was especially grateful, he said, to the members of the Am Kedoshim Society who had walked miles to share in his happiness. He thanked his parents again, and he took his seat.

After the service we all went to the social hall downstairs and there was wine and whiskey and cake and herring and fish and cookies and noodle pudding and a joyous tumult of voices and jostling and people greeting one another and words of congratulation for Saul and my aunt and uncle, who stood together near the long table, my uncle proud, my aunt cool and elegant and smiling, and Saul beginning to look a little tired.

I stood against a wall, chewing slowly on a piece of cake and thinking about the portion of the Torah Saul had read.

"How are you, David?" someone said and I looked up and it was Mr. Bader.

He shook my hand. His fingers were warm and strong.

"I think you are the only person I know who can daydream in the middle of a crowd like this. Aren't you having a good time?"

"Oh, yes. Yes."

"I am very proud of your Cousin Saul. He did splendidly. Were you able to follow the reading?"

"Yes."

"You were? Very good."

"He didn't even make any mistakes with the trup."

He looked at me.

"Not a single mistake," I said.

"You were able to follow the trup?"

"Yes."

"Well," he said, smiling. "Wasting time is not going to be one of your major sins."

"Mr. Bader?"

"Yes, David."

"Can I ask you something about the sidrah?"

"You may ask me anything you wish, David."

"First God tells Noah to take two animals of every kind into the ark; then God tells Noah to take seven of the clean and two of the unclean animals into the ark. Which did God tell Noah to do?"

He gazed at me and was silent for a long moment. All around me rose the happy voice of the celebration.

"Are you able to read Rashi?" Mr. Bader asked and I almost could not hear him for the noise. But I saw the word Rashi formed by his mouth and I knew what he had said.

I nodded. "I understand the Rashi. The seven clean animals were for the sacrifice after the Flood. But, Mr. Bader, when they go into the ark, it says Noah took in two of each animal. It doesn't say two and seven; it only says two. And Rashi doesn't say a word about that."

I stopped, feeling my face a little damp with exertion. I had had to speak very loudly to be heard above the voice of the crowd. I looked up at Mr. Bader and wondered if he had been able to hear me. He was so tall and the noise was so loud.

He had heard me. He bent down and patted my shoulder. "You asked a good question. You aren't satisfied with the answer given by Rashi?"

I shrugged.

"My shrugger," said Mr. Bader. "Between the way you hang your head and the way you shrug your shoulders you have developed a vocabulary that can be understood by half the population of the world. This is not the time to talk about the Flood. I promise I will talk to you about it another time. All right? If I don't congratulate your aunt she will become my enemy and I do not relish that prospect at all."

"Mr. Bader?"

"Yes, David."

"Will you be going back to Europe soon?"

"Yes."

"Are you really in the export-import business?"

He smiled.

"What do you export and import?"

I had the impression the query caught him somewhat by surprise for he mouthed a word that was almost entirely swallowed by the noise and which he clearly regarded as an indiscretion as soon as it had left his lips. I did not react to the word for I was not certain I had heard it correctly. Then I heard him say, "Jewelry and art objects and paintings. Things of that sort, David. I promise you we will talk another time about Noah and the Flood."

He patted my shoulder and moved away into the dense crowd. I stood against the wall wondering if the first word he had spoken and which had almost been lost in the tumult around us had been jewelry or Jews.

I did not see Mr. Bader again until the following spring.

It had something to do with banks and I did not understand it. Also there was the problem of who would take me to and from school once Saul began to attend the Yeshiva high school in upper Manhattan after this year. There were long conversations into the night between my mother and father. Often my aunt and uncle were there too, in our living room or kitchen, talking. Sometimes they all argued loudly. I could understand nothing about the banks but I remember my father's enraged voice. One of the banks had been owned by Jews and they had swindled hundreds of immigrants. He stormed against those bank owners, the veins in his thick neck

bulging with his bitter fury. At breakfast one morning, while
reading his newspaper, he smashed his fist down on the table
and shouted, "The stinking bastards!" Then he threw down
his paper and went from the room. Alex whimpered. My
mother's face was ashen. I sat frozen to my chair listening to
the wild jumping of my heart.

"We have no more money, Mama?" was all I could find to
ask when I felt my heart calm enough.

"Finish your breakfast," she said with a tone of anger in
her voice. "You concern yourself with your studies, David.
That's your job. Nothing else."

And she turned to soothe my brother.

I saw the newspaper in Mr. Steinberg's candy store. But I
was unable to grasp what it was all about. I was happy that
someone called Roosevelt had won the Presidency. My father
had stood a long time in a line waiting to vote for him. My
father disliked standing in lines.

I could not go near my father. He was irritable. He flared
with rage under the slightest provocation: a small act of
mischief, the faintest indication of disobedience. Once he
smacked my brother across the face for dropping his bread
to the floor during a meal. I cowered. My brother screamed.
My mother shouted. My father stormed from the kitchen.

In the middle of December there was a brief meeting of
the board of directors of the Am Kedoshim Society in the
living room of our apartment. Six men attended, in addition
to my father and uncle. My mother served coffee and tea. I
lay in bed and listened to their voices. I could not hear my
father's voice. I do not think he spoke at all during that
meeting.

At the end of December the Am Kedoshim Society went
into bankruptcy. The little synagogue was closed; there were
barely enough people now for a minyan and the rental could
no longer be paid. Sometimes on Shabbat my father and I
prayed in the large synagogue. Often we stayed home and
prayed by ourselves.

My father began to sleep late into the mornings. As the
weeks went by, he became increasingly bewildered. Sometimes I would hear him say to himself, "I cannot understand
it. What has happened? Nothing I do seems to help." Once
he said to my mother, "Your parents and my parents are the
smart ones. They stayed." Sometimes in the night he would
moan in his sleep and once, in the deep blackness of a January

morning, I heard him let out a cry and I felt myself terrified
and wished I could be ill and drugged with medicine so I could
sleep and not be wakened by the sighs and soft moans of pain
I seemed to be hearing often now in the dark.

My brother said to me one evening as he was getting into
his pajamas, "Davey, is Papa sick?"

"I don't know. He's very worried, Alex."

"He hits me all the time."

"If you didn't behave like a wild Indian, he wouldn't hit
you."

"Did he used to hit you too, Davey?"

"Sometimes," I said, after a pause.

"He hits hard."

"Did you touch my books? I told you not to touch my
books. You want to get hit by me, too?"

"I only wanted to see the pictures, Davey."

"Put them back straight. The way I have them. Lined up
straight. I don't want my desk to look as messy as your bed."

He said to me later, looking up from the children's book he
was leafing through, "Is this word 'house'?"

I said from my chair at my desk, "I'm trying to do homework, Alex."

"But is it 'house,' Davey?"

I turned to look at him. He was sitting up in his bed, the
book on his lap. He had undressed himself and his clothes
were strewn all over the floor near his bed. His brown hair,
uncut for weeks, lay across his eyes. He pouted unhappily as
he returned my gaze.

"Show me the word," I said.

He held up the book.

"House," I said. "And go to sleep. It's late."

"How will I learn to read if you won't help me, Davey?
Mama's with Papa all the time. She doesn't like me to bother
her."

My aunt and uncle came over one evening and my aunt
stepped into our room as I was reading Alex a story.

"Well," she said. "Don't let me interrupt, David. I only
wanted to see how you both were and I see you are fine."

"Aunt Sarah," Alex said without preliminaries, "is Papa
sick?"

She gave him a careful smile. "Your father will be fine. We
are all going to see to it that he is well very soon."

Late one night as I sat at my desk I heard a soft noise behind me. I turned in my chair and saw my mother in the doorway. She looked tired but her gaze was firm.

"It's late, David."

"I'm almost finished, Mama."

She glanced at my brother, who lay in his bed surrounded by his children's books which he would not relinquish even in sleep.

"You are a help to me with your brother," she murmured. "I am very grateful to you, my son."

"Is Papa feeling better?"

"With God's help, your father will be all right." She gazed at me steadily and a smile lightened her wan features. "It is good to see you working at your desk this way. It is . . . very good."

"Is Papa asleep now?"

"Yes."

"He woke me last night. Did he wake you?"

"Yes. He has bad dreams. It will pass. In many ways it was easier for him in the war than it is now. He's a man and in the war there were things a man could do. And he did them well, your father. How he did them. And there were Jews who had to be helped and he had ways to help them. But now?" She shook her head sadly. "It is a difficult time. But it will pass. We are all helping and it will pass."

"Will we have to move from here, Mama?"

"Yes," she said. "We will have to move."

One of the middle-aged women who helped in the dining room came over to me during lunch. "You'll fade away," she said. "You'll become like the wind. Why do you sit there like a golem? Why don't you eat?"

I shrugged.

"What kind of an answer is that? From such an answer you'll put flesh on your bones? It will soon be impossible to tell you apart from your shadow."

"She's right," Yaakov Bader said when she went away. He sat across the table from me. "You'll get sick if you don't eat."

"You want my sandwich, Yaakov?"

"I had a sandwich. Why don't you eat, Davey?"

I shrugged again.

Another of the middle-aged women came over to me the

following day. "David Lurie, look at you. You are like a toothpick. There is something the matter with the soup? You want me to give you a different soup? What do you want?"

I stared down at the table.

"How can you study if you don't eat?" she said loudly. I saw heads turning to look at us. "What's the matter with you?"

When I did not respond, she went angrily away.

"Are you all right, Davey?" Yaakov Bader asked. "Can I help you with anything?"

I shook my head.

That night I heard someone scream my name in the chill darkness of my room and knew it was a dream. But I heard my name again, followed now by a gasping cry and a loud sob that ended as if muffled by a pillow. Then, through the blackness, I heard, faintly, my mother's calming words. "It was a dream, Max. That's all. A dream. Yes, my husband. Yes. It will be all right. I make you a promise. It will be all right. Sha, sha. You will wake the children. It will be all right, my husband. Shall I bring you a glass of coffee?"

There was a heavy stirring inside my room.

"Davey?" Alex said faintly. "Where are you? Davey?"

I came up quickly from beneath my covers. "I'm here, Alex."

"Was it Papa?"

"Don't talk so loud. Papa had a dream. He's all right."

"I'm cold, Davey." He was sitting up dazedly in his bed. "I'm scared."

"The steam will come on soon, Alex. Go back to sleep."

"Can I sleep with you, Davey? I'm really scared."

"Come on," I said.

He padded quickly across the space that separated us and climbed into my bed. His hands and feet were cold.

"Papa screamed," he said. "Didn't Papa scream?"

"No talking," I said. "Just go to sleep."

"I thought I heard Papa scream, 'David,' " he murmured drowsily, curling himself into a ball. "Why would Papa scream your name? Were you in Papa's room?"

I was spared the need to respond; as soon as he asked the question he fell asleep. I huddled against the form of my little brother. Just before I fell asleep I thought I heard the soft voice of my mother chanting quietly from a distant room of the apartment.

One of the upper-grade English teachers, a bald-headed man with a roundish face and gentle gray eyes, came over to me during lunch the next day.

"You're not eating, David."

I looked at him and knew I should have felt awe and trepidation. But I was very tired. I looked away and was quiet.

"How's your father feeling?" he asked gently.

I hung my head.

I did not hear him move away but when I raised my eyes a moment later he was gone. The noise of the dining room rang dully in my ears. My head hurt. Familiar pain had resumed its old place behind my eyes. I would be ill again soon. I welcomed it.

The pain remained but I did not become ill. For days I went to school with that vague dull pain behind my eyes. But it did not move from there. And there was no fever and no burning inside my nose or throat.

The bitter days of that winter moved on slowly. A heavy slate-gray darkness began to cloud the periphery of my vision. Inside my classroom or on the street or in the school yard, I began to see small dark shadowy creatures that I knew were not present to my eyes; and at times I could not see shapes that I felt certain were before me. Twice I tripped on the outside stone steps of the school, the second time splitting my lower lip so badly that I was unable to speak clearly for a few days.

My aunt came over to the house alone one night. My father had eaten earlier and had fallen asleep in his living room chair with his head lying awkwardly on his shoulder, his jaw hanging slack. Then, abruptly, he had begun to grind his teeth in his sleep. I could not bear the sound and had gone to my room. I heard my mother putting him to sleep. Now I heard her in the living room with my aunt. They spoke quietly together. I lay in my bed. Alex was asleep.

I heard my mother say sharply, "For how long?"

"Days," said my aunt.

"My God, that is all we need now. No wonder the child looks like a ghost."

"I think it must now be as soon as possible, Ruth."

My mother's reply was indistinct.

"I will help you. You must tell me what to do and I will do it."

Again, my mother's reply was indistinct.

Later, my uncle came over and the three of them sat talking into the night. But I was very tired and did not listen. I lay very still, feeling the pain in my lip and behind my eyes and wondering why I was not becoming ill.

My brother woke that night crying and I went to him and soothed him and walked with him to the bathroom. I sat on his bed until he was asleep and then I went to bed and lay awake a long time listening to the darkness. When I woke in the morning Alex lay next to me on top of my covers, curled into a tight ball. I covered him and dressed to go to school.

One day that week I looked up from my untouched lunch and saw my mother in the doorway of the school dining room. She was watching me. I knew it could not be my mother. But the woman looked exactly like my mother. I closed my eyes and when I opened them the woman was gone.

One week later men arrived early in the morning and brought large barrels into the apartment. I looked at the barrels and felt a trembling begin inside me. Alex stared and grew very still. My mother began to pack up the apartment, with the help of my uncle and aunt. Sometimes Saul came over, too; but he always had schoolwork and was quickly sent home.

Slowly the kitchen cabinets were emptied; walls became bare; rugs were rolled up and stacked against walls; mirrors were carefully taken down; closets became cavernous; the contents of drawers were carefully sifted and selections made for the trash can or the moving van. The drapes were taken down. The apartment began to fill with empty spaces; the empty spaces sent back echoes of our voices.

Night after night my father sat in his living room chair and watched the slow disintegration of the apartment. At first, he had tried to help my mother with the packing. But he seemed unable to participate in the breakup of the house. He would tire easily. A bewildered look would come into his eyes. One night he watched my uncle and aunt move furniture and roll up the living room rug. His chair had been moved over to the wall near the canary who sat in its cage, perched on one leg, puffed up and swaying slightly, and silent for days. My father watched the parquet floor expand as my aunt and uncle rolled up the exotic birds and flowers and jungle animals populating our living room floor and then pushed the carpet to the wall opposite the sofa. His eyes glowed dully.

"God in heaven, Meyer," I heard him mutter. "What is happening to us? What are you doing to my house?"

"I know what I'm doing, Max," my uncle said. "Rest. Take it easy. Why don't you go into the bedroom and lie down?"

"You are taking apart my house."

"We have to move the end tables, Sarah," my uncle said. "Be careful of the lamps."

From inside the kitchen came the sounds of my mother emptying the cabinets, packing the silverware and dishes. The radio was on. The smooth voice came softly through the apartment, and the empty spaces near the walls and windows echoed with the words.

"How could you do this to me, Meyer?" asked my father, a dull bewildered look on his face. "This is how you repay me?"

"This is how I repay you. Later you will thank me."

"We are brothers, Meyer!" My father's attempt at a shout came out hoarsely and seemed to exhaust him immediately. He sat back in his chair, his arms limp and faintly quivering on his thighs. "You know what it means to be brothers, Meyer?"

"Yes," said my uncle quietly, as he moved an end table with my aunt's help.

"You do not know what it means. You are a Cossack! Sarah, how can you let him do this?"

My aunt straightened for a moment and wiped at her damp forehead with the back of her hand. She wore an old dress and her short dark hair was covered by a kerchief.

"Max, do you think Meyer would hurt you?"

My father looked at her sullenly out of the tops of his eyes and said nothing.

"We must move from here, Max. What's left? Nothing. Echoes. Everyone's gone. What's the matter with you, Max? Do you need a war in order to be a man?"

"Sarah," said my uncle quietly.

"Do you want your son to starve to death?" my aunt said. "He doesn't eat in school. Look at him. Look at your son. Can't you see what is happening?"

He turned his dark eyes upon me. I stood near the portiere and felt his eyes rake my face. His jaw hung slack. I could not bear to look at him.

"I do not understand," he muttered. "What? David? What?" A film seemed to settle across his eyes. "David is what?" he said. "David? David?"

My uncle and aunt went to him quickly. They took him into his bedroom. I undressed and went to bed and watched the jumping and swarming of the creatures inside the darkness of my room.

I said to my mother the next morning, "Mama, are we moving because of me?"

"What do you mean?" she asked from the counter where cartons competed with breakfast dishes for space.

"Because I'm not eating?"

"No, darling. Of course not because of you. We have to move. Now we are moving sooner."

"Why can't I eat, Mama? I never feel hungry anymore."

"Everything will be all right, darling. I promise you. Don't you see how we are all working together? It will be all right. You should eat at least a little of your cereal, David."

"I feel nauseous, Mama."

"All right," she said. "Drink your milk and go to school. Don't keep Saul waiting in the cold."

I woke with a sensation of dizziness the next morning and my mother told me to remain home. That afternoon Alex played in the living room and I sat near him staring out the window at the maple tree. My parents were in the kitchen. I looked at the cartons piled neatly one next to the other against the wall opposite the door to my parents' bedroom. They had been removed from the bedroom the night before by my uncle so that they would not be a hazard in the darkness. Alex played quietly with his cars. I went over to the cartons. They had been loosely packed and it was not difficult to search through them. I found the photograph near the top of the third carton beneath a thin layer of letters written in a small delicate handwriting that I had never seen before. The letters were in Yiddish. I began to read the first one and put it down. Then I scooped out the letters and there was the photograph of the men with guns and knives in their hands in the ice and snow of a Polish forest. I looked carefully at the faces in the photograph. It felt odd to be holding in my hands the heart of the firm and solid world molded by my father at the very moment when that world had disintegrated. Standing there, surrounded by the disarray of the dismembered living room, I stared intently for a very long time at the photograph, remembering Mr. Bader's study and my days in the forest when I had entered the rectangle in my hands and joined myself to my father's friends. Now, as I peered into the snowy depths of the forest, the men seemed to stir. Before my eyes, as I watched, they moved slowly and silently from

the world contained by the rectangle. One by one they slipped
away, taking with them their guns and knives and flags until
all I held in my hands was an empty forest through which
blew the winds of an icy and indifferent winter. I replaced the
photograph in the carton, covered it with the letters that had
once been written by my father's dead brother David to my
mother, went over to the window and looked out at the gray
street and the naked maple and the pages of old newspapers
blowing in the wind.

The next day we moved into an apartment house on Washington Avenue two doors away from Eddie Kulanski.

In the rectangle that was my bedroom window I could see
clearly the narrow cement channel of sunless alleyway that
led from the street and ran alongside our ground-floor apartment. The bathroom and kitchen and living room windows
also looked out upon the alleyway and from the two windows
of my parents' bedroom I saw the dense patches of weeds
and brambles and the gray lagoon of cracked cement that
was our back yard. Beyond the broken wooden fence that
bordered the yard was another yard and another fence and
more yards and more fences and the naked unbricked back-
sides of apartment houses and the rear of a furniture shop in
a low building on Third Avenue and, finally, the dark looming girders of the elevated train. There were no trees.

Below my window a steep flight of iron stairs led from the
alleyway to the cellar bakery under our apartment. Along the
right side of the alleyway a stone wall rose to a height of
about ten feet and became the brief cement plateau that met
the red-brick side wall of the adjoining apartment house. Below our kitchen window, which I could see clearly from my
bedroom, was the metal double door that led to the forbidden
darkness of the basement and the furnace room and the last
stop of the dumbwaiter. Cats lounged and played and fought
one another among the cans of coal ash and garbage hauled
out to the alleyway by the janitor, a big-bellied flaxen-haired
Irishman with wet lips and inflamed eyelids who was often
drunk. I kept away from him.

Early each night the janitor would turn off the steam and
I would lie in my bed and listen to the radiator dying. The
contracting metal made knocking sounds that echoed in the
darkness. Then the cold came into the room like a mist filled

with infinitesimal particles of stinging ice and soon Alex would begin to stir restlessly as he searched for the disappearing pockets of warmth beneath his covers. Then he woke and cried softly and called my name. This was not a cold I had ever felt before. It had in it not only the weather but the drab house and the slate-gray street and the worn faces of anguished people. I would take Alex into my bed and we would huddle together against the darkness and the cold. I slept, my brother's body against mine, and was awakened in the predawn darkness by the hissing and spitting of the steam which the janitor sent shooting back into the radiators. My nights were spanned by the death and resurrection of the silver-painted loops of metal below the sill of my window. I dreaded the nights.

I woke and dressed and left Alex asleep in my bed. Carrying my schoolbag, I threaded my way carefully through the clutter of the living room where cartons lay still unopened and where the dinginess of the alleyway sent a pallid light across the furniture and the carpet bestiary on the floor. The hallway from the living room to the kitchen was long and dark, a bleak tunnel with a floor of creaking wood. My mother was in the kitchen, tired, very tired, circles of sleeplessness rimming her eyes. She would try to conceal the fatigue when she spoke.

"Good morning, darling."

"Good morning, Mama. How is Papa feeling?"

"He is the same. But he will get better."

That was the morning litany of those first days on the new street. I ate quickly and left the apartment.

The entrance hall of the house—white and green tile floor, gray walls—was bare and cavernous, filled with sudden pools of cold air. Along the street the wind blew cruelly and stung my eyes. I walked past the Chinese laundry, the tailor, the shoe repair shop, and paused at the newsstand in front of the candy store near the end of the block. There, briefly, I scanned the headlines and looked at the photographs and was awakened starkly to the day. Then I went to school.

In the rectangle of my classroom window I could see the street through which I had just walked. I listened to my teacher explaining the awesome double miracle of the plague of hail in the Book of Exodus—fire and ice simultaneously visited upon those who had enslaved the children of Israel— and saw my brother come out of the apartment house and enter the rectangle, dragging my old tricycle. I watched him riding it up and down the block. He rode skillfully, avoiding with ease the people who walked the street and the groups of playing children. Then my teacher asked me if I would be so good as to pay attention to the blackboard rather than the window. I turned my eyes upon the slate rectangle in front of the room and after a moment found that I had inserted within its borders a sharp unmoving picture of my brother on the tricycle. Then, abruptly, he moved and rode happily about, within the borders of the blackboard. It was an odd sensation, and vaguely satisfying. I closed my eyes for a long moment and when I opened them he was gone. I glanced out the window and there he was, riding around on the tricycle, bent forward over the handlebar and pumping away at the pedals.

During lunch, which I ate at home now, I said to Alex, "I saw you riding around this morning."

"Was I good on it, Davey?"

"You were all right. You ride okay."

"The wheels squeak a lot, Davey."

"Ask Papa to fix them."

"Leave your father alone," said my mother from the sink. "He has other things on his mind now."

"There's a can of oil around somewhere. I'll fix it for you, Alex."

Sometimes my father would come in from the bedroom and sit at the kitchen table while we ate lunch. My mother would give him a glass of coffee and a buttered roll. Then she would serve herself and sit with us.

"You are doing your job in school?" my father asked me suddenly one day during lunch, giving me a sharp burning look.

"Yes, Papa."

"Good. Good. That is the only job left now. There is nothing else."

"Max, don't you want your roll?" my mother asked quietly.

"Where is Meyer?" he said, turning to her. "Why isn't Meyer here?"

"Meyer was here all last night, Max. You don't remember?"

"What kind of brother does not help?"

"He helped me unpack, Max."

"Is he moving? When is he moving?"

"In a few weeks."

"In a few weeks? What is a few weeks?"

"In March."

"Where is he when I need him? Doesn't he realize I need him?"

"He will be here again tonight, Max."

"Tonight?" He was silent a moment, his eyes clouding. His face, gaunt from his weeks of disinterest in food, had beneath the stubble a dull dead gray color. He turned abruptly to Alex. "Are you a good boy? Tell me."

Alex, startled, jumped in his chair. "Yes, Papa."

"You are? Is he a good boy, Ruth?"

"Yes, Max."

"Your job is to be a good boy. Do you hear me, Alex?"

"Yes, Papa."

"You must be a good boy and a good brother. Are you a good brother? Are you?"

"He's a good brother, Papa," I said.

"Yes?" He looked at me. His eyes glowed darkly. He was looking through me at someone behind me. But there was no one behind me. It made me feel cold on the back of my neck to see him looking at me that way. "You are satisfied he is a good brother?"

"Yes, Papa."

"A brother must be good to his big brother. A big brother has a terrible job. Terrible. He must have help. God in heaven, where is Meyer?" His voice choked. He closed his eyes. I sat staring down at my food, trembling with dread.

"Meyer will be here tonight, Max," my mother said again firmly, patiently. "Eat your roll. Shall I bring you another glass of coffee?"

He straightened abruptly and his eyes flew open. The sudden jerking movement of his body sent his tall black skullcap sliding to the floor. Without a word, my mother bent, picked it up, and placed it gently back upon his head. He seemed not to notice at all what she had done. He blinked his eyes rapidly and said, "The German maniac, what is he doing today?"

We were silent.

"What has he done? Where is my paper?"

"It's in the bedroom, Max," my mother said quietly.

"Nu, David? What? You are the brains. What is happening?"

I reported to him what I had read in the headlines and seen in the photographs.

He sat back in his chair, his heavy shoulders sagging. "There will be blood," he muttered. "My nose smells it." He turned his queer burning eyes upon me. "Tell me what to do and I will do it. You have the brains. We must do something. All the brains went to you. You have a job, David." He raised his voice slightly. "Tell me what to do."

I felt a shuddering take hold of me. I saw Alex gaping at him. I turned to my mother. Her eyes were very calm.

"Tell me what to do!" my father suddenly shouted with all the rage that was left in him. The shout echoed and reechoed through the apartment. Alex whimpered. I sat frozen to stone.

"Max," said my mother very quickly. Then she leaned forward and spoke to him softly in Polish.

He became very still.

My mother sat back in her chair.

"What time is it, Ruth?" he asked, sounding dazed. He was not wearing his wrist watch.

She told him.

"The news is on."

"We'll hear the news another time, Max."

He looked at the Ingersoll clock on the counter near the sink.

"Something is wrong with it," my mother said. "It is slow. Maybe it was damaged when we moved. Please finish your roll, Max."

"We should hear the news. We must know what the maniac is doing."

"Will you eat your roll, Max?" said my mother. "You should eat it."

He took a bite from the roll. We ate in silence for a while.

"Was there mail?" my father asked.

"Yes," said my mother.

"From whom?"

"I will show it to you later, Max."

He drank his coffee and finished the roll. He sat back in his chair, murmuring automatically the Grace After Meals. His robe had come undone. I could see his pajamas and the furlike thickness of hair on his chest.

"Are they coming?" he asked when he was done.

"No," said my mother. A cloud covered her eyes and was immediately gone.

"They are all staying?" He sounded incredulous.

"I will show you the letters."

"Not now. I want to lie down now."

She helped him to his feet.

"I am tired. Why am I so tired, Ruth? What did Weidman say?"

They were in the hallway. I heard my mother answer, "He said you will be all right."

"Yes? When? Ah, what does he know anyway? The Bratzlaver was right. Doctors are messengers of the Angel of Death."

I was alone in the kitchen with Alex.

"I'm scared, Davey," Alex said.

"Papa will be all right."

"I have bad dreams about him, Davey."

I was silent for a moment. Then I said, "I think I remember where that oil is. I'll fix the bike. Then I've got to get to school. I don't want to be late again."

But I was late again anyway and drew a withering look from my English teacher as I entered the class and slid into my seat. Later, in the rectangle of window, I saw my mother walk to the grocery store at the far end of the block. She walked very quickly, a short slim figure in a dark coat and with a scarf about her head. Then I saw her walk back, carrying the blue cloth shopping bag. A while later my brother entered the rectangle and rode up and down the street on the tricycle. I thought I could hear the smooth turning of the wheels. It had been a good feeling to fix it.

When my uncle came over that night I helped him and my mother put up some shelves in the kitchen. My uncle was not too adept with hammer and nails. We began to empty the cartons in the living room. The carton with the photograph and the letters lay near the door to my parents' bedroom. I saw my mother pick it up and go with it into the bedroom, closing the door behind her quietly with her foot. She was gone awhile. When she came out of the bedroom she had a strained, almost tortured look on her face; she was just then as she had been during all the years I could remember her: frail, frightened, her eyes timorous and darting nervously about. I thought she had been crying. She kept her head lowered as she went through the living room and along the hallway to the kitchen.

My uncle had opened another of the cartons and had pulled out some books. "What are these?" he asked.

I told him about the books left to me by Mrs. Horowitz. He looked through the carton.

"Are they books with special prayers, Uncle Meyer?"

"What?"

"Against the evil eye and fever and the Angel of Death and for helping people remember things."

"What are you talking about, David? These are books of sermons and explanation of customs. This is a translation of the Bible into German. Here is one on the Bible, also in German, but I don't understand the title. What is *Quellenscheidung?* I'm afraid we do not have time to read books now. Where is the carton with the quilt covers that your mother asked me to unpack?"

I heard my mother walking along the creaking wooden floor of the hallway. She came into the living room, looking composed. She had washed her face. Her eyes were calm. Did we want anything to drink? she asked. She wanted to stop now and go to her room. She especially wanted me to go to bed. In response to my uncle's question, my mother raised her eyebrows, nodded, and indicated the hallway. My uncle put the three cartons of books given to me by Mrs. Horowitz into the back of the hallway closet.

I had a glass of milk and came back into the living room. I saw my father standing in the doorway to his room, leaning heavily against the jamb. His dark blue pajamas were rumpled and his hair was wild and he was staring fixedly at the canary.

"Why don't you sing?" I heard him mutter in a low voice. "Sing."

The canary sat on its perch, a round yellow faintly swaying ball. It had stopped eating.

"Sing," my father said, his voice changing abruptly, a faint note of pleading in it now. "For David you sang. Remember?"

I heard my mother's footsteps behind me and the creaking of the hallway floor. She brushed past me and went over to my father.

"It doesn't sing, Ruth," he said in a forlorn voice.

"Max, it takes time for a bird to grow used to a new place. Please go to bed."

He turned and saw me in the doorway to the living room. "David," he said very quietly.

"Yes, Papa."

"Are you a good boy, David?"

"He is a very good boy, Max," said my mother softly.

"Are you a good brother, David?"

"Yes," said my mother in the same soft tone.

He looked at her.

"What time is it, Ruth?"

She told him.

"That late already? Is there news on?"

"You'll hear it tomorrow, Max."

"My watch is not working. What happened to my watch?"

"Let me take you to bed, Max."

She took his arm.

"What happened to my watch?" he asked again plaintively as they went into their bedroom. "Why isn't it working, Ruth?"

"Did you remember to wind it?"

She closed the door quietly on his answer.

I sensed someone beside me and looked and it was my uncle. I had not heard him come through the hallway.

"Uncle Meyer," I said. "Uncle Meyer." I felt a quivering inside me. I could not control it. It kept rising from somewhere deep inside me. It was rising and climbing and I knew I had to stop it. "Uncle Meyer," I said again. My voice was trembling.

He embraced me. I put my head against him. Then I felt him bend his knees so he could see my face closely. I looked through his gold-rimmed glasses into the young eyes of my father. I looked and trembled and saw the young face of my father. It had aged since the time we had all walked together through the zoo and the meadow to the pine wood and the clearing. But it was still so much younger than the face of my father.

"Now, now," my uncle said, his hands gently holding the sides of my face. "Are you a big boy?"

I nodded slowly.

"You are sure you are a big boy?" he asked, smiling.

Again I nodded.

He lowered his hands to the sides of my shoulders. "Then you will behave like a big boy. There is a time for crying and there is a time for doing. Now is the time for doing. Is your mother crying? David will not cry either. All right? Very good. You are truly a big boy. You are worried about your father. I understand your worry. But do not be frightened. Do you know what David would say now if he were alive? Your dead uncle, my brilliant little brother, do you know what he would say, David? The exact same thing he said when he saw what the Cossacks had done to the Jews in Galicia. 'What should we do?' your father asked him. 'We must protect ourselves and pay back the Cossacks,' my little brother David said. 'How?' your father asked him. 'We must do something that will enable us to build and build so that we can see the results and help ourselves,' my little brother David said." A wistful tone had crept into my uncle's voice. He paused for a moment and took a deep faintly quivering breath. "Dear God, I remember that night as if it had just happened here in this living room on Washington Avenue. 'How?' your father kept asking. 'How?' And my little brother kept answering, 'I cannot tell you how to do it, I can only tell you what must be done. The how you will have to find by yourself.' He kept saying that over and over again. 'The how you will have to find by yourself.' He said the how must be a passion. Do you know what a passion is, David? Something to which you give all your heart and soul, all your thoughts. 'I cannot tell you what is inside your heart,' my little brother kept saying. Your father went away and thought about it. And do you know what he did, your father? He took about fifty of his friends and he joined Pilsudski's army. We thought he had lost his mind. My God, how everyone carried on! All the mothers were hysterical with fear and all the fathers screamed and shouted with rage. Jews should join the army of the Polaks and live in mud and eat pork and maybe, God forbid, get killed—for what? For Poland and the lovely, gentle way it treats Jews? My God, how they carried on; the rabbis they ran to; the screaming that took place in the house and on the streets and in the synagogue. It went on for weeks. Our mother even went to some old thief who had a reputation for casting out demons; she thought your father had a demon in him. He had a demon in him all right. He took forty-nine men into Pilsudski's army with him. I would have gone too but I was already married and your father did not want anyone who might have his mind in Lemberg when he should be killing Cossacks in the Ukraine. David would have gone, but they would not take him because he had very weak eyes. The men who came out formed the Am Kedoshim Society. Now it is all ruined and your father does not know what to do. He is searching for something to do. Wait. You don't know your father yet the way I know him. There is something going on inside his head. He will find something. And we will all laugh. Or we will go into shock. Our mother fainted when she was told he had asked to be a machine gunner. You can kill a lot of Cossacks with them, he told me. He enjoyed taking them apart and putting them together. Machine guns, I'm talking about. Wait. He will find something. We have to help him until he does.

Now—I am tired and it is late and my knees hurt me from being in this position so long. I am not old but I don't have the bones I had ten years ago. Go into your room, David, and go to sleep. Everything will be all right."

"Uncle Meyer?"

"Yes, David."

"Where are all of Papa's friends?"

"What do you mean?"

"Where are they? Have they gone away?"

"Some have gone away."

"To other cities?"

"Yes. One just went to Eretz Yisroel."

"Why don't the others help us?"

"Help? What do you mean, help?"

"Why did we have to move? Why do we have to live here?"

"David, David, your father doesn't want to live on someone else's money. Your father has to decide by himself what he wants to do. No one can decide for him. Can you understand that?"

"I think so. Yes, I think so."

"Now go to sleep."

"Good night, Uncle Meyer."

"Good night, my big nephew. Thank you for helping me put up the shelves. You are a good fixer."

Later I gazed from my bed into the dark rectangle of my window shade. The shade was softly stirred by the minute streams of cold air that blew in through the cracks in the frame. Strange shapes moved within the rectangle, flickering, as if a candle had been lighted somewhere in my room with the flame unseen. A dull reddish glow spread slowly across the rectangle, lighting an array of marching figures. Torches smoked; flags and banners whipped in the wind. A noise filled the room. Is that what it was like, the salute and shout of twenty thousand brown-shirted men? Like the heavy drawn-out thunderous presence of the elevated train rushing along the trestle? They were sharpening their swords. Was Mr. Bader there, watching? We have to do something, Papa! We have to do something!

I slept and was awakened by the dying radiator. The rectangle was dark, black. I slept again and was awakened by my father's sudden hoarse shout. "What happened to it? My life I put into it. What happened?"

There was a brief echoing silence and then my mother's soft soothing voice.

Alex stirred and whimpered softly. I heard him get out of his bed in the darkness.

"Davey?" His frightened voice was next to my ear.

I took him into my bed. The apartment was very still. Lying next to my brother, with my head on the pillow, I could feel the warmth draining out of the room. Often I would see my breath forming clouds in the air if I woke in the night and went to the bathroom or remained awake after the dying of my radiator to listen to my father or to watch the rectangle of my window. That was a month of bitter cold, that February in the year 1933, and each of its icy nights entered my room and spread piercing chill upon me and my brother.

Inside our new apartment a discernible order began to prevail. Curtains were hung, pieces of furniture assigned permanent locations, mirrors put up. In my parents' bedroom I helped my uncle hang the oval-shaped wedding picture; my father was in the kitchen with my mother at the time. When we were alone I stared at the young and glowing faces in the picture, then turned and walked out of the room. The remaining cartons, except those containing Mrs. Horowitz's books, were emptied and piled by the dumbwaiter near our door. The thick ropes creaked and the darkness of the shaft was chilling, but I helped my mother and uncle load the cartons onto the dumbwaiter and then listened to the cracking and thumping as my uncle sent it to the darkness beneath us.

My aunt and uncle came over one evening together with Saul. My father was in bed. Saul wanted to see my room. He stood in the doorway, surveying my desk and small bookcase, the beds, the bureau. He gazed out the rectangle of window. He would not look at me directly.

We were quiet, gazing together at the cats huddled among the garbage cans in the dimly lighted alleyway.

"When will you be moving, Saul?"

"In March, I think. The place has to be painted. My mother wanted some changes in the sockets and things."

"Where will it be, your new place?"

"Not far from here. Clay Avenue. Opposite a small park. It isn't bad."

"Saul?"

He looked at me.

"What's happening to everything?"

He was quiet.

"I'm scared sometimes, Saul."

He began to respond but was stopped by the hoarse cry that came from my father.

"Ruth! Ruth!"

My brother looked up immediately, frightened. I felt my heart jump. Saul looked startled.

"What time is it, Ruth?" my father called. My mother must have gone into the bedroom for his next words were low and indistinct. Then he raised his voice again and there was in it a plaintive tone. "But I cannot see them now, Ruth. Look at me. How can I see them like this?"

"Davey," Alex said softly. "Davey." He was very frightened.

"Papa will be all right. He's just in a bad mood, Alex."

"Can I sleep in your bed, Davey?"

"All right. But go to sleep now."

I pulled down the white rectangle of the shade.

Saul's eyes were large and brooding behind the lenses of his shell-rimmed glasses.

"I hope you move here soon," I said to him.

"What happened?" my father suddenly shouted from his room. There was a moment of shrill tingling silence as the words crashed through the apartment. Then my father said, imploringly, "We must do something, Ruth. Give me an idea what to do."

He grew quiet after that. Later he came out and sat in the living room in his pajamas and robe, listening to whatever was being talked about: the freezing weather, politics, friends. Abruptly he looked at his wrist. He was not wearing his watch. He rose and, without a word, went into his bedroom.

There was a long distressing silence. Then my mother told me to say good night and go to bed. I went to bed but lay awake a long time and found I could not stop thinking of Mrs. Horowitz. I kept seeing her skinny birdlike neck and wrinkled face and hearing her voice. But she was dead and could not help me. I listened to my brother's soft breathing. The radiator died. The cold crept silently into the room like a hungry jungle animal.

My English teacher said in her brassy voice the next afternoon, "What do you see out of that window, David Lurie?"

"Twenty thousand Nazis marching," I said, because that was what I had been seeing.

There was a stir in the room. One of the students laughed, then grew immediately silent as the teacher fixed her gaze upon him. I took my eyes from the window and stared down

at the top of my desk. I was frightened. I should not have said
that. But the words had been out of my mouth before I had
thought what to say. I would have to be careful. I did not
want anyone to know what I saw in my rectangles.

The teacher turned her thin face upon me. "Do you read
newspapers?" she asked. Her voice was low.

I nodded hesitantly.

She peered at me a moment longer out of her large eyes.
"What newspapers do you read?"

I named a Yiddish daily and said I did not actually read an
English newspaper but only looked at headlines and a paragraph or two and at the captions of photographs. "We don't
get an English paper," I said. "My parents don't read English
too well. We only talk Yiddish at home. Sometimes I talk
English with my aunt and uncle and Cousin Saul. And with
my little brother. But not with my parents. My parents know
a lot of languages, but they don't know English yet too well.
But they're both American citizens. They've been citizens a
long time. And we listen to the radio a lot. We hear all the
voices on the radio."

Everyone was staring at me. Why were they all staring at
me like that, as if I were some kind of zoo animal? Even
Yaakov Bader was staring at me.

The teacher too was staring at me. But she said nothing.
After a moment I looked back out the window. A few minutes
before dismissal, as we were writing down the answers to a
surprise test she had given us in geography, she came over to
my desk and asked me in a low voice to remain behind after
class.

I stood alone beside her desk in the empty classroom.

"I am sorry my class is such a boring experience for you,
David." Her thin face, her rouged cheeks, her long skinny
neck—she kept reminding me of Mrs. Horowitz.

I fidgeted uncomfortably.

"I have books at home that might be of interest to you,
David. I will bring you some tomorrow. Take my newspaper.
I am done with it. You may take my newspaper every day if
you wish. Why don't you get a good night's sleep tonight?
Don't you sleep at all? Your eyes are falling out of your head.
And button your jacket when you go outside. If you have a
gift of brains, you have a responsibility to take good care of
your body. You are now dismissed, David."

I went home in the cold wind and found my father in the
living room watching the canary eating. My mother was in

the kitchen doing laundry in the washtub; my brother was seated at my desk looking at one of my books. I had no strength to be angry at him. I lay down on my bed and fell asleep.

My father came to the table in his pajamas and robe that Friday night and made the blessing over the wine at the start of the Shabbat meal. His hands shook and some wine spilled onto his fingers and dripped down onto the white tablecloth. He ate and fell asleep at the table. The tall dark skullcap sat askew on his brown hair. "David is not here," I heard him mutter suddenly. "We will have to find an idea without David." He slept, his head on his shoulder, his mouth slightly open.

I spent the next day reading one of the books given to me by my English teacher. That was the day eight inches of snow fell on New York and the streets lay in a deep entombing silence. From my window I saw the snow fall silently into the alleyway and across the adjoining cement plateau. A wind blew through the alleyway and the snow drifted across the steps to the cellar bakery and the double door of the basement. The garbage cans looked like white misshapen mounds and the cats were all gone somewhere out of the snow.

"The last winter in Lemberg," I heard my father say from the living room. "You remember the snow, Ruth?"

"Yes, Max." I could barely hear her voice.

"It was a cruel winter. But the snow at least covered the burned-out earth. We could pretend the world was clean."

My mother said nothing.

"I would have asked David if he had been alive."

"I know, Max."

"I would never have made such a decision alone."

"It was a correct decision."

"Are you sure David would have said so?"

"Yes," she murmured. "I know David." She said know, not knew.

There was a long silence.

"What do you think I should do, Ruth?"

"You'll find something."

"Why do people think I am able to make decisions? I am a doer, not a thinker. Why did they all come to me and make me decide without David? Why did they come to me all the years we were here? It frightens me to make decisions, Ruth. I am frightened to make a wrong decision about a person's life."

"You do not force your decisions upon them, Max."

"God in heaven, I wish David were here." There was a pause. Then, "Look at the snow, Ruth. Look at it."

"Do you remember it on the trees in the forest outside the farm?"

"Yes."

"I taught David the names of the trees all around the cottage," she said. "He remembers them all. He has David's head. When I wanted to teach David the names of the trees around the farm he laughed and said my father and mother would not count tree knowledge to his dowry credit, only book knowledge. But he learned all the trees in one afternoon and never forgot them."

There was a silence. The wind blew through the alleyway, making a soft moaning sound.

"I miss them," she said. "I see them walking in the snow or riding on the sleigh, and I truly miss them. I will never see any of them, Max."

"You will see them," he said.

"No. I am reconciling myself to it. I will never see any of them again. They will die and be buried in the snow. Like David."

There was another silence.

"I have to find something to do," he said. "Something I can build with. Start very small so it does not involve much money and build and see results."

"You will find it, Max. You will find it. Like you found the idea to bring everyone to America."

"I hope it is a better idea than that, Ruth."

"You are so sure it was a bad idea, Max? Can you see all the way to the end of that idea that you can say with such certainty it was bad?"

He was quiet for a moment. Then he said, in a voice I could barely make out, "You are a wise woman. Not many know how wise you truly are. And how strong. David was worthy of you. Am I worthy of you, Ruth?"

"Do not speak like a foolish man. Would I have let you marry me? If I did not truly care for you and have respect for you I would not have married you. You are my husband and I love you."

"It was my idea to come to America. Only mine. There was no David to blame. I am afraid of making another such decision now, Ruth."

"But you will make it."

"It has to be something small, something I will want to do, something I can build with, something that will hurt no one if it fails."

"Do you want a glass of coffee, Max?"

I heard them get to their feet.

"God in heaven, look at the snow."

"It should make the world clean, Max."

Two days later I slipped on a patch of ice going down the stone front steps of the yeshiva. I had spent a few minutes in the warm vestibule talking with Yaakov Bader and finishing a lollipop. The stick of the lollipop was in my mouth when I fell. It penetrated my throat.

I lay on the sidewalk and felt snow and cinders on my face. There had been shouts as I fell and there were shouts now as I looked at my schoolbag which I had dropped when I felt the sudden loss of traction beneath my right foot. The schoolbag lay very near my eyes and I noted, absurdly, how cracked and frayed its leather was and how worn were the ends of the straps. Someone had me by the arms and was helping me sit up. I started to speak and my tongue encountered a thin rigid object. It pushed against the object and I felt a pressure inside my throat. My tongue curled back and up, trying to push the object out. I coughed and gagged and tore off my glove and put my fingers into my throat. I was coughing and choking. All around me there were shouts and people rushing about and faces close to mine. I had my fingers on the object. It was slippery. I tugged at it and my fingers came away empty. Then someone's hand was in my mouth and I felt the lollipop stick being pulled out of the flesh deep inside my throat. A sensation of moist warmth filled the back of my throat and trickled into my mouth. I coughed and choked and coughed again. Blood sprayed the sidewalk. I looked at my hands and at the front of my jacket. It seemed to me there was blood everywhere. I could see blood on the dirty snow and the schoolbag. I sat and stared in astonishment at the blood on my gloveless hand. Why were they all making so much noise? I started to my feet and vomited.

Then the pain began, climbing steeply to the level familiar to me for years, then on beyond the pain I had known only two or three times before, and then on beyond even that to the unanimous pain that is the weather of the dark land ruled by the Angel of Death. I coughed and vomited again and the pain was beyond endurance. The shouts became a single howling wind. I was lifted on the wind and found my-

self in a violent landscape of crooked gray fields cut by
narrow black-topped roads that had no curves but only sharp
sudden right-angled turns. A red sky arched overhead. The
fields changed to green and white and brown; they creaked
as we moved across them. The wind brought me to a white
meadow; I coughed and the meadow turned crimson.

I could not breathe. I choked and coughed and took deep
grasping breaths. The wind roared in my ears. It came from
a forest and brought the noise of tumultuous foliage and
swaying trees. There were faces everywhere, flickering,
moving in and out of my vision. I took a breath and felt air
flood my lungs. I breathed again and coughed. The dull thick
quivering that had clutched at the base of my neck abruptly
released its grasp. I lay back upon my crimson meadow. The
last thing I saw before the wind lifted me once again and
brought me into the shadowy heart of the forest was the
face of my father faintly silhouetted against the upper part
of my window. It wore a look of horror.

There was silence and cool darkness. Moist leaves brushed
against my face. From somewhere in the darkness came the
lap and wash of water upon a shore. A single firefly flew on a
lone and lazy course through the forest. I cried out and
coughed and lay still.

"There, there," I heard Dr. Weidman say. "There, there.
Everything will be all right."

Icy drops of water tickled my chest and back and I knew
I was alone again and dreaming in the forest. Nearby the
lapping wavelets of a darkly iridescent lake had altered their
gentle thrusting course upon the shore and were turning to
parallel the wet black earth of a flat embankment. The water
ran dark and murmurous into the infinite night of the forest.
Before a stretch of brown viscous earth three figures stopped
and set their torches in the ground. Bent, working swiftly,
two of the three figures shaped a clay man. They permitted
me to mold the head. When it was done they stood around the
clay figure. Prayers were chanted; the secret name of God
was uttered. Water poured from the figure; it glowed a fiery
red; it rose from the earth. The three robed figures vanished.
From its huge height the clay man gazed down upon me.
Golem, I whispered. Something must be done. Something. It
gazed steadily upon me. Then, slowly, it bowed. I clothed
it in a gray woolen shirt and dark baggy trousers and sent it
into invisibility by means of the charm I placed about its
neck. The night was still. The river ran on without end into

the infinite time of my rectangle. And I slept deeply and without further dreams.

I woke and saw my brother reading. He sat propped up on a pillow against the wall near his bed, a book on his knees. He heard me stir and sprang to the floor and stood by my bed, his young squarish face hopeful, frightened.

"You're up," he said eagerly. "You're up."

I nodded but would not use my voice.

"You scared us," he said. "I had nightmares. But you're up. Someone tried to shoot President Roosevelt while you were sick, Davey. I'll get Mama."

My parents told me later that I had severed a small artery and blood had entered my lungs. Dr. Weidman had feared pneumonia and had wanted to take me to the hospital but I had fought going. How did I feel? Was I all right? The throat would be healed very soon. Did I want any more ice cream?

I listened and nodded and would not speak. There was a vague choking sensation inside my throat—I feared the coughing and the blood. I lay back on my pillow. I did not have to speak. I could nod and shrug and shake my head. You could do a lot and still remain silent. Yes, I thought. Yes. You could do a lot. And silence would keep away the coughing and the blood. Two days later I got out of bed and was silent.

I was back in school the following week and I remained silent. A note from Dr. Weidman in a sealed envelope was handed by me to my Hebrew and English teachers. They read the note, stared at me, and nodded. They left me alone. My classmates kept away from me—all except Yaakov Bader.

"Is there anything I can do for you, Davey? Anything? Just tell me."

I shrugged my shoulders.

"Whenever you think you need help, Davey. With anything. My uncle said I should take care of you. When he comes back he'll ask me about you."

I looked at him and raised my eyebrows.

"He'll be back before Pesach, Davey," Yaakov Bader said.

Yes, you could be silent and listen to your teachers and get excellent grades in your examinations. You did not have to talk at all. There was comfort in that. The coughing and the bleeding would not return. And the choking sensation, which never went away, would not worsen. And you could look into the rectangle of the classroom window and watch

your brother on the tricycle and see the way he seemed to
gather to himself friends from everywhere on the block. They
were drawn to him with no effort on his part. He roamed
the street with the exquisite self-assurance of a person for
whom the presence of friends is as smooth and natural as
the presence of water is to fish.

One day the front door of the apartment house was pushed
open and my father came out, leaning on my mother's arm.
It was a cold sunny day and he wore his coat collar up and
his wide-brimmed hat low over his eyes. They walked slowly
and I could see them talking. They stopped in front of the
shoe repair shop and at the newsstand. They walked to the
corner, then turned and went on up the side street toward
the elevated tracks, and I could no longer see them. After
that they were often inside my rectangle as the days went by.
And one afternoon in late February they came out of the
house and walked along the street and I noticed my father
was holding my mother's arm.

There was a fire that night inside the window shade of my
room. The shade glowed red. A vast German building
burned. I gazed at the flames and was frightened. Were the
flames an accident? Their most precious building was on fire.
It had to have been an accident. Golem, I thought.

A brief restless stirring came faintly to my ears from
somewhere inside the chill darkness of the room. It doesn't
know, I thought. How can it know? It's only a golem. It
knows only what I give it to know. It was a long time before
the flames dimmed in my window shade. I closed my eyes
and slept.

Nights later curls of smoke climbed into the dark sky. A
synagogue was on fire. It burned inside my window shade.
From its dark angled roof and the narrow arched windows
in its dome came swirls of dense gray smoke and the wild
leaping of flame. Golem, look what they've done, the brown-
shirted servants of the Angel of Death. We must save the
Torah scrolls! He came then out of the invisibility in which
I had left him and stood beside my bed in the darkness. He
bowed in mute acknowledgment of my words, bringing his
face close to mine, the face I had molded, my face; then he
straightened his massive seven-foot frame and in a leap my
eyes could barely discern was suddenly inside the window
shade. I was inside the window shade plunging into the smoke
and flames that enveloped the synagogue. Through the

flames! Into the smoke and through the flames! The flames tore at me but I felt nothing and I moved swiftly through smoke-filled corridors and burst into the heart of the synagogue where the pews were burning and the flames licked at the curtain of the Ark. A long finger of flame traveled up the curtain and suddenly the curtain was a sheet of flame. I raced through the burning sanctuary and slid open the doors to the Ark. Sacred scrolls in purple and deep red covers, silver crowns and breastplates glinting dully, reflecting the fire. There were six large Torah scrolls there; I would never save them all. I clutched three to myself and sought a wall and lunged toward the stone and crashed through to the street. Bewildered men in dark clothes took the heavy scrolls from me and I leaped back inside. One of the scrolls was burning! I tore at the flames with my fingers, beating them away from the sacred words. I gathered the scrolls into my arms and left them with startled sleepy-eyed men on the street. The flames roared in my ears. I slipped from the rectangle and lay in my bed listening to the long clattering of an elevated train. You did well, I murmured. Slowly, the Golem bowed.

Saul came over to me in the yard the next day during the midmorning recess. He had begun to grow quickly in recent weeks. His face and neck had thinned, his voice had deepened, his eyes had turned sad. There was hair on his upper lip. He seemed awkward, uncertain, and went about in a slouchy, loose-jointed manner.

"How do you feel, Davey?"

I nodded.

"Your throat still hurts?"

I nodded again.

"My mother said your mother told her it's all healed, Davey. There's nothing wrong with your throat anymore."

Oh yes there is, I said, thinking the words.

"What?"

Yes there is, I said. It feels choky and it will bleed if I talk.

He stared at me. "You're driving everyone crazy. Doesn't your father have enough trouble? What's the matter with you?"

I said nothing.

He gazed at me, the sadness darkening his eyes. "We're moving in a few days," he said. "Everything is a mess. I hate it." He kicked at the chain-link fence near which we stood.

"Why does the whole world have to be such a mess? I wish I could live away from the world in some place that's quiet. Does that sound funny to you?"

I shook my head slowly.

He peered at me intently through the lenses of his glasses. "What goes on inside your head, Davey? You're so quiet all the time. What are you thinking?"

I looked down and did not respond.

"My quiet cousin," he smiled sadly. "My brainy quiet cousin. Rabbi Akiva said, 'The fence of wisdom is silence.' Did you know that?"

I nodded. *Pirkei Avot,* three, seventeen, I said, thinking the words.

"We have to have faith in God," Saul said. "But why does everything have to be such a mess?" He continued to talk but I was no longer listening. Down the block, the door to the church had opened and Eddie Kulanski had come out together with a priest. Eddie Kulanski wore his dark winter jacket. I saw him put on his knitted woolen hat. The priest wore a dark coat and hat. They walked along the street and passed within two feet of me on the other side of the chain-link fence, talking quietly. As they passed me, Eddie Kulanski turned and looked directly into my face. He gave no sign of recognition. A shiver of dread ran all through me. Golem, I thought. He's the one.

That afternoon the entrance door to the apartment house was opened and my father came out alone. He stood on the stoop for a moment, gazing up and down the street. Then he walked over to the shoe repair shop and went inside. He was inside a long time. When he came out, he turned up the collar of his coat, walked slowly to the corner, pausing for a moment at the newsstand in front of the candy store, turned the corner and was gone. I looked out of the window at the drab street and the worn houses. My brother came outside dragging the tricycle. I looked away and closed my eyes.

"David," my father said to me in the kitchen the following morning. "Look at me when I speak to you."

I will look at you. I see color in your face and decision in your eyes.

"There is nothing wrong with your voice. Dr. Weidman says you are entirely cured."

But I felt the coughing and the blood. No one else felt it.

"Are you listening to me?"

I am listening.

"There is no reason in the world why you should be afraid to speak."

It's better with silence, Papa. If the whole world were silent it would be better for everyone. And the fixed and quiet photograph would return. Don't we all want the peace and stillness of that photograph? Papa, I need a quiet photograph. And the forest was so still with the snow covering the earth and ice on the trees and the flags silent and not whipping and snapping and no roaring shouts and no hate. Now all the photographs seethe with hate. What can we do? We must do something. But I won't add to the noise.

Golem.

He was there, unseen, somewhere inside the kitchen.

We must do something.

My father turned away, a faint scowl on his face. The radio voice spoke smoothly from the shelf near the icebox.

"The maniac dictator," said my father. "He also built piece by piece, small piece on small piece. He also built an organization."

"For the Angel of Death," said my mother.

Piece by piece. You have to build piece by piece. Are you listening, Golem? The maniac also built piece by piece and now no one knows what to do.

Every night now there were fires and men marching and a din of infinite flags and boots and voices. I would bring the Golem out of his unseen world and we would speak briefly of the day and I would find myself inside the rectangle of my window shade, putting out fires, breaking up demonstrations, shouting down the tumult of rage boiling up from tree-lined boulevards and cobblestone streets. I entered paneled rooms and listened to their schemes; I walked through alleys, watchful, searching for the dreaded cars that came in the early hours. They would see me and flee in terror. *The Golem!* they would cry. *The Golem!* But there were so many of them and I would return and lie wearily in my bed and the Golem would stand in the shadows, looking somehow smaller each night, tireder, shabbier, lines now in the corners of his eyes and his forehead.

In the night the radiator seemed strangely loud and the cold sharper than usual. Alex no longer came to my bed. I missed him. I lay awake and waited for sleep. It came reluctantly and crept into my bed, then slipped away with the first rush of steam into the cold radiator. I lay awake and smelled the bread baking in the ovens.

I was ill with pain and fever the day Mr. Bader returned from Europe. A few days later when he came to the house I was still in bed. I heard his polite, courtly voice in the doorway and in the kitchen and then in the living room. After a while he stood near my bed, peering down at me inside the circle of light cast by the dresser lamp.

"Well, hello," he said, faintly smiling. "You have had quite a time this winter, I hear."

I stirred and gazed up at him from my pillow and said nothing.

"Yes," he murmured. "I understand." He looked older, thinner. He put a finger on the knot of his tie and smiled. "How do you feel, David? I heard of your injury. I am deeply sorry. But Dr. Weidman tells me you are fine, that there was no harm done to your voice. Once I hurt my knee and I felt the pain there long after the injury was gone. I understand how you feel."

I lay very still and saw his craggy face and brown hair and thick eyebrows and gentle smile. His face, always tanned in the past, was now very pale. Had he seen the fires? Had he lost his tan in the glow of German torches? He seemed quieter now than in the past, less self-assured. He touched a finger to his tie again and coughed quietly.

"My nephew tells me he's been watching over you. That's fine. Look at that stack of newspapers. Are they yours? You've read them all? How old are you now, almost ten? Well." He smiled. "Well. I don't know whether to talk to you as if you were ten or twenty. But the difficulty with the voice will be gone soon, won't it? Otherwise how will I teach you your bar mitzvah? How will you learn grammar?" He paused, then coughed again lightly. "A cold. A German cold. I cannot get rid of it. We all had a difficult time this winter, David. But I am certain the difficulty with your voice will be over very soon. Good night, David. Be well. Have a good Pesach."

He went quietly from the room.

But I did not want to use my voice. There was tranquillity in silence. To speak would be to call back to life the troublesome web of scratchy relationships I avoided by moving quietly through the world. Also, I would cough and bleed if I talked, even though the choking feeling seemed almost entirely gone from my throat now. I saw myself coughing and bleeding. I saw the blood spraying the snow. I shuddered and was silent.

I remained silent even through Passover. Seated around

the open extension table in our living room during the first Seder were my parents, my aunt and uncle, Saul, my brother, and I. When my father asked me to recite the Four Questions, I shrank back in my chair.

"What is the matter with you, David?" he said loudly, his squarish features wearing some of his old anger.

The rushing of the blood in my ears drowned out his next words. Saul turned pale.

"Max, Max," I heard my uncle say, shaking his head.

"It certainly won't help to lose your temper at the child," said my aunt.

"David," my father said. "Look at me. It has been a black year for all of us. But now it is coming to an end. Do not make it blacker."

"For heaven's sake, Max," said my uncle.

"Tact is not one of your assets, Max," my aunt said.

My mother seemed panicky with fear. Her eyes darted nervously from face to face. I wanted to tell her not to be afraid, it was comforting to be silent. I said nothing.

Alex asked the Four Questions, his voice echoing through the apartment. He had been reciting them anyway for the past two years; my father had wanted me to recite them tonight to get me to use my voice.

"How is this night different from all the other nights?" Alex chanted. "All the other nights we eat leaven and un-leavened bread; tonight only unleavened bread. All the other nights . . ." It's different, I thought. It's different. Tonight my Golem is resting. But in two nights, after the first days of Pesach are over, we will work again—though it was tiring now, the work, and bore increasingly the mark of futility. I sat in silence at the table before the wine and the matzot and listened to the chanted words that recounted the de-liverance from Egypt. Two nights later, in the darkness of my room, I leaped into the menacing land and roamed troubled streets in search of those who needed aid.

All through that month and into May I would not speak. Dr. Weidman examined me and pronounced me fit; skinny but fit. The shock would wear off, I heard him tell my mother. "Patience, Ruth. Patience. The boy was terrified." My father called him a messenger of the Angel of Death but accepted his reassurance, for he had emerged from his own darkness and was nightly attending a school somewhere in the city. He was learning how to repair clocks and watches.

During the day he was away a great deal of the time at meetings somewhere downtown.

Mr. Bader came to the house one Sunday afternoon, carrying a heavy package which he placed on my desk. "Your job for the next few years," he said, smiling. Then he winked and said, "If you can find where you misplaced your voice." He went out and closeted himself with my father for more than an hour.

The package was a set of *Mikraot Gedolot*, the large multi-volumed work containing the major rabbinic commentaries to the Bible. It was bound in brown buckram, the letters stamped in gold, a floral pattern on the front of each binding along with a picture of a Torah scroll and the Ten Command-ments, all in gold. There were ten volumes, each of them eight inches by eleven inches in size. I made room for them on a shelf in my bookcase. Alex looked at them enviously. I started to tell him to make sure to keep away from them, but I remained silent.

The weather turned warm. Somewhere green buds were appearing on trees but I did not see them. I thought of the trees on my old street and was quiet. From the window of my classroom I saw Alex playing happily. Eddie Kulanski had shed his heavy winter jacket for a pale blue loose-fitting sweater. He remained along the periphery of my nar-row channel of existence like a dormant predator. I thought I saw his cousin on our street one day but I could not be certain.

The Golem continued his nightly forays into the dark fires within my rectangle. There seemed no end to the fires. I thought they would be with me all the rest of my life, until the night in May when they burned the books.

I watched them from my bed. They came along the wide tree-lined boulevard, students, thousands of them, their torches reddening the sky. In a square opposite a university lay a vast heap of treasure, jewels piled on jewels, gold and silver, diamonds, all glittering in the light of the torches. Then flames were put to the treasure, and faces made red and pink and orange by the sudden leaping of the fire laughed as the jewels curled and the bindings smoked and cracked and the pages went brown and the teeth of flame tore into the soul of the world. Books were being burned! Books! Golem! Stop them! He was suddenly by my side, in his gray shirt and baggy trousers, looking strangely small and weary, his face, my face, worn with the nights of sleepless forays against

the hordes of the Angel of Death. Now! Now! A leap, and we
were inside the tumultuous square, the deafening noise, the
laughter, near the curling edge of the smoke and flames that
rose to the black and silent sky. From everywhere books
were being thrown to the flames. The crowd roared. A rage
filled my being and I knew I could kill out of my hate. But
the books had to be saved. Scatter them! Stamp out the
flames! The fire was as tall as a hill and I plunged into it.
Something had to be saved. Something. I reached into the
flames and clutched a single volume and rushed with it into
the wild crowd, shouldering my way out into the sudden dark
silence of the night boulevard. There, beneath a street lamp,
I gazed at the singed pages of the book I had saved. It was
badly burned. I could not make out the title or the author.
What did it matter? I placed it gently beneath a flowering
linden tree and, thick-limbed with fatigue, moved from the
rectangle of burning books into the chill quiet of my bed.

I remember thinking then that they might soon come for
my own books and I did not know what to do. Golem, I
whispered. Golem.

The room was silent.

Golem. Where are you?

The silence echoed faintly.

I peered into the darkness and saw, in a deeply shadowed
corner, a small mound of earth, a gray shirt, and a pair of
dark trousers. As I looked, they dissolved slowly and were
gone.

I lay in my bed and listened to the silence. Alex snored
softly. The apartment was still. The window shade was dark.
I got out of bed, pulled up the shade, and gazed out at the
alleyway. Cats lounged among the garbage cans near the
metal doors of the basement. The sky was dark and tranquil.
I closed my eyes and whispered into the suddenly swarming
darkness, "Let not my thoughts trouble me, nor evil dreams,
nor evil fancies, but let my rest be perfect before Thee." I
whispered, louder, feeling the words move out across my
throat, "Thou shalt not be afraid of the terror by night, nor
of the arrow that flieth by day; of the pestilence that walketh
in darkness, nor of the destruction that wasteth at noonday."
Then I spoke in a normal voice into the night of my room
and said, "In the name of the Lord, the God of Israel, may
Michael be at my right hand; Gabriel at my left; before me,
Uriel; behind me, Raphael; and above my head the divine

presence of God." I repeated that passage of the prayer two more times.

The room grew very silent. I hugged to myself the large firm brown rectangle of the volume of Genesis I had taken to my bed. The window shade scraped softly upon the sill. It remained blank. I closed my eyes and slept and was not awakened by the morning noise of the radiator.

I said to my mother when I entered the kitchen, "What did Papa's father do for Mr. Bader's father?" My voice sounded hoarse. It resonated strangely inside my ears and tickled the back of my throat.

She stared at me and almost dropped the dish of cereal in her hands. "Well," she said, and her voice shook. "No good morning? Nothing? Just a question?"

"Good morning, Mama."

"Good morning, darling. Let me get used to hearing you again for a minute. Yes. Good morning. You and your father are full of surprises this month. You will make a nervous wreck of me with your surprises. Well. Mr. Bader. Your father's father helped Mr. Bader's father and his family escape from Poland into Germany from the police of the Tsar."

I looked at her.

"It was your grandfather's job in those days," she said. "He did it well."

My father came into the kitchen, wearing his pajamas and robe. "Good morning," he said, giving me an intent look. "You found your voice. For a change, Weidman was right."

"Max," said my mother.

"I am glad," he said, still looking at me.

"Sit down and have your cereal," my mother said.

"How do you feel, David?" asked my father, taking his seat at the table.

"I'm all right, Papa. How does my father feel?"

He gazed at me and smiled faintly. "Your father has good days and bad days. Today will be a good day. I need a glass of coffee, Ruth."

"They burned books yesterday, Papa," I said.

He looked at me.

"When will I start studying with Mr. Bader?"

"Soon," he said, narrowing his dark eyes.

"Thousands of books," I said. "Can I start very soon, Papa?"

"I will talk to Mr. Bader," he said in a quiet voice.

"It wasn't possible to stop them," I said. "But there are other ways."

I felt them looking at me as I bent over my breakfast and ate with more appetite than I had had in months.

My English teacher had given me a small blue book called *The Golem*. One afternoon I returned it to her.

"Did you like it?" she asked pleasantly.

"Yes. Thank you."

"Well," she said, surprised. "It's nice to be hearing you again, David."

"But its only a story, isn't it?" I asked.

"Of course."

"There are books that are more than stories," I said. "I like those books better. Storybooks are like air. You don't have anything left when you finish a storybook."

"Oh?" she said, smiling at me in a strange way.

"I don't care for storybooks too much. My little brother reads them all the time. He knows how to read already and he's not even in school yet. But I don't feel I have anything added to my mind when I read a storybook. I don't even like newspapers too much anymore."

"Indeed?" she said. Her rouged features seemed to have paled a little. "What books do you like, David?"

"Books that are true and never change and that you can never stop learning from."

"What books are those, David?" she asked in a very quiet voice.

"They're like something that's in a photograph," I said, suddenly unable to keep back the rush of words. "It's always there and you can look at it and learn from it and it never changes." And it's a comfort, I thought. And I'm tired and I want something firm and fixed, something that won't change every day like the newspapers, something that will make everyone happy that I'm studying it. "I have it in brown rectangles," I said, "but it comes in lots of shapes and colors. It's the most important set of books in the whole world and I'm going to know all of it."

"Well," she said, staring at me. "You are certainly making up for all your weeks of silence, young man."

I felt her still staring at me as I walked through the room and out the door.

In the school yard, Yaakov Bader clapped me on the back when I challenged him to a game of baseball cards, and then promptly cleaned me out. I went over to Saul. He was standing near the chain-link fence with some members of his class. They were discussing a passage of Talmud they had learned that morning.

"Hello," I said to Saul. "I'm all right."

His mouth opened slightly. We moved away from the group and stood leaning against the chain-link fence.

"How do you feel, Davey?" he asked soberly.

"I'm tired. But I'm okay."

"Who isn't tired? The whole world is tired. I'm glad you got your voice back, Davey. What happened? Just like that it came back? You had everyone really scared. You know what the midrash says about the voice?" He quoted the midrash about the three sounds or voices that make people happy: the voice of the Torah, the voice of rain, and the voice of coins. Then he quoted the midrash about how the voice of Jews studying Torah prevents their enemies from harming them. He was into a third midrash when the whistle blew and the recess was over.

Alex climbed into my bed that night. "I was so scared," he murmured. "You used to have such dreams, Davey." He fell asleep and lay with his arm across my chest, snoring quietly.

That Shabbat we went over to my Cousin Saul's new apartment on Clay Avenue. My uncle gave me a gentle embrace. My aunt kissed me lightly on the cheek and threw my mother a knowing glance. My mother looked nervously away.

I waited to hear from Mr. Bader.

He returned to Europe before I could see him again. An emergency, my mother said and would say no more. I spent the summer studying the first of my brown rectangles, verse by verse, with the help of my father, my cousin, and my uncle. I was rarely on the street; I did not like the street. Eddie Kulanski was on it often and sometimes his cousin. My brother roamed the street as if it were an extension of our apartment, always dragging in his wake a cluster of magnetized followers.

In September Saul entered a yeshiva high school in upper Manhattan and Alex entered first grade. In November my father opened a small watch repair service in the window of the shoe repair store owned by the Italian on our block. Mr. Bader returned from Europe. He came to the apartment one evening in December, looking dapper and tired and quite thin. A frown of concern had settled into his dark eyes. He remained in the States throughout the winter and on occasion he visited with us in our apartment; but it was not until the early spring that he had the time to teach me Torah with any degree of regularity. I began traveling to him on Sunday afternoons and Wednesday evenings, taking with me a Hebrew grammar, a notebook, and the first volume of my *Mikraot Gedolot,* the Book of Genesis.

Five

Sky and earth were gray with lingering winter cold. Six people sat in the trolley car, each alone at a window. I looked out my window at the almost deserted Sunday afternoon streets. The car stopped at a drab intersection. On the sidewalk two dogs fought one another over a scrap of bone.

I opened my *Mikraot Gedolot* and reread the Rashi commentary on the first word of the Hebrew Bible, *bereshit*, "in the beginning." Then I reread the Ramban, another commentary. "Listen to how they talk to one another, David," Mr. Bader had said to me the week before in his study. "Look at how the different parts of the page are arranged and you'll understand how Jews have been talking to each other for two thousand years about the Bible. First, there is the text itself in this column of large type; that's the heart of the page. Right next to it are these little markings, Masoretic notes which tell us how words should be spelled and call to our attention unusual words and vowels. They keep guard over the text and make sure it is correctly transmitted. I'll teach you more about these markings later. Would you like another cup of tea and lemon, David?"

I drank another cup of tea and lemon and listened to him tell me about the second-century Aramaic translation of Onkelos, a Palestinian, whose words appear alongside the Masoretic notes; and the eleventh-century commentary of Rashi, a Frenchman, who always refers to Onkelos, cites him, differs or agrees with him, talks to him, listens to him, and very often uses the midrash to explain the text; and the twelfth-century commentary of Abraham ibn Ezra, a wandering Spanish-Italian Jew, who parallels Rashi on the printed page in most editions of the *Mikraot Gedolot* and often differs with Rashi by giving his personal views of the literal meaning of the text in addition to taking account of those who came before him; and the Ramban, who lived in Christian Spain in the twelfth century and who refers often to Rashi and Abraham ibn Ezra, talks with them, argues with them, and adds his own original ideas and often the ideas of the mystics; and Sforno, an Italian Jew living during the time of the Italian Renaissance who tries to understand the Torah as a religious man of the Renaissance. There were other commentaries too on the page, and some that were printed separately in the back or as individual works; but Onkelos, Rashi, Abraham ibn Ezra, the Ramban, Sforno, and one or two others were the greatest of them all. They represented different ways of understanding the text. "You'll learn to listen to their voices, David. You'll listen to the way they talk to each other on the page. You'll hear them agreeing and disagreeing with each other. Sometimes the Ramban gets very nasty when he disagrees with Ibn Ezra. At times he disagrees strongly with Rashi. And I'll show you some commentaries that aren't in the *Mikraot Gedolot* and you'll listen to their voices too. You can pick and choose whichever commentary you like best on a verse. All of them, together with the text, make up the Torah, Prophets, and Writings— our Bible. And don't confuse the Ramban with the Rambam, David. The Ramban is Nachmanides and the Rambam is Maimonides. They were two different people. Now let me show you what Rashi said on the first word of the Torah, and then we'll see what bothered the Ramban when he saw Rashi's words and what the Ramban added. Don't you want your tea, David?"

I finished the passage in the Ramban and closed the book. The trolley car clattered around Crotona Park and into Boston Road, turned into Southern Boulevard, and came alongside the zoo. Two stops beyond the corner where Saul and I used to get off, I climbed down and went quickly to the sidewalk. I stood on the sidewalk waiting for the trolley to pass. Behind me was the stone wall of the zoo. I crossed the boulevard and walked the two blocks to the apartment house where Mr. Bader lived.

There were trees on the street, tall bare sycamores with

the vaguest beginnings of April buds on their boughs. But the chill air mocked the new life of the trees. The wind was raw, a memory of the dark months of winter. And the sky, massed with clouds, seemed to promise snow rather than spring.

I walked through the furnished and carpeted lobby of Mr. Bader's apartment house and climbed the staircase to the second floor. He opened the door to my knock and took my coat. "You look frozen, David. Would you like a cup of tea and lemon? Mrs. Bader is not home. Let me make us some tea." Carrying our tea, we went through the hallway to his study. There, I sat in a chair at his desk, the same dark mahogany desk on which I had first seen the photograph so many years ago, and we studied grammar and Torah.

A week ago I had sat at this desk and he had smiled at me in his gentle and urbane way, adjusted his maroon smoking jacket, put a finger to his dark red cravat, and had explained to me why he had undertaken to teach me. "Your father's father once did our family a favor. He saved our lives by getting us across the border out of Poland. I am now doing your father a favor by teaching his son Torah in a way that he will not learn it in most yeshivas. I did your uncle the same favor when I taught Saul. People exist by virtue of the help they give to one another. That's what I believe. Helping people improves the helped person's life and keeps the helping person human. I know how much rottenness there is in people. If I thought only of the ugliness in human beings, I would despair. So I try also to remind myself of the many people in this world who help one another. And I try to find myself a very bright student from time to time in order to study Torah with him and add a little bit to the good things going on in this world. This year my bright student is David Lurie."

He had smiled and sat back in his tall dark-wood chair. Behind him the dark velvet drapes had been drawn across the two tall windows. The Persian rug and the glass-enclosed bookcases were in shadows. A lamp burned on the desk, casting a vivid circle of light upon my notebook and grammar and the volume of *Mikraot Gedolot*. We would begin with a little bit of grammar, he said. Grammar was dull, he said. But it taught us about the building blocks of a language. Without grammar I would never be able to understand the Torah, he said. And the best way to learn grammar was to practice and memorize.

"I don't think grammar is dull," I said.

He looked at me from behind his desk.

"I like the book you told me to get. But I don't understand something on page forty-two."

"Forty-two," he said, looking at me and touching his cravat. "Yes. Well, your cousin warned me. All right. What don't you understand on page forty-two?"

"It has to do with the construct state," I said, and asked my question.

We spent an hour on grammar.

"It's like mathematics," I said when we were done.

"Oh?" he said. "In what way?"

"I like it. You can build the main groups of words from just the first simple rules."

"I suppose you can," he said. "I never quite looked at it that way."

"Some of the things in this book I learned in school. But I like the way the book teaches it better."

"Well, I'm glad," he said. "I will tell the man who wrote it."

The phone on his desk rang, startlingly shrill in the quiet study. He lifted the receiver and said, "Yes?" He listened a moment and said, "We are fine. Yes. Indeed I shall." He looked at me as he hung up the phone. "My wife apologizes for not being here to greet you and sends you her regards. Her sister is ill. Now let's leave grammar and go to your Chumash. You'll do the exercise for Wednesday. And don't rush too much, David. Don't be in such a hurry to learn everything. Here, let me show you what a page of *Mikraot Gedolot* is really all about. I don't think you learned this in your yeshiva."

He was right; I had never been taught Bible that way in school. For my teacher, the words of the Bible and Rashi were simply there. Our task was to understand, to memorize, and to give back what we had learned. When Mr. Bader was done with that page it quivered and resonated with life.

Mrs. Bader came in a few moments before the end of the second hour and brought tea and cookies into the study. She was a tall handsome woman, well-dressed and well-mannered. Her smooth skin was flushed from the cold air outside.

"It isn't April outside," she said cheerfully. "It's February. Have a cookie, David. Take a few cookies for the ride home."

"How is Edna?" asked Mr. Bader.

"Well, it isn't pneumonia, so we have to be grateful for

that. But she'll be in bed for a while. Are you two men almost done?"

"Almost," said Mr. Bader.

We had arranged to meet together for two hours. After two and a half hours he let me go.

"We should call Ruth and tell her the child will be late," Mrs. Bader said at the door.

"We don't have a telephone," I said.

"Is there a neighbor with a telephone?"

"Yes. He lives upstairs. He's an Italian."

"I will speak to him in Italian. What is his number?"

"He understands English." I gave her the number and she went off to make the call.

"My wife is a very punctual person," Mr. Bader said with a smile. "I have a tendency to lose myself in my work at times."

"Does the export-import business take a lot of time?" I asked.

"What?" he said, and gave me a queer look.

"Will you be traveling a lot again this year?"

"No," he said. "My work in Germany is done. The Nazis have informed me that they would not look kindly upon my presence in Berlin, or anywhere else in Germany for that matter."

Mrs. Bader came back into the hallway. "He will give your father the message."

"Mrs. Bader?"

"Yes, David?"

"Do you know German, too?"

"Why yes," she said. "I know German."

"I was wondering if you would mind if I brought a German book with me and asked you things I don't understand."

"No, I wouldn't mind, David."

"My mother understands German but I found some things in her books that she doesn't know too well."

"By all means, you may bring the book here, David."

"Or I could copy out some of the very hard words and show them to you if my mother won't let me take the books. She doesn't like some of the German books to leave the house. They belonged to my dead uncle."

The two of them looked at each other. Then they looked at me. Somewhere in the apartment a clock whirred and struck three musical notes in an ascending scale.

"It's late," Mr. Bader said. "You had better go home, David."

"Be careful crossing the street," Mrs. Bader said and opened the door for me.

I had gone down the staircase and through the large lobby, pausing for a moment to look at myself in the vestibule mirror. I saw an undersized and very thin youth in a dark wool hat and a dark winter jacket. His face was very pale and decidedly unpleasant in appearance, with gaunt features, dark sunken eyes behind steel-rimmed glasses, two reddish pimples on his chin, a weak mouth, and a crooked nose. I had a memory of once having had a different face, one that I had enjoyed watching gaze back at me. I did not like this face and I looked at it as infrequently as I could. I had buttoned my jacket and gone out into the wintry April night.

The cold weather had continued through the week and now I sat again in Mr. Bader's study. He was teaching me the cohortative and jussive extensions of the imperfect tense. We went rapidly through some exercises. Then he taught me the *vav* consecutive, which I already knew, and stative verbs, which were complicated enough to be interesting. Then we did the *niphal, piel,* and *pual* forms of the regular verbs, and he told me to memorize the conjugations. I told him I had memorized them during the week.

He smiled faintly.

"I have a question on page seventy-four," I said. "I don't understand how one of the words is accented."

"Yes?" he said. "Which word?"

Later we studied the words of Rashi and Ibn Ezra on verses six through nine and he outlined for me some of the points made by the Ramban. I was finding the Ramban difficult to understand. "Be patient, David. Forty-year-old men find the Ramban difficult to understand. There will be things in Rashi you will not understand. Be patient." We read a little segment of the Ramban. There was a tap at the door. Mr. Bader looked at his watch and blinked. "So fast? My God. All right, Miriam."

At the door I said to Mrs. Bader, "Can I just show you these lines in my notebook? I copied them from one of the German books."

"Of course," she said.

She translated the lines. There was something I did not understand. We stood in the hallway near the door.

"Take your coat off, David," she said. "You will get over-heated and catch cold."

When we were done with the passage I asked her a question about the *es sei* and *es seien* forms in German and wondered if they could be compared to the cohortative and jussive in Hebrew. Mr. Bader, who had been standing by patiently and listening, now joined the conversation.

I put my jacket back on and thanked them. Mr. Bader asked me to wait a moment, went away, and came back in a moment with a package in brown paper. "For you," he said. They were dictionaries of German and Hebrew. "They aren't the best," he said. "But they will suit your purposes for the time being. Let's see how long it will take you to outgrow them."

"I think I ought to call your Italian neighbor," Mrs. Bader said. "I am getting a great deal of practice with my Italian, David. But we will see to it from now on that you are not late again. Your mother becomes upset when you are not home in time for supper."

I went out into the cold April evening and spent the trolley car ride looking through the Hebrew and German dictionaries. The two and a half blocks of Washington Avenue from Claremont Parkway to where I lived were dark and deserted. I walked very quickly and came home in the middle of a supper of boiled chicken and potatoes, the leftovers from our Shabbat meals.

"The scholar," my father said wryly, looking up from his plate. "Wash your hands and come in before your brother eats your food."

"So late, darling?" my mother murmured. "Why so late?"

Alex was eating and reading a book. He did not seem to have noticed me come in.

Later I sat at my desk reading and Alex slept in his bed, snoring. There was a chill in the air and after a while I had to go to the bathroom. Crossing the living room, I saw the light on at the desk in my parents' bedroom. My father had converted the desk into a watchmaker's workbench. Every day he brought home with him watches that he worked on into the night. Now he sat bent over a watch movement, a jeweler's glass in his eye, a tiny screwdriver in his hand. At first it had fascinated me to see him take apart a watch and put it together again; the separated pieces of a watch lying on the desk top seemed incapable of being made into something as awesome as the object that marked the passing of time. I remembered him on the stallion and I could barely connect him to those hours in the past. Had that really been my father? All of that world seemed so dim and distant now. Even my trolley trips to that neighborhood had not called back sharply the memories of those years. I could not be truly certain who that horseman had been; but the watchmaker who took timepieces apart and put them together again so they would function properly—that watchmaker was my father. I remembered my uncle's excited assurance that my father would one day decide what to do again with his life. That assurance had conjured up in my mind vivid images of swift decisions, gallant action—a warrior not a watchmaker. I did not know what to make of his decision. But everyone seemed content; there was a settled certainty about people now whenever they were in my father's presence. Friends were once again dropping in. There was even some talk among them about starting a little synagogue of their own in a room in the yeshiva. My father did not like the bigness of the yeshiva synagogue where we now prayed.

Every evening I studied at my desk, my brother studied at the kitchen table, my mother did her housework and wrote letters to her family, and my father repaired watches in the bedroom. Sometimes the canary would burst into song and I would look through my window and imagine I could see a maple in the dim light outside. But I was done with illusions and I knew it was shadows and cats lying among the garbage cans in the alleyway. When I finished my schoolwork I would turn to my *Mikraot Gedolot,* and my grammar, my notebook, my dictionaries. Inside the pages of my *Mikraot Gedolot* I began to move, with enormous difficulty at first, especially when it came to the Ramban, but then with increasing facility, through the centuries of voices. I shuttled back and forth between ancient Palestine and medieval France, Spain, Portugal, and Italy. I listened to them talking to one another about the words of the Torah. I saw the blue waters of the Mediterranean, the white cities of Moslem and Catholic Spain, the vineyards of France, the city-states and hill villages of Italy; for Mr. Bader had told me of the lives of the commentators. Through their voices the text of the Torah took on a luminous quality. I would read a passage of the Bible, read the commentary of Rashi on the passage, read Ibn Ezra, read the Ramban, read Sforno. I read every word and would not go ahead until I thought I understood each word I read. But the Ramban remained very difficult. Often I was happy if I could grasp his ideas in vague outline. I did not understand anything about his secret mystical doctrine. Ibn Ezra too was often very difficult. Sometimes I surrendered to frustration and would sit at my desk late into the night, loathing my ignorance and eager for my next meeting with Mr. Bader, when the difficulties would be explained and clarified. Then, exhausted, I would go to sleep.

The weather remained cold. Spring that year seemed an indistinct copy of the malevolent winter rather than an authoritative time of its own. On the last Sunday in April I came out of Mr. Bader's apartment house, walked the two blocks to the trolley car and, standing on the sidewalk, put my right hand into my jacket pocket and realized that I had lost my carfare. I searched through all my pockets. A trolley car pulled up at the corner, waited, then moved away. I watched it go down the boulevard. Then I walked back to Mr. Bader's apartment.

Mrs. Bader opened the door and looked very surprised. I explained about the carfare. "David, David," she murmured, shaking her head. "Come inside."

I stood in the hallway and heard voices in the living room. The Baders had been alone when I had left them earlier that evening.

"Let me take your jacket," Mrs. Bader said. "I suppose I had better call our Italian friend again. Come into the living room."

Two men were in the living room with Mr. Bader. I had never seen them before. They looked to be in their middle forties, wore dark ill-fitting suits and open-necked shirts. They sat on the sofa across from Mr. Bader, who sat comfortably in an easy chair, his legs crossed. He looked up when I came in and said, "I thought that was your voice I heard, but I didn't believe it."

"He lost his carfare," Mrs. Bader said.

"I didn't take any more money," I said, ashamed. "Just the carfare."

"Just the carfare," Mr. Bader said, and smiled faintly.

The two men looked on curiously.

"I am going to call my Italian friend," Mrs. Bader said cheerfully. "I'm getting to know that Italian very well. Did you know that he had once contemplated a career in opera?"

I shook my head.

"Oh, yes," she said. "But there was a difficulty. He had no talent. He is a happy and honest man, our Italian." She went into the hallway.

"Well," Mr. Bader said, gazing at me. "You lost your carfare. All right. Come here and meet two good friends." He told me their names. "And this is David Lurie," he said, indicating me with a slight move of his hand.

"The son of Max Lurie?" said one of the two men in Hebrew.

"Correct," said Mr. Bader, also in Hebrew.

The two men glanced at each other. They were short and slight of build, with leathery faces and calloused hands. Their hair was thick and combed straight back. They bore the vague resemblance to one another that brothers sometimes have, save that one had red hair and the other's hair was dark brown.

"How is your father?" the red-haired one asked me in heavily accented English. "I have known him for many years."

"He's all right," I said.

"You can speak to him in Hebrew," Mr. Bader said in Hebrew.

"Try German," Mrs. Bader said from the doorway to the living room. She had returned from her Italian friend. "He needs practice in German."

Mr. Bader laughed softly.

"What is your father doing?" asked the one with the brown hair.

"He is working," I said in Hebrew.

"Yes? We heard he was not well."

"He is well now."

"What work does he do?" asked the red-haired one.

"He is a watchmaker."

They looked at me. Then they looked at each other.

"I think," said Mr. Bader in Hebrew, "that we are going to let the son of Max Lurie go home."

"Give your father regards from us," said the man with the red hair. "Tell him we wish him success in his new work. Tell him we said it seriously."

The other nodded.

I went into the hallway with Mrs. Bader. "I can't let you go home this late without eating," she said. "Do you like bananas and sour cream? Come into the kitchen and let me give you something to eat."

I sat at the table in the spacious kitchen and watched her doing things skillfully at the counter near the sink.

"David," she said quietly, her back to me. She hesitated. Then she turned and said softly, "You cannot continue returning home late when you come here."

I looked down at the top of the yellow and white table and was quiet.

"You have your own family, David, and they love you. Mr. Bader and I have great affection for you, but your parents should not be made to feel uncomfortable because you are studying Bible with my husband." She paused. Then she said, "Do we understand one another, David?"

"Yes," I said, after a moment, and hung my head. It's so nice here, I thought. I only wanted it a little longer.

"That's fine," she said brightly. "This and a nickel will help you get back home." She brought the dish of sliced bananas and sour cream to the table. "Would you like some bread and butter?" she asked.

I nodded.

"And a glass of milk?"

I nodded again.

"This isn't supper, David. It is merely a snack." She stood at the counter watching me eat. "Is your father really all right?" she asked. "I haven't seen him in such a long time."

"He's well."

"And his new work is going well?"

"I don't know. I think so. Are those two men in the living room friends of my father's?"

"Friends? No, I don't think I would consider them to be your father's friends. You certainly were hungry, weren't you?"

We stood at the door. I put on my coat and hat.

"You understand what I said to you before about continuing to go home late?" she asked gently.

"Yes."

"Good night, David. You have your books? Did I give you the carfare? Yes. Do you have it? Good. You have everything. Good night, David. We will see you on Wednesday."

I took the trolley car back and walked the chill dark streets of Washington Avenue to my house. Supper was over. My mother sat at the kitchen table writing letters. I told her about the two men I had met in Mr. Bader's apartment. "They send regards, Mama."

"I will tell your father."

"How do they know Papa?"

"They know him. It has to do with Zionist politics."

"They were surprised when I told them Papa is a watch-maker."

"Yes?" she said quietly. "They were surprised? Do you know anyone who is not surprised by that?" She peered at me wearily over the tops of her recently acquired glasses. "I saved you some chicken."

"The men were from Palestine, Mama."

She seemed neither startled nor intrigued by that bit of information. "Your father knows many people from Palestine."

"I liked the way they spoke Hebrew," I said. "It's a different kind of Hebrew."

She sighed faintly. "I must finish this letter, David."

Later I went through the hallway into the living room. My father was at his workbench. I stood near the doorway to my parents' bedroom looking at him painstakingly take apart a watch. The room was dark save for the pool of light cast by the lamp near his head. His hair had begun to recede but it was still dark brown and wavy. He wore a tall dark skullcap on his head when he was home, though in the store he was bare-headed. I saw his fingers separate a piece of the watch from the movement and place it gently on the top of the desk. He was so silent; the room was silent. We never disturbed him when he worked. Looking at him now and remembering the two men I had met in Mr. Bader's apartment, I realized that my father had a life outside our family about which I knew nothing. The meetings he went to; the subdued night conversations with old friends that took place frequently in our living room or kitchen, their voices so low I could not hear; the conferences with Mr. Bader—I knew nothing about any of this save that it had to do with Zionist politics, as my mother always put it. Once he had been in real estate and had failed. Now he was a watchmaker. I could not understand how the two were connected.

I turned away, went past the canary, and found my brother seated at my desk doing his homework.

"You weren't home," he said immediately.

"It's okay, Alex."

"You need it now?"

"No."

"There are some words here I don't understand, Davey."

"What words?"

He showed them to me. I looked at the book. It was *The Adventures of Tom Sawyer*. A friend's older brother had loaned it to him, he said. But he couldn't understand whole parts of it.

"God in heaven, Alex. You're too young for that book."

"I am not!" He stiffened with anger. "I need a little help with it, Davey."

So I sat with him for a while and read and explained to him parts of *The Adventures of Tom Sawyer*. He sat on my chair at my desk, reading aloud and becoming increasingly upset as he went along. The book was clearly too difficult for him.

He slammed the book shut. "I hate it!" he shouted.

"Go to sleep," I said. "In two years you'll love it."

"I hate it!" he shouted again.

"Really? Do you know how many books you hate? All the great books in the world that you can't read yet, all those books you hate. My bright little brother. Don't be in such a hurry, Alex."

That sobered him somewhat. He stared petulantly at *Tom Sawyer,* gave it up with painful reluctance, and picked up another book. He sat at my desk in my chair, reading. I sat on my bed and reviewed the section of *Mikraot Gedolot* I had learned earlier that day, then began to prepare in advance for Wednesday night.

Later I lay in bed in the darkness of the night and listened to my brother's faint snoring. My parents were talking softly in the kitchen. I saw inside my eyes all that I had learned that day; then I went over all the pages my teachers would be teaching in school the next day, for I had read far into all our textbooks. I began to drift languidly into sleep as timber drifts on the surface of a slow-moving river. I felt myself spinning with exquisite slowness in a lazy eddy of cool water when from somewhere deep within the darkness of the river a thought darted upward like a strange creature and, almost asleep, I suddenly found myself wondering if a machine gun had as many parts as a watch and was as difficult to take apart and put together. I came sharply awake and could not understand why I had thought that. The room swarmed faintly and I thought I could hear a vague stirring from the dark shadows in the corner near my bed. I opened my eyes and saw only the dim outline of the window shade. The shade was still. The room was silent. After a while I slept.

Then I was ill for almost a week and when I was able to go back outside the weather had turned warm and there were young leaves on the trees that lined the streets of Mr. Bader's neighborhood. There were leaves too on the trees beyond the stone wall of the zoo, but I did not go into the zoo that spring for I did not have time for lions and tigers.

In late May the weather turned hot. Windows were opened all up and down my street. Women sat near their windows staring into the street and on Sundays men sat in their undershirts drinking beer and listening to the radio.

I would leave the apartment a little before four o'clock in the afternoon and walk quickly by the open windows, hearing vaguely the radio voices that moved out into the street like waves. I walked in and out of the voices and took my trolley and rode to Mr. Bader's neighborhood where, walking through the hot streets, I would often hear those same voices coming through the open windows of new elegant apartments in which men sat not in undershirts drinking beer but in summer shirts sipping amber liquids from tall glasses containing chips of ice.

All though May and into June I walked quickly alongside open windows on Sunday afternoons. Soon it began to seem as if all the radio voices were one voice; and then one day I walked slowly and it was indeed one voice, the deep organlike voice of a man. I stopped at a window to hear what he was saying and a man in an undershirt gave me an angry look and I walked on. I walked slowly now, listening; then I took the trolley and walked slowly again, still listening. The man was talking about President Roosevelt and the New Deal and liberals and Communists. When Mr. Bader let me into his apartment I asked him who Father Coughlin was. He seemed astonished and murmured, "I know you are a bookworm, David. But such a bookworm?" And he told me about Father Coughlin.

"Why do they let him broadcast?" I asked.

"America is a free country, David, and he has a very large following."

"Does he hate Jews?"

"He probably does, but he is not yet being too crude about it."

"They shouldn't let him broadcast," I heard myself say in a voice I had not heard in a long time. "But what do the goyim care?"

He gave me a strange look. "They care, David. He is

attacked quite frequently by gentiles. Would you like a glass of iced tea? Oh, I forgot, you have been taught that Eastern European prejudice against iced drinks. How about a glass of milk? Then we'll go and do our work."

"Why can't they leave us alone? Why do they all hate us?"

"They do not all hate us," he said quietly.

"Most of them hate us or don't care about us."

"Most people don't care about anyone except themselves and the ones very close to them."

"I hate them. I despise them."

"Do you?" he said very gently. "Well, you are certainly your father's son on that point."

"They hate us and kill us."

"Yes. But there are many good souls among them. They help keep the world alive."

"I don't want to talk about it anymore," I said abruptly. "I want to study. Please."

"Of course," he said. "We should not waste our study time talking about Father Coughlin."

We did not talk again about Father Coughlin. But I continued to move in and out of the sound of his voice as I walked the two and a half blocks of Washington Avenue from my house to the trolley and then two more blocks from where the trolley let me off to the house in which Mr. Bader lived. After a while I started walking along the curb of the sidewalk but it did no good, I could still hear his voice. The radios were turned to it and sending it out to the street. All through the coming months when the leaves became full and the streets turned dry and dusty with summer heat I kept walking through the sound of that voice on my way to Mr. Bader to study Bible.

One fall afternoon I saw two boys coming toward me on the street carrying copies of Coughlin's *Social Justice* magazine and felt a sudden shiver of dread. I hesitated, then continued walking. They passed me by without a glance, two tall boys with light hair and blank faces. I took the trolley to Mr. Bader's apartment and found it difficult to concentrate on the words in front of me.

That was the evening we began to study the section on Noah and the Flood. A week later we were deep in the attack by the Ramban on the words of Abraham ibn Ezra to chapter nine verse eighteen in Genesis. "Rabbi Abraham left his path of simple explanations of the text and began to prophesy lies," wrote the Ramban. We spent a long time

trying to understand clearly their differing explanations of
the Biblical text, "And Ham was the father of Canaan," and
their understanding of verses twenty-four and twenty-five,
"And Noah awoke from his wine and knew what his youngest
son had done to him. And he said: Cursed be Canaan, a
servant of servants shall he be to his brothers."

Mr. Bader explained the horrifying deed done to Noah.
"I think you are old enough to understand it," he said. "And
if I am going to teach you Bible I am going to teach it to
you the way it is written. The Torah is an account of man
in his beauty as well as, sometimes, in his ugliness. Now we're
at one of the ugly parts." And he read the commentaries of
Rashi and Ibn Ezra that talked about Noah's having been
emasculated by someone to prevent him from having a fourth
son. Between verses twenty-one and twenty-two is where the
deed is hinted at, he said; and it seems to have been done by
Canaan, the youngest son of Ham; otherwise why would
verse twenty-two state, "And Ham, the father of Canaan,
saw the nakedness of his father"? Why mention Canaan here
at all in connection with Ham unless Canaan was implicated
in that terrible act against Noah? But if the deed was done
by Canaan, Noah's grandson, why are we told in verse
twenty-four that Noah awoke and saw what his youngest son
had done to him? And if it was his youngest son who had
committed the deed, why in verse twenty-five is Canaan,
Ham's youngest son and Noah's grandson, the one who is
cursed? Finally, Mr. Bader said in his quiet voice, according
to the list of sons in chapter six, verse ten, Japheth and not
Ham was Noah's youngest son. But in chapter nine, verse
twenty-three, Shem and Japheth behave very respectably
toward their father and there is no indication at all that Japheth was implicated in the deed.

Those were the problems the commentators faced as they
attempted to explain the Biblical text. When I had prepared
the material in advance I had understood in a general way
the words of the Ramban and Ibn Ezra and very clearly the
words of Rashi. I listened to Mr. Bader's careful explanation
of the Ramban and to his review of Ibn Ezra. Then he
paused and looked at me. Which commentator did I like
best? he asked.

I hesitated. Then I shrugged. I don't know, I said. I wanted
to think about it.

"It is a very complicated section," he said. "They are very
honest about its difficulties and they each give good explanations."

I said nothing.

"You are not satisfied."

I shrugged again. I was very confused.

"The David Lurie answer." He smiled, imitating my shrug. "I thought we had outgrown that. Shall we read some more or shall we stop here?"

We decided to stop and I went home in the chill autumn night thinking about the passage and was back in time for supper.

"Hello," my father said, looking up from the kitchen table. "My scholar is on time today. You look just like my brother David, may he rest in peace, when you wear your sad face. What is the matter?"

I told him I was upset by something in the Torah that I could not understand.

"What?"

"The section about what happens to Noah after the Flood."

He glanced quickly at my brother, who sat at the table reading a book. "Rashi is very clear on what happened."

I shrugged. He sat still, looking at me.

"Please wash up, darling," my mother said, with weariness in her voice. "I am ready to serve supper."

He came into my room late that night and stood by my desk watching me read and I did not hear him. Alex was asleep in the shadows along his side of the room. The curved gooseneck lamp cast a soft yellow light on the books on my desk. Then I heard a cough and I looked up and saw my father's face in the dimness beyond the circle of light.

"How you study," he murmured. "I have been standing here almost ten minutes."

"I'm sorry, Papa."

"No, no, you did nothing wrong. It is good to be able to concentrate the way you do. I was never able to do that when I went to school. I could not sit quietly for too long. You are still bothered by the section in Noah?"

"I don't understand it, and I don't understand how Rashi and Ibn Ezra and the Ramban or any of the others explain it."

"Everything up until now you understood clearly?"

"Not everything, Papa. But this bothers me."

"Why?"

"I don't know. It bothers me. The Ramban is so angry at Ibn Ezra."

"Angry?" His face appeared to float in the shadows beyond the light. The scar on his cheek, reflecting some of the light, seemed a dim white line in the shades of darkness that were the planes and hollows of his cheeks and lips and prominent jaw. "How do you know he is angry?"

I read aloud the words of the Ramban.

"Why do you say he is angry? He disagrees with him, that's all."

"He calls him a liar, Papa."

"Do not take it so seriously, David. It is a way they have of talking. Ibn Ezra says it was Canaan and the Ramban agrees with Rashi that it was Ham. Why are you so upset?"

"But I hear him talking, Papa. And he sounds angry."

"What?" he said, vaguely startled.

"I can see him and hear him. He sounds angry. He doesn't like Ibn Ezra."

"David," he murmured. And again, "David."

"I can't get a picture in my eyes of what happened, Papa. It bothers me. They all try to give good explanations, but they can't really answer all the questions."

Then I remembered something and I thought, It's like God telling Noah to take two animals of each kind and then telling him to take seven of the clean kind and two of the unclean kind, and then the Torah telling us that only two of each kind came into the ark. There had been similar difficult sections. But this one about Noah and his sons upset me very much and I did not know why. "I don't have a picture in my eyes of what really happened and who really was cursed."

"What do you mean, a picture in your eyes?"

"I have to see it in my eyes, Papa, before I can understand it."

He was silent a moment. A block away, an elevated train rushed by on the trestle. My window rattled. I could feel the house vibrate.

"I think," he said quietly, "you want too much. You are only eleven years old, David."

"Mr. Bader doesn't have a picture either, Papa. I have a picture of Noah. But I don't have a picture of this thing that happened to him and who was cursed."

"David," he said, after a long moment,

"Yes, Papa?"

"You are learning a lot from Mr. Bader."

"Yes."

"He is a good teacher."

"Yes."

"I am glad. Because he is doing my job and I do not like

others to do my job unless they can do it better than I can. But I want to tell you something my brother David, may he rest in peace, once said to me. He said it is as important to learn the important questions as it is the important answers. It is especially important to learn the questions to which there may not be good answers. We have to learn to live with questions, he said. I am glad Mr. Bader is a good teacher and I am glad he tells you truthfully that he does not have answers to all your questions."

"I like Mr. Bader. He said he won't be going back to Europe so soon."

"Yes, I think his job will keep him here for a while."

"Is there still a lot of export-import business now in the Depression?"

He looked at me. "David, you are so deep in your books that you do not know what is going on right under your nose. Mr. Bader is no longer in the export-import business. He is the European director of the Jewish Overseas Aid Committee."

I said nothing. European director. It sounded very important.

"It is a big job and he is a good man for it."

Still I said nothing. After a moment, I hung my head.

He stood quietly outside the circle of light, gazing at me. Then his hand came out of the darkness and entered the light and I felt it gently stroke my face. "I understand," he said quietly. "Yes, I understand. But you must understand, too. In order to help Jews I will work on committees, but to make a living I will work only for myself. That is the way I am, David. If you do not like your father as a simple watchmaker, there is nothing I can do about it." He paused for a moment, reflecting, a hard set to his face now. Then slowly his features softened. "You have heard of Rabbi Yosi the Galilean?"

"Yes. In the Gemara."

"What was he?"

"A shoemaker."

"And you have heard of Rabbi Yehoshua?"

"Yes."

"What was he?"

"A blacksmith."

"Some are rich and some are poor. What does how much money a man makes have to do with his wisdom or the good he is able to do for others? There is a man on my committee who may go on home relief next month. He is the best man I have. No one in the entire Revisionist office has as sharp a brain as this man. It is nice to have lots of money and it is terrible to be poor and hungry. But the most terrible thing of all is to be useless. Do you understand me, my scholar?"

I nodded my head slowly, feeling a vague drumming sound in my ears. I heard myself ask, "What committee, Papa?"

He withdrew his hand from my cheek. I saw the play of shadows on his face as his head moved slightly to register his annoyance. "David, you do your job and I will do mine. Your job is to study. My job is—whatever my job is. When it comes time for you to know my job, I will tell you about it. Now I think you ought to let Noah rest a little bit and get yourself to bed. It is very late. Noah will still be here tomorrow and you can worry about him then."

I said suddenly, without thinking the words, "Is Hitler going to kill all the Jews in Europe, Papa?" A faint trembling had taken hold of me, as if the room had begun of itself to vibrate.

I saw him looking at me outside the rim of light, his eyes suddenly narrow. "I do not know what Hitler will do," he said very quietly.

"I see the newspapers, Papa. Isn't anyone doing anything?"

"Yes," he said with bitterness. "They are filling the air with words."

"Words?" I heard myself say. "The Canaanites don't listen to words. We have to save them, Papa. Your father and mother, Mama's father and mother, Aunt Sarah's father and mother. We have to get them out."

He said nothing. He stood there, staring at me, his lower jaw set tight and jutting forward.

"Papa?"

He stirred. "Two cousins are out," he said, still staring at me.

"What?" I said.

"They went to Eretz Yisroel. Your grandparents have decided to stay. They accepted—jobs."

"But he'll kill them, Papa."

"They have jobs," he said. "A person who has a job to do does it and worries later about whether or not he could have been killed. I think you ought to go to sleep now, David."

"The Golem could kill him. He could sneak in and kill him."

"What?"

"He could find him alone in his bed and kill him."

"David—"

"I'm tired," I said. "I really thought they were going to leave us alone for a while." Then I said, "It would be a nice world if there were no goyim in it, Papa." I was very sleepy and my eyes hurt.

"You think so?" my father said. "I doubt it. We would probably start killing each other. Who knows? Go to sleep, David."

His arm came out once again from the darkness into the light and he caressed my cheek. Then he turned and went from the room.

Later I lay very still in my bed and thought, The Golem is dead and cannot do anything. The Canaanites are going to rule the world for a thousand years. The Angel of Death and the Canaanites. It is all one enemy with different faces. Canaanites, Greeks, Romans, Christians, and now the Germans. They will kill as many Jews as they can and the others will flee and hide in caves as they did in the time of the Romans. All the world will be filled with black idolatry. Why do they hate us so much? A face hovered somewhere in the darkness, dim, white, cool, distant. I reached for it but it moved away. Then it was there again and I sought it with my eyes and it moved slowly closer to me and it was the face of the statue in flowing robes outside the church where Eddie Kulanski and his parents used to pray. I looked at the white marble features, at the sweetness and loveliness of that face, at the sad, tender, wistful smile on its lips. It stood very close to me now, and I saw its beckoning arms. Its eyes and face were filled with compassion, but when I touched the stone it was cold.

Through the window of my classroom I saw Eddie Kulanski walking with a group of his friends. He had grown and his wrists stuck out from the sleeves of his jacket. His face was fuller but the gray eyes were still half-closed and his mouth remained small and thin. He carried on top of his books a copy of *Social Justice*. I watched him cross Washington Avenue and go up the block to the apartment house where he lived.

Day after day I watched for him and saw him come along the side street from his school, always in the company of others, and cross Washington Avenue and walk to his house. Once or twice he stopped at the newsstand to look at a magazine.

One afternoon I saw him stop in front of the window of the shoe repair shop and look inside. It was a small shop and my father's workbench was set very close to the window, making it appear as if he were on display. A small sign had been placed in the window among the heels and laces and shoeshine equipment: M. LURIE, WATCH REPAIR. Beyond his workbench were the lathes and workbench of Mr. Donello, the thin, bald-headed Italian who owned the shop. During the first weeks my father had been in that window I had cringed each time I had seen the nakedness of the panel of hooks he had placed on the wall above his workbench. But now it was laden with watches. A second panel had been put up near it and was almost entirely covered with watches. My father worked bent over his bench, oblivious to the faces that stared at him through the window. Now I watched Eddie Kulanski at the window. He leaned forward, peering inside at my father. Then he straightened and walked slowly home.

The next day he entered the store, stayed a few minutes, and went home. I found out from my father that he had left an Ingersoll pocket watch to be repaired.

He returned to the store a few days later and I saw him standing inside near the window, talking to my father. He paid for the repair work and came out of the store holding the watch in his ungloved right hand. He put the watch to his ear. Then he slipped it into a pocket and walked toward his house. He still had that light springy walk and it was not difficult to imagine him as having grown into a precise duplicate of his cousin.

I saw him and thought of him often as the winter months slipped by and rumors began to float in from the fringes of our neighborhood, from the streets beyond the elevated train and the beer factory on the hill and the public library, from the deep east Bronx of Hunt's Point that lay between Bruckner Boulevard and the East River, about Jews molested, attacked, beaten by goyim. On occasion we would read of an event in the newspapers and talk of it in the school yard.

"He's an old man," Yaakov Bader told a group of us on a bitter cold day as we stood near the chain-link fence in the yard. "They were bothering these two kids and he told them to stop and one of them broke his arm. My father knows him."

"What do you mean?" someone said. "Just like that they broke the man's arm?"

"He says they hit him with something but he can't remember what."

"But just like that to break someone's arm?"

"It's nothing to them to use their hands."

"On my block I once saw two of them torturing a cat."

"They're the messengers of the Angel of Death."

Heads nodded sober agreement. Plumes of steam rose from their mouths into the freezing air. An elevated train rumbled by along Third Avenue.

I moved out of earshot and away from the dread in their faces.

One night someone threw a stone through our classroom window. In the morning the janitor swept the glass from the floor and hammered plywood across the open space. It was the window near which I sat. In the weeks that followed it became clear that the yeshiva was in no hurry to replace the glass. I could no longer see the street.

Saul told me one Shabbat afternoon in January that there were platoons of goyim numbering about twenty-five each walking the streets of New York looking for Jews. They would try to sell a copy of *Social Justice* to someone who looked Jewish and if he refused to buy it they would start taunting him and pushing him and then they would beat him and run off. We were in his room when he told me that and I gazed out his window at the brick-paved street that was Clay Avenue and at the narrow section of Claremont Park where a middle-aged woman was walking her dog along a paved path between fields of brown winter grass.

"Why don't the police stop them?" I asked.

"The police are Irish and Catholic," he said, squinting his eyes myopically through the window. "What do you expect?"

"Are you all right?"

"My eyes hurt. I have to get my glasses changed again."

From the living room came the murmur of conversation. Our parents were there, together with some of their friends.

"Is your father going to Boston again for the Revisionists?" I asked.

"How do you know he's going to Boston?"

"I thought I heard Papa and him talking about it earlier."

"Don't have such big ears, Davey." He squinted his eyes again at the woman walking the dog in the park. "I just got these glasses two years ago," he said moodily. "It's the small print in the Gemara, the doctor says."

Alex was in the room with us, listening. On the way back, as we waited to cross Webster Avenue, he said to me, "Everybody is so scared, Davey."

I was quiet. We crossed the wide, brick-paved street.

"You know what our teacher said? He said if we're stopped by goyim we should run away and not fight back. He said a Jew shouldn't fight."

I knew his teacher, a short thin-faced man with a high voice and weak eyes.

"Do your teachers say anything about it, Davey?"

"No."

"What would you do?"

"I don't know."

"I hate to feel this way, Davey. I hate it. The stinking bastard goyim." His cheeks were red with the winter wind and his breath vaporized in the air as he talked. He was almost as tall as I, and very strong. He looked a duplicate in miniature of my father, who was walking behind us talking quietly with my mother. "I hate it," he said again. "It's a bad feeling to feel this way, Davey."

I agreed with him. We walked the rest of the way home in gloomy silence.

Early that March, a week before Purim, one of Saul's classmates was jumped by a group of youths selling copies of *Social Justice* near the Nedick's orange juice stand on Times Square. The Irish policeman on duty waited awhile until he broke up the fight.

In our school yard the following day, Yaakov Bader said, "They broke his nose, and his eyes are all black and blue. My father knows the family."

"Did he fight back?" someone of the group asked.

"I don't know."

"What good does it do to fight back? It only makes them angrier."

"But you can't not fight back."

"I would've run."

"They were all around him."

"The bastards."

They huddled together, talking.

I moved away from them and leaned against the chain-link fence, feeling the trembling of my heart.

The night after Purim, Joey Younger came out of the Blendheim movie theater on 169th Street near Washington Avenue and started down toward Webster Avenue. As he approached Park Avenue, four boys came out of an alley-way and blocked his path. They asked him for money. He gave them all the money he had and turned his pockets inside out to show them he had no more. They asked him if he was Jewish. He said no, he wasn't Jewish. They asked him to prove it. He began to cry. One of them kicked him in the groin. Another struck him across the back with a chain. They fled.

That incident made the *Daily News* and the *Daily Mirror*. The school buzzed with it tensely. There was a faculty meeting and the rumor of an assembly during which we would be told how to act if we were ever stopped in the street by goyim. The assembly did not take place. My Hebrew teacher, a stout man with a short dark beard and a kindly smile, never mentioned the incident. None of the English teachers mentioned it.

Joey Younger returned to school a week later, looking very pale and nervous. I came into the school that morning, passed by the open door of his classroom, and saw him surrounded by his classmates. I had not had anything to do with that class since I had been skipped out of it after first grade. I hesitated in the doorway. Classrooms were territories in which outsiders were sometimes unwelcome. I saw Larry Grossman, the fat boy who had bullied me all through my first year of school but had stayed away from me since that time, standing alone near a window and looking at the group around Joey Younger. I went into the room and edged through the group.

"Hey, Joey," I said. "Hey."

He looked at me and his thin, long-nosed face broke into a sudden smile.

"How do you feel, Joey?"

"I'm okay, Davey." His face wore a greenish pallor. He was as unkempt as always. "I still hurt where they hit me. But the doctor says there were no injuries inside."

"I'm sorry you were hurt, Joey."

"Bastard goyim," someone in the group said.

I moved back out of the crowd and felt a faint push and

looked to my right. Larry Grossman stood beside me. "Hello, shmuck," he said in a nasty voice. "Who asked you to come in here?"

I started to move away. He grabbed my arm. He was fat and had the strength of his weight.

"Let go of me," I said, frightened.

"You're a skinny shmuck, you know that?" He grinned at me. He had wet lips. No one was paying attention to us. They were all crowded around Joey Younger. "I bet your petzel isn't even big enough for a goy to kick."

I pulled my arm loose and walked quickly away, trembling.

During the mid-morning recess, boys crowded around Joey Younger in the school yard. I stood near the chain-link fence with Yaakov Bader, watching the commotion.

"Some way to become a hero," Yaakov Bader said. "The poor kid."

"I grew up with him."

"What kind of kid was he?"

"The same kid he is now. He always kept away from goyim."

"They could have really hurt him with that chain."

"The kick was no pleasure," I said.

"No," he said. "Not there it isn't. I got hit there in a stickball game once. It hurts."

"What do you think is going to happen?"

"I don't know. But I don't think we can walk in the streets alone at night anymore."

I stared through the chain-link fence at a passing horse and wagon.

"Don't look so sad, Davey," Yaakov Bader said. "It's not the end of the world."

"I wonder what the Golem of Prague would do."

"What?" he said.

I did not respond. The horse moved slowly along, defecating onto the brownish remnants of an old snowstorm.

"That Larry Grossman is a mean kid," I said, looking through the chain-link fence.

"Who?" Yaakov Bader said. "That fat kid over there?"

I nodded.

"Is he bothering you, Davey?"

I was quiet.

"Davey?"

"Never mind," I said. "Never mind. I don't want to start any trouble."

My father said to me at supper that night, "I will walk with you to the trolley and then pick you up at the trolley when you come back. You cannot walk the streets alone anymore."

"But you'll be walking the streets alone, Papa?" I said.

"Yes," he said. I saw a strange cruel glint come into his dark eyes. "That might be interesting."

"Max," my mother said quietly, her eyes darting about the kitchen.

"Yes?" he said, turning to her. "What, Ruth?"

But she retreated and avoided his gaze and was silent.

"The stinking bastards," I heard him say as I watched pain and memory crowd themselves into my mother's nervous eyes. "They brought the poison with them to America and that German maniac now gives them the courage to spread it. They will destroy America like he is destroying Europe."

"What will you do if they stop you, Papa?" Alex asked.

"That might be interesting," my father said again. "I know a few things to do."

My mother put her lower lip between her teeth and sat very quietly, rubbing her right hand back and forth across her apron. Her long dark dry hair had come partly undone from the bun into which she had combed it that morning. She looked fragile; she was now as she had been before my father's strange illness. It pained me to look upon the taut dry skin of her face, her thin bony nervous fingers, her frightened eyes. She did the housework and wrote letters; that was her life. And she lived in caverns of fear too easily explored by her when events in America called to her mind Lemberg and Bobrek and whatever darkness she had left behind in Europe. She no longer spoke of her parents or of the farm. She wrote letters instead, long letters, in her flowing curving hand. Often I would mail them on my way to school, letters to her parents and relatives and friends in Poland and now letters to distant cousins in Palestine. Dread lay deep in her eyes that night and cast a pallor upon her face as she pondered my father's response to my brother's question. I do not know what she saw then.

One day on my way through the crowded corridor at school after recess, I felt a hand grasp my right buttock. I turned sharply and looked into the round fat face of Larry Grossman.

"Hello, crooked nose." He grinned. "How are your brains today?"

"Let go of me."

"They feel real good," he said, squeezing very hard.

"Let go!"

"Sure," he said, and pushed me against the wall.

None of the students rushing through the corridor had paid attention to us. I stood near the wall, listening to the deep trembling of my heart.

I avoided him carefully during the next few days, but one morning he came up unseen behind me and grabbed my buttocks with both his hands. I was in the usually deserted section of the yard near the fire stairs that ran down the rear of the building. My eyes hurt and I had wanted to be by myself awhile.

"The brains feel skinny today." He grinned. "Your mama isn't feeding you."

"Get your hands off me," I said, looking frantically around.

He squeezed and grinned. His hands were up under my coat. I wriggled and could not get out of his strong grasp. He was hurting me.

"You bastard," I suddenly heard myself say. "Get your fat dirty hands off me."

He released me and spun me around and grabbed the front of my jacket with both hands. "You called me a bastard."

"Why don't you leave me alone? I never did anything to you."

"You called me a bastard."

"Get your hands off me!"

"Sure," he said, suddenly grinning. His right hand reached down beneath my jacket to the front of my pants. I felt his fingers on me, squeezing. "Where is it, brains? You got nothing there to squeeze. Such a small petzel for big brains Davey Lurie."

Through the red haze that suddenly clouded my vision I saw his pinkish features and small eyes and the spittle on his lips. His fingers were on me. He clutched me to him tightly and I felt smothered. I pushed against him and drew back my foot and kicked him with all my strength on his shin. I felt the metal-capped toe of my shoe strike the bone and heard him grunt with pain and surprise and suddenly I was free. "You fucking bastard!" I heard him shout as I turned. "What did you do? Oh God, you broke my leg!" I fled, terrified, to the crowded section of the yard. Moments later, I saw him limping along near the fire stairs. I leaned against the chain-link fence. The wind pierced my jacket to my bare skin. I felt my skin crawling. It was a long time before I could stop trembling. My head hurt.

I stopped going off by myself and stayed close to Yaakov Bader. From time to time I could see Larry Grossman watching me, in the corridor, in the school yard. I was grateful he did not live on my street.

Saul asked me on Shabbat afternoon in March how my work with Mr. Bader was coming along and wasn't I afraid to walk the streets alone at night.

"My father walks with me. And the streets in Mr. Bader's neighborhood are okay. I'm more afraid of the goyim in the yeshiva than outside." And I told him in a quiet voice about Larry Grossman.

He stared at me through his lenses, a look of revulsion on his face.

There was a long silence. We were in his room. A truck rolled by across the red-brick paving of the street. Alex sat on a chair, reading.

"I can't understand him, Saul. He must be sick."

"You ought to tell the principal."

"He'll deny it."

"The principal will believe you, Davey."

"I don't want to make trouble, Saul. I just keep away from him. He won't bother me when I'm near Yaakov."

"It's disgusting," Saul muttered.

I sat down on his bed. There was the familiar pain inside my eyes. But I did not feel feverish. I covered my eyes with my arms.

"Are you feeling all right, Davey?" I heard Saul ask.

"My eyes hurt a little."

"Why don't you lie down for a while?"

"I can't understand why he hates me, Saul. I never did anything to him."

"The world is full of people like that, Davey."

"Eddie Kulanski at least hates me because I'm Jewish."

"Should I tell your mother you don't feel well?"

"It's a strange feeling to know there's someone who hates you and is waiting to hurt you and you never did anything to him." I looked into the darkness inside my eyes. "I can't understand it, Saul."

"You better let me get your mother."

"Saul?" I said after a moment from the darkness inside my eyes.

"Yes, Davey?"

"Why is my father sending your father traveling all over?"
He was silent.

"He went to Washington and Detroit and Chicago. He even took an airplane."

"It's for the organization, Davey."

I was quiet. A flash of pain traveled from my eyes down across my right cheek. "I don't understand it," I heard myself say as if from a great distance away. "I never did a thing to him and he hates me. And I don't know what to do."

I was ill for a few days after that. When I returned to school I thought I would find out about Larry Grossman and I asked around. He lived about half a mile away on Bathgate Avenue in a welter of shops and pushcarts. His father owned the fish concession in a small market. His mother cooked, did housework, and took care of six children, one of whom, a girl, was rumored to be retarded. Larry Grossman had barely made it through each of his years in the yeshiva and had recently been warned he might have to repeat this entire year. He was undisciplined in class; and in the yard, as I watched him during recesses through the next few days, he seemed a wild charging animal, horned and eager to gore. I had no wish to be gored by him. I stayed very close to Yaakov Bader.

But it was impossible to be with Yaakov Bader all the time. I came into the building from the yard one afternoon and went over to the drinking fountain near the students' bathroom. I was bent over the fountain when I sensed someone behind me. The skin prickled on the back of my neck. I turned and saw Larry Grossman. He had come in from the yard and I had heard nothing. He stood in front of me, blocking the way to the yard door. The corridor was deserted.

"You're asking questions about me," he said. He wore a winter cap with the ear flaps up and tied together. His heavy jacket was unbuttoned and I could see the soiled and crumpled collar of his white shirt beneath the dark blue sweater. "Why are you asking questions?"

"Please get out of my way."

"I don't like you asking about me."

"You're bothering me. Why do you keep bothering me? Why don't you leave me alone?"

"You know what you are?" he said. "You're a piece of shit." He used the Yiddish word.

God in heaven, I thought. Please, please, make him go away.

"I don't like you because you're always walking around like such a big shot with your brains."

I stared at him.

"Lurie with his nose in the air because he's got a big brain. How about the petzel, Lurie? Is the petzel big, too?" He reached toward me, grinning. "Let's see the petzel, Lurie."

I backed away, trembling.

"Who asked you to come into the class, Lurie? You said 'Hey' to Joey Younger and right away everyone in the class makes Joey Younger a hero. Because Lurie with the big brain said 'Hey' to him. Joey Younger the shmuck. Who asked you?"

The empty corridor echoed faintly with his words.

He moved closer to me, pressing me against the wall near the bathroom. "You piece of shit," he said, speaking Yiddish. There was white spittle on his lips and his small eyes seemed inflamed. "My father works his behind off to keep me in this yeshiva and I have to sweat like a dog just to pass an exam and you sit in class and don't even hear what's going on and you know everything. Even the teachers are afraid of you and your brain. What did you come into the room for? Couldn't you have talked to him in the yard? Just because he got kicked in the balls by some bastard goy you have to go and make that shmuck Joey Younger a big hero?"

I stared at him and could not fully grasp what he was saying.

"He was my friend," I said. "We grew up together."

"You haven't said two words to him in years. You did it to get even with me."

"What?"

"You went in and right away everyone said, 'Even Davey Lurie, Max Lurie's son, says Joey is a hero.' You did it to get even with me after all these years, you piece of shit. That's what you are, Lurie. I know you."

God in heaven, I thought. Please get me out of here.

The outside door opened and Yaakov Bader stepped into the corridor. Larry Grossman turned his head, suddenly frightened, stepped quickly aside, then crossed the corridor to his room, opposite the bathroom.

"Davey, are you okay?" Yaakov Bader asked.

I came outside with him and leaned my head against the

cold bricks of the building. The winter air cooled my burning face.

"Was he bothering you?" Yaakov Bader asked.

"He's crazy," I said. Who had spoken to me like that once before? I could not remember. Back in the past. Had it been beneath trees or in the dimness of an apartment? Why would anyone say that to me? Had it been in the zoo or the meadow or the wood? A long time ago. Yes. But I could not remember. "He scares me," I said. "I don't know what to do."

"Let me take care of him for you, Davey. I'll get some of the guys together and we'll do it today."

"No. I don't want anyone to be hurt. No."

He started to argue with me but the whistle blew and we did not talk of it again because Larry Grossman no longer came near me.

Then, in the middle of that March, Hitler suddenly created a new German army of half a million men, and Mr. Bader told me he would be going to Europe again soon.

"For my job, as your father would put it," he said quietly and soberly.

"But who will I study with?" I asked, unable to control the sudden childish petulance in my voice. I did not want him to go away now. Not to Germany. Not to the land of the Angel of Death.

"Study by yourself, David," he said gently.

"But who will answer my questions?"

"Find the answers by yourself. Ask your teachers in school."

"I don't like my teachers too much."

"David, I traveled back and forth very often when I taught Saul."

"But I thought you would be staying here now for a long time."

"Yes," he said. "So did everyone else. But no one thought to ask Hitler and the German General Staff."

He would be leaving before the summer, he said. In the meantime we would continue to study as always. The hours together with him became precious to me as the months of spring turned the trees on his street green with young life. I walked beneath the trees and thought often of the zoo now, for I began to feel it incredible that I had not seen it again in all the time I had been studying with Mr. Bader. And one Sunday afternoon I took the trolley two hours earlier than usual and rode through the sunny streets to the stop where Saul and I used to get off. I entered the zoo and walked its winding paths and stopped for a drink at one of its fountains. There was a brackish, metallic taste to the water. The paths were narrower than I had remembered them, the asphalt pitted, the edges crumbling here and there into the soft shoulders of earth. Inside the lion pavilion the odor of straw and dung thickened the air and clutched at my throat. The giant cats lounged sleepily behind their bars. They seemed old and weary. I circled the elephant pen and watched a baby elephant huddle close to its mother. I walked on past the deer and camels and came up to the goat pen and saw no young billy goats. Beyond the pen lay the length of path that led to the meadow and the pond and the pine wood and the clearing. The meadow was spotted with patches of dead brown grass; a grayish film clouded the water of the pond. Inside the pine wood I stopped briefly at a fallen tree that lay across the vague curving path; it crawled with ants and looked as if a slight touch of my fingers would cause it to crumble. Tall wild grass grew in the clearing. I turned and went quickly back through the wood and the meadow and the zoo and walked to Mr. Bader's apartment.

I asked him during the course of the afternoon why he had so many German books in his library.

"Those are books by great scholars," he said.

"But the Germans are the enemies of the Jews," I said.

"Not much more than the French and a lot less than the Poles and Russians," he said. "Until Hitler."

Were some of the German books about the Bible? I asked.

"Yes," he said. "But they study it differently from the way we do."

Had he studied them in a college or a university?

"Yes," he said.

There was a silence. He peered at me curiously from behind his desk.

"What's the matter, David?"

I was quiet.

"Are you becoming ill?"

I said I did not think I was becoming ill. "Did you ever know my dead uncle?"

His eyes indicated surprise at the question. "No," he said.

"I want to know who he was," I said. "I'm named after him. He was killed by goyim in a pogrom."

"I heard he was a very gentle person with a very brilliant mind. That's all I know, David. Why don't you ask your parents?"

I said nothing. There was a pause.

"You're in a strange mood today," he said.

"Are you going to Germany soon?" I asked.

"I am not able to enter Germany," he said. "I will be going to Switzerland. Yes, soon."

"Is Europe dangerous for you, Mr. Bader? Can you be—hurt?"

He smiled soberly. "I will not be in the dangerous parts of Europe, David."

"Will your organization get all the Jews out of Germany?"

"I don't know, David. We'll help as best we can."

"Where will they all go?"

"Europe and England will take in a few. So will America. But no country will want many of them."

"What do they want from us? Why don't they leave us alone? They must think we're some kind of monsters."

"Yes," he said. "Many do think that. There is a book called *The Protocols of the Elders of Zion* that describes us as scheming to take over the world."

"I know about that book," I said, suddenly remembering.

"Yes? I'm told it's the second biggest selling book in the world. The first is the Bible." He was silent a moment. Then he said, with a pale smile, "Sometimes I think we ought to start a rumor that the book was written and published by those so-called elders of Zion and that all the royalties go to them and help finance their operation. Wouldn't that be a diabolical idea? Jews financing their takeover of the world by the money that they make from gentiles who buy books that warn about Jews planning to take over the world." He chuckled softly. "It's a thought I had recently while shaving. Millions would immediately believe it. It might even kill the sales of the *Protocols*. Ah, well, it's a thought."

"Mr. Bader?"

"Yes, David?"

"What does my father's organization do?"

"You'll have to ask your father, David."

"Does my father have people who don't like him?"

He said, very quietly, after a moment, "We all have people who dislike us, David. Anyone who knows very clearly what he's doing with his life will have people who dislike him."

"I don't know what I want to do with my life and still there are people who hate me."

His eyebrows went up. "Hate you?" he said. "Why do you think anyone hates you?"

"Two boys I know really hate me. One is a Catholic and the other is in my yeshiva. I don't understand how I look to them or why they hate me."

"Did you have a fight with someone in school?" Mr. Bader asked quietly, and when I would not respond, he said, "You are in a mood today, David. I think the best thing I can do for you is stop here and let you go home."

In the days that followed I began to sense that there were matters I needed desperately to know. I said to my father one Shabbat afternoon as we were reviewing what I had learned in Bible and Talmud that week, "How old was Uncle David when he was killed?"

My mother was asleep in her bed; my brother was out playing somewhere with his friends.

"Twenty-three," my father said.

"What was he?"

"What do you mean what was he?"

"A lawyer? A doctor?"

"He was studying to become a teacher of history."

"Polish history?"

"No. Of—what do they call it? Old history. Ancient history."

"He wanted to teach in a Polish school?"

"No, not in a Polish school. In a German university."

"Was he smart?"

"Yes, he was smart. He was like—he was very smart."

"Papa?"

"Enough, now. Enough. On Shabbos afternoons I ask you the questions. Now, explain to me again why you think the Ibn Ezra on this passage is clearer than Rashi."

I came into the kitchen one night for a glass of milk. Our meager supper, the result of a difficult two weeks my father had had with his watch repair service, had left me hungry. My mother was in the kitchen writing letters. Her Waterman's pen scratched softly upon the sheet of paper beneath her hand.

"Mama?" I said, very quietly.

"Yes," she said almost inaudibly, and continued writing.

"Which one is Uncle David in the photograph?"

She seemed not to have heard me. She went on writing a moment longer. Then she stopped and slowly looked up at me. I knew from her eyes that she was not seeing me but was focused beyond me upon an image of her own making. A sudden darkness came across her features as if shadows had leaped upon her from the dim corners of the kitchen. Faint tremors moved across the weak line of her lips. I heard her say, almost in a moan, "What will the end be, David? We cannot do everything. We are only flesh and bones." She blinked and her eyes were moist behind her glasses. Then she looked directly at me and smiled vaguely. "Did you come in for milk, darling? Take some milk." She returned to her letter. I walked out in shuddering dread and was afraid to speak to her again about my Uncle David.

When I asked my father how my Uncle David had been killed he said, "A stinking bastard of a Polak did it," and would say no more. I feared asking him about the photograph. My Uncle Meyer simply said, "He was killed in a pogrom, David."

But I continued going into the kitchen at night on one pretext or another, and one night my mother was not there and the letter she had been writing before she had gone to the bathroom lay on the table. I stood at the table with a glass of milk in my hand and let my eyes run quickly across her flowing Yiddish hand.

"My dear and precious parents," she had written. "I am well and pray to the Master of the Universe that you too are in good health and that your community responsibilities are not overly burdensome. How it hurts my heart to be able to speak to you only through letters but how good it is to hear from you the things you are able to do for Jews in Bobrek. David, my precious David, would have been proud of your work. My own little David grows slowly into a giant though he cannot see it nor can most others around him. He is still so thin and small in size but he swallows worlds with his mind and is not even aware of what he does. His teachers tell me they have affection for him though they admit they are sometimes uncomfortable with him in their classes. His history teacher said she does not appreciate being caught in an occasional error by a sneering twelve-year-old boy. But I think she exaggerates. How fortunate we are to have Mr. Bader here to teach him privately. Do you remember how David used to study privately with that enlightened Hebraist who moved to Lemberg from Warsaw? I look at my little

David sitting over his books and—what can I tell you? How I wish his health were better. How I pray I could take his illnesses upon me. He is often ill and in pain and his bad dreams continue though the doctor assures me that it is not abnormal for a child his age to have such dreams. I remember the dreams my David used to have. Men who are minds dream; men who are bodies sleep soundly. Is that another of your daughter's silly ideas? But I think it is true. Max tells me the business has improved and in these black times that is such joyous news that I thank the Master of the Universe for having sent me such a husband as Max. He is strong again and able to work very hard once an idea is given him. I do my best to think as David might have thought. But it is wearying and the memories often carry with them pain and tears far into the night. Max is the kindest of souls in his own way. Alex will be like him. He will soon be as tall as David and is—"

I heard the toilet flushing. I finished the milk, washed the glass, and went hurriedly from the kitchen.

I could not study that night. My eyes would not focus through my lenses onto the pages of my books. I looked at Alex sitting at the discarded kitchen table my father had rescued from the alleyway and rebuilt into a low small desk. His thick shoulders were bent over a writing book. He worked intently, his features tight with concentration. He labored with enormous difficulty to obtain his good grades. I looked down at the Talmud that lay open on my desk and the letters swam off into the margins and gutter of the folio volume. Quietly I undressed and got into bed.

Alex looked up from his desk. "Are you all right, Davey?"

"I'm tired."

"Are you sick?"

"No. I'm tired. Can't I just be tired?"

He seemed puzzled for a moment, then returned to his work.

I closed my eyes but could not sleep. Later I heard Alex and my parents go to bed. The room was dark. Whispers and the cold black sounds of the night kept me awake until an ash-gray dawn lighted the alleyway and I smelled the warm odor of baking bread. Then I slept and was awakened by my father to go to school.

I sensed throughout the following days that I needed still other eyes on the matters I hungered to know but I could not begin to think how to find them; for I knew no Catholics and of the two Catholics I had briefly known, one, Tony Savanola, had been gone from my life for years, and the other, Eddie Kulanski, had hated me and probably hated me still, though he no longer showed awareness that I was alive. Mr. Donello, the shoemaker in whose store my father had put up his workbench, no longer had children of school age. I did not know what to do.

Then I thought I would ask the librarian. At the end of school on a Friday afternoon I walked along 170th Street, crossed beneath the Third Avenue Elevated just as a train rushed by overhead with a crashing clatter of wheels, went up the long hill past the sour stench of the brewery, and entered the two-story white stone building that was the local branch of the public library.

The librarian I spoke to was a middle-aged woman with rimless glasses and a courteous manner. No, she said. They had none of the textbooks on Catholicism that were used in the junior high schools or high schools in our neighborhood. They had many books on Catholic thought. Did I want one of those?

"I want a textbook," I said. Then I asked her where I could find a copy of the Christian Bible.

She was not-Jewish and knew who I was, had in fact known me for all the years I had been coming to this library.

She smiled and said, "The scope of your reading is becoming quite broad, David. Come, I'll get you a New Testament."

I sat in the reference room reading Matthew in the Christian Bible. I had taken with me my small English dictionary but I used it less often than I had thought would be necessary. I looked up the words "gospel" and "baptize." Then I looked up the words "jot" and "tittle," reread the passage, and did not understand it. There were ideas and images in many of the subsequent passages which I could not grasp, but I understood more than I had come prepared thinking I would; I understood about the Pharisees telling Jesus that his followers were doing "that which is not lawful to do upon the Sabbath day." I understood the words of Jesus about the sick man and the sheep. I read with a cold tingling sensation the account of the blind and dumb man possessed by a devil. Then I began to scan the verses very quickly, looking for the word "Jew." I saw the name Moses near the beginning of a chapter and read the chapter slowly, feeling bewildered at the rage and scorn directed at the scribes and Pharisees.

The Rabbis of the Talmud were being called hypocrites! Then I scanned very quickly and saw the word "Jews" in the account of the crucifixion in chapter twenty-seven. I went back to the beginning of the chapter and read all of it very slowly. I read verses twenty-four and twenty-five, then read them again. I completed Matthew and closed my eyes and sat very still for a long time. I could hear around me the carefully guarded silences of the library. After a while I began to read Mark and I found the word "Jews" in chapter seven and read the chapter slowly. How he despised the Pharisees! Then I realized it was late; I had to be home before the lighting of the Shabbat candles. I turned to the end of Mark and worked backward, verse by verse. I realized that, again, the account of the crucifixion was in the next to last chapter. I read it slowly. Then I turned to the next to the last chapter in Luke and read that. Finally, I read the chapter on the crucifixion and the one prior to that in John. I closed the book and sat in the silent reading room feeling the coldness in my hands and legs. After a few minutes I replaced the book, thanked the librarian, and walked home through late afternoon streets that seemed to swarm with darkness and hate. I was home in plenty of time for Shabbat.

My father said to me the next morning as we walked together to the yeshiva synagogue, "What did you dream last night? Your mother told me she heard you cry out in your sleep."

"I don't remember."

"I didn't hear Davey cry out," said Alex.

"You?" my father said. "When you sleep you wouldn't hear a Cossack if he screamed in your ear."

We prayed in the large ground-floor synagogue of the yeshiva. My father had not succeeded in organizing a separate service. I remember sitting in my seat that Shabbat, following the Torah reading in my Chumash and seeing the words and images of the Christian Bible in my eyes. During lunch my mother asked me if I was getting ill again. I said no, I didn't think I was. But I spent the afternoon on my bed with my eyes closed, still seeing those words and images.

That Monday I came out of my school in the late afternoon after dismissal and, instead of crossing the street and going home, I turned up the side street, went past the chain-link fence bordering our yard and continued walking until I was a few yards from the Catholic church and parochial school. The school stood beyond the church. On the other side of the school was a large yard, paved in asphalt and rimmed by a tall iron fence. I hesitated for a moment as I approached the church, then walked on past it. I slowed as I went by the school, then stopped near the yard. A double-hung iron gate led into the yard. The gate was open. Inside the yard, eight teen-age boys were playing basketball. I noticed their schoolbags and books on the ground near the wall of the school building. I watched them for a few minutes and went home.

For the next three weeks I returned to that yard every afternoon. Twice it was deserted. Shadows slanted across its paved surface. The gate was open. On the first of the two times I found the yard deserted, I saw a briefcase near the school building deep inside the yard. The second time, I saw nothing; the paved ground looked swept clean. The gate was open.

I walked there late one evening after supper and found, it crowded with teen-agers. I went quickly by, crossed the street, and walked back home. On a Thursday afternoon in May I went along the street and stopped and stared through the iron fence at a pack of books that lay in the shadows near the wall of the school that stood perpendicular to the fence. They lay only a few inches from the corner of the ninety-degree angle formed by the juncture of fence and wall, five books held together by a dark brown leather belt. I glanced quickly up and down the block and felt the blood beating inside my head. I knew I could never do it, I could never reach into the dark blood-filled horror that the Catholic world conjured up in my mind. Then I stood on the sidewalk holding the books, feeling the weight of the books in my hand. They seemed heavy as stones. My arms and legs tingled and a chill sweat formed on my forehead. Down the block stood the church, tall, angular, menacing. A black coupe turned into the street from Park Avenue and started toward me. I stood very still, watching with paralyzed dread as it came along the gutter. It went on by, rattling loudly. I opened my schoolbag, loosened the leather belt, separated the books, glancing quickly at the titles, and stuffed them in among my own. I walked stiffly, rapidly, past the church. I was trembling.

In front of the yeshiva I sat down on the stone staircase and took a deep quivering breath. I felt strangely nerveless, yet all of me was quivering and tingling and trembling. I opened my schoolbag and took out one of the books. On the title page I read *Religion: Doctrine and Practice* by Francis

B. Cassilly, S.J. I did not understand what "S.J." meant. Opposite the title page was a picture in color of a man, a woman, and a little child. Four people were gazing at the child, an old man, a young woman, and two youths who looked to be shepherds. They were all inside a barn. Bright yellow circles of light surrounded the heads of the man, the woman, and the little child.

I turned to the Preface and read swiftly: "The widespread popularity enjoyed by this text since its appearance in 1926 is evidence that our Catholic schools consider the fundamental truths of Faith essential to the high-school course in religion." I stopped, turned to the index at the back of the book, and looked for "Jews." Along Washington Avenue people and traffic moved normally. No one paid any attention to a skinny, near-sighted, twelve-year-old Jewish boy searching through a Catholic textbook for mention of Jews. He found it and read at his normal very rapid speed. "The Jews as a nation refused to accept Christ, and since His time they have been wanderers on the earth without a temple or a sacrifice, and without the Messias." A car honked and the Jewish boy looked up briefly, then returned to his Catholic book, read on for a few lines, and then saw these words: "The Jews rejected Christ mainly because they expected Him to found a never-ending kingdom, as was foretold in the prophecies. This He really did, but the kingdom He founded—the Church— was a spiritual one, not a temporal one such as the carnal Jews were hoping for."

I closed the book, removed from my schoolbag the others I had found with it, tied around them once again the brown belt, first making certain I had placed each one on top of the other in the same order they had been in when I had first picked them up in the yard. I left them lying near me on the stoop, reached into my schoolbag, and got out my dictionary. I looked up the word "carnal." I replaced the dictionary in my bag and got to my feet. Then I looked curiously up and down the street and wondered why I could not hear noises of the afternoon. Sound seemed to have been sucked from the street, funneled out of a hole somewhere in the fabric that enclosed us. All the sound I heard, the thin rushing cry that pressed upon my ears, came from within me. I sat down again and stared at the worn and pitted stone of a step. I saw its dull sheen and its tiny cracks. There seemed strange comfort in the sight of that old, dirt-veined stone step. I picked up my schoolbag and the books, stood up, and went down the steps.

I crossed the street and paused for a moment at the news-stand in front of the candy store. There I waited until the trembling stopped and the cry was gone and the drab street returned to normalcy. Then I went into the store of the Italian shoemaker where my father had his watch repair service.

The little bell over the door tinkled softly when the door opened and when I pushed it shut. My father and Mr. Donello looked up simultaneously from where they sat behind their workbenches. Mr. Donello waved at me cheerfully with his left hand. In his right hand he held a hammer. The nails protruding from between his lips prevented him from speaking but I could see the line of his lips go up into a warm smile. He placed a nail on the sole of the shoe on his work-bench and struck it with the hammer. He worked very expertly. I returned his greeting with a nod.

My father took the jeweler's glass from his eye and sat back for a moment. He rubbed his eyes with a thumb and forefinger and said, "What time is it?" Then he laughed softly and turned to look at the two full panels of repaired watches on the wall behind him. As he turned I saw clearly the balding of his brown hair on the back of his head.

"Does Mama need anything in the grocery store?"

"She did not tell me. How was school?"

"I got a ninety-eight in the algebra test."

Mr. Donello's hammer banged loudly upon the shoe. Then he gave the shoe a few rapid finishing taps and removed it from the iron shoe form on his workbench. He stood up, wiping his hands on his blue denim apron. He was completely bald save for a fringe of white hair near his ears and around the back of his head. Often he hummed a song as he worked. His voice was high and reedy. "I could have been in opera," he had told me once cheerfully. "I could have sung in La Scala. I had one small problem. No voice." And he had laughed gaily.

"A ninety-eight in you test," Mr. Donello said now. "That's a very good mark, David." He looked at the shoes on a shelf near one of the lathes, selected a pair, and put them on his workbench. "My boy used to come home from school with terrible marks and I used to say to him why you can't get good marks like the Jewish boys? He never want to work hard to get good marks. Now he drive a truck in Cleveland. Now he work hard. Max, you got a good boy here, a fine boy. David, you be honest like you father and smart like Mr. Einstein and you no have to drive trucks. What?"

"I found them outside near my school," I said.

They looked at the books dangling from the strap I held in my hand. I was standing near the small showcase of inexpensive watches, watch bands, and costume jewelry my father had recently added to his watch repair service. It stood alongside the workbench. The books were dimly reflected in its front pane of glass. My father sat looking at the books. The wings of his nostrils flared slightly; a look of revulsion came involuntarily into his face; then he made his face expressionless.

Mr. Donello cheerfully pointed his hammer at the chair that stood near the second lathe against the rear wall of the store. A small narrow mirror alongside the chair showed me walking through the store and putting the books down.

"I bring the books to the school in the morning," Mr. Donello said. "I know you don't go into a Catholic place. You got a good-hearted boy, Max. He save the books from the rain."

I looked through the front window of the store. A slanting rain had begun to fall. I saw people running for shelter. The sky was dark. From a long distance away came a vague roll of thunder.

"You will get wet," my father said. "Wait until it stops."

I stood in the doorway looking out at the rain. Behind me my father worked intently on a watch and Mr. Donello banged away at a shoe, humming through his mouthful of nails. The rain fell heavily upon the street and school buildings and apartment houses. I saw the stones and bricks wet in the rain. Puddles formed on the sidewalk. Then the sky grew very dark and the rain fell in a torrent and I could no longer see the street through the blur of rivulets on the window of the store. I waited inside the store for the rain to stop. It was a long rain and it did not give me the feeling of having cleansed anything.

The rain was gone in the morning but the sky had not cleared. I walked to my school between the dark puddles on the street. Later in the morning the pavement of the school yard was still wet when we came outside for recess. I stood near the chain-link fence and listened to Yaakov Bader talk about the damage done on his street by the rain. He lived near Jerome Avenue in the Bronx and a tree had been felled by the wind and had crushed a parked car in front of his apartment house. We crowded around him, listening.

"I don't ever remember a storm like that," someone said. "I thought the sky broke open or something."

"We had a storm like that last month," someone else said.

"Not like that we didn't."

Later I stood near the fence with Yaakov Bader and we looked out at the street. His dark eyes brooded. I asked him if his family was upset because his uncle was leaving for Europe.

"They're all worried," he said. "My father is scared the Nazis will get hold of him. He doesn't want him to go."

"But he won't be in Germany."

"The Nazis are all over. My father says he has only one brother and doesn't want him to get hurt."

"What does your uncle say?"

"He's going to Europe in two weeks."

"In two weeks? He didn't tell me that. I was with him Sunday."

"The people he works with decided yesterday."

"But in two weeks?"

"Yes," he said and kicked moodily at the chain-link fence.

We stood together a moment. A warm damp wind blew his light blond hair across his forehead. His eyes were moist with sadness. I could not remember seeing him sad before and I did not know what to say that might cheer him. He stood there, kicking lightly at the chain-link fence and talking about how worried his family was that Mr. Bader would soon be leaving for Europe.

"People say there's going to be another war," he said. "Sooner or later."

"There are lots of people who don't think so, Yaakov."

"I hear about it in the house. They sit around and talk when my uncle comes." He kicked at the fence, striking it lightly with his sneakers. "Do you hear Hitler's speeches? He's a little crazy."

"We hear them."

"My uncle doesn't really want to go. But he has a job to do. They want to save as many Jews as they can." He was silent a moment. "You know," he said, turning to me with a sad smile, "he told us one of the things he regrets most about leaving is he won't be able to teach you anymore."

I felt my heart turn over slowly.

"He said you have one of the best minds he's ever met in his life. He told me to take care of you. He said you'll be a great scholar one day." He kicked at the fence, still smiling sadly. "He said your uncle was going to be a great scholar and now your family all want you to be a scholar and I'm supposed to watch you." The sadness left him slowly. He opened his dark eyes very wide and stared at me. "So I'm watching," he said. "I'm watching." Then he laughed and threw an arm around my shoulder and patted my back. "It will be good," he said in Hebrew. "It will be good."

Outside the chain-link fence an old woman passed by, walking slowly. I turned and leaned against the fence and looked around the noisy yard. Larry Grossman was involved with a game of Johnny-on-the-pony. I saw him run and leap and land on the waiting row of backs. The row sagged and held. I turned and looked out again at the street. Yaakov was talking with some of our classmates. I looked at the tall cross on the roof of the church; it seemed to make darker still the already dark sky. I kicked idly at the chain-link fence. A few drops of rain fell, then stopped. David, someone whispered into my ear. I turned my head. There was no one near me. Yaakov Bader stood a few feet away talking about Babe Ruth. "It's his last year," he was saying. "They want him to be what he can't be anymore. He's too old. You can't make a person what he isn't." I looked out again at the street. David, came the whisper. David. Leave me alone, I thought. Please leave me alone. I knew he was dead and could not whisper but I thought again and again, Please leave me alone. Then I thought, What would it have been like if my father had not married my mother? If my Uncle David had not been killed, then I would not be David and someone else would be my mother's first son. It's because my Uncle David was killed by a goy in a pogrom that I am David. He died and I am David. I am David. Everyone has a different picture of me or wants me to be another Uncle David. But I want to be my own David.

I kicked lightly against the fence and put my forehead to the cool heavy wire. I felt strangely weak and fatigued. The voices of my classmates seemed a comforting balm.

The whistle blew. I walked across the yard with my classmates. I felt a tickling sensation in my lower right leg and I flexed it as I walked and the feeling disappeared. Larry Grossman brushed up against me in the corridor but kept his face turned stiffly away from me. Inside my classroom, I sat down at my desk and looked at the plywood-covered window. Then I opened my Bible and sat back and closed my eyes. The class grew still. The teacher began to talk about the Rashi we had

been studying earlier that morning. I relaxed in my desk and
thought again of what I had thought before. I could not grasp
the idea that I was alive because my Uncle David was dead.
The idea seemed to penetrate through me and double back
and come through me again, and still I could not grasp it. I
was alive because goyim had killed my uncle. There was the
tickling sensation again in my foot and I flexed it and the
feeling was gone. What did it mean that if someone had not
died I would not be alive? I tried to see the idea inside my
eyes but it seemed to slip back and forth through me and I
could not hold on to it. My leg itched and tickled and I flexed
it and pushed down on it and it felt fine. I sat there slouched
down in my desk listening to the teacher's explanation and
thinking of my Uncle David. A train rumbled by along the
Third Avenue trestle. There was the itch again, in the curve
of my foot directly above the tongue of my shoe, and I
reached down and scratched at it lightly. The itch was immediately gone. A moment later a vague throb traveled
through my lower leg like a pulse beat. I opened my eyes
and sat up. I had scratched at the foot with my right hand.
The hand was on the Chumash on top of my desk. I looked
at it. Then I looked down at my foot. Below the rim of my
trouser leg my light-brown sock was stained dark. I raised
the trouser leg and put my hand to my sock and felt the sock
warm and moist against my foot. At that same moment, the
pulselike throb traveled once again through the leg. I withdrew my hand and stared at my fingers. They were red with
blood.

I sat very still for a long moment staring at my fingers. A
vague sensation of choking came slowly into my throat.
Memories tumbled across one another inside my eyes. I
raised my hand and asked to leave the room.

In the bathroom I leaned against the white tile wall near
the sinks and removed my shoe and sock. The upper part of
the foot was covered with blood. The blood formed a ragged
patch of ugly darkness, clotted along the edges and bright red
near the center. As I watched, a thin trickle of blood oozed
out from beneath the clotted edge along the inside of my foot,
traveled slowly down my ankle and fell onto the white tile
floor of the bathroom. Drops of blood lay on the floor, red,
glistening. I stared at them in horror and disbelief and could
not understand what had happened. I wet some toilet paper
and carefully washed away the blood on my foot. Then I saw
the wound. It was a puncture wound almost directly above

the instep. I must have inflicted it upon myself earlier when I had kicked at the chain-link fence. My foot had struck one of the sharp points at the ends of the metal twists in which the fence terminated. But I had felt nothing. Why had I felt nothing? Perhaps it was like cutting yourself with paper; you felt nothing until afterwards. A pool of bright red blood lay inside the wound. I felt no pain, only a dull discomfort. The wound did not look to be very deep. I washed around it again with warm water, then covered it with a thickness of toilet paper and pulled my sock back on over my foot. The sock was damp with blood. I put my shoe on and walked slowly to the classroom. The leg throbbed briefly as I sat down and again at the end of morning when I rose from my desk.

I came out of the school and walked home. The toilet paper was sodden with blood when I removed it in the bathroom of our apartment. I washed the area of the wound again and covered it with gauze and tape. I heard my mother calling me in for lunch. I changed my socks and put the bloodied pair into my pocket. No one has to know about it, I kept saying to myself. I did not understand why I felt that way. It's nothing, I kept saying. It's a little cut. I don't want to make anything big of it. I haven't had an accident in a long time and this is nothing. I had lunch and went back to school. On the way to school I threw the socks into a garbage can in the alleyway of an apartment house.

The pain began in the afternoon. It did not seem to be very bad, but I felt it with a sense of numbing dread. As I walked out to the yard for the afternoon recess, it intensified slightly. A sudden dense warmth traveled briefly along the top of my foot. I went over to the chain-link fence with Yaakov Bader and some of my classmates. There they were, the sharp pointed ends of the metal twists at the foot of the fence. It was a warm windy day. The air was gray. Old newspapers and candy wrappers blew along the sidewalk. I heard Yaakov Bader talking about the latest baseball antics of Dizzy Dean. Later that afternoon we would briefly watch the senior class rehearse their graduation. I wondered if they would do any marching. My leg throbbed faintly. I thought about my own graduation next year. In four weeks school would be over. I had learned more this year outside school than inside. Mr. Bader had told me once that most schools were not set up to teach exceptional students. He had looked at me from across his desk and had smiled and I had felt proud. The light from his desk lamp had cast a golden sheen upon his firm features.

The tall spare body; the soft voice; the dark glittering eyes
beneath the heavy ridge of eyebrows; the smoking jacket and
cravat; the manicured nails—he had been my teacher for a
long time and now he was going away and the Nazis might
get him. Why would the Nazis be after Mr. Bader? Maybe
they thought he was a spy. Maybe they believed he was one
of the elders of Zion. They might throw him into prison or
kill him. I closed my eyes and felt the full steady throb of
pain in my foot. It's healing, I told myself. It's a cut and it's
healing. Every cut causes pain. Since when have you become
a stranger to pain? Big shot! You haven't had an accident in
a long time and all of a sudden you don't know what pain is
anymore. Relax. It's healing.

But when I sat in the classroom later that afternoon listening to our English teacher talk about the graduation play
and the speeches, a sudden swift flame of pain rose from my
foot to my knee. It was immediately gone. The foot throbbed.

After school I walked home and carefully removed the
bandage. The small blackish circle of the wound looked
strangely terrifying. The skin around it was tender and had
turned red. I felt a queer burning sensation now extending
from the wound to the ankle. It seemed such a small wound.
I wished I could move time backward. I would not kick at
that fence. I remembered reading in one of my mother's
German books that camphor was used by many doctors to
cure a variety of illnesses. Of course! That was the medicine
I needed. I had even read about it in one of my Uncle
David's German books. *Der Kampfer ist eine ausgezeichnete
Kur.* My mother kept a box of camphor in a cabinet near the
bathroom hamper. I opened the box and spread some of the
white flakes on the wound. Then I placed a fresh bandage on
the wound and put on my sock and shoe. The wound tingled
faintly but the pain diminished. When I went to bed there
was almost no pain at all, only a vague warm tingling sensation in the area of the wound.

I woke suddenly in the night and lay in my bed staring into
tne darkness of the room and trying to remember what had
wakened me. I had dreamed of a man in a robe lying asleep
in a tent. From the earthen floor of the tent rose a dark
form. Slowly it approached the sleeping man. The face of a
withered crone appeared in the opening to the tent; a brassy
voice had shouted a warning. I had come awake. In the first
seconds of waking I remembered the face and voice as belonging to Mrs. Horowitz.

My leg burned faintly. It felt heavy. But there was no pain.
In the morning I dressed the wound again, using the camphor,
and went to school. Before lunch I looked at the wound and
saw the skin around it was dark red and felt very warm to
the touch. I put a fresh camphor bandage on it and went into
the kitchen.

"Are you feeling all right?" my mother asked me.

I told her I was feeling fine.

"Your nose? Your throat?" she said anxiously.

My nose and throat were fine, I said, and ate lunch. I had
no appetite.

I woke again that night and listened in the darkness to
someone calling my name. David, the voice called as if from
inside a vast cave. The burning sensation in my leg had
reached to my knee. I heard my brother snoring quietly. In
the alleyway a cat wailed in an eerily human voice. When I
inspected the wound before going to school I saw the skin
close to the hole had a bluish look to it.

I was frightened. I bandaged the wound. My father sat at
the kitchen table over breakfast and sniffed the air. "Is someone using camphor?" he asked. There was no answer. "I
smell camphor," he said. Still there was no answer. "I smelled
it last night, Papa," Alex said. Then my mother put hot oat-
meal on the table in front of us and my father said nothing
else about the odor of camphor.

During the mid-morning recess, Yaakov asked me, "Are
you getting sick again, Davey?"

I leaned against the fence and shook my head.

"You don't look good," he said worriedly.

"I'm all right," I said. My head was damp and I felt
feverish. But I knew I could not possibly be having any fever,
for my nose and throat were fine and my eyes did not hurt.

Later, in the classroom, I felt the burning sensation in my
leg spreading slowly upward. It throbbed and pulsed and
moved like waves of heat. Slowly I raised my leg off the floor
and flexed my foot. There was a feeling of flesh suddenly
ripping beneath the bandage. A thrust of pain reached up
along the leg to my groin. I shivered and felt hot and sweaty.
The letters on the Chumash wriggled slowly across the page.
I sat very still, trembling with fear. A sharp steady throbbing
pain settled relentlessly into the top of my foot. I felt all my
body pulsing to the beat of the pain. I was sweaty all over
now and feeling the pain all through my leg. I closed my eyes
and waited for dismissal. Voices drifted over me. The teacher

kept talking about Rashi. He had a quiet voice but it resonated loudly inside my head. With my eyes closed, I could see him in front of the class, short, pudgy, with his kindly face and milk-white hands. I had once answered a question he had put to me by citing a passage from the Ramban from memory and there had been a long silence and he did not call on me too often after that. I listened to his thin voice and to the voices of students. They washed and drifted back and forth across me like gentle waves. I thought someone was calling me but I could not open my eyes. Then a voice separated itself from all the others and I heard Yaakov Bader say urgently, "Davey! Davey!" and I opened my eyes and smiled up at him. I raised my arm lazily and waved and then almost cried out at the pain. Suddenly the pressure of my shoe on the wound was intolerable. I bent, feeling the queer pounding of the blood all inside me, and slipped off the shoe. I gazed at it in astonishment. It was wet with blood. The voices swelled to a roar, then became subdued. Yaakov Bader helped me to my feet. The floor moved crazily. I leaned heavily on Yaakov and another classmate. We were out of the building. They helped me along Washington Avenue. We passed the shoe repair store but my father did not see me. My mother was home. She looked at the wound, put me to bed, and went hurriedly out of the apartment. Yaakov stayed with me. "You'll be all right." Then he said, "Why didn't you tell me, Davey? I'm supposed to take care of you. Why didn't you say anything?" His tormented voice moved darkly through my room. All the voices began moving into my room and I knew I would not be able to endure them. Not all of them together in my room. I closed my eyes and heard my father's heavy tread on the creaking floor of the hallway and knew I did not want to hear his voice now, there were already too many voices calling my name. I sensed him looking at my foot. "God in heaven," I heard his voice say. Then I heard his voice say, "Go call Weidman. God in heaven." Then I was falling slowly into the darkness of a cavern and I heard no more sounds for a long time.

Pain woke me. Someone's hand was on my foot and the pain of its touch sent flashes of reddish light into my eyes. Well, what has the scholar done to himself now? said the cheerful voice of Dr. Weidman. My eyes were closed against the horror on my parents' faces and my brother's bewildered and frightened gaze. I see what the scholar has done, said Dr. Weidman, suddenly no longer cheerful. The scholar should use his brains for practical matters too, he said almost angrily, or the scholar will not survive to a happy old age. Would the scholar like to tell me what happened? It was an accident! someone screamed. I didn't know my foot kicked the sharp points in the yeshiva fence! It was an accident! I opened my eyes and wondered why they were all staring at me. Of course, someone soothed. Of course: I was hot and sweaty and Dr. Weidman was doing things to my leg and deep into my groin. Alex was sent from the room. They were talking together quietly near the window. I saw them through the slits of my eyes, my parents and Dr. Weidman, standing silhouetted against the window and talking. It was queer the way my father kept glaring at me in horror and disbelief and my mother kept wringing her hands and Dr. Weidman kept talking very quietly. They were making plans. They would do things to me. They were talking about me and would do things to me and they would not ask me if they could do them. No one felt it necessary to ask David. Everyone knew what David was and could do what they wanted with him. What would Dr. Weidman do? I would not let him take me to a hospital. I was terrified of leaving my room and my bed. My mouth was dry and my tongue felt thick and gummy. I was burning with fever and could not understand it because my nose and throat felt fine. My head hurt and my eyes ached. That's from the fever, I told myself. You're not sick. The fever is from the leg, not the nose and throat. That kind of fever doesn't count. But the fever was burning inside me and in the night it was worse. I knew I was gasping and crying in the night but I could not hear my voice. I heard my mother's voice chanting incoherent words. I kept my eyes closed but the redness of the fever was still clearly there despite the night. "Ochnotinos, chnotinos, notinos," I heard my mother chant, and I shouted to her to please please stop it and go away. Sha, my father soothed. Sha, my son. My mother rushed from the room and returned a moment later with something in her hands. They sponged my body with a cool tingling liquid. My leg pulsed and throbbed. I could not move it. The pain was in my ankle and knee and thigh and groin. They put warm compresses on the wound and gave me aspirin. After a long while I grew very weary. The warm odors of the bakery ovens filled the room. Finally, I slept.

Later there was sunlight and my mother tried to feed me and I vomited on the bed and the floor. Afterward I lay trembling and sweating in fresh pajamas and the sour odor of vomit would not leave the room. Through the open window I saw the brick wall of the adjoining house and a sliver of pale sky. Then I was very hot again and the burning redness returned to my eyes, moving slowly back and forth, shimmering. I saw a red lake beneath an ash-gray sky. Along the edge of the lake wavelets of yellow fire lapped against a grass beach. A boat moved slowly near the shore, its single occupant bent over a book. David, someone called. The person in the boat looked up into the dull yellow sun that lay like a collapsed ball in the sky. Which David? the person in the boat said. David, someone called again. The boat drifted slowly from the shore. Which David? said the occupant of the boat, staring into the sun. David, came the call. David. The boat was very far from the shore. The occupant stood up. He was short and slight of build and wore a dark robe and cowl. Which David? he called back, speaking into the sun, his arms raised, his hands open. The demon David? The evil eye David? The darling David? The brain David? The arrogant spiteful David? The frightened David? Which David? The boat drifted off slowly, the occupant still standing and speaking into the sun. The cowl slipped from his head, revealing yellowish eyes and pale dim features and long dark tangled hair.

They kept putting warm compresses on my foot and giving me aspirin. I lay burning in my bed, the leg like something evil connected to me, causing me pain I could not bear. Maybe they would cut it off, I thought in my fever and pain. I cried out and felt my mother's fingers stroking my face and head. Sha, my darling. Sha. You will be all right. Master of the Universe, bring him a complete healing. David, are you listening to me? Look at the son who bears your name and intercede for him. David. David. Do you hear me? Sha, my son. I promise you will be all right. David, intercede for me. David! She stroked my forehead and sat murmuring in the darkness. A train charged through the night. The odor of baking bread began drifting into the room. I fell asleep. There was daylight and the long journey of the sun and once again the night.

It was morning and Dr. Weidman was in the room again talking quietly with my parents. A week, he said. At the very most two. But he must eat. Yes, he said. Lymphatics, he said. No, he said. He is better off here. I watched him come back to the bed. How does the scholar feel? he asked cheerfully.

Terrible? I would feel terrible too if I had your leg. But we will make you all better soon. And next time, if there ever is a next time, God forbid, David the scholar will not be so silly. All right? Does this hurt? And this? And this? Some brain. The head of a golem is what you have, if you'll excuse my saying so. No, you must absolutely not move the leg. Read? Of course you can read if you can keep your eyes on a book for more than five minutes. He has a fever of one hundred four and he wants to read. Some brain. Continue the compresses and the aspirin. If the swelling gets worse, call me. And give him something to eat, Ruth. I will cure him and all that will remain will be a sack full of bones. Some cure. Goodbye. Come with me to the door, Max. I want to talk to you.

The fever dropped. My uncle came to visit. And my aunt. And Saul. They stood around the bed, trying to be cheerful. Dread lay across their faces like a dark fog. Mr. Bader came. He sat on a chair next to the bed. Never mind the silliness of what you did. It was an error. Now get well. You must get well. Are you going away soon, Mr. Bader? Yes. I turned my face to the wall.

Yaakov Bader came and stood uncomfortably near my bed, his dark eyes filled with kindness and concern. He fidgeted and stared around the room and talked and was gone.

The fever rose toward evening and there was a pounding in my head; I could not move my head or blink my eyes. I lay very still, feeling the raging of the fever. Sometime during that night I found myself in a green forest near a calm lake. The air was cool and clean and blue. I walked through the forest, calling out the names of the trees. My mother was with me, smiling, her eyes clear and bright as she listened. How still and cool the air was! Something flitted between the trees in the heart of the forest. It was gone. Then it was there again, a vague form moving lightly from tree to tree, coming toward us. My mother stopped and put a hand to her eyes. She removed the hand and her face glowed luminously with a joy that lighted the trees around us. The form moved among the trees, and I stopped, waiting, my heart pounding. Behind me my mother sighed. The form stepped out from behind a maple and my mother went soundlessly toward it and I saw them go off toward the grove of birch near the lake. I was hurt. Why hadn't my mother said, This is David, my son. I would have loved to have been able to meet you, Uncle David, I heard myself say. I would have become your

best friend. Be your own David, murmured the sweet gentle
voice from the trees near the lake. Make your own beginning,
my precious son.

I fell into a deep and dreamless sleep.

I was ill for close to six weeks and when I was well it was
July and very hot. I sat outside on my chair in the sun, my
leg propped up on a second chair, and dozed and read and
dozed some more. My legs had not supported me when I
came down off my bed the first day. I walked holding tightly
to my parents' arms and it was as if I were learning to walk
all over again. I looked into a mirror and did not know who
I was.

I slept a lot that summer, often outside on the chair in the
sun. I had lost eight pounds during the illness. Alex brought
me books to read from the library. Sometimes Eddie Kulanski
went past me, walking lightly on the balls of his feet and
saying nothing. But I was too weary to care about Eddie
Kulanski. He was all burned out of me. After a while it was
almost as if I had never known him.

I sat in the sun and watched people enter and leave the
shoe repair store. My father's little business was doing well.
Toward the end of the summer he began to talk about opening up a store of his own somewhere nearby. His face beamed
and he rubbed his fingers thoughtfully against the cheek with
the scar. "Little by little," he said. "Slowly. Patiently. We
will rebuild it, Ruth." My mother nodded and smiled. In the
evening, when he was away at his meetings, she sat in the
kitchen writing letters.

In the fall I returned to school and in the late spring, three
weeks before the outbreak of the Spanish Civil War, I was
graduated. Mr. Bader returned to the States briefly the next
January, looking thin and tired, but well dressed in a dark suit,
white shirt, and dark tie, his brown hair smoothly combed and
parted in the middle. How was I doing with my studies? he
wanted to know. I was doing well in high school and studying
Bible on my own. He listened to me talk eagerly about Jere-
miah and patted my arm. My father nodded approvingly. A
faint knowing smile flickered upon my mother's thin lips. He
left for Europe a few weeks later. When he returned to the
States in January of the following year I was shamefacedly
unable to report to him significant further progress in Bible.

My high school studies were proving difficult enough to be interesting and were taking up a lot of my time. He seemed disappointed and hurt.

"You've done almost nothing in Bible since I saw you last," he said.

"It's been a hard year. I was sick a lot."

"You've been sick a lot before, David."

We studied together. But it was no longer as it had been before. Much of the excitement was out of it. He left for Europe in March, two weeks after German troops marched into Austria.

That fall, one month after the Munich Agreement delivered Czechoslovakia to Germany, my uncle and aunt traveled to Palestine and were gone ten weeks. Saul moved into the yeshiva dormitory and I rarely saw him. He had grown into a tall thin tense person with thick glasses and a squinting gaze. He would be a teacher of Talmud one day; that was clear enough. He had begun to smoke.

I did not know why my uncle and aunt had chosen that time to go to Palestine, for there were riots and demonstrations and shootings there all the time now. They had a job to take care of, my father said in response to my question, and would say no more. It had to do with Zionist politics, Saul told me. Something about the Revisionist organization. My mother shook her head nervously, murmured some words about having to build things with patience, and told me it was late, I had to go to bed, did I want to get sick again.

I was ill periodically. Dr. Weidman began to talk about surgery. They were waiting until they could be certain I had stopped growing. I dreaded the prospect of surgery. It was a darkness somewhere in the future and I would not let myself think about it.

Early in 1939, Mr. Bader returned from Europe and I studied Ezekiel with him for a number of months. But the passion for Bible was all gone from me now. The yeshiva I attended emphasized Talmud; Bible was not even taught. You were expected to review the weekly Torah reading by yourself. Whatever Bible most of the yeshiva students knew they remembered from the verses cited in their volumes of Talmud.

"They laugh at you in my yeshiva when you talk too much about Bible," I told him. "They think it's for children or for a few hours on a Shabbos afternoon. They only want you to study Gemara."

"Yes," he said soberly. "I'm familiar with that yeshiva attitude toward the Bible. I thought you might have been able to overcome it."

At the end of one of our sessions he handed me a pamphlet entitled *Persecution—Jewish and Christian and Let Us Consider the Record* by the Reverend Chas. E. Coughlin.

"We talked about him once," he said. "You ought to read this. In America the poison is only words so far. In Europe it is already killing Jews. Take it home and read it, David."

I took it home and read it and heard echoes of its hate all around me as I walked the streets of my neighborhood.

That September Germany invaded Poland. Five weeks later Mr. Bader left for Lisbon.

Suddenly, very suddenly, that fall there were no more letters to my mother from her family in Europe. The last letter arrived around the end of September. It had been written in late August by her mother, a somber letter full of foreboding. "But we must have faith in the Master of the Universe," she wrote. "Your father and I send you and Max and the children our wishes for a healthy and prosperous New Year. Kiss our grandchildren for us, my daughter. Perhaps one day they will be able to see the farm. It has been a hot summer but we have had plenty of rain and the trees in the forest are beautiful." The mail service to and from the conquered areas of Eastern Europe was terminated. My mother could no longer write to her family in Poland. She continued writing letters to Palestine. She wept easily that fall and winter, and would lapse into strange staring silences during which she seemed to hear and see nothing around her. The silences deepened and grew lengthier as the Nazi darkness spread itself across Europe.

Six

The yeshiva building occupied an entire block in a gentile neighborhood in upper Manhattan. It had been built in the late nineteen twenties. Its facade was of reddish stone and veined light gray marble; it had spacious windows and a huge green dome that rested upon a sky blue base made decorous with golden arabesques. The building housed a parochial high school and college and a rabbinical seminary. It had been built by Eastern European Orthodox Jews who wanted their American-born children to achieve a synthesis of Torah and modern secular learning. I attended that school for ten years of my life.

It stood on a bluff overlooking the Harlem River. Across from the school was a narrow terracelike park with benches and paved walks and small islands of grass. A stone parapet bordered the outer edge of the park. Beyond the parapet was the brush-covered rock-strewn side of the bluff that dropped about two hundred feet to the roadway and river below. There was a path down the bluff to the river but you did not take it unless you were sure of yourself as a climber. In my junior year in high school one of my classmates tried it alone one afternoon and fell. He was unable to move and no one heard his cries. He lay injured through the night and was not missed until morning. The police found him dead near the boulder that had broken his fall. There was an assembly of the entire school. We were warned not to descend the bluff to the river.

We could see the river from the school and the park. It ran wide and slow and dark. Along the opposite shore were a lumberyard and a shantytown and railroad tracks. Toward the south was the stone and steel bridge that connected this part of Manhattan to the Bronx. North of us the river followed languidly the curving shoreline of Manhattan as its waters branched off from the choppy expanse of the Hudson. We could not see the Hudson from the school.

In the morning I concentrated on Talmud; in the afternoon I studied secular subjects. My Talmud teachers were rabbis who had been trained in the yeshivas of Eastern Europe; the secular teachers were Americans and Europeans who had been trained in colleges and universities. All the secular teachers were Jews but many of them did not observe the commandments. The Talmud teachers were rigid adherents of Jewish Orthodoxy. Many of them wished they could be teaching in one of the other yeshivas in New York where secular studies beyond the state-required minimum were forbidden.

All through my first three years in that yeshiva I studied only Talmud in the morning. Bible was not offered as a course of study. During the first semester of my senior year, this deficiency must have been noticed by someone in the administration and a course in Song of Songs began to be taught one hour a week by a man brought in from the Teachers' Institute, the department that trained Hebrew teachers. This department was regarded as the embodiment of frivolity and light-headedness by the students of Talmud, and as a breeding ground for apikorsim, Jews who are knowledgeable in Jewish studies but who deny the divine origin of the Torah. The hour given to Song of Songs was taken from the Thursday Talmud class. This abridgment of Talmud time was deeply resented by the zealous Talmudists in my class. They flaunted their resentment in the face of the helpless Bible teacher by using the class to catch up on the news during that first fall of the war. The desks of that class were black and white with *The New York Times* and the *New York Post*; the air of that class was on occasion dense with newspaper sounds. Song of Songs, despite the vaunted authorship of King Solomon, could not compete effectively with the news about the German conquest of Poland. The teacher spoke bravely into the dead air of inattention.

He was a short, thin, mild-tempered man in his fifties, with a bald head, a graying mustache, and thick glasses. He spoke in a soft voice made virtually inaudible by the whispers, coughs, and newspaper noises in the class. I would sit in the front row directly before his desk trying to listen while all around me was the rainfall of indifferent disturbance. He was not a bad teacher if you were willing to be taught. From time to time he would appeal in a timorous voice for silence. The class would be quiet for a few minutes; then, slowly, the level of noise would begin to rise. He would order that the newspapers be put away; they would disappear, then reappear, at first surreptitiously, then openly. He would threaten to report the class to the administration; an empty and futile threat, for we all knew that no Talmud student in our school would be punished for not studying Song of Songs. Toward the end of the first month of that class, he was teaching only four or five interested students, who sat near his desk, while the other twenty or so students sat scattered throughout the large airy second-floor room waiting impatiently for the hour to end. It bothered me to see the teacher so brazenly offended and I lost patience one Thursday afternoon when a student sitting some rows behind me loudly riffled his newspaper while turning a page. In the corridor after the class I told him I didn't care if he wanted to remain an ignoramus in Bible, but he was going to have to stop disturbing those who were serious about the class.

He was a tall, stoop-shouldered boy from Brooklyn with a heavy face and dull gray eyes. His name was Irving Besser. I came up to his chest in height.

"Who are you calling an ignoramus?" he said, folding his newspaper and putting it under his arm.

The class had gathered around us, blocking the corridor.

"You are an ignoramus in Bible," I said, using the Hebrew term *am ha'aretz*. "That's your privilege. I'm not asking you to study Bible. I'm asking you to be quiet so I can study Bible."

He put a thick strong finger on my chest and pushed ominously. "I don't like to be called an ignoramus."

"Then don't behave like one."

"Look, Lurie"—he poked me hard—"you better—"

"Rabbi Akiva said that Song of Songs is the holiest of all the books of the Kesuvim. How can you sit there fooling around while we study it?"

"Where did he say that?"

"Rashi brings it into his commentary on the first verse."

There was subdued laughter from the group around us. Irving Besser's face went dark. He was one of the best Talmud students in the high school and rarely did a day go by when he did not prove that in class; but he was indifferent to all his other studies and in constant difficulty with his secular courses. He called his secular studies the "goy part of the day." He would get his degrees with minimal energy. I did not like him and had stayed out of his way until this afternoon.

"You know something else, Besser?" I said. "Someone once said that one third of our study time should be given over to learning Bible. What do you think of that?"

"Who? One of your apikorsishe grammarians?"

"Yes. The Rambam."

The laughter was loud this time.

His face went very dark. "Where does the Rambam say that?"

I gave him the source in the law code of Maimonides. He fidgeted uncomfortably, embarrassed and frustrated.

"You're making fun of me," he muttered, readying his finger for another prod. "You're shaming me."

"I'm sorry if I am. Don't make fun of the ones who are trying to study Bible."

Yaakov Bader, tall, heavy-shouldered, pale blond hair and handsome smiling open face, suddenly slid between us.

"Peace," he said in Hebrew. "Peace, peace, to those far and near." Then in English, "It's time for lunch and not for fighting."

"Why don't you let skinny fight his own battles?" Irving Besser said.

"Because his battles are my battles," Yaakov Bader sang in his toneless voice to the tune of an old melody with similar words. "Besides, you're bothering me also, Irving, and I don't think I want you to do that anymore. Come on, Davey. I'm hungry."

Downstairs, as we waited on line in the crowded school cafeteria, Yaakov said, "Why do you bother with guys like that, Davey?"

"He bothers me."

"The world is full of Irving Bessers. You can't let them all bother you. They can give you ulcers with their righteousness."

We selected our food and took our trays over to a table that had just been vacated.

"What do you hear from your uncle?" I asked.

"The word is that he's in Istanbul."

"Is he going to be away the whole war?"

"I don't know. I'm not even sure what he's doing. No one talks about it. He's saving Jews."

"I miss him."

He gave me a sober smile and bit into his tuna sandwich.

"Are you all set for the history exam?" he asked.

I nodded and picked at my baked fish.

"You memorized the index?" He smiled around his sandwich.

"Try me," I said.

"I believe you, I believe you. I wonder how many guys are going to pass that exam today because of your skinny shoulders."

I shrugged. Often those who sat near me in an exam copied my answers. I did not care and would not stop them.

"I really miss your uncle," I said moodily. "Especially on days like today. My worst days are Irving Besser days."

He made a face and went on eating.

Irving Besser sat quietly with his *New York Post* during our next session with Song of Songs. But the general level of noisy indifference continued. The few of us who studied attempted to ignore it. The Bible class was discontinued the following semester and we returned to the all-encompassing world of the Talmud.

But I did not entirely abandon Bible, for I was teaching my brother the Torah reading for his bar mitzvah. He cared not too much for Bible and even less for grammar. He studied the Torah reading to please my father and on the spring day of his bar mitzvah in his yeshiva synagogue he read flawlessly, and then muttered when he was done, "Thank God that's over with." He read books and remembered most of what he read. But, save for his school texts, he read only stories and novels. It was clear he did not intend to study Bible seriously or read too often from the Torah.

I said to him one night as I watched him reading a novel by Dickens, "Why do you waste your time reading stories, Alex?"

I had to ask it again before he heard me. His face, so much a duplicate of my father's, looked hurt.

"They're great books, Davey. I'm not reading junk. The librarian is helping me find what to read."

"But there's nothing in them. You don't come away with any facts or anything."

"I don't read them for facts. I read them to find out about people and the different kinds of worlds they live in."

"You find out more about people from a page of Gemara or Chumash than you do from a story."

"But it's not the same thing, Davey."

"Okay. It's not the same thing. Are you going to sleep?"

"When I finish the chapter."

Late one night I looked up from my Talmud and listened to a strange soft choking sound and saw my brother crying. He was sitting at his desk near the window, reading *Oliver Twist* and crying. I stared at him in astonishment. He sat there, hunched over his book, and I could see clearly three-quarters of his face and the tears that flowed down it. He turned a page and wiped at his eyes and went on reading and crying. I could not understand it and went back to my Talmud.

He was rarely without a book in his hands from that time on; and it was almost always a novel or a collection of stories. He read as he ate; he read as he walked in the streets; he read as he rode the buses to and from school; he read in the bathroom.

He told me one night that he thought he might like to teach English literature. I was astounded.

"Why?" I asked.

"Because I like it."

"Why don't you teach Hebrew literature? Why English literature, for heaven's sake?"

"There is no Hebrew literature. It's only fifty years old and it has one or two great novelists and two or three great poets. English literature is a thousand years old and has a library of great novelists and great poets."

"I wonder how overjoyed the goyim will be having a Jew teach English literature."

"It's mine if I make it mine," he said firmly and somewhat cryptically. "I won't ask them to do me any favors."

He was only thirteen and I thought his remarks presumptuous. I envied him his fervor, though I was certain he would change his mind a dozen times before he decided finally on what he would do with his life. Thirteen and he was talking about teaching English literature!

Saul came over with his parents one cold Shabbat afternoon early in January. We talked for a while about the war. He looked tall and gaunt and was still having trouble with his eyes. He was now studying in the highest Talmud class in the school. His teacher was Rav Tuvya Sharfman. "A phenomenon," Saul called him, his thin voice rising excitedly. His pale hands and long thin expressive fingers danced and gyrated and described circles in the air as he spoke. He dressed sloppily—tie awkwardly knotted, shirt collar unbuttoned, brown hair uncombed, shoelaces trailing behind him. "Everyone said he was great," he went on in solemn rapture, "but you have to study with him to know how great he really is." At this point he swiftly pulled a handkerchief from a pocket, placed it in front of his nose, and sneezed loudly. Alex, who lay propped up on his bed with a book, read on undisturbed.

The two of us looked at him. He lay with the upper half of his chunky frame resting upon his pillow, which he had placed against the wall near his bed. His squarish face was fixed upon the book that lay before him on the twin hillocks formed by his knees. He had spoken a brief greeting when Saul had first entered the room, then had slipped back into the world of his book. He was reading *Great Expectations*. He had been reading Dickens all that fall and winter. He had also begun to write sketches and stories in a pad which he carried with him to school, concealed somewhere in his desk, and showed no one.

"You used to look like that when you studied Chumash," Saul said. "If a bomb fell in the street he wouldn't hear it."

I looked away and was quiet. From the living room came the sounds of our parents' voices. They were talking about the war.

"Anyway," Saul said, returning to our conversation, "I'm staying on and will probably end up teaching Gemara there. Hints have been dropped."

"That's great, Saul."

"I have about three more years to go after I graduate and then I'll have smicha."

"Rabbi Saul Lurie. It sounds wonderful."

He squinted at me through the lenses of his glasses. Then he looked again at Alex. "The Rambam didn't trust the human imagination," he said. "Where does he get it from?"

"Mama says she used to write poetry when she was a little girl."

"Does he have to read all that for school?"

"You went to the same school. Did you have to read all that?"

"Novels are for women."

"According to the Rambam?"

He smiled and squinted his eyes. Then he rubbed his eyes wearily and I saw the tobacco stains on the index and middle fingers of his hand. I had a sharp image of him sitting in the large study hall of the yeshiva, his table piled high with volumes of the Talmud and commentaries. He studied from a standing position, in his shirt sleeves, stooping over the folio volumes, shuffling pages, smoking, murmuring to himself, straightening his thin body, staring off into space, then stooping again over the volumes. All around him was the din of more than one hundred rabbinical school students studying Talmud; he was oblivious to it. Wreathed in cigarette smoke, alternately squinting and staring, he carved out of the books on the table his own world of the mind. I would pass by the study hall on my way to a class or out of the building and look in on him and see him studying, and I would carry that picture of him inside my eyes for a long time. But he looked very tired and I told him so now and he smiled wryly and said, "Most of one's knowledge is acquired at night."

"Also the Rambam?"

"Of course."

Alex stirred on his bed, rearranged his pillow against the wall, fluffed it up, and settled into it again—all without taking his eyes from his book.

"We are sure Dickens did not write with divine inspiration?" I asked.

"There aren't many things in this world I'm sure of," Saul said. "But that I'm sure of."

"You're lucky Alex hears no evil when he reads. Listen. Is it still forbidden to ask what your father does when he travels for the Revisionists and my father?"

"He organizes."

"What does he organize?"

"The organization."

"Do you know what he does, Saul? Seriously."

"He gives talks in private homes, raises money, and organizes youth groups."

"Everybody is so busy doing things," I said. "Everybody."

He looked at me. I gazed out my window at the alleyway and stone wall. A train rushed by along Third Avenue, rattling the windowpanes.

"Busy," I said. "Busy, busy. Everybody has a job."

He squinted his eyes at me and was quiet.

"You want to go to the movies after Shabbos?" I said. "Is there anything at the Blendheim or the Luxor?"

"I have a date tonight, Davey."

I gazed out the window, tipping my chair back.

"Davey?"

I looked at him.

"What did Dr. Weidman say?"

"He said quote soon unquote."

"Will you have it when he says?"

"I don't want to think about it."

"Some of the girls, when I talk to them——"

"All right," I said. "You told me."

Sometimes the mother or father of a date would open the door to my ring. I would see their eyes alight on my face, then circle nervously away. They would be very polite. The girl would be sweet and chatty. Sometimes girls would even take my arm as we walked through a subway station or along a street and I would feel a tightening in my groin. We would sit in a movie or a theater and afterward we would have coffee and cake and I would listen to their talk and watch the way their eyes kept brushing across my face. Then I would take them back home and, later, lie awake in my bed, remembering their closeness, feeling their fingers on my arm. I would sleep and wake wet from strange fearful dreams. None of the girls I took out on blind dates would go out with me again.

"I'm thinking of your good, Davey," Saul said.

"All right," I said. "All right. What does the Rambam say about surgery for a flattened nose that makes you sick with fever ten days out of every month?"

"The Rambam says to listen to your doctor."

"I'm scared, Saul. I don't even want to think about it. Weidman says they have to go into the sinus cavity pretty close to the brain."

"He said that? Why did he say that?"

"I asked him to tell me the truth."

"Who says it's good to know the truth all the time?"

"I'm so scared I can't even dream about it yet."

Alex sighed, stirred faintly, and was quiet. We looked at him.

"Just the way you were," Saul said after a moment. "Exactly the same way."

"Yes," I said, bringing my chair forward and staring out the window at the oncoming night. "I seem to remember."

My mother was also remembering, but in dark silences that were like descents into a void. After the letters had stopped coming from her family in Poland, she began occasionally to sit in the living room near the canary and reread old letters. Sometimes I would come out of my room after a night of studying and find her asleep in an easy chair, her head fallen forward, her mouth slack, a letter crumpled in her hands. She looked pale and thin, her hair long and loose and already threaded with strands of gray. I would wake her gently and she would be startled at first and I would hear a sharp intake of breath and see her eyes go very wide; often I had the impression I had brought her back from memories and dreams far more pleasant than the world upon which she opened her eyes. She would swallow the saliva that had accumulated in the pools of her slack mouth as she had slept; then she would manage a shamefaced smile.

"Your mother fell asleep again in the chair." She said it as if apologizing and asking for understanding at one and the same time. "I was reading letters." Then she added, "I can't write to them anymore, so I read. What time is it, David?"

I would gather up the letters and help her to her bedroom door. I was only a little taller than she. At the door she would raise her dark eyes to me and smile wanly. "My little David." She stroked my hair and the side of my face. Her fingers were dry and rough. She would kiss me and I would return her kiss and she would go into the room, opening the door wide enough for me to see my father asleep in his bed. One night I woke her in the chair and walked her to the door and she murmured, still not fully awake, "What have we done to you, my darling?" then turned and went into her room. I stared at the door and for some strange reason was seized by a moment of uncontrollable shuddering.

My parents rarely spoke together now in the kitchen or living room during the early nights. My father repaired watches in the bedroom; my mother read old letters or wrote new ones to her cousins in Palestine.

In the weeks that followed the German conquest of Poland, my mother's silences grew longer and deeper. She continued doing the housework, preparing our meals, washing, ironing, baking for Shabbat, scrubbing floors, changing the bed linen; but she spoke very little and often not at all. And as Europe was swiftly consumed by the German army, as Denmark, Norway, Holland, Belgium, and France fell, as the Battle of Britain raged and waned, as the Germans began their race through Russia, she ceased to read her old letters and, for periods of time that were often days in length, simply would not utter a word. If we spoke to her she would nod or respond with a yes or a no or an expression on her worn face. But she initiated no conversations, participated in none of our table talk. She moved about the house like a cloud of silent darkness.

I found her asleep one cold winter night in the living room long after our radiator had died. The air was chill; when I touched her hands they were icy. She stirred and woke, startled, and gasped loudly. She seemed for the very briefest of moments a frightened little girl.

"It's very late, Mama."

"I'm sorry, darling. I fell asleep again in the chair."

"Let me help you up."

She held my arm as we crossed to her door.

"Why does Papa let you fall asleep here?"

"I tell him to go to sleep. I can't sleep. I have dreams." We stood at the door and she smiled weakly and gazed up at me. She pulled her robe close about herself and looked around the room. Then she looked at the doorway to the hall, as if expecting someone. After a moment, she shivered and her dark gaze fell upon the reflection of her face in the large decorative wall mirror, a remnant of our previous ornate style of living. She shuddered visibly.

"They should have come," I heard her say in a barely audible tremulous voice. "Master of the Universe, what did they do?" She looked again around the room. Her hair lay long and loose upon her thin shoulders. Then, silently and without a further word, she opened the door to her room, slipped inside, and closed the door quietly behind her. I stood very still, and for a long moment thought I could still see her face in the mirror.

I dreaded the night I would again be wakened by her murmured incantations. In school one afternoon I asked Saul what the Rambam said about charms and spells. He quoted by heart, as if automatically, "One who whispers a spell over a wound, at the same time reciting a verse from the Torah, one who recites a verse over a child to save it from terrors, and one who places a scroll of phylacteries on an infant to induce it to sleep, are not in the category of sorcerers or soothsayers, but they are included among those who repudiate the Torah; for they use its words to cure the body whereas these are only medicine for the soul."

I had asked him the question in bitter jest. The response turned the jest to bile in my mouth.

But she did not return to the old darkness of spells and incantations. Perhaps she finally recognized its infantilism and worthlessness; perhaps she thought it unworthy of use in the case of her parents; perhaps the menace was not immediate enough: they were, after all, thousands of miles away and not deathly ill in the next room with a very high fever or a punctured throat or a seriously infected leg. Instead, she began to pray morning and evening from the Book of Psalms. And she became rigidly, zealously, almost compulsively wary about her observance of the commandments and about our own religious behavior. "Did you pray yet? Then come and have breakfast." "Did you wash your hands yet? Then come and make Hamotzi." "Did you pray the Afternoon Service yet? It's almost sundown." "I must light candles no later than four-twelve. A moment later it's Shabbos." "Your tefillin look worn. You should take them to a scribe." "You should get up now and go to synagogue or you'll come too late for Borchu." "Who put the meat spoon in this drawer? Who? You will make my entire kitchen unclean."

She continued this way for months. Alex chafed under it but said nothing. My father would nod, thank her for reminding him to check his tefillin, to pray the Afternoon Service, to do this or that, to avoid this or that; he was extraordinarily meek in the face of her relentless watchfulness over our religious lives. Sometimes in the early evenings after supper I would sit at my desk and hear him talking with my mother in the kitchen before he went into the bedroom to work on his watches. "You will hear from them," he said. "How long can the war last? Soon you will hear from them, Ruth." But as the war in Europe went on, he ceased his vacuous soothing and bore with patience and expressions of gentle gratitude my mother's need to make firm the outlines of the world immediately around her. Still I remained upset over the way she would fall asleep in a chair in the living room during the chill nights of winter and I talked to my father about it one Shabbat morning in early March on the way to the yeshiva synagogue. Alex was in bed with a slight cold and I thought this was as good a time as any to tell him how I felt.

"There is nothing I can do," he said into the icy wind that blew along the street.

"I don't understand. I found Mama asleep in the chair

last night without a blanket. She was freezing cold. She'll catch pneumonia."

"She will not catch pneumonia. You will catch pneumonia if you get yourself excited and overheated in this weather."

"Why don't you help Mama to bed after you finish your work at night?"

"She does not let me. Every night she tells me she wants to sit up by herself a while longer."

"Then give her a blanket."

"No," he said. "I do not want your mother to start using the chair for a bed. That is not good for her."

"I don't understand."

"Where is it written that you must understand everything? There are things between a husband and wife that no one else has to understand."

"She's my mother."

"Yes," he said. "Your good head should therefore tell you that I know her longer than you do. I tell you that I know her better than you do. She may lose some of her family in Europe. But she will be all right."

"What do you mean?"

We crossed at the corner of Washington Avenue and 170th Street.

"It is only rumors. But they have a smell of the truth about them."

"Are the Germans killing Jews?"

"Yes."

I shivered in the wind. "Is anyone doing anything?"

"It is not officially known as yet. When it becomes officially known, then governments will meet and decide that nothing can be done."

"Nothing?" I said. "Nothing?"

"David, the Jews are doing nothing to save themselves. Why should the goyim help us?"

I was quiet. The wind stung my eyes. We stood at the foot of the stone steps that led up to the yeshiva building, the stone steps down which I had once fallen with a lollipop stick in my mouth.

"Between the mentality of Tulchin and the mentality of the Hasidim, we will lose many European Jews because of this war." He hunched down in his winter coat, his hands deep in his pockets. He looked up and down the deserted Saturday morning street. "There are those who are trying to smuggle weapons into the ghettos. Certain friends are helping. I tell

you this because you are no longer a child. Do you understand?"

I nodded slowly, staring at him.

"Jabotinsky was right. We should have got them out. But I
could not get out my own family. So we must save what we
can. And we must be patient. Until after the war."

I stared at him. His face was grim. The scar on his cheek
was starkly white within the flesh reddened by the bitter
wind. It occurred to me at that moment as we stood there in
the March cold outside the yeshiva that his eyes were seeing
this war in a way utterly different from mine. I saw it in
newspaper photographs, in movie newsreels, in the images I
conjured up for myself as I listened to radio broadcasts; but
this man, my father, had led men in combat, had killed men
in war, knew the smells of battle and death, and was able to
enter the photographs and newsreels and radio broadcasts to
see the war. In that same way, he could see Jews being killed.
And again I shivered in the winter wind.

I woke one night that April in the second year of the war
and heard voices in the apartment. I felt it to be a dream but
realized quickly enough it was not. One voice was that of
my mother crying; the other was that of my father speaking
to her softly, gently, soothing. I could not make out what
they were saying but it went on a very long time until silence
settled deeply once again into the apartment. Then I heard a
stirring inside my room and Alex quietly called my name.

"I'm awake," I whispered.

"What happened?" he whispered back.

"I don't know."

"Something is going on. They're hiding something from us."

I was quiet.

"I don't like that," he whispered. "I can't stand it."

Still I was quiet.

"I can take almost anything. All the nagging and the gloom
and doom over this place. I can take that. But I can't take
being treated like a baby. They keep everything from me."

"They used to keep everything from me too."

He stirred in the darkness. "Used to?" he whispered. "Used
to?"

I said nothing.

"What's going on, Davey?"

"I don't know."

"Davey."

"I really don't know, Alex."

"I can't stand it," he whispered, his voice muffled as if he had abruptly turned his head away. "Don't they realize I'm not a baby anymore?"

In the morning I said to my father in the living room as he was removing his tefillin after the Morning Service, "Are the rumors true, Papa?"

He stopped, stared at me, nodded once, then went on unwinding the black leather strap from his left arm. I watched the muscles of the arm move. Had he killed men with that arm? It was strange how frequently these days I thought of my father as a soldier. A few weeks ago I had asked him if he ever had any photographs of himself in uniform. Yes, he said. But they had all been destroyed in a pogrom.

"I told your mother because I do not believe in concealing such matters," he said now.

"The Germans are killing Polish Jews?"

"Polish Jews and Russian Jews. The picture is not clear. But they are killing Jews."

I told it to Alex. He stared at me.

"What do you mean?"

"Just what I said."

"How does Papa know?"

"He knows." I stared out the window at the people on the street. The world was the same. Nothing was changing. The same street, the same stores. "He knows," I repeated. "It's his job to know."

Then I was ill for a while and when I returned to school I had to work hard to catch up on what I had missed. And then it was summer and fall. Alex was in high school and was reading novels and writing into the nights; Saul was working for his ordination; my uncle's law business was doing very well and he was traveling a great deal for the Revisionist organization; and my father was talking about opening his own store and moving from the neighborhood, perhaps to Clay Avenue. He began looking at store sites. At first he would go out alone in the late evenings or early mornings. My mother would sit alone waiting for him to return. One evening during supper she announced abruptly, "I must get out of the house." She looked around the kitchen, blinking nervously. "I cannot stand it any longer, Max."

We stared at her in silence.

"I am going to look at a store tonight," said my father very calmly.

"Yes?" she said. "Where?"

"Near the Concourse. A nice walk." He sniffed at a forkful of baked potato and said, "We will go together, Ruth."

She nodded. They went out together after supper. The next night they went out together again to another site. They were out often together that fall and Alex and I were in the apartment alone.

I remember one cold rainy night of that fall with particular vividness and poignancy, a November night after an entire day of rain. I had been to see Dr. Weidman in the morning. "It's time, David," he had said, his aging pink face sober. "I want you to have it done in the summer."

I lay on the examining table and felt myself beginning to tremble.

"I will get you the best man in the city. We will have it done at Mount Sinai."

"The summer?" I heard myself say in a voice that was suddenly dry and dead. Then again, absurdly, "The summer?"

"Yes," he said. "It is definitely time."

I wanted to say something that would effect a delay, cause him to change his mind, give me another year. Next summer? Next summer was only eight months away.

"Are you sure?" I heard myself say in a tense rising voice.

"David," he said quietly. "I am absolutely sure."

I rode to school in a bus and sat in my Talmud class looking out at the rain. It fell in a slant and a wind came across the river and blew it along the wide cobblestone street. Toward late afternoon it changed briefly to snow. Then it became rain again, thick, grayish, dirty-looking, as it fell onto the city from the darkening sky. I walked to the bus stop after school and rode home and felt the rain let up and then stop as I walked home.

During supper I told my parents and Alex what Dr. Weidman had said.

I saw my mother's face freeze. My father looked at me and his face was suddenly drained of expression. Alex's mouth opened slightly and he took a sharp deep gulping breath.

No one said anything. For what seemed to me to be an interminable length of time I heard nothing but the simmering of the kettle on the stove and the ticking of the clock on the shelf above the sink.

My father broke the silence. "If Dr. Weidman says it is time, then it is time. We will have it done."

Sweat ran down my back. My hands were icy cold.

"I will call him in the morning," my father said. "Did he say who will do the operation?"

"The best man in the city," I heard myself say.

"I will talk to him in the morning. It will be all right, David."

"I'm a little scared, Papa."

"It will be all right, I tell you. Everything will be all right."

"Dr. Weidman said they have to go near the brain."

My mother's eyes flew open.

"Whatever they have to do they will do," my father said after a moment. "Afterward you will be a new person."

Two days before my father opened his watch repair and jewelry store there was a heavy snowstorm. We watched it from our kitchen window during supper. "It is a good sign," my father said. "Snow is an excellent sign."

"On the farm snow in early spring was considered a blessing for the year," said my mother.

I looked at them. They seemed excited, eager for the future.

"The customers won't consider it a blessing," Alex said.

"It will be a good year," my father said. "I feel it."

He opened the store in the first week of March, three months after the Japanese bombed Pearl Harbor and America entered the war. It was located on a busy corner two blocks west of Grand Concourse in a neighborhood dense with recent apartment houses and stores. On the front window, in large gold letters, were the words JEWELRY & WATCH REPAIR. In the lower right-hand corner was my father's name: M. LURIE. When I rode by on the bus back from school the first day the store was open, I saw it crowded with customers. It was crowded with customers the second and third days too.

"The trouble is the bride is too beautiful," said my father at the kitchen table later that week. "I am so busy waiting on customers I can no longer repair watches."

"Max," my mother said quietly.

He looked at her.

"Is it difficult to wait on customers?"

"It is a job that a person with sense can learn," my father said.

She nodded and was quiet. The next day as I rode by in the bus I saw her inside the store behind the counter. The store was crowded. She wore a pale blue woolen dress, had her hair combed back in a bun, and wore a thin gold necklace. The store stood at a bus stop. The bus was crowded and many passengers were getting on and off. I watched her a long time. The bus pulled away from the corner and she receded from view.

At the kitchen table that evening she said buoyantly, "I think I will enjoy being a business lady."

My father smiled around the drumstick he had been chewing. Alex and I looked at each other.

"Yes," my mother said, her eyes shining. "I think I will like that very much."

Every day I would ride by on the bus and see her in the store with my father. It was a large spacious glittering store. In its front and side windows rings and watches nested in folds of black velvet. It was always busy.

Two weeks after he opened the store my father announced at the kitchen table that he felt it was time for us to move to a new neighborhood.

"Closer to the store," he said. "Your mother agrees."

"Where?" I asked.

"Your mother and I are looking."

They would go out together after supper and be gone for hours. I would be alone with Alex. The snow was all gone. The weather carried with it a vague tinge of warmth. I saw the summer and the darkness and I did not know what to do.

They came home one night from one of their forays. I heard them in the hallway putting away their coats. "I need a glass of coffee, Ruth," my father said. A moment later he was in our room. They had found an apartment, he said.

Alex looked up from his writing pad.

"Where?" I asked.

He told us. His face wore a controlled smile of pleasure. "Hard work," he said. "And a little luck. And patience. Piece by piece. I told you."

We were all delighted that we would be near my aunt and uncle and Saul. We moved during the last week of April when warmth was unmistakably in the air and the trees in the park on Clay Avenue had begun to open their buds. It was a lovely first-floor apartment in a large six-story house with an elevator and an entrance hall furnished with mirrors and lamps and chairs. The room I shared with Alex looked out on the wide brick-paved street and the park. I could see the trees above the tall stone wall that bordered the park. I would be able to watch them turn green.

My aunt and uncle came over the first night to help us get settled. But Alex and my father had already put up the beds and were arranging the living room furniture and there was little for my uncle and me to do. We stood near a window talking quietly while Alex and my father finished unrolling the living room carpet.

"This is different from the last time you moved, isn't it?" said my uncle in his gentle smiling way. "Do you remember?"

I remembered vaguely a time of darkness and horror.

"Yes," he said. "This is different." He watched Alex and my father handling with ease the heavy living room sofa in response to my mother's directions.

"You should replace the carpet, Ruth," said my aunt.

"We bought it when we were married," my mother said as if in the carpet's defense.

"And the curtains," said my aunt. "You will need new curtains. There is an excellent place on Fordham Road and Grand Concourse."

"That's quite a pair, your father and brother," said my uncle to me. "They move furniture around like it was matchsticks."

I looked out the window at the wide dark street. "Uncle Meyer?" I said very quietly.

He looked at me. It was my father's face looking at me. Alex and my uncle and my father. Squarish shape and hard bony features and brown wavy hair and protruding lower jaw and small gray eyes.

"Are the Revisionists going to fight the British after the war?"

He blinked his eyes and regarded me in silence. Slowly the gentleness seemed to ebb from his face; and then it was indeed my father's face, with all the hardness I had so often seen in it over the years.

"We will have to break heads after the war," he said in a low voice. "There will be no way out of it. Weizmann and the others will bow to the British and behave like gentlemen. Let them, the fools. We will have to smash heads."

I stared out the window at a passing bus.

"It will be a beautiful apartment, Ruth," came my aunt's smooth, elegant voice. "You all deserve it after what you've been through."

I looked at my uncle. The gentleness had returned to his face. He smiled. "He would surprise us all. Do you remember I said that?"

I thought I could remember and nodded.

"There will be other surprises," said my uncle. "He is a clever man, my brother, once he finds an idea. Very clever. Let me help you unpack some of those cartons."

We worked together for a while on cartons of books and papers. I had not looked for or seen the photograph of the armed men in the forest. I had lost interest in it. The cartons of books given to me by Mrs. Horowitz I shoved into the back of one of the two closets in the room I was to share with Alex.

In a very brief time the apartment was set up and we moved about in it as if we had lived there for years. Quickly, very quickly it seemed, the ash-gray bleakness of Washington Avenue, the dark alleyway, the cement back yards, the grinding noise of the elevated trains, quickly it all began to dim. There was not much in any of it worth remembering as I sat during our first week in that apartment gazing out of my window at the park and thinking of the summer that lay ahead.

There were many little synagogues in the neighborhood and two or three large ones. My father decided we would pray in the same synagogue attended by my uncle and cousin. It was an intimate place in a small detached house on Teller Avenue three blocks from where we lived. I prayed there on two successive Shabbat mornings and could not abide the gross errors that studded the Torah reading and made corpses of dozens of words. The Torah reader was an old white-bearded man. He had been reading for years and Torah reading was his tenured post in that little synagogue. He knew no grammar and had his own mysterious system of notes and tones. After the second Shabbat I told my father I could not stand it and would look around for another synagogue in which to pray.

"Why don't you study Gemara while he reads the Torah?" Alex asked.

"You're supposed to follow the Torah reading," I said heatedly. "You're not supposed to be doing anything else."

"Okay, okay," Alex said. "My religious brother."

"It says so. You want to see it?"

"No. If you say it says so, then it says so."

"How can you stand his reading, Papa?"

"I have heard worse Torah readers than that old man. If I am able to read the Torah at eighty-two I might also not care too much how I read it."

"The people who listen might care."

"Find another synagogue," my father said. "I did not know Mr. Bader taught you to be such a fanatic about Torah reading."

"I'm not a fanatic, Papa. He's impossible to listen to."

"All right. Go to another synagogue."

I began attending other synagogues. In one, the Torah reader was fine but I could barely hear him over the loud conversations of the congregants. Three times during the Torah reading the rabbi, a man in his late twenties or early thirties, rose to appeal for silence and cited the religious requirement that the Torah reading be followed with scrupulous care. The conversations about the war, health, family, business were blithely resumed each time a moment after he returned to his seat. I did not think I would go back.

"I've never seen anything like it," I told my father later during our Shabbat dinner. "It's a marketplace, not a synagogue."

"How many synagogues have you seen, David?"

"I'm beginning to miss the yeshiva synagogue. Peace and quiet and a good Torah reader."

"I do not miss the yeshiva synagogue," said my father in a hardening tone.

"I wish Mr. Bader were reading the Torah around here somewhere."

I saw my mother give me an uneasy look from her side of our dining room table.

"For all I know, Mr. Bader may be reading the Torah in Lisbon or Istanbul these days," said my father a little grimly.

"I've never heard such talking during a Torah reading," I said.

"People work hard all week," my father said. "They have very little time to see their friends. So they talk in the synagogue during the Torah reading."

"It was a desecration, Papa."

"The people who talked committed a wrong. Do not make more of it than it was."

"Mr. Bader taught me to—"

He cut me short with an abrupt wave of his hand. "I know what Mr. Bader taught you. I asked him to teach it to you. Find yourself another synagogue and do not make such a fuss."

"The way the rabbi kept pleading with them to be quiet and they just went on talking."

I saw Alex and my mother exchange an uneasy glance. Before my father could reply, Alex broke into the conversation with an account of the beating a boy in our yeshiva had suffered at the hands of some goyim that week, and we lost the thread of our talk about Torah reading.

The following Shabbat I went to a large synagogue on the other side of the park from where we lived. The Torah reader was fairly good. The rabbi, a balding man in his early forties, preached in a high-voiced frenzy. He juggled Talmudic passages with dazzling ease and exhorted his congregants to ever-increasing devotion to Torah-true Jewish life. Brilliant morning sunlight came through a sliver of window above the Ark. I could see branches of trees with broad green leaves against the blue radiance of a clear sky. I turned away from the window and the gesticulations of the rabbi and gazed down at the volume of *Mikraot Gedolot* on my lap; the synagogue made the volumes available to its congregants together with the prayer book, and at the end of the service you placed them both in the small rack in front of you. I let my eyes wander idly through the words of Ibn Ezra. I knew them by heart. I knew the page by heart. I knew it all by heart, all the precious pages my fingers now touched. I looked up at the podium in the center of the synagogue where the Torah reader had stood earlier that morning chanting the sacred words of God to Moses at Sinai. I imagined I could see myself at the podium now, thin, short, face very pale from a recent illness, myself as I had stood reading the Torah when I had become a bar mitzvah six years ago. A boy. Dark suit, white shirt, dark tie. Swaying slowly as he chanted the words of the Torah from the scroll that lay open before him. The story of Joseph and his brothers and the dreams and the pit and slavery. And the sense of the hushed congregation all around me, following the words. My father standing beside me and reciting the opening blessing over the Torah. "Amen," from the congregation. "Amen," I said, and took up the chant where I had stopped when I was done reading for the second man who had come up to the Torah, an old friend of my father's from the days when we had lived near the zoo. "And it came to pass, when Joseph was come unto his brethren, that they stripped Joseph of his coat . . ." I chanted and stopped and listened to my father recite the closing blessing. My father stepped aside. A moment later my uncle stood beside me next to my father. He recited the blessing. I took a deep breath. My knees were a little weak but I felt a strange soaring exultation. I was reading the Torah! I knew it by heart, had known it by heart for weeks; but you are not permitted to read the Torah in the synagogue from memory alone; so I fixed my eyes on the black squarish unpointed hand-lettered words on the parchment and read in my high thin voice. "And it came to pass at that time, that Judah went down from his brethren, and turned in to a certain Adullamite, whose name was Hirah." I heard my uncle murmuring the text as I read. Out of the corner of my eye I saw my father, his face empty of expression, following the reading in the Chumash he held in his hands. The synagogue was very still. I read on. "And Judah saw there a daughter of a certain Canaanite whose name was Shua . . ." And I read on to the end of the story of Judah and Tamar, my voice trying to match the rise and fall of the drama of the text. I was perspiring. It seemed to me I had never heard the synagogue so silent. I did not look around as my uncle recited the closing blessing and the fifth man, another of my father's friends from the Am Kedoshim Society, was called to the Torah. He recited the opening blessing. I chanted the account of Joseph in the house of Potiphar. And still there was that silence in the synagogue, as if I were alone, as if mannequins were crowding the seats all around me. Barely a cough. Only the silence and my voice in the silence chanting of Joseph and the wife of Potiphar. A sixth man was called to the Torah, and I chanted of Joseph in prison; a seventh man, and I chanted of Joseph deciphering dreams, and concluded, exultantly, with the words, "Yet the chief butler did not remember Joseph, but forgot him." And a stir like the winds in the forest behind the cottage we had once owned moved through the congregation. I saw my father's face, flushed, proud, slightly incredulous. I scanned the balcony where the women sat and saw my mother. She sat staring at me, her mouth open. All around her women talked to her but she seemed not to be listening. She had upon her face a luminous look that seemed blinding to me, a look that for the briefest of moments washed away the dead years; and I loved her then, loved her so very much, wanted so very much to walk

down from the podium and go upstairs to the balcony and
embrace her and say to her that all the pain and all the
darkness had been worthwhile. Worthwhile, Mama. Wasn't
it worthwhile? I tried to make it worthwhile for all of us, all
the nights of fever, all the horror, all the nightmares, made
worthwhile in a Torah reading by a boy who was becoming
a bar mitzvah. But I remained on the podium and recited my
own blessing over the Torah and read my own portion, the
Maftir, repeating the last four verses of the portion I had
read before. Then I recited the closing blessings and the Torah
was lifted from the podium and the congregation rose and
proclaimed, "This is the Torah which Moses set before the
children of Israel, according to the commandment of the
Lord by the hand of Moses." And then I stood alone at
the podium chanting the prophetic reading from Amos. And
when I was done a rain of candy poured from the balcony
and voices shouted "Mazel tov! Mazel tov!" and I saw my
father surrounded by his friends and I came down from the
podium and people were shaking my hand and then my
father held me to him in a strong embrace; I felt his hard
muscular body against mine; and he kissed me; and later my
mother held me to her, gently, tenderly, and I felt her tears
on my cheek and she stroked my face. Was it worthwhile,
Mama? For all the years. Was it worthwhile?

The rabbi raised his voice very suddenly to make a point
and I looked away from the podium and closed my eyes. The
palms of my hands were cold and sweaty. My head felt damp.
I found the strident voice suddenly unendurable. I opened
the volume of *Mikraot Gedolot,* then closed it. I was unable
to concentrate on the words. I wished he would finish. I
looked around to see if others were as uncomfortable as I
was. No. He seemed to have the entire congregation spell-
bound. It was a very large congregation of about eight hundred people. I turned my eyes back upon the podium. As I
did so, I noticed, seated two places away to my left, a dark-
haired man in his twenties reading a book. We were separated
by an elderly man who was listening avidly to the sermon. I
looked at the book and saw that it was in English and its pages
were divided into columns, two columns on each page. The
man reading it was clearly oblivious to the sermon emanating
from the front of the synagogue. I thought it singularly dis-
tasteful for a person to be reading an English book during a
synagogue service and was about to look away when he began
to shuffle the pages of the book and I noticed columns of

Hebrew type. He shuffled pages toward what I thought was the end of the book; but when he stopped, I saw him looking at the table of contents. An English book printed as a Hebrew book would be! I had never seen or heard of such a book before, unless it was one of those books where the table of contents appeared in the back. I scanned the upper half of the page swiftly; his hand lay across the lower half. I read:

The Creation Chapter, The Garden of Eden, The Flood, The Tower of Babel and the Diversity of Language. The Deluge and its Babylonian Parallel, Are There Two Conflicting Accounts of the Creation and the Deluge in Genesis?, Abraham, The Binding of Isaac (Akedah), Alleged Christological References in Scripture.

His hand concealed the rest of the page. I glanced at the right-hand page and read very quickly:

AUTHORITIES. Jewish and non-Jewish commentators—ancient, medieval and modern—have been freely drawn upon. "Accept the true from whatever source it comes," is sound Rabbinic doctrine—even if it be from the pages of a devout Christian expositor or of an iconoclastic Bible scholar, Jewish or non-Jewish. This does not affect the Jewish Traditional character of the work. My conviction that the criticism of the Pentateuch associated with the name of Wellhausen is a perversion of history and a desecration of religion, is unshaken; likewise, my refusal to eliminate the Divine either from history or from human life.

I began to read the next paragraph, but he had found what he was looking for in the table of contents and was shuffling pages again.

I turned away. The rabbi was concluding the sermon. His voice and arms flayed the air around the pulpit. Then he was done and we rose for the Kaddish preceding the Silent Devotion. The man two seats away from me put his English book into the rack before him and prayed quietly from his prayer book.

During the repetition of the Silent Devotion, he picked up the English book and continued reading it. Each time he concluded a section he went back to the table of contents. I watched carefully as he flipped the pages. Once he turned too far and I saw the title page:

THE
PENTATEUCH
AND
HAFTORAHS

Hebrew Text, English Translation
and Commentary

Edited by

DR. J. H. HERTZ

Chief Rabbi of the British Empire

He continued to read off and on until the conclusion of the service. I lost sight of him for a moment in the crowd that moved toward the rear doors of the synagogue at the end of the service. Then I saw him leave the synagogue, go down the long flight of stone stairs to the sidewalk, and go up the street, carrying the book under his arm. A block away he removed the black skullcap from his head, put it into his pocket, turned into the side street, and was gone.

I wondered who he was. Not an Orthodox Jew, certainly. Tall, dark-haired, well groomed, strong tanned features. Possibly a student in a non-Orthodox rabbinical school. Otherwise he would be in the army. Or the navy. He looked like someone who belonged in the navy. I would probably never see him again. Unless I came back to this synagogue. But I did not think I would be back. My head still ached from the sermon.

I went down the stone stairs and walked slowly through the park. The trees and grass were green with life. It was the end of May. I walked along the curving paths and heard the call of birds in the branches over my head.

That afternoon I lay on my bed. The sunlight entered the window and shone upon my shelves of books and my desk and the wall next to Alex's bed with its *New York Times* maps of the war and upon the ceiling above the maps. The window was open. I could hear the traffic on the wide street and the noise of children playing. The Germans were consuming the world. Arrows showed their new advances in Africa. I did not follow the war in the Pacific as closely as I did the one in Europe. The Germans were swallowing everything, and killing, killing. I could not understand such a people. What pleasure was there in killing? I lay on my bed looking at the maps on the wall and the sunlight on the ceiling and thinking of the summer and the surgery and of how helpless I really was, small and always ill and helpless before the oncoming rush of darkness. Only a single breath ago, it seemed, the surgery had been eight months away. Now—four weeks? Five weeks? I did not know. I would be seeing the surgeon in a few days for the first time. "Are you sure?" I had asked Dr. Weidman again this past week. "I am absolutely sure, David." And his pink face had been chillingly sober.

I felt all through me the coldness of vague dread. Laughter floated into the room from the street outside. I got to my feet and stood by the window and looked down at the street. Neighbors sat on chairs in the sunlight or stood around talk-

ing; children played. I turned away and a moment later found
myself wandering through the sun-filled apartment. Had we
really lived in darkness all those years? But now that we were
in sunlight I had a new darkness approaching. I could not
turn from it; there were no streets or alleyways down which
I could run. I wandered aimlessly through the rooms of the
apartment, and the sunlight seemed strangely cold to me now.
I came back into my room and sat at my desk and opened a
book. And suddenly I remembered where I had seen the name
of Wellhausen before this morning.

From the closet near my desk I pulled out the cartons of
books left to me by Mrs. Horowitz. I could not remember
which carton the book was in. I went through all the cartons
very quickly and could not find it. But I was certain it was in
one of those three cartons. I had a picture of the book inside
my eyes. I began to go through the cartons once more, slowly
this time. I found the book near the bottom of the second
carton. I replaced the cartons in the closet and sat at my desk
and looked at the book. It was a slim volume titled *Die
wichtigsten Instanzen gegen die Graf-Wellhausensche Hypo-
these*. It had been written by a Rabbi David Hoffmann
and published in 1904 in Germany. I looked at the table of
contents, then turned to the Preface and read the following
words in the first paragraph:

> Virtually all the new scholars of the Bible have come to the
> single conclusion that the Five Books of the Torah are com-
> posed of four sources. The source which these scholars regard
> as the major and fundamental one, which starts with "In the
> beginning God created" and to which they link the laws of
> sacrifice, priesthood, and purity and impurity—this source is
> signified by these scholars with the letters P or PC (priestly
> code); the Deuteronomy source is given the letter D, and the
> other two sources—E and I; in E, God is, according to their
> words, referred to always as Elohim, and in I, God is most
> frequently referred to by the name Yahweh. The letters IE
> indicate a book that is made up of both these sources.

The footnote to this paragraph read as follows:

> Bible scholars speak always of the six books of the Torah
> (Hexateuch), because they maintain that the Book of Joshua
> was in ancient times joined to the Five Books of the Torah.

I read the paragraph again. Then I looked up from the
book to the window. A queer tingling sensation had spread

across the back of my neck. The book was a thin dark-covered volume of stiff yellowing pages. An odor of decay rose from it, and I had a sudden sharp image of the interior of Mrs. Horowitz's apartment with its fetid air and the dark form of her dog moving about silently in the shadows. The book lay on my desk, waiting, and I felt its presence with a sense of apprehension and sharp excitement. It had been a long time since I had felt this way about a book. Sources, I thought. Sources. There was another German book somewhere in those cartons with the word "sources" in its title. Something about spells and sources. I turned away from the window and resumed reading.

I finished a little more than half the book by the early hours of the morning. My head ached and my eyes hurt. I saw the gray wash of dawn on my window shade and smelled the warm odor of baking bread—until I realized the odor was an illusion carried into my new room from all the dark years of the past. I lay in bed and tried to sleep. After a while I rose and went to the window and pushed aside the shade. The street was in shadows from the sun in the east behind me, but to the left, where the line of buildings fell away to the outdoor stone stairway that connected the cliff of Clay Avenue to the canyon of Webster Avenue, the sun shone through like a river of brilliant gold. The street wore a Sunday morning stillness. After a while I dressed and prayed and had breakfast and went to school.

Yaakov Bader said to me in the yeshiva study hall that morning, "You look terrible, Davey. What happened? Big night?"

"Very big. Did you ever hear of Graf and Wellhausen?"

"No. Are they a new comedy team?" He was in high spirits. He had met this girl last night, he said. Brooklyn College. Orthodox. Father an attorney. Who were Graf and Wellhausen?

I told him they were a new comedy team. "A German comedy team. They make bad jokes about the Bible."

But he seemed in a dazed ecstasy over his Brooklyn College girl and had not heard me.

I looked around the study hall and saw Saul standing over his table, staring down at his folio of Talmud. The table was piled high with books. The hall was crowded and noisy, and he was about ten tables away from me. He had already been deep in study when I had arrived earlier and I had not wanted to disturb him.

During the morning I left the study hall and went up to the library on the second floor. I checked the catalog. There was nothing on Graf or Wellhausen. I checked it again. There was no category called Bible Studies or Bible Scholarship or Bible Criticism. I looked for David Hoffmann and discovered a number of books under his name in the area of Talmudic and midrashic studies. A brief biographic entry on one of the cards told me that he had been rector of an Orthodox rabbinical seminary in Berlin and toward the close of his life was regarded by Orthodox German Jewry as their supreme authority on matters of Jewish law. He died in 1921. The book I had read last night was not listed in the catalog.

I went over to the chief librarian and asked him if there were any books in the library on or by Wellhausen.

He sat behind a cluttered desk near the stairway that led to the third-floor stacks. He was a short thin-faced balding man who wore his rimless glasses down on the tip of his nose and knew every book in that library. He looked up at me from behind his desk. His brown watery eyes seemed to float above the rims of his lenses.

"Who?" he said.

"Julius Wellhausen."

"Who asked you to read Wellhausen?" He had a gentle voice. I wondered at the hardness that now crept into it.

"There's nothing by Wellhausen in the library?"

"David Lurie," he said. "If it is not in the catalog it is not in the library."

"Or Graf? Nothing on or by Graf?"

"For whom are you reading these people?"

"For no one. For myself."

"They were anti-Semitic German goyim who tried to destroy the Bible. Why should we have their books? Do we have *Mein Kampf*?"

I told him I did not want to cause any trouble, I had merely been curious about them. He told me I was better off being curious about more important matters. I thanked him and went back downstairs to the study hall to finish preparing for my Talmud class.

On Sunday our Talmud classes ended at one o'clock. There were no English studies. I met Saul on the sidewalk outside the school. He was talking with Alex. We walked along toward our bus stop. The air was bright and warm. People eyed us in the street as we passed them in our skullcaps.

Saul looked pale and distraught. He walked with his shoulders stooped, his eyes cast down, his knees bent slightly forward. He was developing the sort of curving posture I saw on many of the Talmud teachers in the school. Alex walked tall and straight and fast, impatient to get home.

I asked Saul if he was all right. He said Rav Sharfman had called on him to read the Gemara in class that morning and had destroyed him. "I didn't know how much I didn't know," he said miserably. "It was terrible. He called me stupid."

I told him to console himself, the Ramban had called Ibn Ezra worse names than that. Then I asked him if he had ever heard of Graf or Wellhausen.

He had never heard of Graf and only vaguely of Wellhausen. Who were they?

"German goyim who tear pieces from the Torah."

"Now I remember," he said. "They're anti-Semites."

"Is that what you were reading last night, Davey?" Alex asked.

We had come to our corner and were waiting for the bus. It was a narrow side street and it led to the wide cobblestone avenue and the bridge that spanned the river.

"You're reading those goyim?" Saul asked me.

I told him what I had been reading.

"All night you were reading," Alex said.

We saw our bus up the block, moving slowly along the narrow street.

"Hoffmann attacks them for what they do," I said. "I never even knew about any of this. It's terrible what they do, Saul. They destroy the Torah."

"Who takes them seriously, Davey? They're a bunch of anti-Semitic goyim. German goyim yet."

The bus pulled up to the curb and we climbed inside, paid our fares, and went up the aisle looking for seats. The bus was fairly crowded. People kept looking at our skullcaps. We sat down together on the last seat beneath the rear window.

"I don't understand how I never knew about this before. The goyim are destroying the Torah and no one in the yeshiva says anything about it."

"Who cares what the anti-Semites say about the Torah?" Saul said. "They should all lie in the earth."

We were talking Yiddish. In front of us a middle-aged heavy-faced man with light brown hair and a large veined nose turned around, looked at us for a moment, and turned back. The bus moved quickly across the bridge. The river ran smooth and slate gray far beneath us. Overhead the vast expanse of sky was deep and blue and cloudless.

"I think we should care, Saul. I think it's wrong to ignore what they say."

"Ah, it's all nonsense," he said. "Don't get yourself involved in it, Davey."

"It's not nonsense, Saul. Rabbi Akiva says in the Gemara that there isn't a single extra letter in the Torah, and these goyim change words and move around whole sections of the Torah."

The bus stopped. The man in front of us got up and moved to a seat five rows away. The bus started up again.

"They say the Torah wasn't given by God to Moses. They say whole parts of the Torah were written after the Prophets."

"Parts of the Five Books of the Torah were written after the Prophets?" Alex asked incredulously.

"That's what Hoffmann says they say."

"They're crazy," Saul said. "They're anti-Semites and you should stay far away from them."

"I'm not reading them. I'm reading Hoffmann."

The bus had come off the bridge into the Bronx and was on the wide brick-paved avenue that led to 170th Street.

"I don't know where you find the time to read everything," Saul said, staring moodily out the window. "I only have Gemara to worry about and I haven't got enough time to study it right." •

"My brother the brain," Alex said. "Davey eats books, Saul."

"One more day like today with Gemara and I'll also start getting sick all the time. What a terrible day. Stupid. He called me stupid."

"The Ramban called Ibn Ezra a false prophet," I said.

"No one ever called me stupid before." He was staring out the window and not listening to me. "In front of seventy people he called me stupid."

"Were you?" I asked.

He turned to me. "What?"

"Was what you said stupid?"

He looked back out the window. "Yes."

The bus entered the shadows beneath the Jerome Avenue elevated train and emerged into an uphill street lined with stores. We rode in silence. At the stop before the tunnel that led beneath Grand Concourse, I gazed out the bus at the dark interior of my father's store. The gold letters on the window glittered in the sunlight. A rich lustrous glow emanated from my father's name. M. LURIE. I imagined I saw him sitting astride the stallion on the street in front of the store. What a laughable picture! But I did not laugh. I turned my eyes away from the store and glanced at my cousin and brother. Saul sat slouched down in his seat, looking forlorn. Alex was reading another of his novels. I felt sleepy but strangely exhilarated. I closed my eyes and began to review inside my head some of the pages in the book I had read through the night. I spent the rest of the day reading the book and finished it a little after midnight.

That Tuesday I took a subway to a tall building in midtown Manhattan and rode up in an elevator to the office of the surgeon whose name had been given to me by Dr. Weidman. He turned out to be a tall ruddy-faced man in his fifties with smoothly combed light brown hair and large freckles on the backs of his hands. His name was Dr. Bernstein. I lay on the examining table and watched the freckles as his fingers probed my face. He spoke softly as he probed. "Does that hurt? And that? How's your father? You will give him my best regards, won't you? Sit up and let me have a look at it." He was using instruments and lights. "I haven't seen your father in a while. We grew up together in Lemberg but I came here before the war. You have frequent colds? Well, I think we can take care of that. We'll need some pictures and we'll schedule the surgery for the first week in July. Yes, we'll make all the arrangements. My nurse will notify you. Do give my regards to your father. Ask him if he remembers the day I pulled the stunt with the cat. Goodbye. We'll see you soon."

His nurse sent me to another office on the same floor. I stood in front of a machine in a dim room and a man in a white frock told me to hold perfectly still and he went out. I heard clicks and whirring sounds. He told me to move my head to the right and to the left. There were more sounds. A few minutes later I was outside on the street, walking very quickly toward the subway. I took a train farther downtown and, in a Hebrew bookstore, purchased a copy of the Hertz Commentary. Then I took another subway to the main branch of the New York Public Library on 42d Street. I walked quickly up the tall front stone stairway and went inside and checked the catalog for books by David Hoffmann. There were many books under his name, including the one I had just completed. I took out a book on Leviticus and another on Deuteronomy, neither of which was in my school library. I noticed there was another volume to the book I had read, published in 1916, and I took that one out too. Laden with books, I came out of the library and turned up 42d Street to the subway. The street was very crowded. On the corner I stopped for a moment to watch the news flashing across the *Times* building. The Germans were advancing toward Tobruk and El Alamein in North Africa. Inside the concussing rush and roar of the train I began to read the Hertz Commentary. I looked up "Bible criticism" in the index and read all the passages on it in the book. I looked up the bibliography and saw a list of medieval Jewish authorities and commentators, most of whom I had studied with Mr. Bader. I saw two additional lists of modern commentators, one of forty-eight Jews, the other of twenty-six non-Jews. I had never heard of any of those commentators except David Hoffmann, some of the Jews, and a few of the non-Jews who had been mentioned in the Hoffmann book. I sat in the train, reading the Hertz Commentary. I made it back to school in time for my afternoon college periods and read the Hertz Commentary all through my classes.

During the free period I went downstairs to the library and leafed quickly through all the writings of David Hoffmann that I could find in the stacks. Somewhere in one of the books by Hoffmann that I read that day I saw underlined in faded black ink his justification for his writings against Biblical criticism. He regarded those writings as "a sacred task, a necessary way to respond decisively to these new critics who came as oppressors to do violence to the holy Torah." I remember nothing about the rest of that day save that I spent it reading the Hertz Commentary. Late in the night I put it aside and leafed through the Hoffmann books I had taken from the library.

Alex woke, stared at the clock near his bed, stared at me, and said, "For God's sake, Davey. Go to sleep." He rolled over, sighed, and was immediately asleep. I sat at my desk in the circle of light cast by my lamp, and read. After a few minutes I was conscious of someone else in the room with me. I turned my head and saw my father in the doorway. He wore his pajamas and robe. His tall dark skullcap was on his uncombed hair.

"My scholar," he murmured. "Do you have any idea what time it is?"

I looked at my watch. It was after two in the morning.

"Go to sleep," he said. "You will make yourself sick."

"Soon," I said.

He gazed at me for a moment in silence, then shook his head slowly. "You have no idea how much like my brother you are." He closed his eyes. His lips went momentarily stiff and his face emptied itself of expression. Then he opened his eyes and smiled vaguely. "You have time for a glass of tea with your father? Me with my store and you with your books —we have no time even to talk to each other. A glass of tea, yes? And you will tell me what you are reading so late at night. I am not the most educated Jew in the world, but I am far from being an ignoramus. I saw the German book on your desk today. I am curious to know why my son is reading a German book. Come, join me in a glass of tea. I am sorry we are able to talk only at two o'clock in the morning. But it is better than not talking at all."

We walked together through the silent apartment and he turned on the kitchen light and put on a kettle of water. He sighed as he sat down in his chair. "Once I was able to stay up through the night and then do the work of two men the next day. In the war there were weeks I did not sleep at all during the night. Twenty minutes, an hour. I would sleep on my feet or on my horse. Not anymore. I envy you your young strength."

It seemed astonishing to me that my father should be envious of my strength. I had poured myself a glass of milk. I sat sipping it.

"Your mother looks all right these days, doesn't she?" he asked softly. "I was worried about your mother. But I think she will be all right now. She is very good with the customers in the store. I have a tendency sometimes to be—impatient."

The kettle boiled. He got up and poured himself a glass of tea. A darkness of fatigue lay across his face and clouded his eyes. I had never seen him this tired before save during the fearful months many years ago when we had moved to Washington Avenue. But those memories had begun to drift away. In the daytime, dressed, working, he radiated good health, exuberance, self-control, mastery; now in the night he seemed strangely tired, worn; the lines were deeper on his forehead and around his eyes. There was gray near his temples; his once thick wavy brown hair was receding seriously, revealing a somewhat ungainly upward-sloping head. He blinked his eyes, then rubbed at them with the fingers of his right hand. The stubble on his face accentuated the forward thrust of his lower jaw. The scar stood out clearly. He sat sipping his glass of tea.

"The store is a lot of work," he murmured. "It is a great success. God has been good to us. But it is endless work."

"Can I help?" I asked.

"Yes. Do your job and study. That is how you can help. The books that you are reading, this German book, they are for school?"

"No, for myself."

"What books are they?"

I described the Hertz Commentary and the Hoffmann book. He sipped slowly from his glass of tea, the cube of sugar between his teeth. "Higher criticism of the Torah," he said, speaking the words in English. His eyes narrowed and the wings of his nostrils flared slightly. Then he said, resuming his Yiddish, "Why do rabbis write about such matters?"

"To show how wrong it is."

"And Hertz uses goyim to help him?"

"Goyim who are Bible scholars."

"I need goyim to help me defend the Torah of Moses?"

"Goyim are attacking it."

"Nu, so what? What haven't goyim attacked that belongs to us? Why should a Jew waste his time on such nonsense?"

"Papa, some Jews fight with guns, other Jews fight with words."

"This Hertz and Hoffmann are important people?" he asked, after a moment.

I told him that Rabbi Hertz was the Chief Rabbi of all the Jews of the British Empire and Rabbi Hoffmann had been in his day the greatest authority on Jewish law for the Orthodox Jews of Germany.

Beneath his robe I could see clearly the firm outline of his shoulders. "I am uncomfortable with German books in my house," he said after a while. "It is like having here a member of an evil family. I did not mind so much when they were lying in the cartons out of sight in your closet. But now I see the German books on your desk and it disturbs me, even though you tell me they were written by a rabbi. I have known many rabbis who have been wrong. And I cannot begin to tell you how much I hate the Germans and everything that is German. That land is inhabited by the hosts of the Angel of Death. Whatever they touch they poison. But if my David thinks it is important for him to read German books,

all right. I will ask you not to read them in my presence. Tell
me something. You are considering becoming a Bible
scholar?"

"I'm only reading, Papa."

"Yes," he said. "I see how you are only reading. Your
Uncle David was also always only reading." He was silent a
moment, wreathed in memories. Then he put down his glass
and said, looking at the surface of the table, "We owe the
dead an obligation. That is the most difficult job of all. When
two people believe in the same thing and fight for it and one
dies and the other lives—what a debt he owes. I wonder if
goyim understand this." He stared down at the table. "I
wonder how many Jews understand this." After a moment
he said, "Yes, Jews understand this. They may not do anything. But they understand it. I try to pay my debts. That is
how my father was, and that is how I am. I will owe my little
brother nothing." He lapsed again into silence. Pools of darkness had formed around his eyes. "I loved him," he murmured. "I was wild. My uncles called me a goy. I played with
goyim and fought with them. I was more with them than I
was with Jews. I loved their—wildness. My little brother
taught me a little about gentleness. Not enough. It is an effort
for me to be gentle. Then the war came and he was married
and the goyim killed him. He was the kindest and gentlest
person I have ever known. The stupid goyim. They killed the
wrong Jew. They should have tried to kill me. I am the threat
to goyim. Instead the fools killed him. Stupid goyim. What
did they care? Another dead Jew they could laugh about as
they got drunk. The stinking bastard idiotic goyim." All the
weariness had washed off him as he spoke. He sat straight,
his short stocky figure rigid, and turned upon me dark burning
eyes. "I owe you a debt. It was my fault your mother fell
when she carried you. Your injury was my fault. No matter
what your mother may say to you, it was my fault. I should
have supported her arm. I will pay part of my debt to you
this summer with your operation. I am not able to repay you
for your years of suffering. There are a few debts in this
world that cannot be repaid. I can only ask you to forgive
me. I also ask you to remember whose name you carry. It is
the name of my dead little brother. You want to fight the
goyim with words? All right. Good. Fight them with words.
My little brother would not have been troubled too much to
see you reading German books if you were thinking to use

them as weapons. I will fight them with guns. When this war is over there will be a Jewish war. I do not know how many Jews will be left in Europe after this war, but Bader and others will try to bring them to Eretz Yisroel and then our war will begin. You will fight with words and I will fight with guns."

I stared at him and felt myself turning cold. "What war?" I said. "What do you mean?"

"Against the British," he said. "We are building an army in Eretz Yisroel to fight the British, and we are building an army here to help them fight the British."

I kept staring at him and did not know what to say. A dark fatigue seemed abruptly to descend upon me. I felt desperately the need to lie down.

"It will take years," he said with a fierceness in his voice. "Three years, five years, ten years. But we will win. We would win sooner without Weizmann and his gentlemenly way. With a goy who wants to kill you a Jew should not be a gentleman. That was what I tried to teach my little brother in return for what he taught me. I failed. He died gentle. Most Jews who are dying now are gentle. There will not be many gentle Jews left after this war. I think—I think I will have another glass of tea. My stomach is bothering me again. Go to sleep, David. You look like you are falling off your feet. You want to fight goyim, you have to be strong. Go to sleep."

I heard myself say, with great effort, "What army, Papa? What do you mean?"

"We are doing the work of Jabotinsky. If he had not died, he would be doing this work. But because a leader dies suddenly does not mean his work should come to an end. His followers become leaders. This is all I care to say. It is not your job. Look what time it is. Your job now is to go to sleep so tomorrow you will be able to read your books with a clear head."

I left him in the kitchen pouring himself another glass of tea. Later, I heard him shuffling about; I had the impression he was pacing slowly back and forth between the kitchen and the living room. Then I heard my mother's voice call out softly from their bedroom, "Max? Max?"

The pacing stopped.

"Max?" my mother called again, a little louder this time.

"I am here," I heard him answer. "I am all right."

"What are you doing? Come to bed."

"Soon," he said.

I heard her come out of their bedroom and go through the living room to the kitchen.

"What's the matter?" I heard her say in an agitated tone.

His reply was indistinct. There was a momentary silence. Then I heard their quiet voices coming from the kitchen. They were still talking together in the kitchen when I finally fell into a haunted sleep.

I would take the Hertz Commentary to school with me and in my free periods sit reading it either in the library or, if the weather was warm and sunny, on a bench in the little park overlooking the river. Sometimes a classmate would come over and ask what I was reading and I would show him the book. Most of them seemed unimpressed. One of them told me he had once heard his sociology professor refer to higher Biblical criticism as higher anti-Semitism. Another informed me that Hertz had been a graduate of a non-Orthodox rabbinical seminary.

Yaakov Bader came over to me one afternoon and I talked to him for a while about what I was reading. He listened. I talked for a long time. He asked what the difference was between lower and higher Biblical criticism. I told him "lower" dealt mostly with the text of the Bible and "higher" dealt with literary analysis and historical and ideological matters. For example, I said, if you change the second word in Genesis from *bara* to *bro*, that's lower criticism; but if you say that the Book of Deuteronomy was written after the period of Judges, that's higher criticism. He replied jovially that the higher could end up getting you into the lower, and he pointed toward the ground.

"What're you reading that stuff for, Davey?"

"It's important. I want to know what the goyim are saying about the Bible."

"Why?"

"Because it interests me."

"Does it interest you that you have an English lit class now?"

I looked at my watch. "I forgot," I said, and rushed from the park. I was late to the class.

All through the rest of that month I sat in the park or in the library every chance I had, reading the Hertz Commentary. Saul saw me in the library one day and came over to my table. It was raining outside. He stood next to me peering down at the book; then he muttered, "They told me you were reading this. I didn't believe it."

I looked up at him. His thin sallow face was shrouded in gloom.

"This is a real stealing of time from the study of Torah," he pronounced unhappily.

"Hertz didn't think so."

"Hertz graduated from a goyishe seminary."

"Hoffmann didn't think so."

"It's stealing time from Torah, Davey. I'm telling you."

The librarian came out from behind his desk near the staircase to the stacks and informed us that the study hall downstairs was the place where you studied in a loud voice, not the library.

Saul walked away, looking troubled and unhappy.

I saw him two days later in the study hall. He seemed these days to be carrying about him a permanent pall of gloom. He passed my table on his way back from the bookshelves where he had gone for a medieval commentary text. I asked him if my Hertz was still making him unhappy. He looked over at Yaakov Bader, whose head was buried in his volume of Talmud, and said in a low voice, "I'm so scared I can't sleep nights anymore."

I asked him what he was scared about.

"My Gemara class," he muttered. "The whole class is scared."

I told him it was the end of the year, why were they all suddenly so scared?

"You've been in a fog all year, Davey. Nothing's changed. I've been scared all year but you've been like a piece of stone. 'They have eyes and they see not,' " he quoted in Hebrew.

"You told me he was a great man."

"He's a phenomenon. That's why we're all so scared. You know what it's like to be studying with the greatest Talmudist in the world?"

I told him I didn't know. He went off gloomily, in that stooped and curving posture of his, holding the heavy black-bound folio volume of the medieval commentary in his pale white hands.

That Shabbat morning I ventured into a non-Orthodox synagogue and discovered that the Hertz Commentary was used by the entire congregation during the Torah reading.

The reader, a middle-aged man, was excellent. I held the Commentary in my hand and realized that sooner or later I would have come across it; the encounter in the synagogue a few weeks ago when I had first seen the Commentary was not as extraordinary as I had thought. And the Hertz Commentary would have led me directly to Hoffmann and Wellhausen and the others. The rabbi of the non-Orthodox synagogue preached smoothly and clearly. But I would not return to that synagogue; an organ was played during the service and I felt my Orthodox religious sensibility violated. I decided to return to my father's synagogue and endure in silence the carnage inflicted upon the text of the Torah by the aged reader.

On the second Shabbat in July we came out of the little synagogue, my parents and brother and I and Saul and his parents, and walked in the warm blue air of the late morning toward 170th Street. I heard my father and uncle continuing the conversation they had begun while removing their prayer shawls inside the synagogue after the service. Discussions had been taking place between the Revisionist party in Palestine and the Labor Zionists in an attempt to work out a compromise plan whereby the Revisionists would rejoin the World Zionist Organization from which they had seceded in 1933. My uncle, in a loud voice, was expressing his anger at "Weizmann, Ben-Gurion, and that fuzzy-headed socialist crowd." He wanted the largest number of Jews brought to Palestine in the shortest period of time, he said; not small-scale immigration based on the slow procedure of immigration certificates. It was always surprising to me how loud and angry his gentle voice would become whenever he discussed Zionist politics. My father said he favored support of private initiative and private capital investment and that the way the socialists were building the country would create a nation of lazy workers and daily strikes. He favored compulsory arbitration, he said, and agreed with my uncle that the Revisionists should remain separated from the World Zionist Organization. Meanwhile Saul was explaining to Alex a passage of midrash on today's Torah reading. Alex did not appear especially interested; he was probably burning to get back to the Thomas Wolfe novel he had been reading all week. My mother and aunt talked about a lovely little bungalow colony near Hunter, New York, that my aunt had heard about and the possibility that all of us might be able to go up there for

.two weeks in late August. We turned into 170th Street and
went past the little grocery store and delicatessen and corner
service station.

"Are you feeling well, David?" asked my mother anxiously.

"I'm all right, Mama."

"You must not become ill now."

I was quiet. She was smartly dressed in a dark blue summer
dress and a yellow wide-brimmed flowery hat. She had put on
weight; her waist and arms and legs had thickened; but her
face had remained pale and taut, and her eyes would not look
directly at me as she spoke.

"Everything will be all right," she said. "I swear to you,
David."

I did not respond.

Two days later I entered the hospital.

I lay in a white bed in a large white room and men and
women in white clothes kept coming over to me and doing
things to my body. It seemed to be no longer my body. I had
a low-grade fever. They came over with needles and injected
them into my buttocks and they came over with water and
told me to drink. My body suffered the injections and drank
the water. The man in the bed to my left had white hair and
spoke hollowly through a tube in his throat. He was skeletal
and he wheezed and coughed hoarsely, echoingly, through
the night. I listened to him and felt all the dread of the world
upon my body. The fever did not abate and they kept putting
needles into me and giving me water. You'll be fine, young
man, just fine, said a nurse in a white starched dress and cap.
She smiled. She had uneven teeth and seemed kind. It was
night. The man next to me coughed chokingly. Someone in a
bed farther down cried out and there were the sounds of
scurrying feet and whispers. I kept my eyes tightly shut. They
had followed me to the hospital, the dark leaping forms, and
I could not sleep. David, I heard someone whisper, and I
turned my head and opened my eyes. I saw the darkness of
the wall to my right and the faint yellowish light of the nurses'
desk reflected off the ceiling. Deep shadows lay in the corner
over my head where the ceiling joined the wall. David, came
the whisper from the shadows. My David. I closed my eyes.
The old man wheezed and coughed and seemed to be stran-
gling. Oh my God, I thought. What did I ever do to be
punished this way? I saw them inside my eyes, leaping about.

What were the words? Ochnotinos, chnotinos, notinos. David! came the sharp whisper. I lay still and listened to the hospital night. Finally, exhausted, I slept, and was immediately awakened by a form in white. How are we this morning? the form said. Next to me the old man lay very still, wheezing softly. White sunlight streamed through the windows. The white form was doing things to the body that was no longer mine. I closed my eyes. The form went away. Later it returned with a small pill and water. I took the pill and lay in my bed and felt my body sink deeply into the mattress. I could not lift my arms or legs. Two men in white came with a stretcher table. They wheeled it alongside my bed. Easy, kid, one of them said. Don't be no hero. They helped me onto the table and covered me with a sheet. I watched the ceiling slide by above me. Good luck, kid, someone called from a bed. David, came a whisper close to my ear. I closed my eyes and felt the rolling motion of the stretcher. The air was cold against my face. I felt my head upon the pillow. Soon it would no longer be my head. I did not know what they would be doing to it but I knew it would no longer be my head while they did it. People in surgical gowns and masks would take it from me for a while. I lay still, feeling the terror and the strange coldness of the air as it brushed against my face. Then the air grew still. The stretcher came to a stop. I opened my eyes and found myself alone in a narrow corridor. I lay very still and listened and heard only silence. Then a warm hand very gently caressed my forehead and the side of my face and I closed my eyes. I listened to the silence. There were dark shapes within it, swarming, waiting. A door opened somewhere and I opened my eyes. A white form approached, murmuring words in a gentle voice, and put a needle into my arm. The ceiling moved again, briefly. Strong arms supported me as I was moved to another table. Close your eyes, David, someone said. And keep them closed. We are washing your face. I felt fingers on my nose and cheeks and forehead and lips and jaw, strong fingers, washing briskly the face that was no longer mine. Then they were tying down my arms. Then they were tying down my forehead. These are local anesthetics, David, a gentle voice said. We will need you to be awake for the surgery. If at any time you feel pain, you are to tell us. I kept my eyes tightly shut. Tiny pricks of pain entered my nostrils. There were clinking sounds and the murmur of voices and I opened my eyes briefly and stared into a light and masked faces and I closed my eyes. I felt something

touch my face and move briefly across it and then I knew it
was really no longer my body and everyone became very
busy with the still silent form on the table. I left this form
and wandered about in the dark corners of the room and
found in a juncture of wall and floor an opening; it was a
warm narrow cavern of smooth walls that glowed faintly red
and I let myself rush into it and thought how merciful it
was to be out of that room. I kept running downward and
thinking it was so good to be away from there. Once, when
the surgeon began to use the bone saw, I came swiftly from
the cavern onto the operating table. The grinding of the saw
on the bones of my face filled me with unutterable terror; and
just when I thought I could no longer endure it, the grinding
ceased. Someone kept using a suction tube. After a moment
I felt myself again able to wander away from the inert form
on the table. I sought the solace of the cavern. But I was
drawn back to the table when hands grasped my nose tightly
and completed the breaking of the bone. I lay helpless and
disbelieving beneath strong and swiftly moving fingers. Then
I drifted away, not knowing any longer whether to be afraid
or merely to weep, and I found the cavern once again and
this time tumbled into it and let myself fall. I do not know
how long I fell. When I stopped, I lay suspended in reddish
darkness for what seemed to me to be a long time. Then I
began to rise. And again I felt a warm hand caress my face
and forehead. David, came a distant whisper. My precious
David. Again the hand caressed my face. My soul, said the
whispered voice. My life. Are you afraid? Do not be afraid.
I promise you a complete healing. And I felt myself gently
embraced.

There was silence. The bands about my arms and head
were loosened and removed. I was lifted and put down and
the ceiling slid by again above me. I was lifted again and
felt the bed beneath me. The angle of the sunlight on the
windows had changed. Was the skeletal old man still here?
And the man with one leg, was he still in the bed near the
nurses' desk? And the old man who had undergone cataract
surgery? And the young handsome blond-haired boy who
was in for cancer tests? And the jovial ladies' man with his
right leg in a cast up to his hip? Were they all still here? My
face was thickly bandaged. I was tired; I could not remember
ever having felt so tired before. I saw reflected sunlight on
the ceiling and a vague dance of shadows as an orderly

passed by wheeling a stretcher table. I closed my eyes and fell immediately into a deep sleep.

I woke in a lake of blood. Grayish light came through the windows. I saw my pillow soaked with blood. I could not move; a vast weariness had settled upon me all its mountainous weight. I thought to call out; but two nurses were suddenly beside me, holding me and changing the pillow. I lay back and once again fell into a deep sleep.

I was in a forest and a wind moaned through the trees and I woke and listened to the old man wheezing and coughing in the bed next to mine. It was night. He coughed and choked and breathed hollowly through the tube in his throat. I slept again and when I woke it was still night. I thought of the beach and the lake and my mother reading beneath the elm tree. A warm breeze blew across the tall grass and rippled the surface of the water. Saul was in a boat on the water reading a book. Alex was in the tall grass searching for frogs. A horse and rider came up the dirt path from the main road.

I woke sharply. Two forms in white had come to change my bandages.

Later that day I was helped from the bed by an orderly and found I could barely walk. My legs melted beneath me. In all the years of my illness and accidents I had never felt as weak as I felt now. He helped me to walk. In the bathroom mirror I saw a pale haggard face into which were set two eyes surrounded by skin that had turned a sickly blue-black color. The thick bandage gleamed in the mirror. I turned quickly away, shaken. Later I lay in my bed and slept. A nurse woke me and did things to my body. I turned my head slightly at her command and noticed that the bed next to me was empty and the old man was gone.

I was in the hospital a week. They all came to visit: my parents, Alex, my aunt and uncle, Saul, wearing stiff smiles designed to conceal their shock at the sight of my bandaged face and blackened eyes.

"The doctor is satisfied," my father said. "It went well."

"We are all going to the country and you will be able to rest," said my aunt.

"We took two bungalows," said my mother. She did not look at me as she spoke.

Alex kept glancing at me and looking away. Saul stood at the foot of the bed, pale with shock, a queer fixed smile on his thin face.

"You have been through a lot," my aunt said. "You need a rest."

"We have all been through a lot," said my mother.

I came home and spent a week in the house. Toward the end of that week I returned to the outpatient clinic of the hospital and had the stitches removed. I looked in a mirror and barely knew who I was. My face was pale, emaciated; a greenish pallor lay in the hollows of my cheeks; the broken ridge of the nose and ugly bulge of cartilaginous tissue had been repaired; patches of coagulated blood still showed beneath the skin around my eyes. I slept a great deal and sat in the park reading. The sun warmed my face. At the end of the second week in August we left the city.

I rested and had a pleasant time. Our bungalow was on the shore of a small lake. My aunt and uncle and Saul had a bungalow a few yards away from us. There were trees and a sand beach. The weather was warm and sunny. There were thunderstorms twice while we were there but they came in the late evening and did not upset the day. Saul and I lounged around reading or went rowing out on the lake. He liked to row and I sat in the boat with my book. "Why are you reading that stuff, Davey?" he asked me one day in a mournful tone. "You're getting in deeper and deeper." "Watch out where you're rowing," I said. "You're getting shallower and shallower." Alex swam and read novels and went horseback riding with my father over at a nearby stable. My uncle lay in the sun. My mother and aunt sat in the shade, talking; sometimes they put on bathing suits and went into the water. One hot day I entered the water and my uncle taught me to float and breathe and kick. Then he taught me the crawl. I had forgotten most of what my father had once taught me about swimming.

One morning my father invited me to go horseback riding with him and Alex. We were having breakfast. I saw my mother give me an anxious look. I thanked him and said I did not think I would like it.

"How do you know what you won't like until you try it?"

"I'm a little afraid," I said.

"It's fun, Davey," Alex said.

But I would not go. Later I saw them cantering through a grassy field beyond the lake and I marveled at the swiftness with which Alex had learned to ride.

"He rides well, your brother."

I turned. My mother had come up silently behind me. We stood beneath the plane tree in front of the bungalow, gazing across the small lake and watching them ride.

After a while I heard my mother say, "How do you feel, David?"

I told her I felt fine.

"You look well," she said, and let her eyes move slowly across my face. "You look—" She turned her eyes away. "You look rested," she murmured, her pale face flushing slightly.

The following morning my father again invited me to go horseback riding with him. I declined.

"God in heaven, David, the whole world is not only books and books. There are other things too."

He was angry. We all stared at him. My mother's lips quivered.

I said I would go with him. My mother gave me a panicky look but remained silent.

Later that morning I walked with my father and Alex along a curving dirt path through fields of wild grass. Grasshoppers jumped and whirred through the warm air. I do not remember what we talked about. I was tense and sweaty and wished I had not acceded to my father's request. Why was he so eager to have me ride a horse? The fields fell away and we crossed a meadow. A low white-painted stable lay a few yards beyond a draw. We skirted the draw and came up to the peeling white wooden posts of the corral. A man in jeans and boots and a wide-brimmed straw hat came out of the stable. The odor of dung and horses was very strong. I remember the three horses he and my father brought out. I remember the ease with which Alex slipped a leg into the stirrup and mounted. I remember sitting on my horse and feeling astonished at how high I was. I remember feeling the horse moving slowly beneath me. My father was talking to me. I remember the sun on my face and head and my hands sweating and Alex riding off by himself somewhere and my father still talking to me. I remember very little else. We walked back to the bungalow through the fields. I could still smell the odor of the dung and the sweat of the horses. I swam and lay on the beach in the sun and thought I could still feel myself moving on the horse.

The next morning my father asked me again if I wanted to go horseback riding with him and Alex.

"No," I said.

"You did not enjoy it?"

"No."

"Why?"

"I just don't care for it."

"You looked pretty good on that horse, Davey," Alex said.

"Come with us," said my father.

"I've had my thrill," I said. "Leave me alone."

He looked at me. A sudden electric silence filled the kitchen. My mother's face drained of color. He said, explosively, "Don't you dare talk to me that way!"

"I'm sorry. I apologize. Please. I have no interest in horses."

He finished the meal in a raging silence. Then he quickly chanted the grace and left. Alex followed him out.

"David," my mother murmured, turning to me.

"It's okay, Mama. Don't worry. It's okay. No more horses."

"Don't make him angry at you, David. Please."

"I understand. It'll be okay, Mama. I promise."

She came out of the bungalow a while later and walked over to where I was sitting on the beach. There was a warm wind and I heard it in the trees. She stood facing the lake. The sun shone upon her pale features. I heard the wind loudly in the trees.

"Do you remember their names?" she asked softly.

"Names?"

"Of the trees." She seemed shy, hesitant.

"Yes."

She smiled deeply. "He never forgot the names," she murmured. After a moment she turned to me. "Your father loved his brother very much," she said. "He was also very jealous of him. Of his—mind."

"I understand," I said.

"No, you do not understand at all," she said. "But I am happy you remember the trees."

She turned and went slowly back inside the bungalow.

Later I saw my father and brother in the field beyond the lake. They rode to the edge of the lake and let their horses drink. Alex saw me and waved. I waved back. My father ignored me. Saul and my uncle lay sleeping on a blanket; my mother and my aunt sat in wicker chairs beneath the plane tree. I sat on the beach and went back to reading Wellhausen's *Prolegomena to the History of Ancient Israel.*

I had finished the Hertz Commentary and was reading the scholars Hertz had attacked.

We returned to the city in a heat wave. I sat in the small synagogue on Rosh Hashanah. My father led the Morning Service, his stocky frame garbed in white, his voice firm and strong. The white-bearded old man read the Torah and left desolation in his wake. The heat wave continued. In the days that followed Rosh Hashanah, I sat in the park beneath a tree, reading. In the last week of September I started my third year of college and chose history as my major subject. One Shabbat afternoon in late December I looked up from the German book I was reading and gazed out my window at the falling snow. I realized with quiet astonishment that I had not been ill since the summer.

All through that winter, as the German advance into Russia and North Africa was finally halted, I read German books on Bible scholarship. I could not read them in my father's presence. If I was in the living room with a German book and he came in with his newspaper, I would have to leave and continue reading in my own room. Once I brought into the living room the Moses Mendelssohn translation of the Bible into German—one of the books given to me by Mrs. Horowitz. It made no difference to my father that it was the Bible and that the translation had been done by the greatest German Jewish scholar of the eighteenth century; he told me to take the book from the room. Another time I brought in a book on midrash and preaching from the times of the Prophets up to the modern period—another volume left to me by Mrs. Horowitz. The book was in German and he ordered me to remove it from his presence. I told him the author, Leopold Zunz, had been one of the greatest German Jewish historians of the last century. He asked me if I was reading the book for school. I told him I was reading it for myself. He told me the German Jewish scholars of the last century had been responsible for the destruction of Torah Judaism. He did not want to be in the same room with anything German. I brought the book into my room and read it at my desk.

On Friday afternoon I would come out of school after my English classes and take the subway to the 42d Street library. I would bring back with me books for Shabbat reading. He sent me out of the living room late one Shabbat afternoon in March and I went angrily into my room where, unlike the living room, we did not leave a light burning all through Shabbat. I read by the dying light of the day until my eyes would no longer focus on the page.

"You're lucky you don't love Goethe," I told Alex one night.

"Nothing lucky about it," he responded with a thin smile.

"My lousy luck scientific Bible criticism was started by German goyim."

"Your lousy luck will get lousier if you keep reading this stuff, Davey."

"What do you mean?"

"I hear talk in school."

"What talk?"

"Someone heard two of the Talmud teachers talking about you."

"I have to read these Germans if I'm going to answer them back."

"Are you planning to answer them back, Davey?"

"I don't know enough to answer anyone back."

"Why bother?"

"Why? Why? Listen to this and you'll understand why. Listen to how they sneak the anti-Semitism in even when what they're saying has nothing to do with the text they're commenting on. Listen."

I read to him from *Theologie des Alten Testament* by Walther Eichrodt, translating as I went along:

"It was not until in later Judaism a religion of harsh observances had replaced the religion of the Old Testament that Sabbath changed from a blessing to a burdensome duty."

"How about that?" I said. "Isn't that beautiful? Shabbos is 'a burdensome duty.' And listen to this."

I read to him from an earlier page of the same book a passage dealing with what the author called "the powerful and purposive movement in the Old Testament." Alex sat propped up against the wall near his bed, listening half-heartedly.

"This movement does not come to rest until the manifestation of Christ, in whom the noblest powers of the Old Testament find their fulfillment. Negative evidence in support of this statement is afforded by the torsolike appearance of Judaism in separation from Christianity."

I looked up at Alex. "How do you like being called a torso?"

"I've been called worse things than that by goyim."

"But he's supposed to be a great scholar, Alex."

"Didn't the Jewish scholars answer them back?"

"The Jewish scholars in the last century wrote almost nothing about the Torah."

"They were smart. They had good Jewish heads. Who cares what those anti-Semitic goyim say?"

"That's not the reason. They were afraid of what the Jews would say."

"What is that supposed to mean?"

"Some of the Jewish scholars thought the goyim were right."

"About what?"

"That the Torah was created by Jews and not by God."

He sat up very straight and looked at me. "Don't play around," he said. "What are you trying to do?"

"I'm not playing around, Alex. I'm reading."

"Tens of thousands, maybe hundreds of thousands of Jews are dying for a Torah created by men?"

I did not respond.

"You ought to take that stuff and flush it down the toilet," he said. "The best way to answer an anti-Semite is with your fist, not by reading the garbage he puts out. You read enough garbage about anything, you begin to believe it. And you better not bring those books to school anymore, Davey."

"Why not?"

"Because my name is also Lurie and I don't want any trouble. I don't have your brains and I sweat for every A I get. I don't want problems."

"Who's going to make problems for you?"

"My friends are asking me why you're reading these books. I like having friends. And I don't want any of the Talmud teachers to start thinking your books are rubbing off on me."

"Oh, come on, Alex."

"No, you come on, Davey. You're so buried in books you don't see what's going on right in front of your nose. Are you waiting for a personal invitation from the registrar for a private talk?"

I stared at him. He was angry. His face was flushed and his lower jaw jutted forward sharply.

"It's not that kind of a yeshiva," I said. "What are you

talking about? The yeshivas you're talking about are down-town and in Brooklyn."

"Maybe," he said. "Let someone else find out for sure. I want to graduate and not have problems. Keep your books in the house."

I was bewildered by his words and I promised him I would think about it. The next day Yaakov Bader told me that some of the members of our class had approached him and re-quested that he speak to me about not bringing the German books on Bible criticism to the school anymore.

I stared at him. "I can't believe it," I heard myself say.

He gazed at me sadly. "It's true, Davey."

Now I was angry. "Who the hell do they think they are?"

He made an effort to calm me. "They all have families in Europe, Davey."

"So do I have family in Europe."

"But it's the Torah, Davey. It's not just any kind of book. You're reading how the Germans take apart the Torah."

I told him no one had a right to tell me what I could and could not read. I wanted to think about it, I said. On the bus back home that evening, I decided to read the German books at home and to take with me books on the Bible written in English. As I rode past my father's store, I saw it was very crowded. My father and mother stood behind the counter, waiting on customers. My father was laughing at something one of the customers had said. I looked away and closed my eyes.

That Shabbat afternoon my father came from his bedroom into the living room and sat down in his easy chair. His face wore the residue of his nap. He yawned and took up his paper and looked at me. I was reading an English book. Alex sat on the couch inside *Moby Dick.* My mother was still napping. The volume I held in my hand was titled *The Book of Genesis* by S. R. Driver, an English Bible scholar whose writings had been consulted by Hertz in the preparation of his Commentary. I looked at my father and remembered a passage I had read in this book a few hours earlier and I turned back to reread it:

> It follows that the Bible cannot in every part, especially not in its early parts, be read precisely as it was read by our fore-fathers. We live in a light which they did not possess, but which it has pleased the Providence of God to shed around us; and if the Bible is to retain its authority and influence among us, it must be read in this light, and our beliefs about it must be ad-

justed and accommodated accordingly. To utilize, as far as we can, the light in which we live, is, it must be remembered, not a privilege only, but a duty.

I read the passage a third time, then flipped back to the chapter I had been reading when my father had entered the room. The chapter was called "The Historical Character of the Deluge." A few minutes later my father rose and, without a word, went to the kitchen. Alex and I looked at each other. I heard my father pouring himself a glass of tea. He did not return to the living room.

I returned home very late that night from a date with a Brooklyn girl. Alex was asleep. I undressed quietly and sat at my desk for a while, reading. Someone came softly into the room and stood in the shadows beyond the light from my desk lamp. I looked up from the book and saw my mother. She had on her light green housecoat. Her face was pale and dim; her hair was combed out and long.

"David," she murmured. "How late it is."

"Did I wake you? I'm sorry."

"I was awake." She and my father had had friends over and they had left late and she was unable to sleep. She had been awake in her bed and had heard me come in. She sat down wearily on the edge of my bed and gathered to herself the broad spread of the housecoat. "You are going to make yourself sick again staying up so late," she said.

"No I won't," I said. "I'll be all right, Mama."

"David."

I looked at her and waited.

"The books you are reading on the Torah are making your father very upset."

"I'm not reading them near him. Not the ones in German."

"Your father came into your room tonight and looked at the books. The ones in English. Then he brought out one of the German books and asked me to read some pages to him."

I did not say anything.

"He was angry," she said. Then she said quietly, "I am upset too, David, that you are reading such books."

"I'm reading them to fight them, Mama. They're destroying our Torah."

She sighed and was silent a long time. Alex's soft snoring breaths rasped irritatingly against my ears. "Let others fight them," she said finally.

"Which others? Goyim? Or Jews who don't know a thing

about Yiddishkeit? It's our Torah they're destroying. Why shouldn't Jews defend it? Papa fought goyim when they attacked Jews."

"It's not the same thing, David."

"Why?"

"He did not have to read their books month after month."

"No," I said. "He only had to kill them. That saved him from contamination."

"David," she said, her voice trembling. "I will make believe I am not listening to you talk about your father this way. What I am saying to you is that no one can read such books without being affected by them. In this I agree with your father."

"What did David read?" I asked suddenly. I had not wanted to ask that. I did not even know where the question came from.

Her mouth fell open. "What?" she said almost inaudibly.

"Uncle David. What did Uncle David read?"

She was deathly still.

"Were there fights between Uncle David and Papa's father? Were there fights between Uncle David and Papa?"

"David," she murmured, and her eyes glazed.

"Please, Mama. Please. I don't want ghosts. All my life I've had ghosts."

"David," she said pleadingly, her eyes glazed and not looking at me. "I do not want fights."

"Mama, I'm going to read what I want to read. No one will stop me from reading. I don't want to know about the fights Papa had with his brother."

She shuddered visibly and drew the housecoat tightly around her. Her face was a pale moving blur of dim whiteness in the shadows beyond the light. "David," I heard her say softly, wearily. "You are brilliant. Are you going to use your mind to be cruel?"

I did not respond.

She rose to her feet. "Good night," she murmured, and went slowly from the room.

I sat at my desk and listened to the pounding of my heart. The palms of my hands, sweaty and cold, itched as if insects were crawling upon them. I rubbed them against my pajamas. My mother seemed still to be in the room. I closed my eyes to ward off her pale thin face.

It hurt that no one believed me. It hurt that they thought me close to or already beyond the borderline of orthodoxy because I was reading scholarly books about the Bible. It hurt that no one understood I had entered a war zone, that the battlefield was the Torah, that the casualties were ideas, and that without the danger of serious exposure the field of combat could not be scouted, the nature of the enemy could not be learned, the weapons and strategy of counter-attack could not be developed. It hurt that no one around me seemed to understand any of that. I felt myself a lone combatant on a torn field of battle advancing fearfully and without support against a dark and powerful foe.

When my heart grew still I opened my eyes and found myself looking at the book on my desk. After a moment my eyes focused upon the words and I continued reading. I was in the section in the book by Driver where he compares the story of the Flood in Genesis to the story of Utnapishtim in the Babylonian Gilgamesh Epic. I opened the first volume of my *Mikraot Gedolot* to the portion on Noah. I read slowly and carefully.

In the course of the next morning, Yaakov Bader said to me, "You're making a lot of people angry at you, Davey."

"What do you mean?"

"They don't like to see you with those goyishe books on the Torah. They asked me to talk to you."

"What is this, a new reign of terror? Now it's the books in English?"

"I can't blame them, Davey."

He looked deeply unhappy. It angered and upset me to see him that way. Sadness was an unnatural state of being for him; he could not conceal it and it drained the light from his always cheerful face. I told him I would think about it.

During my classes that afternoon I began to notice classmates giving me furtive glances. As I entered the class in Roman history, Irving Besser, tall, stoop-shouldered, and gallant defender of the Talmud against the menace of Bible, brushed against me in the doorway. Some of my books dropped to the floor. He neither apologized nor helped me pick them up. During the surprise quiz thrown at us by the teacher at the start of the lecture, Irving Besser sat in the desk to my right, copying furtively from my paper.

The next afternoon I was sitting on a bench in the little park overlooking the river when Saul came over to me. It was a warm day and I sat with my face to the sun. He sat down on the bench, looking mournful.

"I didn't get a chance to talk to you this morning," he said.

"Tough class with Rav Sharfman?"

"Like the splitting of the Red Sea. Listen."

"Your friends want me to stop reading books on Bible criticism."

"In my class that's already an old story. The girl you dated Saturday night called me."

"Yes?"

"For God's sake, Davey. I told you she's a very religious girl."

"I didn't touch her, Saul. I didn't even hold her hand."

"Why do you have to talk with a girl like that about the— what is it called?—the Gilgamesh Epic? You got her upset."

I stared at him.

"She was really angry," Saul said.

I did not know whether to rage or laugh. I felt a cold falling sensation inside myself.

"She didn't tell me I was upsetting her."

"She was afraid to."

I looked at him. "Afraid?"

"My God, Davey, no one wants to come up against your brains. They all talk to me and Yaakov and ask us to talk to you. They're all afraid of you. Every time someone opens his mouth, you have ten quotations from ten different books to show him how wrong he is."

I was quiet.

"You want me to give you phone numbers, you have to stop talking about things that make you sound like an apikoros."

"All right," I said.

"Don't you have an English lit class now?"

"I can live without *Tintern Abbey*. I'll memorize it for the exam."

He raised his eyes and hands heavenward in a gesture of exasperation and went away. I sat on the bench for a while longer, reading. Then I went over to the stone parapet and looked down the clifflike slope to the road and river below. A barge moved slowly along the river in the direction of the Hudson, pushed by a tugboat. Wide-winged birds circled overhead.

That Friday afternoon I took the subway to the 42d Street library and talked for a while with one of the staff members of the Jewish Division. I returned home with four Hebrew books, two by someone called Yehezkel Kaufmann and two by two medieval Spanish Jewish Bible scholars. I sat in the living room on Shabbat, reading in Hebrew *A History of Israelite Religion* by Yehezkel Kaufmann. Three volumes of that work had already been published and the author was still writing, so it did not seem I would run out of Shabbat reading material for a while. The author was opposed to classic European Biblical criticism and offered his own theory as to the human origins of the Torah.

In the weeks that followed, I sat at home, rode the bus, sat in the park or in dull classes, reading books on the Torah in Hebrew by Yehezkel Kaufmann and by some of the great Spanish Jewish Bible scholars of the early medieval period, whose works Mr. Bader had never told me about when I had studied with him. I read the tirade of Jonah ibn Janach, the greatest of the Jewish Bible scholars of tenth- and eleventh-century Spain, against Talmudists who, he said, trifled with the laws of the Hebrew language and did not read the Bible accurately. I learned his concept of Biblical ellipsis by which he explained omissions of letters and words; for example, the meaning of the word *sharshot* in Exodus 28:22 is unclear; Ibn Janach explained it as being an elliptical form of the word *sharsharot*, "chains"—which fits perfectly the meaning of the verse. I learned his concept of substitution, which assumes that the biblical writer intended one thing but wrote another; for example, in Exodus 19:23, Moses is told to "set bounds about the mountain and sanctify it." But verses ten and twelve indicate clearly that it is not the mountain but the people that constitute the object to be restricted. Therefore, concluded Jonah ibn Janach in his *Sefer Ha-Riqmah*, the text *wrote* "mountain" but *intended* "people." I read a work in Hebrew that informed me of the singular fact that Jonah ibn Janach produced what in effect were over two hundred emendations of the text of the Bible. I read that Isaac ibn Yashush, another eleventh-century Jewish Spanish Bible scholar, appeared actually to have emended the text of Genesis 36:33 and had read "Job" in place of "Jobab," and I remembered Ibn Ezra's attack on that emendation. I also remembered how, in a comment to Exodus 25:29, Ibn Ezra himself argued that there is an error in I Chronicles 28:17 and how the Ramban sharply attacked Ibn Ezra for that remark. I went back to my *Mikraot Gedolot*, reread Ibn Ezra on Genesis 12:6, 22:14, Deuteronomy 1:2, 31:9, 3:11, and began to think that he really had attributed post-Mosaic origins to a number of verses in the Torah, something I had never seriously considered when I had first studied those verses with Mr. Bader or by myself after Mr. Bader had left for Europe. Then I read Yehuda Halevi, the great medieval Jewish philosopher, who asserted that even the vowels, syllable divisions, and accents in the Torah went back to the times of Moses. I read the view of Abraham, son of Maimonides, who maintained that the peculiarities in the Torah text were impenetrable mysteries handed down by tradition. I read others who seemed to my Orthodox eyes on the borderline of heresy, though nowhere in the writings of the Spanish Jewish scholars did I find an explicit statement that cast doubt on the integrity of the Biblical text.

I was having a strange time with my Hebrew reading. All through my junior and senior years in college I read Hebrew books on the Bible. My parents and friends stopped bothering me. But I was reading Hebrew works by classical scholars who probably would not have been permitted to teach in my yeshiva. On the day before the Allied invasion of Normandy I discovered that Judah ben Barzillai, a tenth- to eleventh-century Jewish Bible scholar who lived in Barcelona, had reported that many of the Biblical scholars of his day came perilously close to being heretics. Then I stopped reading for a while and stayed close to the radio in our kitchen, listening to the news of the war.

Two weeks later, on a Sunday afternoon, I was graduated from college. I have retained no memories of that graduation other than vague images of a crowded auditorium, speeches, awards, and hot weather.

I remember Irving Besser saying to me afterward on the street, "Nice of you to leave one or two awards for some of the other guys, Lurie."

Yaakov Bader said, "Cut it out, Irving. You graduated because of Davey's small shoulders and your big eyes. Don't complain."

Irving Besser glared at him and walked away.

I returned to my reading. On Shabbat I read the Hebrew books. Inside my room or outside alone on a bench in the park I read books in English and German. I found that there were English and German books without an echo of prose-lytizing or anti-Semitism. I spoke to no one of what I was reading and no one seemed interested enough to ask me: my parents were busy with the store, Alex was reading and writing stories, Saul was studying in panicky fashion for his ordination exams in the fall.

In the early summer my father asked me if I would help him with the store and I readily agreed. Three times a week he sent me downtown to the jewelry district in and around Third Avenue and Canal Street. There were watchmakers with whom he now subcontracted, for he could no longer handle by himself the watch repair volume of the store. There were diamond merchants whom he phoned in advance of my coming and who had ready for me gleaming rings and watchbands and necklaces. There were distributors of watch parts who read my father's instructions on the small yellow envelopes I handed them and skillfully fitted into the watches contained in the envelopes stems and crowns, mainsprings and balance wheels, and other parts whose names I never bothered to learn. I was surprised to discover that many of the people my father did business with in the Canal Street area were his old friends from the Am Kedoshim Society. Some of them greeted me with astonishment. "My God, this is little David?" one of them said loudly. He ran a store off Canal Street that replaced crystals in watches. "Hey, Jack, this is Max Lurie's boy! You used to be such a skinny kid we thought the wind would carry you away." It was later while walking toward the East Broadway station of the subway that I remembered he was the man who had wrestled with my father during that picnic in the pine wood years ago. How many years? I went down the subway steps into the dank coolness of the station, holding tightly to the black leather bag containing watches and diamonds.

Back and forth I journeyed that summer between my father's store and the stores on and around Canal Street. I would wait in the cramped odorous little closet of a store run by one of the best watchmakers in the city, an old white-haired Jew to whom my father sent repair work he would entrust to no one else. Overhead ran the Third Avenue elevated train; a block away was the Canal Street station. All around me were the derelicts of the Bowery, sleeping in the doorways of stores, on the streets, wandering, drinking, staggering about. I saw the flophouses in which they slept, the places where they ate, the gutters where on occasion one of them died. I would go from store to store and wherever I went I saw clocks and watches. Time stared at me from a thousand shelves. For the derelicts of the Bowery time seemed to have ceased; but I was learning about time and about history and memory.

That summer I began to read Gibbon's *The Decline and*

Fall of the Roman Empire. I remember I finished reading
the final volume late one morning while I sat on a blanket
on the shore of the lake outside the bungalow where we
lived during the last two weeks of August. I put the book
down on my blanket and covered it with a towel to protect
its binding from the sun. I sat on the blanket for a long time,
looking up at the sky. I could not remember ever having felt
that way after finishing a book. I wanted to embrace Mr.
Gibbon, to thank him, for I understood now, finally, the
texture and dimension of history. I felt warm and excited and
was deeply grateful to that industrious, scribbling Englishman.
The lake was very still. After a while I went in for a swim.
When I came out I sat alone on the beach and let the sun dry
me. Saul was inside his bungalow studying Talmud; the sun
had begun to bother his eyes, he had said. My uncle had returned to the city for the day on business. I heard my mother
and aunt talking gaily beneath the tree near our bungalow.
Overhead birds wheeled slowly in a cloudless sky. As I gazed
across the lake I saw my father and brother gallop on fast
horses through the tall grass of a distant field. I lay back and
closed my eyes and felt the hot sun on my face. I let my head
fall beyond the edge of the blanket onto the hot sand of the
beach. I dug into the sand and felt it crumbling beneath my
hand. I scooped up a handful of sand and let it sift between
my fingers. I lay on the blanket in the sun and felt the sand
sifting slowly between my fingers onto the beach. After a
while I went into the bungalow for another book.

We returned home on a cloudy day in the last week of
August. In September I entered the class of Rav Tuvya Sharfman and began my studies for rabbinic ordination.

I remember the night in the second week of October when
we danced with the Torah scrolls in our little synagogue. It
was the night of Simchat Torah, the festival that celebrates
the completion of the annual cycle of Torah readings. The
last portion of the Five Books of Moses would be read the
next morning.

The little synagogue was crowded and tumultuous with joy.
I remember the white-bearded Torah reader dancing with one
of the heavy scrolls as if he had miraculously shed his years.
My father and uncle danced for what seemed to me to be an
interminable length of time, circling about one another with
their Torah scrolls, advancing upon one another, backing off,

singing. Saul and Alex and I danced too. I relinquished my
Torah to someone in the crowd, then stood around watching
the dancing. It grew warm inside the small room and I went
through the crowd and out the rear door to the back porch.
I stood in the darkness and let the air cool my face. I could
feel the floor of the porch vibrating to the dancing inside the
synagogue. It was a windy fall night, the air clean, the sky
vast and filled with stars. The noise of the singing and dancing
came clearly through the open windows of the synagogue. An
old cycle ending; a new cycle beginning. Tomorrow morning
Moses would die, and the old man would read the words re-
counting his death; a few minutes later he would read the first
chapter and the beginning three verses of the second chapter
of Genesis. Death and birth without separation. Endings leading to beginnings. And then, on Shabbat, he would read all of
the first portion of the Book of Genesis: the Creation, Adam
and Eve, the Garden of Eden, Cain and Abel. And the following Shabbat he would read the story of Noah and the Flood.
And then Abraham and Sarah and the Covenant and Isaac
and the sacrifice and Rebecca and Jacob and Esau and
Joseph and . . .

The back porch faced out on a brief patch of lawn and a
tall elm. I could not see the leaves in the darkness. But I had
seen them earlier in the day during the Morning Service; they
were dying with the fall.

The noise inside the synagogue poured out into the night,
an undulating, swelling and receding and thinning and growing
sound. The joy of dancing with the Torah, holding it close to
you, the words of God to Moses at Sinai. I wondered if
Gentiles ever danced with their Bible. "Hey, Tony. Do you
ever dance with your Bible?"

I had actually spoken the question. I heard the words in
the cool dark air. I had not thought to do that. I had not even
thought of Tony—yes, I remembered his name: Tony
Savanola. I had not thought of him in years. Where was he
now? Fighting in the war probably. Or studying for the priest-
hood and deferred from the draft as I was. Hey, Tony. Do
you ever read your Bible? Do you ever hold it to you and
know how much you love it? Do Christian Bible scholars write
about Jesus the same way they write about Abraham? Do
they say that it's all only stories? Hey, Tony.

I thought of the street and the maples and the zoo and the
meadow and the pond and the clearing in the pine wood. I
thought of Eddie Kulanski. Hey, Eddie. Do you ever read

your Bible? I wondered where he was. I hoped he wasn't
dead. I hoped he was killing Germans. That's what you're
good for, Eddie. You're a good killer and the war is helping
you to kill the right people. Kill a lot of Nazis, Eddie. That's
what you're perfect for. But don't get yourself killed. I don't
hate you enough to want you to get killed. Why was I thinking
of Eddie Kulanski? I could see him in front of me in the darkness, cold sleepy gray eyes, small mouth, pointed features. I
felt a silent swarming in the leaves of the elm.

The door to the porch opened and closed behind me.
"Davey?" It was Saul. He came over to me and we stood
together near the porch rail. "It's hot inside," he said.

I felt his presence as a comforting warmth.

"What are you reading now?" he asked.

"Spinoza."

"Oh, God!"

"That's appropriate for Spinoza," I said, laughing.

"I tried reading Kant once," he said, after a moment.

"And?"

"I went back to the Rambam."

"Thank God for Maimonides! The refuge of the Orthodox
Jewish rebel. Do you want to go for a walk?"

"Davey."

"What?"

"Are you all right?"

I looked up at the sky and the stars. "I'm a little frightened,
Saul. I don't know what to do."

He was quiet.

"I've stopped reading all those goyishe books about the
Torah. I'm really frightened of what they're saying. Come on
for a walk with me, Saul. A quick walk through the park."

"I'm exhausted, Davey."

"All right," I said. "All right." I felt a sudden agitation and
restlessness and a surging of blood in my ears. "Let's go back
inside."

But once inside the noise was deafening; I felt it thickening
the air through which I moved. A child, riding an adult's
shoulders poked me in the face accidentally with the stick of
his Torah flag. I put my hand to my face; there was no blood.
I looked around and saw my father seated at one of the
tables, talking with my uncle and some friends and drinking
beer. There were people still dancing with the Torah scrolls.
Alex was dancing again. As I watched, Saul was handed a
scroll and he too entered the circle of dancers. Behind the

gauzy curtain near the front of the synagogue was the women's section. My mother and aunt were there but I could not see them. The synagogue was packed. I edged through the crowd and came outside onto the street. There was a crowd here too, but less dense. I walked quickly beneath the trees toward the park. The night was cool upon my face. The skin throbbed faintly where the stick had jabbed me. I touched my face again. No, there was no blood. I crossed 170th Street and entered the park.

The cement path led directly off the sidewalk through a wide opening in the stone wall. It curved and branched and narrowed, winding along between grassy fields. There were trees and benches and a few people walking about. I wandered aimlessly through the park, sat for a while on a bench listening to a tree in the night breeze, then walked along following a sudden steep dip in the path. Here in the heart of the park I seemed to be alone. I sat down on a bench, feeling the hardness of the slats against my back. I had been doing a lot of sitting on park benches these past years. They were good places for reading. Yaakov Bader kept saying there were too many distractions when you read in a park; he read in the school library or at home. I liked parks. I had the world visible to me while I read. It was important to have it visible so you could see how your reading changed it.

An elderly couple passed by slowly, talking in Yiddish about the war. Their footsteps made soft tapping sounds on the path. They looked at me as they went by, a gray-haired couple walking very slowly, the man leaning on a cane. Did they have family in Europe? I had never seen them before. I had lived on this street more than two years, and every day I saw faces I did not recognize. Had I known everyone on my street near the zoo? I could not remember. There were many things about that street I could no longer remember.

I looked up at the underside of a nearby tree. My eyes, accustomed now to the absence of light, saw the shifting shades of darkness as the tree responded to the breezy night air. I shivered and pulled closer to me the light coat I wore. I hungered for the comfort of my school. In its large, light-filled study hall I could lose myself in the centuries of accepted thought. We would maneuver to be audacious as we displayed our acquired wisdom and skill in the Talmud; but the paths were clear; they had been trod by prior generations. There was comfort in that and only terror in the thought of striking out alone beyond the boundaries of the past. I loved the past. Why should I leave its warmth and solace-giving strength? I wished for the festival to be at an end so I could once more be at school. I had had enough of goyim and secularists and borderline heretics. They created a world of endlessly shifting sands and I hungered for the world created by the Master of the Universe.

I walked back to the synagogue and arrived too late for the Torah reading but in time for the last prayer of the Evening Service.

The weeks that followed were among the loveliest I have ever known. Saul took his ordination exam and passed and the family celebrated his achievement with a kiddush in the synagogue and a party in my uncle's apartment. Saul, flushed with joy, his pale face still filled with awe and disbelief at his accomplishment, was congratulated, pounded on the back, hugged, kissed. "Rabbi," everyone kept calling him. "Rav Shaul Lurie. How does it feel? Rav Shaul Lurie." I noticed that many of the old members of the Am Kedoshim Society were at the party. "What are you doing with yourself?" they kept asking me. And I kept saying I was going to the yeshiva and studying Talmud with Rav Tuvya Sharfman. "You will follow in the footsteps of your cousin?" I nodded. There were smiles. The paths of generations would be walked again by the young of the Lurie family. They had reason to be happy.

It was a long gentle fall with only an occasional harshness to the winds. Slowly the leaves turned and fell and the grass in the park took on its brown winter look.

I learned to love to walk that fall. Sometimes I would rise very early and if it was a sunny day I would dress and pray and eat and walk all the way to school. It was a very long walk but I had ridden on buses for so many years through these blocks that I felt them all to be my own, and easy familiarity shortened the miles. I went past the stores and the houses of 170th Street, saw in windows the blue stars that signified families with men in the armed forces and an occasional gold star that marked the war's deadly cost.

One night I asked Alex to walk to school with me the next morning.

"Are you crazy?" he said, looking up from his book.

"Come on," I said. "It'll do you good. You're the athlete."

"You are crazy," he said, and returned to his novel.

I did not ask him again for a while.

I walked and enjoyed the fall and the slow coming of the cold weather. I loved crossing the bridge to Manhattan and looking out at the city and the river below. There on the bluff stood the school, its green dome glistening in the sunlight. I hurried toward it, eager for the day.

From nine in the morning until noon I sat in the study hall and prepared with Yaakov Bader for the Talmud class. At noon we went down to the cafeteria for lunch. A little before one o'clock about eighty students entered the classroom across the corridor from the study hall. We sat crowded in it, pressing tensely forward against the old battered desk and chair in front of the room. Promptly at one o'clock Rav Tuvya Sharfman entered.

A hush would instantly pervade the room, a sudden draining of all extraneous sound. We were in the presence of the greatest Talmudist in the Orthodox Jewish world, a world in which excellence in Talmud is the highest of human achievements.

I remember with all the vividness of a photograph my first class with Rav Tuvya Sharfman. I had seen him in the school building from time to time but I had never been close to him. He entered the room and silence entered with him, together with an awesome sense of the generations of greatness he carried within himself. He was a tall, thin man in his late forties with dark hair and a dark Vandyke beard. He wore a neat dark pin-striped suit, a white shirt, and a dark tie. His face was long and narrow and somewhat saturnine in appearance, with thin outward-turned lips, a sharply beaked nose, and large black eyes. He had a long thin neck and thin bony white hands. His was a lineage of Talmudists extending back in time to the period immediately following the Crusades. A rich wine merchant had turned over his business to his brother soon after a mob of Crusaders had rampaged through the nearby German countryside slaughtering Jews. He had gone off to study Torah in a distant academy of learning. The line had continued unbroken and its descendant was now my Talmud teacher. He had come to America from Eastern Europe in the twenties with ordination from his grandfather and a doctorate in philosophy from the University of Berlin. I felt generations of Talmudists staring at me over his wide shoulders. I was excited by their beckoning eyes.

We were studying the Talmud tractate *Berachot,* which deals with various important prayers, blessings, and benedictions, the occasion and manner of their recitation, the

significance of their words. He had brought in with him a
dark-bound folio of the Talmud. He placed it on the desk,
opened it, and surveyed the class. His large eyelids drooped
somewhat, giving his eyes a hooded, birdlike appearance. I
sat directly in front of him, a foot or so from his desk. He
stood behind the desk and said abruptly in a faintly nasal
raspy voice, "You all prepared the Mishnah and the Gemara.
What is missing from the Mishnah?" He spoke English with a
vague trace of an accent. "What does the Mishnah leave out?"

The Mishnah we had prepared was a series of terse legal
statements describing the times one is permitted to say the
Shema prayer, "Hear O Israel the Lord our God the Lord is
One." It begins by asking, "From what time in the evening
may the Shema be recited?" and goes on to a series of responses to that question.

I did not understand his question. He repeated it, this
time in Yiddish. "Nu, what is not said in the Mishnah? The
Mishnah asks 'From what time in the evening may the Shema
be recited?' What does the Mishnah not ask?"

Most of the students had entered the classroom in a condition of panic. That condition now swiftly deteriorated into
paralysis. They sat in various attitudes of frozen terror,
staring blindly at their volumes of Talmud, afraid to raise
their eyes and meet the large hooded black eyes of Rav
Sharfman.

He waited. The air became heavy and stifling with silence.

I scanned the Mishnah once again. It had to be an absurdly
simple answer, something we were all looking at but could
not see. He had asked the question for effect. He wanted to
make an important point. What had I heard about him? He
was interested not so much in the words on a page of Talmud
as in the invisible threads that tied various pages together.
He was alluding to assumptions, presuppositions, the unstated
scaffolding that lay behind the terse statements of law and
legal skirmishing. I looked at the Mishnah and there it was,
suddenly, clearly, the answer, like a singing inside my head.
Keeping my elbow on my desk, I raised my right hand.

His long thin neck turned slightly inside his white collar as
he looked at me and waited.

"The Mishnah does not state that we are supposed to say
the Shema. It assumes that the Shema must be said."

I felt everyone in the class looking at me. Now that I had
given my answer, it sounded a little inane. But what else could
he have meant?

The hooded eyes blinked once. I thought I could hear the lids go up and down.

"That is correct," Rav Sharfman said in English with no emotion on his face. "Did you all hear that? Without that assumption, the Mishnah has no meaning." He looked at me and said in Yiddish, "What is your name?"

"David Lurie."

The eyes fixed themselves upon me, unblinking. "You are Lurie," he said in Yiddish. Then he said in English, "A base hit, Lurie. Read the Mishnah."

Saul had told me about the way he occasionally would punctuate his classroom remarks with baseball terminology. Still it was strange hearing the words "a base hit" from the lips of Rav Tuvya Sharfman. From somewhere in the classroom came a nervous giggle. Yaakov Bader gave me a smile.

I read and explained carefully the words of the Mishnah. Then I read and explained the commentary of Rashi to the Mishnah. He let me go on without interruption. Then I read and explained the long commentary of the Tosafists. Finally he stopped me with an abrupt sideways motion of his right hand and called on someone else to read the Gemara.

I sat with my eyes on the text of the Talmud, feeling a tide of exhilaration wash over me. At one point during that afternoon, as I sat there with my eyes on the page, I sensed his eyes upon me and I looked up and saw him gazing at me. I turned my eyes back down to the page and felt my face warm. It would be a good class. I was exultant.

The weeks of that autumn moved gently by. I lived in the world of my school, inside the crowded classroom of Rav Sharfman and the text of the Talmud I studied every day. My father's business was very successful and he began to talk about opening another store somewhere in the Bronx. My mother delighted in her role as a business woman; she dealt with customers and salesmen, and answered the phone; on occasion she traveled to the Diamond Exchange downtown in Manhattan, carrying with her the black leather briefcase. Alex read novels and wrote stories and poems which he sent to magazines and received back in the mail together with printed rejection slips. Then one day one of his poems was accepted by a college magazine in the Midwest. He was radiant with joy. It was a fine autumn.

But in the middle of December the sudden German offensive in the Ardennes forest, which broke through the American lines and seemed to shatter all the advances of the summer and fall, turned the year suddenly dark. I looked at the war maps on the wall over Alex's bed and saw again the poisoned sword of the Angel of Death. We listened to the news broadcasts on our kitchen radio.

"Stinking bastard Germans," my father muttered.

"Where did they all suddenly come from?" Alex asked.

"How could it be such a surprise?" I asked.

"Somebody was not doing his job," my father said.

"What does it mean, Max?" asked my mother fearfully.

"It means more months of war," said my father. "Half a year. Maybe a year. The bastards."

I walked to school on a cold late January morning and saw gold stars in windows where blue stars had appeared before and felt the distant war translated into discernible grief. Saul told me the brother of a girl we knew had been killed in the Ardennes offensive.

"They found out yesterday." He was gray-faced with shock. The war had never been this close to us before. I saw her inside my eyes, a sweet round-faced cheerful girl with long brown hair and brown eyes. Her brother was dead in the war.

I called her that night and expressed my feelings of sympathy. Yaakov and Saul and I went by subway from school to her home in Brooklyn that Sunday. The family sat in mourning. The mother, a young woman made pale and old with grief, huddled in a corner surrounded by friends. The father kept saying, "He wanted to go in. He wanted to fight the Nazis." He was in his early forties, and he seemed dazed. "He died fighting Nazis. If he had to die, that was a good way to die. Oh, God. Oh, my God. He was such a good kid. God, God." The girl could hardly talk but sat with tears streaming down her lovely face. We left and took the subway and rode in silence. Yaakov got off at 161st Street to change trains for his home in the West Bronx. Saul and I left the train at the 170th Street and Grand Concourse station and climbed the stairs to the street.

It had begun to snow. I pulled my collar up and walked carefully on the slippery street.

" 'Once God gives permission for Satan to destroy, he destroys the good together with the wicked,' " Saul quoted.

"Yes," I said, talking into the wind. "I know that Rabbinic remark. I don't understand it."

"The remark?"

"No. The reality."

We walked home in silence.

The cold winter weeks went slowly by. I listened to the radio and read the papers and saw the pictures and newsreels of the war. When I woke early to sunny days I would walk to school despite the bitter cold. Once I dared Alex to walk with me and he accepted the challenge and we walked together. He spent half the time rhapsodizing about Melville and the other half asking himself out loud how he had ever let me talk him into taking such a walk. I did not walk with him to school again. Once I asked Saul to walk with me. He was teaching Talmud now in the high school department of the yeshiva. He looked at me as if I were insane.

One day in March Rav Sharfman called on a student who was inadequately prepared. The student, a nervous high-voiced Brooklyn boy, started reading, ran words together incorrectly, stopped, read the passage again, this time correctly, and began to explain it. Rav Sharfman let him talk. The student's face became flushed; his voice grew higher. He mired himself in a swamp of contradictory explanations. Finally he stopped and sat in pale trembling silence, staring down miserably at his volume of Talmud.

"You're not prepared," Rav Sharfman said in English with contempt.

The student began a lame excuse. A wave of the hand stopped him.

"Prepare or don't come to my class. You warm up before class, not during class. Understand?"

The student nodded, shrinking with shame.

"No excuses," Rav Sharfman went on. "No excuses in this class. Now, Besser, continue reading."

A few minutes later we were tangled in a passage of Talmud from another tractate that bore vague allusions to our own. Someone in class mentioned a similar passage in a third tractate. Then we were comparing the commentaries on the three passages, all of whom tried with varying degrees of success to reconcile the contradictions between the passages. I raised my hand because I had just remembered a medieval commentary on a somewhat similar passage of Talmud in another tractate I had studied many years ago.

Rav Sharfman was bent over the pile of open volumes on his desk.

"Rebbe," I said.

He looked up and fixed upon my face his large black eyes and gloomy countenance.

I gave him the explanation of the medieval commentary.

"That's nonsense!" he said. "Absolute nonsense!"

There was a stir in the class behind me.

"But it's the Meiri. I remember—"

"Lurie, if the Meiri was in my class and said that, I would throw him out."

He looked back down at the books on his desk. I saw eyes go wide all around the room. The Meiri is one of the greatest of the early medieval Talmud commentators. Rav Sharfman stood tensely behind the desk, pursing his lips, tugging occasionally at his Vandyke. He turned pages impatiently, moving from book to book. We sat in silence and waited.

Finally he looked up and said in Yiddish, "We will do it this way. Listen, all of you."

He spent forty minutes explaining the various passages in a way that eliminated the contradictions with ease.

We talked about that explanation for days, in the corridors, in the cafeteria, in the study hall. We went over it again and again. We were awed by it, all of us who were his students in that classroom.

That was how those weeks went by, those last weeks of the war against Germany. One evening Rav Sharfman gave a talk in the study hall to commemorate the anniversary of his father's death. He spoke that evening of the struggle to be a man of Torah. His voice was soft, subdued. He spoke of hardships and deprivations, of the joy of discovery, of loneliness. I heard he was to give a lecture at a Jewish community center in mid-town Manhattan and I took a subway and sat in a crowded hall and listened to him speak of Kierkegaard and Rudolf Otto and the anguished search for faith. Into this talk he wove words of Torah, legal statements, passages of midrash. "My God, he's great," I heard someone say afterward. "I couldn't follow him after the fourth sentence," was the response.

In class he was the master Talmudist. Somehow he had adopted the language of the baseball field and made it on occasion the controlling metaphor of his relationship to his students. "You struck out there, Lurie," he said to me one afternoon, and I shook my head with dismay. "Okay, you're on first base," he said to Yaakov Bader after a lengthy struggle with a difficult passage. "Now make it to second." It had seemed strange to me at first to hear that kind of language used even occasionally by a Talmudist. I wondered about it aloud one night in Saul's presence.

"He's always talked that way," Saul said.

"Good morning, Rebbe," I heard myself say thickly, and cleared my throat.

The bridge and the avenue were heavy with traffic. A bus turned from the avenue onto the bridge with a roar of its accelerating motor and a gush of fumes.

He turned to continue walking and I walked beside him.

"I notice you from time to time as you cross the bridge," he said, looking straight ahead. "Where do you live?"

I told him.

He glanced at me and glanced away. "That's a long walk."

"I enjoy it."

"Do you walk by yourself?"

"Yes."

We walked half a block in silence. He looked down at the two books of Talmudic commentaries I was carrying.

"What are you reading?"

I told him.

"What are you reading that is not required for class?"

"I don't have much extra time."

He turned, then, and gave me a long look. His large black eyes moved slowly across my face.

"I heard once that you used to read many books not required for your classes," he said.

We were on the corner facing the school. We crossed the avenue.

"I used to read books on the Bible," I said, using the word *Tanach*, which is the acronym for the three sections of the Hebrew Bible.

"Yes," he said. "That's what I heard."

We entered the wide metal front doors of the building. With a brief nod, he turned to the right and went up the short flight of steps and through the doors to the administration offices. I turned left and went along the corridor to the study hall.

I noticed during the course of that week that he was always alone, except when he was with his students in the classroom. Other teachers of Talmud would stand together in the corridors, chatting, or sit together in the study hall. He sat alone and walked about alone.

I met him again one morning in the last week of April as I turned off the bridge onto the avenue. He slipped into step beside me.

"Good morning, Lurie."

"Good morning, Rebbe."

"You have courage to take such long walks."

"I like it. I have time to think."

He was silent a moment.

"What are you reading?"

"Commentaries."

"Lurie."

"Yes?"

"The books you once read. Which were they?"

"I read lots of books, Rebbe."

"Tell me their names."

"All of them?"

"In the last two or three years. Not the books for school."

He listened with no trace of emotion on his features as I named the books. He interrupted me with a raised hand and asked me a question about one of the books I had mentioned. I responded. He asked me questions about a second and third book and I responded to those as well. From the nature of his questions it was obvious he had also read those books. They were books on scientific Biblical criticism. One of them was *The Book of Genesis* by S. R. Driver.

We crossed the street and entered the school and separated inside the large entrance hall. I watched him go up the stairs toward the administration offices.

I was puzzled by his queries. I had the impression he had been waiting for me at the end of the bridge but I could not be certain. In the classroom he continued to relate to me in his normal manner. I struck out and hit a double that afternoon.

When I rode by the store later that day I noticed that my mother was not behind the counter. I came into the house and discovered she was in bed. She had felt very tired, she said, and had gone home.

"I am pampering myself," she said to me from her bed. But she would not look directly at me and I did not like the greenish cast to her skin and the white blotches on her cheeks.

"We are going to have a little problem with your mother," my father said to Alex and me in the kitchen that night. "The war is ending and your mother is waiting to hear about her family. Our job now is to be patient and strong. Do you understand?"

Alex and I looked at each other. We understood.

I heard my mother cry out in her sleep that night, shouting Polish words I did not comprehend. My father soothed her and she grew still. I lay awake a long time afterward, fighting back the whispers that moved back and forth across the dark floor of my room.

She felt well enough to return to the store later that week. But she was tense and easily upset. Small failures would strain her timid resolve. She was now what I vaguely remembered her having been when I was a child: fearful of hurt, timorous, withdrawn. One evening that week she began to speak of her childhood on the farm outside of Bobrek. We listened in silence to the spinning out of her years before the darkness of my Uncle David's death. My father sat stiffly in his chair, not a trace of emotion on his face. We were in the kitchen. From the living room came the sudden singing of the canary. My mother's voice faltered and grew silent.

I walked to school the next morning and had before my eyes my mother's haunted face. The memories of her past whispered themselves at me during the Talmud class. The trees, David. How they would sing in the summer wind. And there was a horse I loved. And Papa taught me to ride it. Jewish girls don't ride horses, he said. But this Jewish girl I trust. I named the horse Balak and rode him and felt the wind on my face. The farm, David. The forest, David. The sky, David. The rich black earth, David.

Through the veil of whispers came a knife edge of anger. Someone had called my name. I looked at Rav Sharfman.

"Are you dreaming?" I heard him say.

"I'm nightmaring," I said without thinking the word. I heard the swift beating of my heart and sat stiffly in my seat, waiting.

But he said nothing more to me and turned away and went on explaining the passage of Talmud I had drifted away from moments before on the tide of whispers.

After the class I waited until everyone had left and apologized to him for my lack of attention. I told him about my mother.

He closed the volume of Talmud on his desk.

"We are all waiting," he said in Yiddish with no emotion on his face. "The entire Jewish people is waiting." He glanced at the books I held in my hand, then looked away and went slowly from the room.

And then the war in Europe was over. We sat around the kitchen table listening to the radio. I heard my father take a long tremulous breath. A slight flush had risen to his squarish face.

My mother blinked her eyes nervously. "Max? Will we know soon?"

"Yes," my father said. "We will know soon, Ruth."

He did not look at her as he spoke. Instead he looked out the window at the pale sunlight on the street.

I woke very early one day that week and set out to walk to school. It was a warm sunny day. I avoided the tunnel beneath Grand Concourse and used the street. I stood a moment at the corner of Grand Concourse waiting for the light to change and glanced at the morning papers in the newsstand. At the corner of Jerome Avenue, I looked at the papers again. I bought one of the papers and looked at the photographs. I folded the paper and walked quickly to school.

In class that afternoon Rav Sharfman called on me to read. I read and explained and he did not interrupt me. His eyes remained upon my face as I spoke. The class was very still. At one point a passing bus drowned out my words and I stopped and went back over what I had said. His hooded eyes regarded me without expression. Finally he stopped me and clarified a complicated point in a late medieval commentary. He told us the explanation had been the insight of his grandfather. That was the first time he had ever mentioned any member of his family to us in class. Then he dismissed us.

"Did you see the pictures?" Yaakov Bader asked me in the corridor.

"Yes."

"In the afternoon papers?"

"No."

"Besser has a paper."

I went over to Irving Besser and looked at the photographs.

"You have family there?" I asked him.

"My father's family. Brothers, sisters."

"Where?"

"In Lodz," he said.

We looked at the pictures together a moment longer.

"I can't believe it," he said.

"Believe it," I told him. "It's a photograph."

I felt a queer whispering sound in my ears. It was gone a moment later.

I rode back home on a bus later that day and saw my parents in the store behind the counter. The store was crowded. Alex was home listening to the radio. The afternoon newspapers were strewn all over the kitchen table. I looked at the photographs. Then I went into my room and closed the door and lay down on my bed. I covered my eyes with my hands. It made no difference. I saw the photographs inside my eyes.

My mother came home in a while to prepare supper. Later I heard my father enter the house. We sat around the table eating.

"We knew a lot about what was going on," my father said. "But we did not know this. A nation of maniacs. They should be destroyed."

"They have been," said Alex.

"Wiped out. Every last one of them. Like Amalek."

"We ought to poison their wells," Alex said with grim humor.

"Cut it out," I told him.

"Somebody ought to do something," he said bitterly.

"Aren't we tired of blood?" I said. "Hasn't there been enough blood?"

"Only Jewish blood does not make the world tired," my father said.

"Max," my mother murmured, raising her eyes from her plate. "How soon will it be now?"

"Very soon, Ruth. There are Irgun boys in the camps."

I looked at him.

"They are leaving the Brigade and infiltrating the camps," he said.

"How do you know?"

"It is my job to know."

"They're deserting the British army?"

"To hell with the British army! You think all we have to worry about now is the British army? Look what nice gentlemen we all were to the goyim. You know what it cost us? *That* is what it cost us!" He pointed to the newspapers piled on the kitchen counter. "Stinking bastard goyim. They are drinking our blood."

My mother could not finish her meal. She went to bed.

The phone rang. My father went out to the hallway. He spoke briefly and returned to the kitchen.

"Nothing," he said. "No word."

"Whom do you have looking?" I asked him.

"Everyone," he said.

"Where?"

"All over."

"How are you doing that?"

"I am looking for others too. So I look for myself. I am going to stay with your mother for a while."

"Is Mr. Bader looking?"

"Yes."

"Where is he?"

"On his way to a German castle."

I stared at him.

"His headquarters," he said. He went out of the kitchen.

Alex and I did the dishes. The phone rang again. I heard my father come into the hallway.

"The Jewish people is going to have a big phone bill these next few months," Alex said.

"What is Mr. Bader doing in a German castle?" I asked.

"The Nazis left behind a few Jews who aren't dead. Somebody has to figure out what to do with them."

My father hung up the phone and returned to the bedroom.

I lay awake a long time that night in the darkness of my room. The street light made a dim rectangle of my window shade. I looked through the darkness at the shade. A truck rumbled along the street, rattling the window. I envisioned the trolleys and trains near the streets where I had once lived, clanking and rattling and rushing by. Hey, Eddie. Eddie. Have you seen a concentration camp? Did they look good, all those corpses of dead Jews?

I walked to school the next morning in a light rain. There were more photographs in the newspapers. Now the magazines were out and they had photographs too—large, sharp, black and white and starkly horrifying. Every day now there were photographs. All through May the flow of rectangles continued across the ocean onto the pages of our newspapers: hills of corpses, pits of bones, the naked rubble of the dead and the staring eyes and hollow faces of the survivors. I saw a photograph of dead children, eyes and mouths open, bodies twisted and frozen with death and I tried to enter it and could not. I bought the papers and magazines and saw the photographs of the chimneys and the furnaces and the death trains and tried to penetrate the borders of the cruel rectangles—and I could not do it. They lay beyond the grasp of my mind, those malevolent rectangles of spectral horror. They would not let me into them.

I came off the bridge early one morning in the last week of May and saw Rav Sharfman on the corner, his back to me. Had he been waiting? I came over to him.

"Rebbe?"

He turned slowly and fixed upon me his large eyes. "Good morning, Lurie," he said in Yiddish. "You have begun to walk again?"

I told him my mother was not well and often woke us in the night.

He murmured a word of sympathy. We began to walk. He walked briskly, slightly stooped forward. He had on a dark gray suit and his dark battered hat. We walked awhile in silence. Then he asked abruptly, "What has your father heard?"

"Nothing. They were all in Auschwitz and were moved to Bergen Belsen. That's all we know."

"Who was moved?"

"Everyone in my mother's and father's families. There was one transfer of people from Auschwitz to Bergen Belsen and they were in it."

We walked on for a block. At a corner we stopped to let a line of cars go by.

He said to me, "They destroyed an entire civilization. The Nazis have taught Western civilization that not only making cars but also committing murder can become a mass production industry. You are aware of that." He did not wait for my response. "If Western civilization is finished, we are all finished. There will be nothing with which to water the roots. Nothing. What are we doing about it, Lurie?" Again he did not wait for my response. "I am as far away from your father's politics as I am from a belief in spirits and demons. But I admire your father. He is doing something."

I felt a rush of blood into my face. We crossed the street and entered the school.

In the course of the Talmud class that afternoon I offered an answer to a question he put to us and his face darkened. "That is nonsense!" he said in Yiddish with an impatient wave of his hand. "Next! Next!" He called on someone else for an answer. I interrupted and tried to defend myself.

"Lurie, you are talking nonsense!"

I cited the early medieval commentary whose words I had used as a starting point for my answer.

He cut me short. "Don't tell me what everyone else says! Tell me what you say! Can't you think? What's the matter with all of you? I could sell you the Brooklyn Bridge and you would buy it because Sharfman told you to buy it! I could teach you nonsense and you would accept it as Torah! Have your brains been paralyzed? Lurie, open your eyes and look at the Gemara and tell me what bothers Hillel."

I was angered and confused by his rush of words. I offered him what I had originally thought to be the answer but had withheld because it contradicted the commentaries.

From a few seats away came Irving Besser's immediate reaction. "That can't be right, Rebbe. It contradicts everyone."

"It contradicts, Besser?" said Rav Sharfman. "So? The commentators understood everything? It is all finished? We have nothing to say? We are swallowers, Besser? We can make no living waters of our own?"

Irving Besser stared at him, a flush rising to his face.

We sat very still. Rav Sharfman, his face dark with his effort to control anger and agitation, surveyed us with a look of contempt.

"Does anyone know what I am saying?" he asked. "Do I speak to the wind?" His eyes fell upon mine. "He who understands will understand. Yes? Now I will explain to all of you why the answer of David Lurie is correct."

Yaakov Bader said to me in the corridor after the class, "What was that all about, Davey?"

I shrugged.

"I never heard him talk like that before," Yaakov Bader said. "I never heard any rebbe talk like that before."

"He's not just any rebbe," I said.

I went home by bus that afternoon and passed the store and saw that my mother was not inside. I found her at home in bed. Alex was with her. His face was pale.

I came into her bedroom.

"Mama?"

She had her face to the wall. She turned her head to me. Her eyes were dark and flat and dead.

"David?"

"Yes, Mama."

"Do you remember the names of the trees, David?"

My voice faltered. "Yes, Mama."

She gave what sounded like a laugh. "It will not add to the dowry, but Papa will be pleased. He loves the forest."

I stared at her and went icy cold with dread.

"Can I get you anything, Mama?"

"No, darling. We should go back now."

I went to my room and lay down on my bed and could not

stop trembling. Later my aunt and uncle came over and were together a long time in the kitchen, talking quietly.

Two days later I walked to school and again met Rav Sharfman on the corner beyond the bridge.

"You did not walk yesterday?" he asked in Yiddish.

"My mother was up most of the night."

"I am sorry to hear that. Was there bad news?"

"There's no news."

"Have you seen the pictures in this morning's papers on Bergen Belsen?"

"Yes."

"Incomprehensible barbarians. My mind cannot grasp it. Be careful, a car is coming." We stopped at a corner, then crossed quickly together. "You gave a good answer the other day."

"Thank you, Rebbe."

We walked on a few steps. He gave me a sidelong glance.

"You understood my words?"

"Yes."

He said nothing.

"There is danger," I said. "I could lose . . . everything."

He looked at me, his hooded eyes narrow, the prominent nose flaring slightly. "You want there to be no danger? You are afraid to take risks?"

I was quiet.

"It has to come from you," he said. "No one can give it to you. If it comes from you, then the risks will be worth taking. And the price will be worthwhile."

I looked at him.

"Yes," he said. "You will pay a price, Lurie."

We entered the school and separated. It was during the Talmud class that afternoon that I realized he had been speaking only in Yiddish to us for weeks and that the baseball terminology had disappeared from his vocabulary. He said to us in exasperation at one point during the class after a poor response from a question he had put to a student, "You want ordination from me? I will test you and give you ordination. All of you. You will give me back everything that I have taught you and I will give you ordination." He used the Hebrew word smicha for ordination. "But remember this: You must feel upon you the weight of God and the responsibility of the generations. Know that there is a law that if a watchman gives an object to another watchman, the second watchman must guard it with care. If through negligence it is damaged, the second watchman is liable. I will give you the ordination my grandfather, may he rest in peace, gave to me. If you are neglectful of it, you will be liable to my grandfather and to his grandfather and to his grandfather. You will have to go to the graves of those against whom you transgress and ask them to forgive you. But, remember, you may be unable to do that. You may not know where the dead are buried."

I felt his eyes rest heavily upon my face. There was no movement in the class, no sound.

Then he called on me to read.

I met him again the following morning as I came off the bridge.

"How is your mother?"

"Not well, Rebbe."

"I am sorry. There has been no news?"

"Nothing."

We walked in silence.

"All the books you are carrying are for class?"

"No."

"Which ones are not?"

I showed him a Hebrew book on the Bible.

"It is a shallow work," he said with contempt. "I detest shallowness. It is the biggest problem with Bible scholars. Their shallowness."

I was quiet. We crossed a side street together.

"Words and fables and stories," he said. "That is all they see. Man and God they cannot see. They are shallow people."

"They're mostly goyim and secularists, Rebbe."

"I am aware of who they are, Lurie. The few Jews in it are shallow too."

We walked on in silence.

"A shallow mind is a sin against God," he said. "A man who does not struggle is a fool."

I was quiet. The blood beat heavily against my eyes.

He gave me a sidelong glance. "Do you know how many students I have spoken to this way over the years? Once every five or ten years I find one such student. I have many boys studying Talmud in my classes. I have few students."

His face was utterly without emotion. The turned-out lips were moist and seemed vaguely curled with contempt. He maintained between us a distance immeasurably wider than the few inches that separated us as we walked. I had heard and read of such rebbes. Unlike the Hasidic rebbe, who controlled the inner and outer life of his followers, the Lithuanian rebbe, antagonist of Hasidim, deliberately sought to make room for the intellectually brave to chart their own lives. He was shy of prying into the lives of his students. Distance with such a rebbe was an act of love.

We entered the school together and parted in the hall.

When I rode by the store that afternoon I saw that it was closed. An icy panic suddenly choked my heart. The remaining few blocks to my house were a nightmare of torturous waiting. I raced up the stairs and threw open the door to the apartment.

My father and aunt and uncle were seated at the kitchen table. Alex had heard me enter and was coming toward the door. His face was ashen. I did not see my mother.

They had heard that afternoon, Alex said in a trembling voice. No one had survived.

I felt my books slipping from my grasp. I clutched at them. A voice said, "There were over a hundred people in both families. What do you mean no one survived?" It was my voice that had spoken but I had not felt myself say the words.

No one had survived, Alex repeated.

"That's impossible!" the voice said. My tongue was thick and dry inside my mouth. "How do you know?"

There had been a cable from Mr. Bader, Alex said.

I saw someone enter the hallway from the living room, carrying a black bag. For a moment I did not recognize him. He had a round pink face and graying hair.

"Hello," he said. "I haven't seen you in a long time. I'll bet you don't miss me." It was Dr. Weidman. His face was grim. "Your mother is sleeping." He went past me into the kitchen. I wondered where Saul was. "Max," Dr. Weidman said quietly. "I want to talk to you."

My father rose with heavy effort from his chair. How old he suddenly looked, the deep lines in his face, the dark circles around his eyes, the network of tiny dry wrinkles in the folds of his skin along the front of his neck. He went with Dr. Weidman into the living room.

I stood in the kitchen doorway looking at my aunt and uncle.

"We're absolutely sure?" I said. "How can we be so absolutely sure from a cable?"

My uncle looked up. "We are sure."

"How are we sure?"

"There are witnesses who saw them on the day they arrived

at Bergen Belsen. Witnesses who knew them from before the war."

"You mean witnesses who survived Bergen Belsen?"

"Yes."

"How do we know they were *all* killed? Why do we believe the witnesses?"

"Bader spoke to them."

"In Bergen Belsen?"

"Yes."

"Mr. Bader has been inside Bergen Belsen?"

"What do you think he is doing in Europe, spending Jewish money to have a good time?"

"Meyer," my aunt said softly. "Control yourself."

"I am sorry," said my uncle. "I apologize."

I leaned against the jamb of the doorway. A red haze had moved across my vision. I shook my head but the haze remained, a film of reddish color over my eyes.

My father and Dr. Weidman came along the hallway toward the kitchen.

"I have to go," Dr. Weidman said. "You will call me, Max, yes? We should all meet under happier circumstances. Goodbye. David, it's a pleasure not to have seen you in so long. Professionally, I mean. Goodbye."

He went out. My father sat down at the kitchen table. They all sat there, staring down at the table. I left them and went into my room and put my books on my desk. Alex stood at the window, staring out at the street.

Something occurred to me. "Aunt Sarah's family too?"

Everyone, he said, not looking away from the street.

"That's more than a hundred and fifty people."

I deserved an A in arithmetic, he said, still looking out at the street.

I lay down on my bed and covered my eyes.

"Where's Saul?" I asked.

"In bed with flu."

"Does he know?"

"Yes."

I lay very still with my hands over my eyes. But the reddish film remained and I could see it across the darkness of my vision.

In the early hours of the morning I came suddenly awake from the horror of a nightmare and listened to my mother screaming. She was screaming in Yiddish, "Don't touch me!

Stay away from me! Help me, God! Help me!" Her words trailed off into choking sobs. Alex and I rushed from our room. My father was coming out of the bedroom. "A bad dream," he said. "I will bring her water and a pill." He went along the hallway in his bare feet. Alex and I returned to our room.

I could not sleep. Out of the folds of darkness that lay across the walls and floor of the room came sibilant whispers. A huge monstrous form rose out of the darkness. There was a beating of wings. A sword glinted murderously. I opened my eyes and felt the deep trembling of my body and the curling horror that clutched at my soul. I lay awake, trembling, my eyes open, defying the darkness. The sword gleamed and moved back and forth in the black air of the night. I stared at the sword, at its poisoned point. I thought in my horror and dread that I would mouth ancient formulas of protection. But I remained silent. Slowly the giant form grew dim, taking with it the wings and the sword. The room was still. In the silence I heard a faint whispering sound. Alex was crying softly in his bed.

I rose very early that morning and prayed and walked to school. As I came off the bridge I saw Rav Sharfman on the corner, waiting for me. I came up to him.

"We heard yesterday," I said.

He turned upon me his large eyes and waited.

"No one survived," I said.

The eyes blinked. The face remained without expression. He murmured ancient Hebrew words of solace. Then I heard him say in Yiddish, "I do not understand those words. How many were they?"

"About a hundred and fifty," I said. "Everyone."

"All at Bergen Belsen?"

"Yes."

"You are certain?"

"Yes."

"Errors are made."

"The man who informed us doesn't make errors."

"Who is he?"

I told him.

"Of the JOAC?"

"Yes."

He fell into silence. We walked along together.

"You carry heavy baggage with you now," he said.

"I'm afraid."

"Then don't do it. Remain in the yeshiva. It will be"—he hesitated—"very comfortable for you here."

I said nothing. We entered the school building in silence. I went into the study hall and sat down at my table. Most of the tables were still empty. A number of dormitory students stood near the podium, praying the Morning Service. I sat staring at my closed folio of Talmud through the red haze that would not leave my eyes. The study hall began to fill with students. Irving Besser came by and went to his table. I saw Yaakov Bader enter the hall. He caught my eye and waved at me, then stopped for a moment to talk with a classmate. I saw him laugh and pat the classmate on the arm. His uncle used to do that to me, pat me reassuringly on the arm. I thought of his uncle and saw the years of journeying back and forth on trolleys between Washington Avenue and the apartment where I had studied Genesis. The voices, David. Listen to the voices talking to one another across the centuries. Yaakov came over to the table and said a cheerful "Good morning." I told him about the cable.

He sat down slowly in his chair and leaned back, tipping the chair dangerously but restoring its balance in time. He brushed a faintly tremulous hand across his pale blond hair. He seemed not to know what to say. His dark eyes were wide and moist.

I opened my volume of Talmud and told him we had better start preparing for the class.

He stared at me. After a moment he nodded slowly. We sat at the table, preparing for our Talmud class.

Later that day I sat in the class and could not keep my eyes upon the words in my volume of Talmud. I gazed out the tall wide windows at the street, and there, upon the cobblestones, saw the photographs of Bergen Belsen. Grotesque forms with skeletal arms and legs and rib cages and heads lay stacked like macabre cordwood on a stone ramp. Behind the ramp was a sloping slate roof. Off to the right there were trees and a patch of sky. I sensed a shudder of dread deep within myself and looked away and rested my eyes upon the volume on my desk. But the words would not enter my eyes and I turned away and gazed once again out the windows. I saw a deep rectangular pit scooped out of the earth. Women SS guards in long-skirted uniforms were filling the pit with dead bodies. In the foreground two stocky women, standing with their sides to the camera, their faces turned toward the pit, were lifting off the ground the shrunken corpse of a woman. One held the corpse by both legs, the other by its right arm. The upper portion of the torso was turned to the left, the breast dangling loosely downward. A few inches in front of the two SS women, in the immediate foreground, lying directly on top of the lower border of the photograph, was the body of a young girl. She lay face down, the curve of her shoulder coming to just below the line of her lower jaw. I could see one side of her face. The eye was half-open. She seemed pretty even in ghastly death. There was no sky in that photograph.

I saw other photographs. I saw them through the windows and could not penetrate them. Rav Sharfman's raspy voice went on and on over a passage of Talmud but I needed to enter the photographs of Bergen Belsen and I could not do it. I did not understand it. I saw them and could not enter them. I could not walk inside them. I stared out the window at the photographs in the street and did not know what to do.

At three o'clock that afternoon I came out of the Talmud class and walked quickly downstairs to the locker room. I left my books in my locker, then went back upstairs and out of the building. I crossed the street and entered the little park. I sat for a few minutes on a bench, looking at the river. It was a warm day. The afternoon sun was behind me; I felt it hot on the back of my neck. I rose and went to the stone parapet and looked down the side of the bluff to the roadway and river below. There was light traffic on the roadway. The river looked dark and still. Across the river lay the railroad tracks and the shantytown and the lumberyard and farther along the river in the direction of the Hudson was a factory of some kind with two tall chimneys pouring smoke into the air. I looked at the chimneys for a while. The red haze lay across everything my eyes saw. I felt cold. A tightness spread itself slowly inside my throat. I would enter those photographs. Somehow I would enter those photographs. I sat down on the stone parapet and looked carefully down the side of the bluff. I saw its trees and boulders and scrub brush and the dirt path that ran along it like a wedge of raw skin. After a while I climbed down off the parapet and walked to the small break in the stonework where the path began. I left the park and started down the bluff.

The path was a little more than two feet wide. For a few yards it ran almost perpendicular to the bluff, slanting gradually downward between boulders and leafy trees. I walked it with guarded ease. To my right was the earthen wall of the bluff, leading upward to the park; to my left was the almost sheer drop to the roadway and the river. I walked slowly and with care. Overhead an aircraft droned by, vibrating the air. I did not look up. The path was strewn with small stones. I felt them through the soles of my shoes, painfully reminding me of the pebbled bottom of the lake shore near the cottage where we had lived years ago. It was strange how I suddenly remembered that lake and Saul rowing me along the shore and Alex digging along the beach in his efforts to get to China and sometimes in the water along the shore a dead fallen tree, black and moldering, with green moss on its underside where it lay in the water and its stripped branches jutting from it grotesquely like—like the arms and legs of the frozen dead. I stopped on the path and rested.

There was no sunlight here and the air was cool and redolent of moist earth. After a while I went on. A small tree, growing directly out of the side of the hill, sent its branches across the path, partially obstructing the way. Its exposed roots clung as if in desperation to the dark brown earth of the bluff. I bent low and went carefully beneath its branches. One of the branches brushed against my shoulders and snapped with the sound of a dry twig. I went on down past the tree and suddenly, after a few feet, the path turned as if it were being pulled upward along the right side. It turned and flattened and began running straight down the bluff between brush and trees and boulders. I looked up. I was about fifty feet below the top of the bluff. A moment later I halted.

My legs shook, the muscles tensing as if in anticipation of the descent. A tugboat made its slow solitary way down the river. I turned sideways, leaned forward into the side of the bluff, bending my right leg, and started down. Slowly, moving sideways, leaning hard into the bluff, I continued downhill. Prickly brush pulled at my trousers. Here the path was almost indiscernible; it did not seem a path at all but a vague shallow draw. I went carefully across a cluster of small rocks. Then the earth suddenly seemed to give way and slide out from beneath me. Stones and pebbles and loose soil cascaded downhill. I slid feet first and then threw myself heavily upon the earth and clawed with my fingers. I came to a stop a few feet above a boulder and lay without moving.

My heart pounded against the dark soil. I glanced over my shoulder and saw the boulder, its surface pitted as if from some disease. I looked up. The bluff towered over me now. I was a little less than halfway down. I released my hold upon the ground and let myself slide slowly toward the boulder. I clutched the earth. My feet touched the boulder. I lay upon the near perpendicular earth and rested.

My hands were badly scraped. The forefinger of my left hand was cut and bleeding. My trousers were curled up over my knees. I turned my head and looked up at the afternoon sky and saw it red and filling with smoke. I closed my eyes and lay very still. After a while I began slowly to move around the boulder. I held tightly to myself its hard cold pockmarked surface and made my way around it and saw the steep folds and undulations, the stretch of corrugated earth and rock-strewn cliff that remained between me and the roadway and river. The path was gone. I slid and slowed myself, clutching the earth. I slid again, steeply, almost tumbling into a headlong fall, but grasped a bush, feeling its branches scratching at my face and slowing my descent. Rocks and pebbles slid with me down the bluff. I saw its earth against my eyes, the intricate patterning of its various stones and wild leafy shrubs in the dark moist soil. I stopped near a scraggly bush and laid my head upon the earth.

For a long time I lay very still, feeling the thick beating of my heart. Sweat ran down my face and stung my eyes. I started downward again and slid, grabbed desperately for earth, slowed, then slid again. I cried out, for I was beginning to roll. And then, abruptly, the earth beneath me altered its contour, slanted sharply and began to level. I fell heavily to the foot of the bluff in a shower of pebbles and soil.

I rose to my feet and brushed at my clothes. The forefinger of my left hand had been split by a rock and was bleeding profusely. It left stains of blood on my jacket and trousers. I looked up. The bluff loomed monstrously above me. I could not see the school. On the roadway a car passed by, the driver looking straight ahead. I put my handkerchief around the bleeding finger. Then I crossed the roadway and the length of grass along its side and stood at the low stone wall that bordered the river. The water was gray, its current swifter when seen from here than from the parapet above. I could hear it running quickly and lapping upon the stone embankment. It ran dark and foamed white as it licked at the stones; then it foamed dark too, and then red, and I looked and saw the river running red, and I closed my eyes. But the redness would not leave. I opened my eyes and all the world was red. Across the river a train moved slowly upon the bed of rails and I saw it was a freight train. I had seen many such freight trains before, running long and often slow upon

these tracks, with strange shapes on flatbed cars covered by
tied-down tarpaulins, the boxcars sealed. This train moved
quickly. I watched it go past the shantytown and the lumberyard and on down along the river past the factory with the
two tall chimneys. I closed my eyes and leaned upon the
stone wall. It had been an ordinary freight train but I had
seen through its sealed doors a multitude of writhing human
beings packed together riding in filth and terror. I turned
away from the river and felt the heavy beating of my heart.
Again I looked up at the bluff. Then I looked away and began
to walk along the river. How red it ran, licking and foaming
at the stones. For a brief interval the low wall fell away,
leaving only the embankment. I came upon a length of wet
earth where water lapped across the stones of the embankment onto the flat of the ground. I bent down and touched
the earth, felt its clayey softness, and scooped out a handful
and brought it to where the stone wall began once again
above the embankment. I put the earth on top of the wall. It
oozed upon the stones, wet and gleaming red beneath the red
sky. My fingers played with it, shaping it. You did nothing, I
said. Nothing. You died in the flames of the burning books
and then you did nothing. But what could you have done, my
golem? Who can expect miracles anymore from clay?

I left him there beneath the red sky and walked on along
the river. The shantytown lay almost directly across from me.
I stopped and stared at its shacks and hovels. Then a cold
wind blew across the river and someone called my name. I
shivered and looked again at the shantytown and saw in its
depths huddled beings waiting for death. I looked down the
river at the lumberyard and saw rows of barracks behind
electrified fences. I looked farther down the river and saw the
factory and the chimneys pouring smoke from burning flesh.
I closed my eyes again and saw the photographs. I lowered
my head and trembled and knew now I could never have entered those photographs; instead they had entered me. And
the wind blew again across the river and again I heard my
name.

David, he murmured. David.

The wind blew cold and I shivered.

You climbed down well, he said in the wind. You climbed
down very well. Did you see the stones and the earth and the
boulders? Did you see?

Yes.

These are the roots, my David.

Yes.

Do you see the roots?

I was silent.

Do you see the roots, my David?

Yes.

Who will water the roots? he murmured. Who will give them new life? The leaves are already dead.

I opened my eyes. The red world pushed heavily against my vision.

David, he said softly. David. Will you start again?

The wind touched me with an icy finger as if it blew from a winter sky.

I'm afraid, I said. I'm so afraid.

Yes, he said. Yes. I understand. But will you start again?

They kill us, I said.

Yes, he murmured into the wind.

I hung my head and leaned heavily against the stone wall. The wind gusted across the river, bringing distant echoes to my ears. I brushed at my eyes and saw before my face the blood-stained handkerchief. I shuddered and closed my eyes. And, slowly, I nodded.

My David, he murmured. My precious David. What a burden you take upon yourself.

I bowed my head in silence.

How you have grown, he whispered. It is so good to see how you have grown. You are making your own beginning.

I bent low and leaned my head upon the cold stones of the river wall. Then I felt myself weeping for all the years of pain I could remember and all the years of pain I knew lay yet before me. I wept a long time near the river, my head upon the stones. The wind grew slowly warm; the air grew still. I became silent. Below me the waters of the river lapped gently against the embankment. The river ran with a silken sound, gathering in little pools upon the stones, murmuring softly the hopes of all beginnings.

After a while I straightened and opened my eyes to the blue afternoon sky. I wiped my face with my handkerchief, cleaned myself up as best I could, and took a cab home.

Rav Sharfman said to me in Yiddish when I came off the bridge the following morning and he saw my scraped face and bandaged finger, "What happened to you, Lurie?"

I told him I had tripped and fallen in the park.

"Take care of yourself," he murmured. "You have an obligation."

We stood together for a moment on the corner. It was a warm June day. I could see the river below the bridge and the steep drop of the bluff. The sun on the surface of the water stirred within me a quiet ecstasy.

"How is your mother?" he asked.

"Not well, Rebbe."

"I am sorry to hear that."

We began to walk. I told him briefly of my decision.

He turned his face to me without breaking his stride. Beneath the wide brim of the dark battered hat the hooded eyes gleamed. Passion, controlled but clearly apparent, entered the saturnine countenance. A minute play of smiles moved across the curling lips. Then impassivity returned to his face and he said, "It is a good decision."

I thanked him.

"But I do not envy you the price you will pay."

I said nothing.

"No one will understand what you are going through. They will call you a traitor. It will become intolerable."

Still I said nothing.

"But you will withstand them. You have your roots in this world. Others with roots elsewhere are not able to make such a decision."

I was moved by his words and his faith in me. And I understood the echoes that linked him to his world and would not relinquish him to the world outside. His self-appointed task was to send others and to wage his own dark war in the solitude of his own torn, restless soul.

He asked me if I would stay on to study for ordination. I told him I would.

"I will give you your test any time you are prepared."

"The Rebbe will give me ordination despite what I told him?" I ventured the question that had been on my mind through much of the night.

We had stopped at a corner to let cars pass. He turned toward me, contemptuously. "I will not investigate your ritual fringes, Lurie. That is between you and your obligations to the past. Are you telling me you will not be an observer of the commandments?"

"I am not telling the Rebbe that."

"What are you telling me?"

"I will go wherever the truth leads me. It is secular scholarship, Rebbe; it is not the scholarship of tradition. In secular scholarship there are no boundaries and no permanently fixed views."

"Lurie, if the Torah cannot go out into your world of scholarship and return stronger, then we are all fools and charlatans. I have faith in the Torah. I am not afraid of truth."

We crossed the avenue and entered the school together. The entrance hall was deserted. He turned to me. I felt his eyes move across my face. He said to me in Yiddish, his voice rasping, "I am not bothered by questions of truth. I want to know if the religious world view has any meaning today. Bring yourself back an answer to that, Lurie. Take apart the Bible and see if it is something more today than the *Iliad* and the *Odyssey*. Bring yourself back that answer, Lurie. Do not bring yourself back shallowness. Study Kierkegaard and Otto and William James. Study man, Lurie. Study philosophy of religion."

I bowed my head beneath the rush of his words.

He was silent. He regarded me without expression. "I do not envy a Jew who goes into Bible today. Goyim will be suspicious of you and Jews will be uneasy in your presence. Everyone will be wondering what sacred truths of their childhood you are destroying. Merely to destroy—that is a form of shallowness, Lurie. Do you understand?"

"Yes, Rebbe."

"Lurie."

"Yes, Rebbe."

"Come and see me from time to time."

I thanked him.

"If I tell you that you are coming too often, you will understand."

"Yes, Rebbe."

"I have wings enough only for one man."

I looked at him. His face was impassive. He turned and walked away, alone, his tall form moving quickly up the stone stairs. He went through the metal doors and was gone.

He called on me that afternoon to read and explain. He called on me again the following day and the day after that. For all the rest of that month he called on me every day. I would read and explain. At times he would let me go on for a short while. At other times I would read for over an hour.

Once I read for the entire two hours of the class. I walked out
sweating and drained. It was clear enough that my ordination
test with him had already begun.

I dreaded the hot weeks ahead. I had decided to wait until
we were all out of the city and resting in the bungalows before
telling my family. But I could not tell them that summer. In
July I helped my father in the store and in the last two weeks
of August, when we lived in the bungalows near the lake and
the summer camp, I saw my mother resting in the wicker
chair beneath the tree, color returning slowly to her weary
face, my aunt and uncle and father hovering over her, caring
for her, and the very last thing I would do then was destroy
their efforts to restore the delicate balance of their lives.

I studied Talmud with Saul or alone. Alex read novels and
wrote stories and poems. I swam and went on long solitary
walks through fields and woods, naming aloud the trees I saw,
reciting to an occasional rabbit a Talmudic insight I had recently acquired, speaking to the birds that wheeled overhead.
I spoke my heart to the world around me. My own immediate
world was unapproachable and there was in me the need to
speak, for they all saw me studying Talmud and were certain I was following in the path of Saul; and I burned with
the shame of my betrayal of their trust. So I justified myself
to the listening wind: You see, people have taken the book
that I love and have emasculated it. We died for its ideas,
and they have drained those ideas of life. Yet there is something in what those people claim; but they cannot have said
it all. I stake my life on that. Listen to me, rabbit. The Torah
is not the word of God to Moses at Sinai. But neither is it
infantile stories and fables and legends and borrowed pagan
myths. I love it, bird. I want to find out what it is. Am I
crazy? I have to go to the secular world for new tools to find
out what it is. My Orthodox world detests and is terrified of
those tools. Do you understand? Does anyone understand besides Rav Sharfman? I want to know the truth about the
beginnings of my people.

My mother said often that summer that her only consola-
tion now was her children. At the kitchen table in the bungalow, she would lapse suddenly into silence, her face emptying
of life. Then she would stir and smile faintly and gaze at me
and Alex out of her large brown frightened eyes. I could
not bear to look at the fear in them. It was like witnessing
dread in the eyes of a child.

She said once, "If only one of them had survived. We could

have talked about it. He could have shared it with me. Only one. I do not understand it, Max."

"The goyim themselves do not understand it, Ruth," said my father. "Who can understand what cannot even be imagined?" And his face stiffened with the permanent rage he carried within him now against all the gentile world. Through that rage he gazed with absolute indifference upon the dropping of the atomic bombs on Japan and the termination of the war in the Pacific.

We returned to the city in September. On the afternoon of Simchat Torah, after a night and morning of joyous dancing with the Torah scrolls in our little synagogue, I took Alex away from one of his novels and went with him for a walk in the park opposite our apartment. I told him that in the spring of the coming year I would be taking my ordination test and in September I would begin graduate studies for a doctorate in Oriental studies.

We were walking along the path between the rolling fields of grass. He stopped and gazed at me, puzzled. What did I mean, Oriental studies? he asked.

I explained to him that the study of Bible was part of the Oriental studies departments in many graduate schools.

"You're going for a doctorate in Bible?" he said. "You're going to study the Torah with goyim?"

"Jews and goyim."

He was not angry; he was concerned. "My God, Davey. The yeshiva won't give you smicha."

I told him that would not be a problem.

"Is it worth it?" he asked. "You'll be hurting yourself."

"What do you mean?"

"Papa will get angry. You'll lose all your friends. Is it worth it for stories?"

"What stories?"

"If you keep quiet, no one knows what you think. Why do you have to study it and publish books about it and make a fuss and get everyone upset?"

I stared at him.

"God, Davey, I read Darwin a while ago and it's all a bunch of Sunday school stories. I get more out of a good novel. Why are you making such a fuss over it? Why don't you go for a doctorate in history?"

I stared at him and did not know what to say. He prayed every morning, observed the commandments, went through all the motions. He had taken the more common road and I had not even been aware of his journey. And his observance of the commandments—it would probably all begin to disintegrate the day he left home. We had lived together as brothers all these years and neither of us had known of the other's deepest intentions. It was strange and sad.

"I think you're nuts," he said. "But you're my big brother and I'll love you anyway. Now can we go home so I can get back to my book?"

He returned to his novel and to his normal routine. I would gaze in astonishment at the seriousness with which he conducted his charade. Sometimes he would hesitate as he put on his phylacteries in the morning and I would turn away, bewildered at my own inability to have seen before my eyes the swift vanishing of my brother's faith. But he had covered it well; he continued to cover it well. And I said nothing.

One day in the fall I sat with Saul in the park across from the school and told him too. I had seen him that morning rushing to the high school class he taught and had asked him to meet me in the study hall. I wanted to talk to him, I said. We sat in the park and I looked at the river. An autumn wind blew coldly against my face and stung my eyes. I turned to him and told him and watched shock and sadness enter deep into his blue eyes. He drew his coat tightly around him. He listened in silence. I heard the wind in the dying autumn trees and inside my eyes saw the steep drop of the bluff and the path and the descent and the boulder and the sliding of stones and earth to the river below.

He said, very quietly, "You are going out to an evil culture." He used the traditional Hebrew phrase for a Jew who abandons the tradition and becomes, in the eyes of that tradition, a renegade.

"No, Saul. Please."

"I knew it would happen, Davey. You were never satisfied with answers people gave you. I knew, I knew. But it hurts."

I was silent and without defense. For he was right; I was indeed moving away from his world.

We sat for a while looking at the river and listening to the wind. Dimly I saw myself walking with him along the curving paths of the zoo near which we had once lived. I closed my eyes. That had been so long ago; I could hardly remember it now.

"Saul."

He looked at me, the sadness dark upon his thin narrow face.

"I'm trying to do two years of Talmud in one. Will you help me if I need it?"

"Sure," he said. "Of course I'll help you, Davey. What does one thing have to do with another? I'll study Talmud with you any time you want." He was quiet a moment. Then he shook his head. "Why does it have to be Bible, Davey? Can't you go for anything else? Why Bible? You'll hurt Yiddishkeit, Davey. You'll affect lives."

"I don't love anything else enough to want to invest my life in it."

He was silent. Then he asked, "Will you publish?"

"Yes."

"Books and papers?"

"Yes."

"About this piece of the Torah being from this date and that piece from that date? Things like that?"

"Yes."

Again he was silent. He gazed at a cluster of leaves blowing in the wind around our feet. Then he looked up at me with defiance.

"It's the Torah of Moses, Davey. With all my heart I believe that. If you teach anything else, you destroy it."

I did not respond. A moment later he rose.

"I'll help you with Talmud any time you want, Davey. I have a faculty meeting in a few minutes." He hesitated. "Be careful what you write, Davey. It's the Torah of God to Moses that you'll be writing about."

He walked slowly away in that stooped shuffling gait of his, bent forward slightly, his eyes upon the ground before him. I sat and looked at the river. It shone like cold silver in the pale afternoon sun. I shivered in the wind.

All through that winter I studied Talmud. From time to time I asked Saul for help. I would go to his apartment and we would study together in his room. I was studying the tractate *Chullin*, which deals with the dietary laws and the laws of ritual slaughter. It is a difficult tractate and he had already mastered it. He was very helpful to me. But as the weeks went by I began to notice a cooling of the relationship between us. There were fewer intimacies volunteered by him; he appeared reluctant to give me the names of girls I might date. I do not know if he was fully aware of the slow drawing away from me that I felt him going through: no more of his easy dipping into the midrash; no more jokes and light gossip about members of the high school Talmud faculty. I had chosen to move out of that world; he was simply reacting naturally to my self-inflicted estrangement.

At the same time, Alex began to move toward me. Often deep into the night, with our lights off and the winter winds gusting along the street, he would share with me his dreams. He wanted to teach English literature; he wanted to write poems and novels. He hungered for the world he felt was being denied him by his tradition. He mocked what he called Jewish totems and tabus. He had read two books by Freud, one book on anthropology, and a work on comparative religion. And *On the Origin of Species* by Darwin.

"That one knocked me out, Davey," he said into the darkness.

"When did you read it?"

"About half a year ago. It really knocked me out. Six days of creation. Sure."

"Didn't you read the Rashi on that? He says—"

"I know what Rashi says. I know all the answers. You think because I read novels I'm a jerk?"

"I don't think that, Alex."

"I know all the questions and I know all the answers. The questions are better than the answers."

I stared into the darkness and I did not respond. I had traveled a parallel road and had taken a different turn. I understood what he was saying and had no answers as yet to give him. And so we would talk into the night, softly, as if we had become comrades in a secret revolt.

My mother did not fully recover from the news of the destruction of her family. She was able to return to the store in the fall but she was no longer the cheerful business lady she had affected to be in the past. She had lost weight and could not seem to regain it. Her nightmares grew less frequent. I would find her often staring out the window at the street, the sunlight on her pale drawn face, and I knew she was gazing upon memories of sunlight on trees and a distant love that the world had ground to dust.

I came over to her once as she stood by the living room window and kissed her cheek. It was winter. Snow lay deep upon the street and blew in white gusting waves through the air.

"We would play in it," she murmured. "I loved the snow."

"I was always afraid I would get sick in it," I said.

She looked at me and smiled faintly. "Are you afraid of it now?"

"No, Mama."

"I'm glad." She gazed out the window, her gaunt face momentarily serene. "David loved the snow," she said. "He would write messages to me in it and they would freeze in the wind and my sisters and brothers would come by and read them and point to me and laugh. Don't we love the snow, my David?"

"Yes," I said. "We love the snow."

In the early spring I told my father. I chose an April night when Alex was at an English seminar and my mother was visiting my aunt. My father sat in the living room, reading his Yiddish newspaper. I was at my desk, staring in blind panic at my folio of Talmud and seeing nothing. I heard him shuffling the pages of the newspaper. I felt myself shivering, felt the coldness in the palms of my hands, felt strangely weak as if I were about to come down once again with the illness that had plagued all the growing years of my life. I could not do it; I could not tell him. Then, strangely, there rose before my eyes the image of Rav Sharfman waiting for me at the end of the bridge. I saw him, tall, dark-suited, in that battered dark hat he always wore, waiting for me. I came up to him and he turned. A dark light burned in his eyes, a passion carefully controlled and revealed to few. Good morning, Lurie, I heard him say. You like to walk? I also like to walk. And I rose and felt him walking with me into the living room where my father sat in his easy chair, his tall black skullcap on his head, reading his Yiddish newspaper. In the cage the canary perched in silence on one leg, rocking gently, a roundish ball of yellow feathers. It was a warm night. The window was partly open. A wind stirred the curtains.

I sat down in the easy chair across from my father and asked if I could interrupt his reading. There was something very important I wanted to tell him, I said.

He put down his newspaper and removed his steel-rimmed reading glasses. The light of the floor lamp fell across his thick shoulders and balding head. He was in his fifties now but he looked older, ravaged by his endless wars with the world. In moments of relaxation such as now, when he felt no need to hold himself a warrior, the cruel gouging of age was clearly discernible in the lines in his face, in the folds around his eyes, in the fleshiness that had once been a trim square face. He blinked wearily and yawned and rubbed his eyes. He wore a white shirt open at the neck, dark trousers, and brown slippers. Curls of gray-brown hair lay in the opening of the shirt, ending abruptly with the white skin at the base of his neck. He yawned again, pointed to the newspaper, and said that Truman might yet be a good President after all; he knew how to make decisions; he knew how to deal with the Russians; he was not the weakling and the simpleton people had thought him to be. Did I want a glass of coffee? he said. Maybe we could go into the kitchen.

I did not want any coffee, I said. I wanted to talk to him.

He looked at me then and his small gray eyes narrowed a little. A vague guardedness began slowly to enter him as if he were drawing together all the various parts of himself. He straightened himself in the easy chair; some of the fleshiness disappeared from his face as his prominent jaw with its marked underbite stiffened. He looked at me, and waited.

I had half hoped that Saul or Alex might have made some allusion to my plans, thereby easing my way somewhat. But it was clear they had said nothing. I would have to do it all myself.

I told him I had been thinking about what I wanted to do after I received ordination.

He looked at me and sat up quite straight and folded his muscular arms across his chest. He waited. Behind me I heard the curtains stirring in the warm wind that blew in through the open window.

I told him I had been thinking about it for months, as a matter of fact for almost a year. I did not want to teach in a yeshiva, I said. I wanted to go on for a degree in a university.

His eyes narrowed till they seemed closed. I saw a sudden flaring of his nostrils. Still he remained silent.

"A degree in Bible," I said, speaking English and using the English word. "I want to study Bible." I had already applied to a university, I said. I was waiting for an official answer. But I had been promised acceptance.

"You did this behind my back?" he said, his face stiff.

I did not reply.

"What kind of a son does this behind a father's back?" he asked. He was not angry; he seemed hurt but strangely calm. I was frightened by that calm; I had expected an immediate raging reaction to my words.

I told him I had not known what to do or when to tell him. I had been frightened, I said. I apologized for doing that behind his back. I had felt the need to have it done before I spoke to him, I said. I had wanted to speak to him about a certainty, not a possibility, I said.

"You were frightened to tell me?"

"Yes."

"I frighten you?"

I lowered my eyes and did not respond. The canary, awakened by our words, stood on both legs now on its perch.

"I am sorry I frighten you," he said. "Even so, you should not have gone behind my back."

I apologized again.

He waved aside my words with a brusque movement of his arm. "I am not interested in hearing your apology." He leaned forward in the chair. "Tell me what it means to study Bible in a university. Your teachers will be goyim?"

"And Jews."

"The Jews are observers of the commandments?"

"I don't know. They may be. I'm not certain."

"It is unimportant to you that they may not be observers of the commandments?" His voice, capable of ringing loudness, was low and calm. "You will study the Torah with goyim and with Jews who are like goyim? What do they know of the Torah?"

"They know a lot, Papa. They—"

"How can a goy who believes in Jesus or in nothing teach a Jew the Torah? How can a sinful Jew teach the Torah?"

"They're great scholars, Papa. They teach a new method."

"Scholars," he said, in English, his voice rising slightly and edging into contempt. "Scholars." He muttered something in Polish which I did not understand. Then he said abruptly in Yiddish, "You are searching for truth, yes?"

I stared at him.

"Yes, I know. You are searching for truth. You will turn over the whole world in your search for truth. My brother David used to tell me he was searching for truth. He did not care what precious ideas he threw aside once he thought them untrue. I did not like that about my brother David. He was gentle in everything except the use of his mind. No, I did not like that. It is as much a curse to be born with too much brains as too little."

"Papa, I don't want to throw anything aside."

"No?" he said. "You already have. You are going out to an evil culture. You have entered the world of the goyim." He said it calmly and with studied sadness as if he were reporting a battle casualty to a superior officer. "You do not want to throw anything aside. What more could you throw aside than the Torah?"

"I'm not throwing the Torah aside, Papa."

"No? Then why are you going to a university to study it? What you learned with Mr. Bader and in the yeshiva was not enough? You are not satisfied with that as the truth?"

I wanted to say, It was beautiful; listening to the voices of the centuries teaching me Torah—that was beautiful. But, Papa, listen. The medieval commentators used the most advanced knowledge of their day to understand the Torah. But they did not have the tools we have today. They did not have anthropology, archeology, comparative religion, linguistics, a true grasp of the texture of history. I do not know what kind of commentaries Rashi, Ibn Ezra, the Ramban, and the others might be writing were they alive today; they might be helping me penetrate the precious rectangles of Torah I hold in my hands. I wanted to say all that, but I remained silent. For my father was right: what I had studied with Mr. Bader and in the yeshiva was not enough. It could not be the entire truth.

"You see," he said, stirring in his chair, his face darkening. "I am correct. It was not enough. It is exactly like my brother David."

He was silent then, sitting back in the chair with his eyes closed, the skullcap like a dark and severe crown on his head. The canary ruffled its wing feathers, hopped down to its water dish, and drank. My father said nothing for a long time. I remembered the months of his illness after the world he had built had suddenly been shattered in the early thirties. Nightmares long forgotten, dark wastelands of memory, suddenly flooded my mind. He had rarely if ever conveyed the impression of being a compassionate man; yet he had helped so many people, had given so much of himself to others. And he had suffered so terribly. What a strange fusion he was of duty and selflessness!

I sat and looked at him, feeling the sweat on my back and the iciness on the palms of my hands. The canary hopped back to its perch and pecked into its breast feathers. The silence dragged on, became dense with dread. Somewhere in the house a clock ticked. I had never heard a ticking sound in the living room before. I took a deep tremulous breath. My father stirred and opened his eyes.

"I could forgive you anything," he said without preliminaries. "But I cannot forgive you going to the goyim to study Torah. Do the goyim come to us to learn their—what do you call it?—New Testament? I will tell you about the goyim. They either hate us too much or love us too much. They will never understand us and be natural with us. After the way we have been slaughtered you want to go out to the culture of the goyim? You want to mix Yiddishkeit with goyishkeit? You think that will make Yiddishkeit stronger? I will tell you what will make Yiddishkeit stronger. I want to bring Jews here because this a good land. I want to build yeshivas here. I want to build Eretz Yisroel. I do not want to mix Torah with goyim. I want to rebuild what was destroyed in Europe. That is what I want to do. And I will do it, if God gives me the strength. Go ahead. Go to your university to study with your goyim or your Jews who do not care about the commandments. I had no way of stopping my brother and I have no way of stopping you. At least you will not go there an ignoramus. At least I did my job. You were taught Yiddishkeit."

"Papa—"

But he would listen to nothing more. "I do not want to hear another word, David." He had raised his voice. The canary, suddenly agitated, began to fly about excitedly inside its cage, making wild fluttering sounds with its wings. "I want to talk practical matters with you." He paused. "Where will you go to school?"

I told him.

"Good. It would be—unpleasant—if you were home. We will tell your mother you are studying Hebrew or history or some such subject. I do not want to upset her now."

I said nothing.

"You will need money to live. You will tell me how much you need and I will give it to you. You are still my son and I am not a cruel or vindictive person." He rose to his feet. The newspaper fell to the floor. He reached down for it and picked it up. Then he looked at me. "I did my best," he said in a flat tone of voice. "The Torah says if a man marries and dies and has no children, then his brother should marry the dead brother's wife and give the first-born son the dead brother's name. You know this law and you know it is possible with ease to avoid such a marriage. I loved my brother despite all his arrogance. I loved him. I have continued my brother's life. It is your job to continue his good name. Now I am going into the kitchen for a glass of coffee. Is there anything else you want to tell me?"

I had nothing more to say.

He went into the kitchen. I heard him puttering about at the sink. I went into my room and lay down on my bed. The apartment was silent. I could not stop trembling. How miserably I had failed! I had not even been able to begin explaining myself to my father. Who would ever believe me? I want to understand the Torah as it was understood by those who wrote it. I need to learn this new critical method so I can discover the truth about the beginnings of my people. I want to know who I was so I can understand better who I want to be. Why can I say that to myself with such ease but am unable to say it to others? Have I read too many books? Am I talking a language of shorthand? I felt alone, so absolutely alone. And at that moment I saw myself, as if through a silver mist, coming slowly off the bridge. And there on the corner, waiting, was Rav Sharfman. He turned to greet me, his dark hooded eyes without expression. We walked together toward the school.

That night I woke and heard a man crying. It was the most terrifying and anguishing of sounds—a stifled, gasping series of choking, wrenching sobs. I could not bear the sound and slid beneath my covers and brought my knees close to my chest. I slept in a fog of confused images and shifting visions and dreams. A murmurous voice penetrated my sleep. I came into dazed wakefulness beneath my covers and thought I heard my father's voice chanting softly from the Book of Psalms. I raised my head from beneath the covers. A dark form stood at the foot of my bed. "Papa?" I whispered. "Papa?" The murmuring ceased. The form remained very still. I did not know if I was awake or asleep. I felt my eyes closing and a blackness descending upon me. Fingers brushed lightly across my cheek. I could feel the fingers through my sleep. Then the side of a face touched mine and lips brushed across my forehead. I knew I was asleep and had dreamed it. Then, suddenly, I opened my eyes and stared into the darkness. The form was gone. But there lingered unmistakably in the darkness, like the trace of a vanished hope, the faint warm odor of coffee.

In the last week of June I was ordained and in the first week of September I left home.

The test for ordination was given to me by Rav Sharfman and two other members of the Talmud faculty. I remember it as a four-hour ordeal comparable in intensity only to the oral defense of my doctoral dissertation which I underwent years later. In a small room, at a dark-wood table, we ranged over hundreds of pages of Talmud and the minutiae of Jewish law. At the start all three posed questions; some time in the third hour the other two sat back and Rav Sharfman alone directed the questions at me; darts of questions. He would ask a question and I would begin to answer and he would see I knew the answer and would stop me and ask a new question. I came out of the room shaking, exhausted, feeling the same dry-mouthed fatigue I had experienced after the descent to the river, and the same pulsing ecstasy. I had done well. A wisp of a smile had played across the thin curling lips as he had dismissed me.

My mother grew strangely calm the week I was to leave. She did my laundry; she ironed my shirts; she taught me some simple cooking skills, for I would be living alone in an apartment near the University of Chicago. "David wanted to study for a degree," she murmured as she helped me pack my bags. "You will study for him, darling. Yes?" Her eyes filled. I held her to me and stroked her hair.

"We will send your books to you," my father said to me at one point during the week when we were alone in the kitchen. "And also the books of Mrs. Horowitz. Is there anything else?"

I could not think of anything else.

"If you need money you will let me know. I am still your father. You need never feel shame with me."

I thanked him.

He hesitated, looking down at his glass of coffee. Then he raised his eyes and I felt upon my face the full impact of his stern strength. "Whatever you do," he said, "do not become a goy." And he turned his face away and put his hand over his eyes.

During my last Shabbat in the city I walked with Saul and my aunt and uncle in the park. It was a hot windless day. Saul said to me, "Will you be back in the winter?"

"I don't know."

"If you think I can help you in any way, will you write to me?"

"Yes."

"I hope you don't hurt Yiddishkeit with what you're doing, Davey. We've been hurt enough in this century."

"I don't want to hurt Yiddishkeit, Saul."

"No? You already have. The whole yeshiva knows what you're doing. You know what effect it will have? You were one of the best students they ever had."

I did not know how to respond to that.

"Even Yaakov Bader feels hurt, Davey."

I choked back the memory of the bewildered pain I had inflicted upon my caring friend when I had told him of my decision.

"Anyway, let me know if you ever think I can help you. How many cousins do I have?"

And he turned away from me, concealing the sadness that had entered his eyes.

My uncle wished me luck in a pained and poignant way. My aunt let me kiss her cheek. I returned home to a silent apartment, stared at my bed and my desk, and felt a wrenching loneliness. I lay down on my bed. The door to the apartment opened and closed. I heard footsteps in the hallway and the living room. It was Alex. He came into the room and sat down on his bed.

"It's hot out there," he said.

I turned my face to the wall.

He was silent for a long time. Then he said, "I'll write to you, Davey. I'll become the family letter-writer."

"I only want to study the Bible," I said. "They all act as if I've become a heretic or something."

"You have," he said. "In their eyes you have."

I was quiet.

" 'A sinner who makes others sin,' " he quoted. "You'll write books and others will read them. In their eyes you're the worst kind."

"All right," I said.

"We shouldn't fool ourselves," he said. "Especially if we're interested in truth."

I left the following day. My mother's strange calm remained with her even as I went through the door of our apartment. Alex embraced me. I felt my father's iron handshake all the way downstairs to the cab. I boarded a train to Chicago.

I sat at a window and looked out at the river. Docks and boats glided by. The river was bluish gray in the morning sun. Above us flashed the underside of a bridge. I saw a shanty-town and, across the river, a low stone wall and a towering bluff. On top of the bluff stood a reddish building, its green dome glistening in the sun. I looked at the rocky side of the bluff and thought I could see the huge boulder that had broken my fall and had also barred my further descent. I could feel its scarred surface on my fingers and palms as I sat in the train. I saw myself circling that boulder and felt again the sickening slide and fall to the ground below. It had been a feeling of sheer terror, that helpless slide and fall. And I felt it now again, that terror, as I sat looking out the window at the river and the bluff and the school and the two tall smoking chimneys that suddenly came into view. I closed my eyes. What was I doing? I had left behind a secure life and was going out on an insane search for intangible beginnings. Who cared about beginnings? The present was what everyone really worried about. I had made a grotesque mistake! I must go back! A wind moved across my face. Sh, someone whispered. Calm yourself. It is loneliness and fear. Did you think it would be easy to make your own beginning? I listened to the rasping voice within the whisper and grew still. I opened my eyes. The middle-aged man seated across from me smiled and wondered if I wanted to read his *New York Times*. He was finished with it, he said. I thanked him and took it from him and sat reading it as the train moved smoothly around a bend and smoothly and swiftly along the wide dark-blue waters of the Hudson River.

That was my first long journey into ancient beginnings, a train ride to Albany and Cleveland and then on to Chicago. The following year was 1947 and, with millions of our people everywhere, I exulted in the new beginning we were making on our ancient land. During the years that followed I longed to make a journey back into other recent beginnings but could not. I had seen a photograph in a newspaper of a dedication ceremony in Bergen Belsen: the camp had been turned into a vast parklike cemetery. Stone walls, grassy fields, paved lanes, groves of trees. I remember gazing at the photograph and hungering to enter it. But its borders remained impenetrable.

Then a few years ago I began writing a book on Genesis that took a sudden unexpected turn; it became necessary for me to do research into Bible manuscripts to be found only in Frankfurt and Erfurt. I was frightened, I hesitated, and even considered putting aside the book, but my wife and my colleagues urged me not to. In the end, the need to make that journey, both for the book and for myself, overcame the cold nervous urge to avoid it. I flew to Germany.

For days I worked in the Frankfurt Municipal Library with rare manuscripts and Bible fragments. Then I rented a

car and drove along a beautiful autobahn to Erfurt. It was
an April day. My hands were cold and sweaty on the steering
wheel. To find Germany so new and clean and vibrantly alive
had unnerved me: I had expected rubble somewhere. The
borders of the highway were smooth and grassy and there
were lovely bluish hills in the distance. I arrived in Erfurt in
the evening and spent a few days there with the Erfurt
Codices. Then, finally, I set out on my journey into the final
beginnings of my family. I stared through the windshield,
enmeshed in memories. I drove swiftly, and I remember
thinking to myself, Slow down, don't have an accident. I do
not remember the road I took, or how long I drove.

I stood beneath a cloudy sky before a stone entrance wall
on which was written *Lager Belsen 1944 1945*. I had seen
that wall in the newspaper photograph. I could not move. A
paralysis of terror had seized me. I wanted to turn and rush
away. Then he was there, Rav Sharfman, by the entrance
wall, stern and tall and gloomy of countenance. Come, he
murmured. You must see the remnants of the beginning of
your family's love for the Torah. But I could not move. You
must enter, he said. You have nothing to apologize for. You
have only to give thanks and to remember.

Still I could not move.

Beyond the stone wall were paths and knolls and trees. I
was alone. The air was cool. I had wanted to come; now I
wanted to flee. I could not confront this horror.

Then from beyond the stone wall someone called my name.
Papa? I said. Papa?

In dreams I visit here, he said. No one knows. You will
tell no one.

David, someone murmured from beyond the stone wall.
Come.

Uncle David? I said. Is that you?

The dead can journey too, he murmured. I sleep in Lemberg but all my beginnings lie here. Come.

I put on my skullcap and entered Bergen Belsen.

I walked along deserted paved paths between massive stone
walls on which were words that read *Hier Ruhen 2000 Tote*
—"Here rest 2000 dead"—*April 1945; Hier Ruhen 2500
Tote April 1945; Hier Ruhen 5000 Tote April 1945*. Weeds
covered the mass graves. A trembling took hold of me. The
gray April sky seemed to lower itself toward the earth. The
day had darkened.

Papa? I said.

There was silence.

Uncle David? I said.

Only the silence.

I walked along slowly, a strange dryness in my throat and a dull ache inside my eyes. What had my father told me years ago when I first began studying with Mr. Bader? It was a tradition in our family that went back generations. We were Torah readers. My own father, your grandfather—how he loved to read the Torah. He would work in the mill and chant the words to himself, the precious words. How can a Jew not know the Torah?

He is buried here somewhere, my grandfather.

Papa? I called. Papa?

Silence.

Uncle David? I called. Uncle David?

There was only the silence.

They were all here, grandparents, uncles, aunts, cousins. Who lies beneath my feet? I am walking on the dead of my family's beginnings.

I found myself on a path leading to a massive stone wall that bore the words *Hier Ruhen 1000 Tote April 1945.* I stopped on the path. They were standing by the wall.

Ah, my brother, murmured my Uncle David. I am grateful. And he moved closer to my father and held him for a moment in a gentle embrace.

I tried, said my father. It was my job to try. We could have done more together as father and son. But the world kept coming between us, stealing my time and strength. And he went out to their evil culture.

I bowed my head.

To another culture, said my uncle gently. To bring new life to our roots.

To an evil culture. Look how it slaughters us.

Yes, said my uncle. I know. I know.

I tried, said my father. David, how Ruth and I tried.

You did well, my big brother, came the murmured words. He turned to me.

David, he said. David. Look at me.

I raised my eyes.

He made a gentle sweeping gesture with his arm. Here is the past, he murmured. Never forget the past as you nourish the present.

I was silent. Slowly I nodded my head.

He turned to my father. Thank you, he murmured. Our David is giving new life to my name.

I closed my eyes. A wind brushed against me, lingered for a moment, and was gone. I opened my eyes and found myself alone. After a while I recited the Mourner's Kaddish. Then I walked back between the graves to the car and drove away.